MEET ME IN THE MIDDLE

Also by Alex Light

The Upside of Falling

MEET ME IN THE MIDDLE

ALEX LIGHT

HARPER TEEN
An Imprint of HarperCollinsPublishers

HarperTeen is an imprint of HarperCollins Publishers.

Meet Me in the Middle
Copyright © 2022 by Alex Light
All rights reserved. Printed in the United States of America.
No part of this book may be used or reproduced in any manner whatsoever without
written permission except in the case of brief quotations embodied in critical
articles and reviews. For information address HarperCollins Children's Books, a
division of HarperCollins Publishers, 195 Broadway, New York, NY 10007.
www.epicreads.com

Library of Congress Control Number: 2021948116
ISBN 978-0-06-313617-5

Typography by Corina Lupp
22 23 24 25 26   PC/LSCH   10 9 8 7 6 5 4 3 2 1
❖
First Edition

To Mom, for everything.

1

EDEN

A QUICK GOOGLE SEARCH tells me there was once a woman who woke up after being in a coma for twenty-seven years, and I cannot wrap my head around that. That's nearly ten thousand days of idling, of being stuck somewhere between reality and another world altogether. I try to imagine what that must feel like, to close your eyes and see an endless stream of black. A never-ending void. It's so terrible I close the internet tab.

I don't need to spend much time wondering what that woman's family must have felt like. I know that feeling all too well.

Ten thousand days. It's insanity. I've been waiting on Katie to wake up for five months now, and it's broken me into so many pieces I stopped counting.

"Order up!"

I deliberately ignore Manny's voice booming from the kitchen and delve deeper into my mental distress. Typically when I begin thinking of my best friend's state in the hospital down the street, I check out seconds after and try to think of anything else. But tonight, I'm feeling oddly masochistic. Maybe I can conquer this brain of mine—or at least put a leash on the damn thing. Before any of that can happen, the bell behind me begins to wail. I know Manny is purposely pressing down on it over and over again to annoy the shit out of me. Not that it's working. At all.

"*Eden*," Manny grits out. The level of disdain he can force into one word is truly remarkable.

I'm well caffeinated and well rested, so in that moment I vow to tone down my regularly moody self by at least, like, 35 percent. I let my phone slide into the pocket of my apron, muster a smile, and spin around. Manny watches me with that familiar thinly veiled annoyance that teeters on amusement. His olive skin is flushed from being in the kitchen, and the narrowing of his eyes is comically offset by the slightest curve of his mouth.

If anyone can look angry in a nice way, it's Manuel Álvaro.

"Need something, boss?" I ask innocently because I am a very good employee. And technically, he's not my boss. Manny's barely two years older than I am. His dad, on the other hand, *is* my boss. But he's not here right now.

Plus, Manny and I already kissed once. Any air of authority he may have had left the moment his mouth touched mine.

"Just for you to, you know, do your job." He slides a plate of chicken and potatoes down the counter, then crosses his large

2

arms across his chest. It's difficult work to drag my eyes back up to his face. "Think you can handle it?"

"Can I handle walking a plate of food to a customer sitting fifteen feet away? What a ridiculous question," I say, taking the plate. "Of course I can't." Manny's laughter follows me across the restaurant to where Earl, one of our regulars, is sitting in the corner booth—the same booth he's been sitting in every Friday night since I started waitressing here two months ago. Same booth, same drink, same meal, same lousy tip. Although I can't really blame him for the last one. I haven't exactly been a ray of sunshine lately. More like a permanent storm cloud hovering around, waiting to drench everything and everyone that walks beneath.

But, as I mentioned, the level of caffeine flowing through my body is truly remarkable, and I'm determined to not be a pain in the ass for once in my life. So, for what might be the first time, I smile at Earl as I set his plate down. He responds with a scowl.

"Extra potatoes?" he asks like he always does.

"Of course," I say, because getting yes-I-remembered-your-fucking-potatoes tattooed on my forehead seems a bit excessive.

Earl digs in as I stand there like a freak, watching a sixty-something-year-old man eat. Finally, I remember to walk away. Good choice. I do a quick once-over of the restaurant. Pollo Loco is unnervingly dead for a Friday night. Aside from Earl, there are two other customers here. Manny's parents opened this place last year, serving up Portuguese food to a small Toronto neighborhood

3

that's lined with sketchy businesses and fast-food shops—my cuisine of choice, personally. Before Pollo Loco rose from the ashes, there was an old-fashioned diner here that specialized in deep-fried food that led you on a one-way track to a heart attack.

Manny *swears* that Pollo Loco used to be packed every single night. To put it in his words, "That stupid Mexican place ruined everything." A meek reference to the Chipotle that opened down the street a few months ago. Like a black hole, they sucked all the customers right up. Apparently. Not sure I buy it. But the food here is amazing, so maybe he's got a point.

Itching for someone to annoy, I head past the front counter and push through the door to the kitchen. Manny's standing at the large metal table, rolling out a slab of dough into a perfect rectangle. Without having to ask, I know he's making pastéis de nata, a Portuguese dessert that's a creamy egg custard nestled in a flaky pastry. I can eat five in one sitting, theoretically speaking. I definitely haven't done that on numerous occasions.

"Got anything for me?" I ask like a dog begging for scraps. Manny, like the angel he is, pulls a plate with a single pastel de nata on it out of thin air. "Have I mentioned that you're my favorite person in this entire world?"

Manny blinds me with that eager grin. "Not lately, no."

I take a seat at the table and dig in. The pastry is buttery heaven, and the custard makes me stifle a moan. In ten seconds flat I manage to inhale the entire thing.

Manny stops rolling the dough. He points the rolling pin at me in a very accusatory way that I'm not entirely fond of. "Is that the first thing you've eaten all shift?"

"Maybe."

"Eden," he groans like I'm single-handedly responsible for the nonexistent gray hairs on his head. "Not like you work five feet from a kitchen with an extremely talented chef who'll cook you up whatever you'd like."

I make a big show of looking around the small space. "Extremely talented chef . . . where?" Manny doesn't bother humoring me anymore. He shuts me up by tossing a handful of flour at my face. I brush it away, stick my tongue out at him in a very dignified way, and continue to eat all the pastry crumbs off my plate.

"We should close early tonight," I say.

Manny rolls his eyes at my bad idea. I watch as he expertly folds the dough into a square, wraps it in plastic wrap, and sticks it into the fridge like he always does. That way, the brunt of the work is done for tomorrow morning. And he claims the dough is easier to work with after it's been chilled. Not that I'd know—he keeps me away from it like it's the *Mona Lisa* and I'm a child with sticky fingers.

After he's washed his hands and snapped a towel around his neck, Manny hits me with a quick shake of his head. "We can't close early," he says.

"Why not?"

His thick brows draw together. "Because we close at ten. It's only eight thirty." God, no twenty-year-old should be such a stickler for the rules. If he weren't so damn attractive, it would almost be annoying.

I feel the need to point out that, in the past three hours, only four customers have walked in, so I do. Manny counters with, "Things might pick up soon." We both know the real reason why he won't lock up early. It's simply a game of whether he'll admit to it.

"And I might sprout wings and fly away," I say.

"We're not closing early, Eden."

"Why not? It would be so fun," I push. "There's a whole world out there, Manny. Aren't you dying to see it?" Manny snatches the towel off his neck and begins wiping down the counter. He's now avoiding eye contact, which means I'm wearing him down. "Don't be so lame. C'mon, we can go get donuts. Or I'll buy you a cane, set you on someone's porch, and you can yell at children to stop running around, if that's more your speed. Is it, Manuel?"

At that, he stops scrubbing. "Why would I want to yell at children?" he asks with complete sincerity.

"Forget yelling. You can speak to everyone in a very civilized, friendly tone as long as said speaking takes place outside these four walls. You in?" At this point I'm practically bouncing at the thought of leaving work early.

Until Manny caves and says what we've both been thinking: "My dad won't like that, Eden." Hope deflates from my chest like a balloon because, if there's one thing we can agree on, it's that disappointing Manny's dad should be a federal crime.

The first time I met Mr. Álvaro was when he interviewed me

on the sidewalk bench across the street. He's, like, seven feet tall and covered in tattoos, which is enough to make you do a double take. But then he smiles and the hardness chips away, teddy bear softness peeking through the cracks. He might be the nicest person I've ever met—Manny included, which says *a lot*.

The doorbell chimes and I'm reminded that I'm at work. Manny eagerly peeks through the window that separates the kitchen from the dining area. I know he's hoping to see another customer, but it's only Earl leaving for the night. I shoot Manny a look that says, *See, I told you no one else is coming*, then head over to clean Earl's table because I *am* on the clock.

I pocket the two dollar tip, add his dishes to the cart, and wipe down the table. By the time I'm finished, the other customers have left and I'm alone with my thoughts, which are by far my least favorite company to keep. My fingers itch for distraction. I head back to the cash register and collapse on my little stool, propping my feet up on the counter's edge and probably violating a dozen different health codes. My phone is in my hand, and I have the article on the comatose woman open in seconds. I read every paragraph this time, even the ones about her family's happiness at this "miracle." Something bleak and gray snakes its way around my heart. Envy? Guilt? I'm not too great at identifying my feelings these days.

Something broke in me after Katie's accident. Like the internal switch that makes you feel empathetic and kind and caring and all those sweet little adjectives just shut off with a simple *flick*. All I can really feel is tired. Sometimes sad. But like I said, I try not to dwell on that for too long. If I do, it's suffocating.

Like Manny, I find myself staring at the restaurant door, hoping for someone to walk in, hoping for a distraction before I begin to spiral out like a spool of thread. I'm waiting for the day I'm unable to wind myself back up anymore.

Then heat radiates through my skin. Manny has sidled up against me, his arm pressed into mine. I scrunch my eyes shut for a minute and breathe because I refuse to unravel today.

When I meet Manny's gaze, he's smiling. I don't understand why I'm constantly surprised by that. Maybe it's because he makes happiness look so easy.

"I have an idea," Manny says. He's trying to play it off, but the guy is nearly bursting at the seams.

"Do tell."

Manny raises his hand. A pair of keys is dangling from his finger. "Wanna get out of here?"

It takes us twenty minutes to clean and lock up. I'm standing on the sidewalk outside, hands fidgeting with the straps of my bag, watching as Manny locks the door. The excitement I feel is a testament to how utterly uneventful my life is. If leaving work early is enough to make me breathless, I may need to consider picking up a hobby. Or expanding my social life. Either-or.

Manny loops his arm through mine and guides us down the street. To my relief, he heads west at the intersection, not north, which leads to Katie's hospital. Tonight, I'm trying to step *outside* my life. That hospital is a looming reminder of my bleak reality.

I want to ask Manny what changed his mind about leaving early, but I really don't care. I'm just happy to be *free*. And part of me fears if I bring it up, he'll change his mind right back.

The city streets are bustling, and the air has lost its humidity now that the sun has set. It also smells faintly of sewage, because the city refuses to let you romanticize it in any capacity. Manny leads us past the laundromat—which I'm positive is a front for something illegal—and keeps walking. Convenience stores, used bookstores, bubble tea shops. I don't even bother asking where we're going. I'm just happy to be heading somewhere that isn't my apartment building, a hospital room, or the restaurant.

When we pass by Chipotle, I jerk to a stop. We stare through the large windows and I know we're thinking the same thing— that the insanely long line of customers should be at Pollo Loco instead.

"I'm going in there," I say, bouncing on the balls of my feet like a boxer trying to pump themself up before a fight.

Manny steps in front of me, blocking my view of the line. His face is creased with concern. Shocker. "What— Why?" His eyes are wide and anxious.

"To advise them that their money is better spent at a family-owned restaurant down the street."

"Eden." Manny takes my hand in his and begins dragging me away from the door. My feet literally slide across the concrete. I plant them firmly and hold my ground. I cross my arms like the eighteen-year-old child I am.

"I'm simply trying to save your family business, Manny," I say.

The corner of his mouth kicks up. "Is that what you're doing?" I nod. "Our business isn't yours to save. Now, can we keep walking before you get permanently banned from Chipotle?"

I huff out a disapproving breath and fall into step beside him. "I'd like to see them try to ban me." We pause at the intersection. I realize again that I have no clue where we're going. "Where are you taking me?"

"The park," Manny says a bit anticlimactically. He shuffles on his feet as we wait for the light to change. I assume he means Trinity Bellwoods Park, which is only a few blocks away. "I like being outside after work," he continues. "Being stuck in that kitchen all day messes with my head."

The traffic light switches to red. I take a step and Manny reaches out to stop me, his arm barricading my stomach. He looks both ways because of course he does, then takes my hand and hurries across the street. I want to make fun of him for being such a complete nerd. For some reason, I don't.

Instead, I say, "You should talk to your dad about hiring another chef so you don't have to work all day." When business began to die down, so did the money. Manny told me how his dad had to fire the two other chefs because he couldn't afford to pay them. Now he's the last one standing. Mr. Álvaro helps Manny in the kitchen whenever he can. Still, I can't imagine the pressure

10

Manny must feel, holding all that weight on his shoulders.

"It's not that easy," Manny says simply, any trace of cheerfulness now gone from his voice.

"Money?"

Manny nods, his jaw a tight line below the glow of the streetlights. "The root of all problems, huh?"

"Tell me about it," I say with all the exhaustion in the world.

Of course hiring new staff isn't that easy. Whenever money's involved, it rarely is. And I'm a struggling eighteen-year-old waitress here, living with a roommate in one of the country's most expensive cities, so I know a thing or two about a tight budget.

I briefly consider donning a balaclava and robbing a bank. Anything that'll make this easier on Manny and his family. Although getting arrested would really dampen things.

Up ahead, the park comes into view. Lush, tall trees flank the grass, and the tennis court's lights are already on now that the sun has nearly set. I can hear the balls being thwacked around by rackets. Even this late, the park is bathed in a warm glow, and tons of people mill around, mostly sitting on the grass or walking their dogs along the pathways. I realize that Manny was right—being outside after work is sort of nice. At least it's better than my standard subway ride home and subsequent collapse into bed.

We walk through the gates leading into the park, then ditch the sidewalk for the grass. Manny finds a quiet spot beneath a tree and sinks down. I'm about to drop too when he shrugs off his jacket and places it down for me. For the briefest moment, I wish my patchwork quilt of a heart weren't ripped apart, being held together by cheap tape and Band-Aids. Maybe if it were a full, functioning, beating organ, I could be with someone as wholesome as Manny.

But he deserves a lot better than me. And I definitely deserve a lot worse.

I sit on his jacket and cross my legs, making sure to keep my shoes off the soft denim. Since I apparently can't take a hint, I keep prodding. "You should just talk to your dad," I say. "At least let him know you're struggling. Don't you think he'd want to know?"

"I'm not struggling," Manny says. He holds out his hands in a sweeping gesture and grins widely. "See? Perfectly fine."

Sure, he looks perfectly fine. That's probably a bit of an understatement. But what I'm focusing on are the bags beneath his eyes, like faded blue smears of paint. And the way he's always yawning. Or now, when he tips his head back against the tree trunk and his eyes droop closed, like he could fall asleep right here on the grass.

"Maybe *I* can be your sous-chef," I tease. At that, Manny's eyes snap open, like the thought of me cooking is the equivalent to downing three shots of espresso. "Is that the term? Doesn't matter. I can roll out dough and beat an egg. Really, how hard can it be?" I'm picturing myself in a fancy white apron with one of those tall, stiff hats on. The look on Manny's face tells me that he's picturing me burning down the kitchen. "God, Manny. Tell me how you really feel."

So he does, of course. "You'd be a terrible chef," he says.

"I didn't mean that literally!" I look around for something

to throw at him. A branch. A small but effective rock. Nothing. Nature and its treacherous ways.

"Because," he continues, "the customers would never get their food. You'd eat it all."

"You eat one pastry in front of someone and they think they know you," I grumble.

But he has a point. He knows it too, because his eyebrows jump up. I can tell he's stifling a laugh, waiting for me to deny it. "Well? Am I wrong?" he asks.

"It's simple quality assurance," I say in what I hope is a very informed way. I try to think of more smart-sounding words to spit out that can further my case.

I can't.

"How so?" he pushes. And now that I'm on the receiving end of the teasing, I don't like it very much.

Thankfully, a woman brushes by us with her dog trailing behind. It buys me a few seconds to come up with an answer. The dog stops trotting around to pee, and I notice it's wearing a neon-pink sweater that says BITCH on it in silver sequins. I turn to Manny with my jaw basically unhinged. His face is entirely lit up. It's the funniest thing I've seen in a long time.

Manny is hunched over, laughing into his hands in what I'm assuming is supposed to be a discreet way, but somehow manages to call even more attention to himself. I'm thinking that this is the happiest I've ever seen him, and it's because of a dog in a ridiculous sweater. Meanwhile I've been spewing comedic gold since the moment we met and what do I get? A shake of the head and a disapproving stare. Pft. Maybe I should wear a sweater that says BITCH on it, too.

The woman, finally catching on to Manny's laughter, tugs at her dog's leash and stomps away, making it crystal clear she knows we're laughing at her. Like, as if we couldn't.

"Wonder if that sweater comes in human sizes," I say, thinking out loud.

Manny, because he's a predictable man, shakes his head at me, still laughing. His dark curls brush over his forehead in a very distracting way. "I'll buy you one for your birthday," he says.

"I'll accept nothing less."

"You were saying something about quality assurance," Manny points out. Again, I search the grass for a weapon.

"Was I? Doesn't sound like me."

"Sounds exactly like you."

"Fine. Quality assurance, yes, hm. What I meant was . . . You need to taste your food before serving it, Manny. It's Chef 101," is what I settle on.

"Huh." The sole syllable comes out with equal amounts of shock and— Wait, is he *impressed*? "You're actually right."

"Try not to look so shocked. I watch *Chopped*."

Now he looks even more surprised. "Is that what you do in your spare time?"

"Wouldn't you like to know."

"I do," Manny says gently. "That's why I'm asking."

I think that if I sat here for the next three hours rambling on about myself, Manny would listen the entire way through. More than listen. He'd commit everything to memory. He'd take mental notes and color coordinate them. Maybe he'd even help me. But then this facade would crack. Eden, the silver-tongued girl who takes nothing seriously, would crumble into Eden, the soppy little mess who can't seem to get her life back on track.

I'm not even sure I'm capable of opening up to someone anymore after spending months building up barricades around my heart like a wild animal. Twigs, shards of glass, dried-up leaves. Whatever I could get my hands on is plastered to my chest like the world's worst armor. It will have to do. It keeps all the darkness in and any trace of light away.

And Manny is turning out to be the source of much light.

"I mostly sleep," is what I say. Maybe I can bore him enough with the realities of my life that he'll stop asking.

To be fair, the easier course would have been to not hang out with him after work at all. But something in that article about the comatose woman made me want to step outside that restaurant, step outside *my mind*. Maybe because, if I dwell on it too much, I worry I'll never feel the relief the woman's family was lucky enough to feel.

I worry that Katie will never be here again. Not like she used to be.

"I don't believe you." Manny's words are a sharp tug back to reality.

"What?"

"That all you do is sleep," he says slowly. His eyes search my face like he noticed my mind slip away for a minute.

"Oh. Well, too bad." My conversation skills are unmatched. Or I guess it's difficult to hold a conversation with someone when you're trying to have them learn the least possible amount about you.

"Seriously, Eden," Manny says. "We've been working together every day for, what, two months now? And the only thing I know about you is your name and that you're a terrible waitress." He says the last part with the cutest smile, and I can barely even muster the energy to dispute it.

"My life is boring. You're not missing out on much." *Except for all the sad shit no one wants to hear about.*

"Try me." He speaks those two words like a gentle caress. Like I'm made of glass and anything sharper would break me in two. Or scare me away. It's so earnest that it makes me consider telling him everything.

Since Katie's accident, there hasn't been a single person I've wanted to pour my heart out to. Not my parents. Not my roommate. Not a therapist or any other stranger. Manny is the first—and even then, I still refuse to.

There's one other person who knows what I'm going through. One other person who can relate. Sadly, I have no clue where he currently is.

A heavy sadness settles over me. I push it off like a blanket.

I cross my legs and stare down at the patch of grass between my thighs. My fingers pick at the green strands, plucking them up, then shredding them whole.

"No, thank you," I say.

"For what it's worth, *you* can ask *me* anything about myself," he says. I look up to find Manny staring into me with a level of eagerness I wasn't prepared for. This guy—this nice, great guy—is just waiting, waiting for me to take the bait. Waiting for me to give him the pieces of myself I lost months ago.

I should let him down gently. I should say something nice. But niceness and compassion don't come too easily to me.

"And why would I want to do that?" I say with a smile this time. I can give him that.

"Because it's what people do, Eden. Talk to each other."

"I don't like talking."

He shoves his hands into the pocket of his hoodie. "Unless it's sarcastic comments. Right?"

"Bingo."

"You're impossible."

"Nothing is impossible, Manny," I say with another smile. I'm too generous tonight.

"That's what I'm hoping for." Something in his face changes when he says that. He gets wistful, thoughtful. It reminds me of the night he kissed me. Tenderly. Softly. Like he was about to admit to something I didn't want to hear.

"Anyway," I begin, throwing a bucket of cold water over

17

whatever this moment was turning into. "Back to the hiring stuff. I'm just looking out for you. You're only twenty, with the work ethic of a middle-aged man. You should be out having fun. Doing whatever weird shit guys do on Friday nights." Although I'm nearly positive that whatever normal guys do, Manny does the opposite. He must spend his Friday nights volunteering at a food bank or wearing red-and-white spandex as he saves the city by anonymously fighting crime.

Now I'm realizing I have no idea what Manny actually does outside of work. I never thought to ask. Weird.

Manny plucks out a handful of grass and tosses it at me. "Bit of a pot-calling-the-kettle-black situation, huh?"

"Am I supposed to understand what that means?" I ask, brushing the grass off my clothing.

"I'm saying it's a bit ironic having *you* get on my case about not having a social life."

"Are you inferring I don't have a social life, Manny?" I ask, pretending to be offended.

"No," he says. "I was implying it."

"Whatever, nerd. Either way, you're wrong. I'm a bumble of activity. You should be thankful I even managed to squeeze you into my very busy schedule tonight."

Manny chuckles. I watch his brown eyes dance in the dark. "Right. I'm sure it was difficult to squeeze me into your ten to two a.m. time slot that says *consume unhealthy amounts of television.*"

I can't even deny it because he is absolutely correct.

With my last shred of dignity, I say, "You're changing the subject."

Manny lets out a long breath, signaling this topic is nearing its end. "I'm not asking my dad to hire anyone else, Eden. I can't risk him hiring someone more attractive than me. How will I survive without being the sole target of your constant attention?"

"I don't know," I say honestly, fighting back a smile. "You might combust into a thousand pieces."

Manny leans back against the tree trunk as he laughs. He kicks his left foot in the air and crosses his ankles. "I just might." He grows quiet, his eyes trailing to the grass. "So," he begins, his gaze shifting back up to mine, "when are you going to let me take you on a date?"

And there it is.

If I were any other person in the world, my heart would grow two sizes and I'd run home to write seventeen pages about this exact moment in my diary. I would detail the smallest smile on Manny's face and that raw vulnerability that's enough to make you kiss him on the spot. But this patchwork heart of mine doesn't work like that. Instead, what I feel is annoyance, because now I have to let him down gently.

In retrospect, kissing Manny probably wasn't the greatest idea. Any idiot with a pair of eyes can tell that he's the type to catch feelings. But I was dumb, stressed, and feeling lonely. All it took was one glance at Manny's bare chest as he stripped out of his work shirt for me to practically pounce on him in a way that was incredibly hot and not at all desperate. Like, at all.

Maybe a little.

Hindsight is always twenty-twenty, and I'm realizing now that our moment in the kitchen began a little thread that led us here to *this* moment, with Manny's heart on the line and me being the one having to break it. Or at least bruise it a little.

"Manny . . . ," I begin, because I am a wuss and the English language has left my brain in a single-file line.

Manny's sneakered foot knocks against my knee. "Jeez," he says with a laugh. "This doesn't sound good." I work up the nerve to look him in the eye. Bad move. The embarrassment on his face shreds whatever was left of my heart to pieces.

I scootch across the grass until we're side by side, our backs against the tree trunk. Maybe not looking him in the eye will make this easier. "Listen—"

Manny cuts me off. "You don't have to explain yourself, Eden. You can just say no. I'm a big guy. I can handle rejection."

Aaaaand I hate myself. My head somehow finds its way onto Manny's shoulder. In another life, maybe I could be whole and warm and worthy of someone like this.

"I think you're my only friend," I tell him. "And one of the best people I've met. Can we just stay like this? Please?" I don't want to elaborate. I just want him to get it. To get this—to understand this small piece of me that I'm offering.

20

I feel the warm pressure of Manny's head resting on mine. The relief that floods through my chest nearly knocks me over. "Nicest thing you've ever said to me," he says. I can hear the smile in his voice.

"Don't get used to it," I say, wondering if he can hear the smile in mine.

2

EDEN

MANNY INSISTS ON WALKING me to the subway, and I don't put up a fight. It's so late that the streets are dark and quiet, the only light coming from the lit-up windows of the twenty-four-hour convenience stores. If it weren't for the six-foot-three boulder trudging along beside me, I'd be glancing over my shoulder. To my relief, Manny has smoothly moved on from all mentions of dating, love, and nauseating romance in general. I breathe easier at that, letting my thoughts drift away as he talks about a new item he's trying to convince his dad to add to the menu at Pollo Loco. I'm not really listening. Instead, my mind pulls up a scene from a chilly spring day when Katie gave me bangs on the edge of her bathtub, when we headed downtown the next day to look at apartments. We walked down the city streets like we owned them, pointing out restaurants we planned on trying and memorizing the layout of the city.

The memories are hazy now. They've turned gray around the edges, crumpled like a book that's been dog-eared one too many times. I can still remember little moments: Katie's hand in mine, warm and firm; the foil-wrapped burritos we ate for lunch; this brightness blooming in my chest, like we were on the cusp of the rest of our lives. But everything else feels far away, like trying to find stars and not realizing you haven't taken the cap off the telescope. I can't remember the names of the streets we walked down, or if we walked down them at all. Did we take the bus? Catch an Uber? I can't remember what the buildings we explored look liked, if they were tall and shining into the sky, or if they were beaten and broken, with rust-lined balconies.

In the spaces within me that the memories fade, guilt grows. I'm losing pieces of her. Every single day, they fade away, growing further from reach. It's only been months. That's nothing in the span of a lifetime. It's insignificant. If I'm forgetting about her now, what will I be able to remember in five years? In ten? The thought is so chilling I almost start to cry.

To my right, Manny walks beside me. And all I can think is that it should be her.

Now, every day feels like a waiting game, like I'm suspended in limbo and there are only two possible outcomes: Katie wakes up, takes my hand, and pulls me right out of this nightmare and back into our life of driving late at night and eating takeout for dinner; or Katie never wakes up—then the rest is too horrifying to even think about. Because now, however small it might be, there's still the tiniest possibility that she does wake up. And the second her eyes open, the game resets and we're back, stepping into our futures because they are *ours*, tethered together. But if she doesn't, then this is it. This bleak day-to-day existence switches from being my current reality to being *the rest of my life*. I can't have that. I need the light at the end of the tunnel, even if it dims a little every day.

It's exhausting to feel as if you have no control over the path your life takes.

We stop at the entrance to the subway station and I'm winded like I've completed a marathon. This happens all the time: my body feels physically exhausted from the laps my mind is running. It happens when I let myself freely think about Katie, which is why those memories are locked up behind an iron door, held down with thick restraints.

Manny towers above me, watching me with wide, careful eyes. I let the restraints slip the loosest bit and he morphs into someone else entirely. His brown curls turn into loose waves, black as spilled ink on a sheet of paper. His soft eyes harden into cool blue, warmth freezing into ice. I can see the slope of Truman's smile, can remember the feathery weight of his touch. I want to sink into him like a still pond. I want to fall backward, tumble into the before.

But the wind howls against the brick of the buildings, slashes into the metal of the streetlights, and every trace of him blows away, wisps melting into the night air. It's Manny before me, staring like he wants to ask me what's wrong, knowing full well the

24

answer he'll get is far from the truth.

"You okay to get home alone?" is what he says. His eyes say, *Let me take the subway with you, Eden. Let me walk you into your building and hold your hand in the elevator. Let me tuck you into bed and make sure you're okay—make sure whatever place you just wandered into isn't hiding under your bed or waiting in your closet.*

"I'll be fine," I say. I've done this alone hundreds of times. I can do it hundreds more.

Before I can run down the stairs to the trains, Manny pulls me into a hug, crushing me against his chest. I want to feel safe, to feel protected. Instead I feel suffocated, like an animal left to fend for itself on the streets for so long it begins to suspect any form of affection. My body stiffens. I don't know if Manny realizes, because he keeps squeezing me like I'm Humpty Dumpty, like he can put all my pieces back together again.

"Manny," I croak, pushing against his chest. He lets go instantly, clears his throat, and shoves his hands into the pockets of his jeans. We both sense that something is off. That *I'm* off. We both happily step around it. I'm the elephant in the room.

"I'll see you tomorrow," he says. I'm running down the stairs, now halfway underground, when I hear Manny call, "And don't be late!"

I don't respond. I can't make any promises.

At this time, there's barely anyone on the subway: an older man with graying hair who's resting his head against the paneled glass; a girl my age with her feet kicked up on the seat in front of her, thumbing through a book decorated with sticky tabs. I take the last seat in an empty row of three. The advertisement directly in front of me is for some fall festival, with photos of fresh maple syrup sticking to snow before being wrapped around Popsicle sticks. It's a Canadian stereotype come to life, and now I'm craving pancakes. Dammit.

The subway ride is barely five minutes, but I still dig through my bag for my headphones. By the time I manage to unknot the cord, the voice on the intercom says, "You've arrived at St. George station," and the train's doors are pulling open. I remind myself to buy AirPods, then do a mental tally of the money I currently have in my bank account and, yeah, never mind. Making rent this month is probably more important. . . . Probably.

I'm weighed down with exhaustion from working, socializing— is that what Manny and I did?—and just existing in general, so I take the escalator instead of the stairs. Up, up, up. Seconds pass and I'm pushing through the gate, out of the station, and bursting back onto the eerie streets. My headphones cord reminds me that I'm broke, but it's straight now, so I plug it into my phone and shove them into my ears. I tell myself I don't care what comes on when I hit shuffle, then continue to skip every single song until the one I'm searching for pops up: "Robbers" by The 1975. It was Katie's favorite— And there is it, the memory pushing against my mental door, trying to slip through the cracks. *No*, I think, *not tonight*. I skip the song. I'm not doing this again.

26

A random song by a random band I saw in concert years ago starts playing, and it's not great but it'll do. And by that, I mean there's no emotions attached to it, no memories that are ready to be dug up and played on an endless loop in my mind for the next hour.

I turn the volume higher. Higher. Then higher again, until I no longer hear my sneakers slapping against the concrete or the whir of the cars driving by. I walk from memory—I could close my eyes and still end up standing in front of my building. I pass by the Asian grocery store with the freshest and cheapest fruit. I take a left at the Starbucks. I listen to one more song and I'm there, standing beneath the looming building that stretches right into the night sky. It's the exact building Katie picked— *Nope.*

I smack my fob against the pad and the door swings open. The lights are bright and yellow, the floor covered in worn beige carpet. Robert, the security guard, sits at his desk and smiles at me as I enter. I walk past the weird vertical water fountain thing that still isn't working, and straight to the elevators. I press the up button. There's a new poster taped to the wall. It's of a slot machine, advertising a weekend trip to Fallsview Casino in Niagara Falls. I think back to the AirPods, the one-hundred-and-something dollars in my checking account. I really cannot afford a gambling addiction right now.

The elevator takes too long to arrive because it always does. There are only four and one's currently out for renovations. I'm annoyed and my exhaustion grows with every passing second. I'm starting to feel like my body is filled with stones. Still, I head to the stairs. By the time I reach the fifteenth floor, I'm gasping for breath and my chest is heaving too quickly for someone who's only eighteen.

The hall is long and straight, covered in maroon carpet that's been stained from decades of wear and tear. It's so different from the building my family used to live in, with its polished mahogany floors and bright white walls. The walls here are the color of faded manila. It's dreary and depressing. Nothing like what Katie and I envisioned. But in the battle of aesthetics and affordability, the latter obviously won.

I walk down the corridor, past the elevators directly in the middle—two on each side—and my door is the first one on the right. No one told me renting a unit directly next to the elevators was a bad call. All night long you can hear the rhythmic squeak of them moving up and down the shafts. We've grown used to it, though. Now it's nothing but white noise that fills the eerie silence.

Apartment 1519. I slide my key into the lock and shove the door open. I'm already envisioning peace and quiet. A quick shower before jumping into bed, wrapped in a weighted blanket, and watching reruns of *Brooklyn Nine-Nine* until I fall asleep without a single damaging thought entering my mind. I've learned that if you constantly overstimulate your brain with music, social media, or any other distraction, it's easier to avoid thinking about all the moments from your past you're trying to forget.

But when the door swings open, my promised peace turns into very real chaos. Ramona's shoes are flung across the narrow hallway, her coat sitting in a lump on the wooden floor instead of hanging off the coat hook that is literally *right there*. I hang my jacket and bag on the brass hook and kick past her mess. The hall opens into the living room, which is much worse. The heather-gray couch we hauled in from the thrift store sits in the middle of the small room, fully covered in empty cardboard boxes. Package slips and Bubble Wrap are piled into a mini mountain on the coffee table. They spill onto the carpet and are shoved into the couch cushions. It's like Canada Post has exploded in our apartment. Or, more accurately, Ramona finally made it down to the mail room to pick up all her packages. All these boxes were filled with useless products that brands have sent over in return for a sponsored Instagram post to her nearly one hundred thousand followers. Most of them will end up flying down the garbage chute.

I'm not delusional enough to call myself an organized person who has her life together, but dammit. Even this is too much for me.

I pry the headphones from my ears and swing the cord around my neck. "Mona?" I call, wading farther into the destruction. I step around the garbage on tiptoes, trying to find some inch of bare floor to walk on.

Ramona doesn't respond, but I can hear her buzzing around in the kitchen, talking to herself—or, more likely, talking to her followers. Our apartment is small enough, barely eight hundred square feet, that I can cross the living room and enter the kitchen in five steps.

Our kitchen is all unflattering fluorescent lighting and old, battered wooden cupboards. There's no dishwasher, so dirty plates and cups are piled high in the sink. I want to blame that on Ramona until I spot my half-filled cereal bowl in the pile, exactly where I left it before running off to work this afternoon. Ramona stands in front of the fridge, her honey-blonde hair woven intricately into some fancy braid she undoubtedly learned from YouTube.

Her soft blue T-shirt has *donuts are life* stitched onto it in white cursive. She has one for each of her favorite foods and rotates through them depending on what she's filming for the day. Sure enough, there's a box of half-eaten donuts on the kitchen island, next to her phone, which is propped up on a fancy tripod.

"Honestly," Ramona is saying, eyes locked on her phone, chocolate donut in one hand, "you would *never* know this donut is vegan. It's so light. Like, *so* fluffy." She takes a bite and holds what's left of the donut right up to the camera, pulling the dough apart with her fingers. "Do you see that texture? It's literally a cloud, you guys. I really can't believe how good this is." She takes another bite, chewing while she grins into the camera, then spots me hovering in the doorway. "I've got to pause the livestream for a second. My roommate just walked in." She taps her phone, then turns to me, wispy bangs falling into her eyes. "I left you some chicken chow mein in the fridge. I ate all the spring rolls, though. Sorry."

"It's fine, I ate at work— What happened in the living room?" I ask.

Ramona's face flushes, and she chews away at the pink polish covering her nails. "I'll clean it in the morning. I promise. This new high protein cereal company sent me, like, two dozen boxes to promote this weekend. I think there are seven grams of protein per cup or something."

"Is that supposed to be a lot?"

Ramona shrugs. "No idea. It's in the cupboard if you want to try." The cupboard creaks as I open it. There are at least ten pastel boxes of cereal stacked neatly on the shelves. I pull out the pale orange one—peanut butter Crunchy O's. I skim the nutrition facts and, huh, she wasn't kidding about the protein.

"Robert's going to hate you if you keep clogging up the mail room," I say, ripping the box open and plunging my hand into the plastic bag.

"I've started leaving a coffee for him on his desk every morning. It balances out. So? How are they?"

I pop a few of the circle puffs into my mouth. "A little cardboardy," I say. I nod at her phone, the half-empty donut box on the counter. "What are you working on?"

Ramona slides the box across the counter toward me. *Blossoms* is written on the top in purple cursive. "There's this new vegan bakery that opened last week on Queen Street. Everyone's been bugging me to review them." She rolls her eyes, but I know she loves it. I know she's happy. Then she glances at the clock and back toward me. Her eyes widen when she notices it—the change in my routine. "Why are you home so late?"

I crunch on some more cereal because this is where Mona and I draw the line. She talks about her work, her brand deals, her days spent running around the city in search of the cutest bakery or underrated café to post on Instagram for her followers to eat up. She shares and shares and shares like a broken faucet that can't be turned off. The water just keeps spilling out. But I'm the opposite. An old, rusted tap that nothing drips out of anymore.

"Where were you?" she prods, leaning her hip into the counter, like she's cozying up because she knows it'll take a while to get even the smallest scrap of information out of me.

It's our routine song and dance. She asks. I avoid it. Eventually I sulk off to my bedroom and shut the door. She tries again the next day. Her efforts are useless.

"Well?" she asks again.

Maybe it's because she's asking so nicely, or maybe because the fluorescent lighting makes her blonde hair look like Katie's did under the summer sun. Or maybe it's just because answering is the quickest route to the end of this conversation that I find myself saying, "I walked around a little after work with Manny." Ramona rolls her eyes. She knows about my job at Pollo Loco, about Manny and his dad. "What's wrong with Manny? You can't hate him. It's like hating a puppy."

"I don't *hate* him. I've never even met him," she reminds me with a glare, as if to say *And whose fault is that?* Well, excuse me for keeping my work life and personal life separate. I can't have these equally depressing parts of me colliding. The world might end from incurable sadness. Or worse, Manny and Ramona will talk about me like two disappointed parents.

"Spare me, Mona. I've already listened to one person my age try to parent me today. I can't do this again." I hold up the box of cereal. "And this tastes like crap, by the way."

She swats my hand away from the box and tries some herself. Her face instantly scrunches up like she's sucked on a lemon. "Oh my God. It's like eating sand."

"And now we have fourteen boxes of sand in our cupboards."

She bursts out laughing. It's not the first time Ramona has been sent sponsored products that are terrible. First it was the cauliflower oatmeal that made our entire apartment smell like feet. Then the grain-free brownie mix that was, essentially, a brick made of cacao. The worst was the stuffed cookies that spoiled in transit. We both got food poisoning and had a contest for who could throw up the most. I won.

"I'll do a giveaway," she offers.

"Or we can just throw it out?" I move on from the cereal and hunt through the fridge for the leftover Chinese. "Though throwing out that much food feels wrong." I think about Manny, packing up all the leftover food at the end of the night to donate to food banks or hand out to people sleeping on the streets. I hate that his goodness has infiltrated my brain like a parasite. Yuck.

"Good point. Giveaway it is," Ramona says. She turns back

to her phone, fingers hovering over the screen. "I'm resuming my livestream. You've got three seconds to grab whatever you want and hide in your room. Three, two . . ."

I grab the chow mein in one hand, the box of donuts in the other, and I'm out of the kitchen before she can finish her sentence. "Tell your followers not to buy that cereal!" I call back when I'm safely in the living room, kicking through empty boxes.

"Use the code RAMONA25 for twenty-five percent off your purchase!" she yells back, then I hear her raise the pitch of her voice into that high, sugarcoated sound and she's back to talking about donuts.

Our living room is dark, save for the light of the moon pouring in from the floor-to-ceiling windows. There's no view of Lake Ontario, but . . . But, well, nothing. There is no bright side, really. It's the wrong building, wrong roommate. Nothing against Ramona—she simply isn't the person I'm supposed to be doing this with. It's a replacement life. A compromise. A last-ditch attempt to hold on to some sort of familiarity when everything changed.

When I lie in bed at night and squeeze my eyes shut, I can still see the red and blue lights dancing across my eyelids. I remember how brightly they lit up the night sky. How the ambulance's wailing siren broke through the stillness of that kiss. How everything flipped upside down in a matter of seconds.

Now, standing in our living room, I see the door to Ramona's bedroom is cracked open, a sliver of her bright, rainbow-hued life spilling out. The walls are covered in Polaroid photos hung from string lights, the smiling faces of friends and her twin sister flicking against the wall. Her polka-dot bed is piled so high with pillows there's barely any space to lie down. Potted plants cover the floor and dressers, even though Mona always forgets to water them and they wither away. She empties their pots and drives to Ikea to buy new ones, saying, "I'll be more careful this time." She never is.

I walk past her bedroom door to mine, which is shut tight. I turn the knob and the door pushes open, the old hinges creaking. My room is bathed in darkness. There are no windows, no exterior wall to let in sunlight or moonlight. It's like living in a tomb. My twin bed is shoved against the wall, plain gray sheets crumpled into a wrinkled mess at the bottom. A secondhand desk, my old MacBook my parents bought me when I started high school, and my dad's old desk chair that scratched up the wooden floorboards. There's no decor. No plants or photos hanging on the walls. It's lifeless. There's no trace of me in here, like someone came along with a pair of scissors and cut off any connections to my life— both who I am and who I was.

Mona calls it my cave, like it's this bleak, cold, uninhabitable den that I've chosen to live in.

In reality, it's temporary. I saw no point in decorating the walls only to strip them bare when our lease ends in a year. I moved into the city for Katie. I wanted to do that for her. I wanted to live out this version of her dream because she wasn't able to. But it was nothing like I thought it would be. There are no midnight walks through the quiet streets. No takeout and red wine. No sprawling on the couch and going through entire seasons of her favorite shows in a matter of days.

There's no her.

When I moved out here three months ago, I thought I would wake up one morning and everything would fall into place, like this life and this city would fit me perfectly, like a snug sweater. Like I'd grow into this building, this job, this roommate, these streets, and these false pretenses. Instead, everything got worse. I went through with my and Katie's life plan without Katie—the most essential piece in this entire puzzle. Without her, everything feels off. Incomplete. This life is two sizes too big.

Even starting university in the fall doesn't seem possible anymore. Nothing does.

I sink into the chair and roll myself toward my desk. My old laptop takes a minute to fire up, so I hit the power button and dig into the chow mein. I can still hear Mona speaking through the too-thin walls. The noodles are dry and hard. I eat them anyway. I think about Manny offering to cook for me at work. *An extremely talented chef who'll cook you up whatever you'd like.* I hate that I keep saying no, keep pushing everyone away like some sort of reverse magnet.

I shake off the thought. My laptop's screen brightens, and I abandon the food. My fingers fly across the keyboard in a memorized, well-rehearsed routine. I open up Instagram and the first thing I see is the notification for Mona's livestream hovering at the top of the page. I ignore it and go to the search bar. I type in the account name. At this point, I could do it in my sleep. I pull up Truman's account and it's the same as it has been since four months ago. Every post has been deleted. His bio is now erased. His profile photo is his reflection in a store window. I refresh the page one, two, three times. Nothing happens. Four hundred eighty-four followers. He's following seventy-two accounts. That's it.

I begin to pull up Katie's page and stop myself. I don't want to see her last post, dated the night of Truman's party. It was of the two of us, heads touching, grinning wide, lying on her bed with our feet kicked into the air.

But more than that, I don't want to read the comments. The last time I checked there were nearly one thousand of them. *Miss you so much. Hope you're back soon. We haven't given up on you, Katie.* It's a thousand different ways to say the same thing. I never left a comment. I've never even liked the photo. I didn't know she posted it until it was too late. Until she was already gone. I was too busy that night to check my phone and see the notification: *@Katiefalls tagged you in a post.* Seeing it the next morning was a feeling I can't describe. How. How was she there? How did we take that photo twelve hours before and now she was just . . . gone? I couldn't bring myself to like it, to leave a comment. It felt so wrong, knowing she wouldn't see it. Knowing the notification would hover on her phone screen indefinitely.

I'm spiraling. I know I am. And I can't stop it. Sometimes it feels good to find the twisted sort of comfort that only that past can bring me. Sometimes I let it bury me completely. I let myself soak fully in the memories of us until it almost feels like she's still here and the past five months have been a dream. I want to do that now, but I won't. I can't.

I exit the browser and shut my laptop. My clothes smell like the food Manny cooks, so I strip out of them and into my sweats before climbing into bed. My closet is overflowing with dirty laundry, and I tell myself I'll head into the basement tomorrow to wash it. I'll knot all the garbage bags and drop them down the chute. I'll take Ramona's cardboard boxes downstairs and dump them into the recycling bins. I'll wash the dirty dishes in the sink. I'll do a million different tasks to distract my mind from the one thing it wants to fixate on.

I slip beneath the covers, and in the silence, in the dark, I'm a boat that's taken on water. It rises up my toes, past my ankles, inching toward my knees. I'm frantic and running, patching up the holes with loose scraps of fabric, shoving them deep into the wounds. I patch up one hole and another breaks free. I'm exhausted. Out of breath. My mind is telling me to stop. To stand still. *Just lie down. Let the waves rock you to sleep. Rest.* But my body has a mind of its own. It keeps moving, keeps trying. It won't give up on me. Not yet.

And then my phone chimes, a beacon in the darkness. I reach for it on the floor, squinting against the light from the screen. It's some notification. I can't read the words—my eyes are still adjusting to the brightness. I click on it blindly and my phone unlocks, the Instagram app popping open. It takes me a minute to register what's happening, and then I'm on Truman's page. I bolt upright because something is different. *@Trumanfalls has posted for the first time in a while!* The zero has turned into a one.

There's one new post.

My fingers shake as I click on it.

The photo is dark. I squint at the screen, trying to make it out. It looks like an empty room. Light wooden floors. Barren white walls. The camera's angled toward the floor, showing the tips of his black-and-white Chucks. There's a flimsy white table and something on top of it, too. I zoom in. It's a painting canvas. Beside it are bottles of unopened paint, two or three paintbrushes. The caption is one word: *home*. I look at the tagged location. Toronto.

He's back.

3

TRUMAN

WHAT I FEEL IS bone-deep exhaustion. Physical, mental, emotional.

I'm tired of waking up in an empty bedroom because I'm too drained to unpack any of the boxes that finally arrived from Montreal. I'm tired of my phone blowing up with endless texts from my mom, detailing lists of errands for me to run the second the sun rises. Speaking of, I'm kind of fucking tired of the sun rising every day, too. I'm tired of the weird knot that's been in my shoulder for days now and is slowly creeping its way up toward my neck. My friends did warn me that taking a six hour bus ride back into the city from Quebec wasn't the best idea.

When I told them I couldn't drive myself because I planned on sleeping the entire way, they countered with, "Then take a plane," but boarding a plane for an hour long flight felt like something only rich snobs did. No, thank you. Not to mention how much

I dislike flying. I never could understand my sister Katie's obsession with the sky. So ultimately, I decided to ignore everyone's suggestions, because nineteen years on this planet has taught me absolutely nothing.

The bus was crammed with a sketchy group of teens who were high as kites—not that I was jealous; I don't do that anymore—too many screaming babies to count, and a dude who listened to the same song on repeat for the entire ride.

In retrospect, maybe this feeling of exhaustion is warranted after all.

My bedroom in my family's new apartment is still completely unfurnished. The mattress is flat on the floor, which probably isn't the best for my back and makes getting out of bed a pain in the ass. I need to buy blackout curtains for the windows, so right now all the sunlight is streaming in at full brightness, making it impossible for me to sleep in later than . . . I reach around on the floor for my phone and check the time. Seven thirty. The sun is making it impossible for me to sleep past *seven thirty*. There were times I didn't go to bed until seven thirty.

What I want is to tear the sun from the sky and sleep for the next month. What I do is unlock my phone and read the texts from my mom. *Can you please pick up fresh flowers on your way to the hospital? The ones your father bought last week have died. Thanks.* I type back a thumbs-up emoji, sit up in bed, try to massage my right shoulder, but the knot only tightens, the pain shooting farther up into my neck. I leave it alone. If my body decides today is the day to just mess up my entire bone structure, then so be it. It can do whatever the hell it wants at this point.

I pad out of my bedroom and down the wide hallway lined with knockoff artwork and thin sideboards my mom has topped with fake plants, fake books, and very real family photos. Katie's smiling face watches me walk by, all the way into the living area.

Even though my family has only been living here for two months now, you'd never know it by how elaborately my mother has decorated every inch of space, like she's expecting the photographers from *Lifestyle* magazine to show up any second and do a two page spread on her design techniques. I mean, she is a well-known interior designer, so it's not completely impossible. Fairly unlikely at best.

This morning, I'm the only one home. Just how I like it. The quietness is inviting, this stillness I can feel in my bones, my brain. The marble floors in the kitchen are cold as ice beneath my bare feet. I turn on the Keurig and stand, watching as it whirs to life, the power button blinking blue. Coffee drips into the mug and I drink it in big, greedy gulps while it's still piping hot. It's the only way to do it. It burns my tongue and prickles the roof of my mouth, but everything around me comes into focus, blurred edges now sharpened.

The entire house is dusted in three colors: white, beige, and this shade my mom refers to as *pewter* but is really just gray. The artist in me can appreciate her choices—layered rugs covering the living room floor, off-white leather L-shaped couch, white-and-gray marble on the kitchen counters, shiny metal pendant lights with gold accents hanging over the kitchen island. It looks perfect. It probably *would* fit the front page of any magazine. The only problem is it doesn't feel like home. Maybe that's because I've only been living here for twelve hours. Or maybe it's because all my memories are stacked away in our old house.

My parents didn't move, not exactly. Selling our old house wasn't a possibility. The idea of throwing all those memories away—throwing Katie's bedroom away—was suffocating. When they transferred Katie to Mount Sinai, a hospital here in the city, they did it because they knew Katie's dream was to live in Toronto. She would have done so if it weren't for . . . everything. My parents wanted to be closer to the hospital, since my mom seems to live there these days and was getting sick of staying in hotels. My dad already worked in the city, so it eliminated his nearly two hour commute. My parents rented this unit in the building across from the hospital and started splitting their time between homes. It's the kind of ease that comes with having money. That ability to uproot your life in a matter of days when most people would have spent years saving, planning, prepping.

It didn't take long for me to decide to move in here permanently. One, it has a killer view. Two, the memories in here aren't as loud or as suffocating. But I moved all my shit in back in June, right before I headed over to Quebec. I never had a chance to unpack.

The front door slams open. I expect to see my mom, but it's Milo rounding the corner. Milo, who doesn't have a key.

Maybe I'm still half-asleep. Maybe he's not here.

"God, you look like shit," he says.

I swallow another sip of coffee, wince as it hits my throat. "You sure you want those to be the first words you say to me in two months?"

"Do you expect me to say that I've missed your lanky ass? Because I haven't." He takes in the space, the floor-to-ceiling windows, the way everything screams *money!* Milo whistles. "Whooooa. You're living like a king in here," he says, then goes on to make himself at home, rifling through the fridge and pulling out aluminum foil–wrapped dishes of leftover lasagna and fried fish and plastic containers of stuffed olives. "I have missed this." He grabs a plate and takes a seat on one of the leather stools.

Then the coffee really kicks in, because I realize something. "How'd you even get in here?"

Milo reaches into his pocket and slaps a key ring on the counter. *My* keys. Crap. How tired was I last night? "You left these in the door. You're lucky it was me who wandered in and not some fucking weirdo."

"Remind me of the difference?"

Milo pins me with the look, the one I've seen him give countless guys before unleashing himself and pounding their faces in. One second it's bone and skin, then nothing but blood. He's got a real habit of falling for girls who aren't into monogamy.

I catch my reflection in the glass cupboard and wince. I look like a malnourished twig next to him.

"Late night?" he asks, nodding to either the coffee I'm gripping too tightly or my hair, which is doing God knows what on my head.

"The bus didn't reach Union until almost midnight."

"If only someone had advised you not to take a bus. Wait a second—"

"Is this why you broke into my house? To annoy the shit out of me?" I ask.

"Not much else to do on a Friday morning." He stops shoveling lasagna into his mouth for a second to slide the keys across the counter toward me. "And I didn't break in."

The barstool groans when I sit down. The key ring sparkles under the bright lights. For a second I'm relieved it was Milo who found them sticking out of the door. If my parents had, they wouldn't have yelled at me. The opposite. They would've handed them back to me like it was no big deal, which is almost worse. I wish they'd yell. I wish they'd treat me as they did before Katie's accident, like a work in progress.

Ever since Katie's accident, I've been getting a free pass. I'd get home long past midnight, stinking of alcohol, and my mom silently cleaned my vomit off the floor; I showed up for dinner three hours late and my mom pulled a Tupperware out of the fridge. "I saved you some," she'd say, smiling. There were no consequences. No repercussions, no matter how bad I got. And I get it, I really do. They were just thankful I was there, alive, breathing next to them.

"How's your sister?" Milo asks, staring me right in the eye when he mentions her. He's the only person who can. Everyone else needs to look away—the sidewalk, walls, their feet, wherever.

"Same as before," I say. Still tucked away in a hospital bed with her eyes closed. I wish I had a timeline, a big calendar stuck to the fridge with a specific date circled in red marker that'd say *KATIE WAKES UP!*

"Need anything?" Milo huffs out, his übermasculine way of saying he's here for me.

"Yeah, for you to stop eating all my food. Seriously, man, are you sure you're not a machine?"

He eyes my scrawny body. "Not like you're eating it," he says.

"I *am*. I just don't . . . gain weight, I guess. Whatever. Fuck you."

The door slams open again. This time, I'm certain it's my mom because, at this point, who the hell else is there? Then a flash of fiery red hair rounds the corner.

"Morning, boys," Santana says, sliding effortlessly into the kitchen like she lives here. She walks right up to the island and taps her long red nails against the marble. Milo's staring at my ex-girlfriend with his jaw open, half-chewed pasta noodles hanging out.

"There's no chance I left two sets of keys in the door," I say.

"Didn't need a key. The door was unlocked," Santana says, smiling brightly, the gap between her two front teeth on full display.

I shoot a glare at Milo. He shrugs it off, his eyes instantly going back to Santana, who he's clearly hung up on in a real subtle, not obvious way.

"What are you doing here?" I ask, because it's pretty clear Milo's brain has malfunctioned.

"I came to see you." She turns to Milo then, acknowledging him for the first time. "What are *you* doing here?"

"Same thing," he says. "Came to see Tru."

Santana eyes the mountain of food he's in the middle of eating with the slightest look of disgust. Her face is an open book. She can't hide any emotion. Milo notices too, because he makes a big show of putting the fork down and pushing everything a few inches away.

The fact that the three of us are sitting in a room together is a miracle. Our past is, to put it lightly, pretty messed up. Santana went to high school with me. We spent all of grade twelve doing the on-again, off-again thing. Then I graduated, took a year off, and we kept at it. Back in May we were on again. We thought it could work that time—my family had just moved down here to be closer to Katie, Santana had just moved here to kick-start her modeling career. We met up one night at some dive bar because we aren't the five-star-restaurant, foods-you-can't-even-pronounce kind of people. Long story short: I got there early, spotted Santana's car, and got too close before realizing she wasn't inside it *alone*. She wasn't dressed, either.

My initial response was to *try* to punch the guy with my lanky-ass arms, but that guy ended up being Milo, this two hundred fifty pound Greek dude with muscles the size of my head. I thought it best to keep my hands to myself.

The night ended with Santana and me breaking up, Milo unscathed, and the three of us somehow sitting at the bar together, drinking cheap beer and laughing over how miserable our lives were. We're dysfunctional, but we work.

"How was art camp in Montreal?" Santana asks as she fills a glass with water from the tap.

"Art *camp* is something parents send their kids to when they need a break from them, San," I say.

"Sorry. How were the whimsical two months you spent in Quebec, honing your craft and becoming the world's next Michelangelo?"

I look at Milo. He shrugs like, *Don't bring me into this.* "It's too early for a dose of sarcasm that heavy."

Santana rolls her eyes, twirling a long red curl around her finger. "Seriously, Truman. How was it?"

Truthfully? Fine. Spending two months away in another province was less about improving my art and more about improving my mental health. When it comes to art, it's the one thing I'm sure of. I know I have a future with it. I know I can be great. I believe in my talent, and that's mostly because one person convinced me I should a long time ago in my old bedroom. . . .

Now, I push those memories of Eden away. We had our

moment. It only took us seconds to mess it up.

"Montreal was anywhere but here," I say, eyes locked on the dregs of coffee left in the bottom of my mug.

We all go silent. They nod like they understand, but they don't. Of course they don't. They try, though. That's what's important.

"Have you given Angelo's offer any more thought?" Santana asks, sweeping the heaviness under a rug with one swift hand.

"Who's Angelo?" Milo pipes in, finally finding the balls to speak.

"No," I say truthfully, ignoring him.

"Truman, he needs an answer. He's blowing up my phone every single day," she says. She takes her phone out of the pocket of her jeans, which are so tight I'm shocked she managed to squeeze it in there. Santana holds the screen up to me. It's all her missed calls, and every single one of them is Angelo. "I'm either blocking his number or giving him yours. Then you can deal with it directly."

"Who's Angelo?" Milo asks again.

Santana's eyes dart to him, then back to me. She can't look at Milo for more than a few seconds. Why? She either has a thing for him after their one-night (one-hour?) stand, or she's doing it on my behalf. She refuses to clarify which it is. Either way, doesn't bother me. I'm over Santana, for real this time. Those two could ride off into the sunset together and I wouldn't bat an eye.

"You haven't told him?" she asks me. I pretend to be distracted with a faded stain on my shirt. Santana heaves a sigh like she's sick of our shit, then explains. "Angelo is a photographer. I met him at a modeling gig I did a few weeks back. He mentioned he owns his own studio and has an art show coming up, so I showed him some of Truman's paintings and he loved them. Now, Angelo wants to showcase some of Truman's work at his next show, but Truman's been giving him, or more specifically *me*, the runaround."

"Why didn't I know this?" Milo asks. Then to add fuel to the fire, he adds, "And I still haven't seen any of your artwork."

"Seriously, Truman? How are you two even friends? You don't tell him shit." Santana grabs her phone and taps, taps, taps as I sit there like a fly on the wall while they discuss my life. "Here," she says, holding the phone out to Milo now. "This is his secret Instagram account. Totally anonymous."

"I like how you know it's a secret and yet you've told two people about it now," I say, rejoining the conversation. I watch as Milo scrolls through the posts. There are about three dozen or so, all photos of paintings I've done within the past year. Santana's right: it's completely anonymous. There are no photos of me and I go by the alias *Capote*. Like Truman Capote, this writer my dad always talks about.

No one knew about the account until Santana was taking selfies on my phone one night and opened up Instagram to post some. She wouldn't let it go until I showed her the canvases stashed in an old milk crate in my closet.

Milo does a low whistle, handing Santana back her phone. "Those are really good, dude. Like, *real* good. And you've got almost ten thousand followers, you famous shit."

"If Milo thinks you're talented, then that means something," Santana says.

It's weird to see someone as big and burly as Milo blush. "What's that supposed to mean?" he asks.

Santana juts her hip into the counter, flicking her curls behind her back. "It means you never tried to get with me again after that night, Milo, so you're clearly not too great at recognizing when a beautiful thing's in front of you." Huh, so maybe she *is* into him. His face goes from pink to beet red. Poor dude. "Anyway," Santana says, ignoring Milo's discomfort and turning back to me, "are you doing the show or not?"

"I'll think about it," I say. I'm teetering more toward no, but I'm not fully there yet.

"You said that three weeks ago."

"And I'm still thinking."

Santana shakes her head, finally sick of us. "Whatever. I have to go. I have a photo shoot I should've been at ten minutes ago. I'm sending Angelo your contact information tonight, so he's your problem now." She tugs the strap of her purse up her shoulder, tucks her phone back into a skintight pocket, and leaves without a single look at Milo. The guy has sunk so far down into his chair that he's almost on the ground.

"What the hell is going on with the two of you?" I ask when the door slams shut.

"Hell if I know," he grumbles.

***

Milo spends an hour venting about Santana. How she's beautiful. How he hates her. How he's probably in love with her. He eats his way through another few Tupperwares of food before finally leaving. This time I double-check there are no keys in the door before locking it.

My mom mentioned Katie needs new flowers, so that's what I'm going to do. I shower and riffle through my luggage for something to wear, settling on whatever smells the least dirty. At this point, I either have to do laundry or put it off long enough that my mom does it for me.

It's nearly eighty-five degrees out, the humidity making my shirt instantly stick to my skin when I step outside. I push my sunglasses up the bridge of my nose and head right, toward the florist. It's nine o'clock and the streets are packed with the early morning commuter rush. Everyone's fresh off the subway, pushing past one another and running to cross the road before the light changes. This is what I love about being in the city, how it's a natural distraction.

The florist is a block before the hospital. I could stop at the gift shop on the first floor for flowers, but Mom insists Katie's flowers must be freshly picked, the brightest and the fullest. I don't argue with her because she's right. The flower shop is bright and perfumey, the smell so strong it clings to my clothes. The woman at the counter smiles at me. It's not my first time here. I smell roses, lilies, and other ones I don't know the name of. They all smell the same to me. I pick the most colorful bunch because that's what Katie would want, and have them wrapped in bright yellow paper, like the morning sun. I pay the woman in cash and she smiles, not asking for details. We both ignore the way my hands shake.

The closer I get to the hospital, the worse the shaking gets. Then it starts in my chest too, making it too hard to breathe. I'm thinking I need to sit down and take a break, but Mom's already been waiting long enough, so I keep walking. I pick nervously at the leaves hanging off the flower stems. They fall to the ground, leaving a bright trail on the concrete.

It's been two months since I last saw Katie. I went into her room to say goodbye before leaving for Montreal. My mom sat in the old tweed chair and cried, my dad beside her, a firm hand on her shoulder. I knew they couldn't understand why I was leaving. It was difficult to explain. How do you tell your parents you need to get away because every single day it's getting harder to breathe? Harder to wake up in the mornings? Harder to live?

Although I try to forget it, it's been two months since I last saw Eden, too. It was the same day: same spotty fluorescent hospital lighting, same beige hallways. I was making an exit, halfway to the elevator, when the doors groaned open and she was there. I only saw a sliver of her at first, but it was enough to stop me in my tracks. By the time the doors fully opened, I was crouched beside the vending machine, hiding like a coward.

We never agreed that we'd move forward by avoiding each

other. After the night of Katie's accident, it was just what we started to do. I couldn't look at her without remembering what we did that night—without reminding myself that if I hadn't been with Eden, I could've been with Katie, could've prevented her from leaving the party and getting in that car to begin with.

There was too much guilt. Every time I saw Eden, it was a reminder of how I failed my sister. Every time she saw me . . . Well, I don't know what she feels when she sees me. But she hasn't looked me in the eye since that night. That can't be a good sign.

Mount Sinai Hospital doesn't look like a hospital. It's another building that lines a street filled with thousands of them. It's all concrete and windows, towering high enough into the sky to be daunting. To make you feel small. I stop walking. I freeze up like I always do. I can't help but picture Katie in there, behind one of those streaked windows on the seventh floor, alive but not really. I'm hit with the same realization I always am: *It should've been me.*

I want to sit on the steps leading to the entrance for a minute or two. Maybe an hour. But if I do, I might never get up and go inside. I go through my usual routine: deep breath, stare at the floor, count to one hundred, then head inside. The automatic doors swing open and it's twenty-seven steps to the elevator. My stomach drops as it lurches to the seventh floor. Then it's down the hall, make a right, then a left, and Katie's room is right there: 708. There's a blue gurney outside with a faded yellow blanket on top. My eyes settle on all the details: the nurse reading a chart at the end of the hall, the kid sitting on the floor, phone flipped horizontally as he probably plays some game his parents tried to distract him with. This is what I do—how I ground myself before walking through her door.

Because then I'm inside her room and my lungs deflate.

I always think seeing her will eventually get easier. It never is. It's always the same as the first time: the shock, the anger, the disbelief. The urge to cradle her to me. To cry. To sit down and never get back up.

My mom's sitting in the chair next to Katie's bed. The blinds to the window are fully open, a pool of sunlight streaming into the room. I notice the vase of flowers on the windowsill. My mom was right about them being dead. The petals are brown and hardened, sagging out of the ceramic vase.

My eyes drink in every detail—the way the ceiling light flickers, the scraps of paint chipped off the walls, the muted TV playing a rerun of *The Big Bang Theory*, my mom's coat and purse draped over the table—before flickering over to Katie. Usually I need to look at her in short intervals. I glimpse her face for a second, then stare out the window for ten. I touch her hand, then the cool metal of the bed she lies in. But today's different. After not seeing her for two months, I'm feeling something like deprivation. I stare at her and stare at her and keep staring without looking away, without flinching. Her blonde hair is fanned around her pillow, soft and pin straight. She's propped up in bed, the blanket drawn to her waist, showing the pink cotton pajamas my mom must have dressed her in.

She looks like she's asleep. Like if I kill two hours, then come back, she'll be sitting upright, talking to my mom, her laughter echoing down the hall.

My mom spots me in the doorway and stands up. I notice the way she drops Katie's hand, gently placing it onto the bed.

"You brought the flowers," is what she says.

I'm thinking that it's been two months. Sixty days since I've seen her. And this is what she says first: the flowers.

She grabs the bouquet from my hands and I'm about to hug her, but she just walks away, right over to the window, and picks up the old vase. I watch her toss the wilted flowers into the trash can before placing the new ones inside. A water bottle is on the table. She grabs it and empties it into the vase. She does it out of habit. This little task she's done every week now.

I stand there watching, waiting for her to say something, waiting for her to ask about Montreal. Ask how I am. *Anything*.

She finishes with the flowers, turns back to me, and wipes her hands on her jeans. "How was the new apartment?" she asks. "Do you like it?"

"It's nice," I say. My voice sounds lifeless. Faraway.

"Have you unpacked?"

I shake my head. No. No, I haven't.

I can't tell if she's still upset at me for leaving for two months. She saw it as me abandoning Katie instead of what it really was: me having to save myself. I tried to explain that to her. That Montreal wasn't about art school and some random hobby. It was about me being able to breathe again, because the air in this hospital room, the air in this entire city, felt stale and dry. It smelled too much like her. Like the memories. I saw Katie's face everywhere I went, and I just needed to get away for a minute, go somewhere that was untouched by her, somewhere where I could walk down a street without my chest tightening up, without having to sit down for ten minutes to avoid collapsing.

I don't think my mom understood that. To her, I left. It was as simple as that. Even when I tried to explain that Katie would want me to go, she still didn't buy it.

"How is she doing?" I say, because Katie is our primary topic of conversation these days. I grab the black folding chair from the table and drag it over to Katie's bedside. I sit next to her, take her hand.

"The doctors haven't seen any changes," she says. "If they had, I would have texted you." It's probably an offhand comment, but it feels like a dig, a cheap shot. Another reminder that I was gone.

"Are you still talking to her?" The doctors say she may be able to hear us. That there've been cases of comatose patients waking up and recalling exact conversations people had with them. It may not be likely, but it's something. Any scrap of hope is worth clinging to.

My mom settles into the seat across from me. I notice the gray hairs lining her roots, the ones she usually dyes black whenever they start to peek through. It's a mystery to all of us where Katie's blonde hair came from. My mom and dad have raven-black hair; I do, too. But Katie? She's as bright as the sun.

"I am," my mom says, taking Katie's other hand in hers again. "I was just telling her how your grandmother called this morning from Rome. She's flying out to Germany tomorrow, says she sent us a postcard in the mail a month ago, but it hasn't turned up yet. Strange."

"Strange," I repeat, running my thumb across the back of her hand, her yellow-painted nails. "Is this the same color she used to be obsessed with?" I ask.

My mom smiles, nods. "It is. I found it in a drawer in her bedroom. The shade is 'morning light.' Remember how much she used to love it?"

Of course I remember. "She used to paint my nails with it. Dad's too."

We both go quiet, lost somewhere in the past. I remember warm summer days, falling asleep on the couch. I'd wake up to my fingernails painted every color of the rainbow. Sometimes she did my toes, too. That was Katie: awake when everyone else was asleep. Sneaking color into our world.

It triggers another memory, one I haven't lingered on in a while: Katie's obsession with the sky. It's why she loved that nail polish color so much, because it shone like the sun. It's also why she spent way too much time in the summer lying in the grass, staring up at it.

My mom sighs and she's back here in the present with me. "She wouldn't want this," she whispers so quietly I'm not sure if I heard correctly.

"Where's Dad?" I ask.

"He's been working very late. His firm has taken on a big corporate case. Sexual assault allegations against a CEO."

"Who's he representing?"

"The women," she says.

"Good."

We lapse into silence.

It took me a lot of three a.m. Google searches to fully understand what happened to Katie. The doctors tried to spell it out as plainly as they could, but my brain checked out the second I walked through these hospital doors. It is nearly impossible to decipher medical jargon when your sister is lying in a bed down the hall, her life on the line. I completely blacked out. It's like what my high school teachers used to tell my parents at parent-teacher interview night: *Truman doesn't pay attention in class. He's in another world entirely. The lessons don't stick. They go in one ear and out the other.*

When I was alone in bed those first few nights, the world quieted a little. That tightening ache in my chest dulled the slightest bit, so that I could actually breathe without having to remind myself to. I stayed up for hours searching WebMD and Wikipedia. *What does it mean to be in a coma? Can someone in a coma still hear you?* I'd read result after result until I fell asleep with my phone in my hand and the white light of the screen still pressed into my eyelids.

The gist of it is that when the collision happened, Katie wasn't wearing a seat belt. A thought that, months later, brings me to a boil. I can't count the amount of times I told her to always wear it. It was the first thing I'd say whenever I drove her around: *Put your seat belt on or I'm not going anywhere.* Then she'd stick her tongue out and buckle in. But that night I wasn't there to remind her, so she didn't wear it. When the car struck hers, the impact caused her to fly through the windshield. The doctors said the severe head trauma caused her comatose state. They said that brain imaging research has suggested that patients in a coma can still hear you, but it isn't conclusive. I thought that maybe it was just a thing they said to suckers like me, to give you the smallest dose of hope to keep you pushing forward. It worked.

It sucked, but it worked.

"So, Montreal," my mom says. I wait for her to elaborate—ask how it was or what I did. She doesn't.

"It was fine," I offer. I scramble to add something else before silence hits again. "The art professor said he saw a lot of promise in me." His words, not mine.

Her tight-lipped smile doesn't exactly scream *tell me more.* "That's great, Truman."

I keep sitting there, waiting for her to ask the question. She rambles on again about my grandmother's two month trip through Europe, about her recent adventures after divorcing my grandfather and taking half his money. After Germany, she's off to France. Greece. Switzerland, maybe. I zone out.

I'm staring at Katie, waiting and waiting and waiting. *How are you doing, Truman?* I keep waiting. She never asks.

That night I decide it's time to unpack. I do a load of laundry first, dumping everything from my luggage straight into the machine. I stand there for the entire forty minute wash cycle, watching the clothes spin left and right, soap suds sticking to the fogged glass. The soft whir is calming, hypnotic. I'm thinking about nothing. Literally nothing. My mind is a blank canvas in the silence. I keep all the lights off aside from the dim spotlights in the kitchen.

When my clothes are clean, I fold them up and stack them into piles. I place them in the drawers of my dresser, one by one, unnecessarily meticulous. I make my bed, the mattress still on the floor. I drove down to our old house after leaving the hospital, which is never an easy thing to do. I was in and out in a few minutes. I grabbed whatever felt most important: my banged-up easel, a milk crate full of some of my old paintings, cases full of paints and brushes. When I'm done with the clothing, I unpack those, too. My easel goes near the window because I need the natural light, although I prefer to paint at night. I stack the old paintings on the shelf in my closet, flip the milk crate upside down and use it as a table. I unpack the bottles of paint and line them up in a straight row on top. The brushes are next.

My room is still empty. It still doesn't feel warm. But this is better.

I think about painting something. I stare at the canvas and wait, but nothing comes to mind. Ever since Katie's accident, my creativity has dried up like an old creek. The images and scenes that used to flood my mind, to the point where I couldn't think straight until I painted them, just . . . stopped. In Montreal, I painted because I had to. I went off prompts—a landscape, an old woman's face, a bowl of fruit. But it wasn't the same. It didn't come naturally anymore.

I think about Katie and the sky. That nail polish color— *morning light*. It feels like something is there, the tiniest piece of inspiration, but it's buried too deep inside me. I can't reach it. Not yet.

I'm frustrated. I want to create but I can't. I need an outlet, something other than painting. I fall back into bed and lean against the pillows. I look at my phone for the first time all day. Two texts from Santana: *Have you decided yet??* Then: *I gave Angelo your email. Good luck.* It gets me thinking about my anonymous art account, so I open Instagram. I haven't posted in three weeks, the last one a grainy photo of a painting I did of a pond at sunrise. The prompt was *stillness*. It wasn't my favorite, but the post still got nearly one thousand likes.

Then I switch from my art account to my personal account. The first thing I see is a new photo from Santana, her face airbrushed with makeup, hair straightened and hanging past her waist. She's wearing this tight gold dress, her eyes covered in sparkles. Probably an outtake from her photo shoot today. I see that three hundred people have liked it, Milo included. I roll my eyes.

I look at my own profile: zero posts. I deleted them all months ago. After everything happened, people I barely knew started flooding my posts with comments saying *so sorry for your loss* and *I'm here for you*. They acted like Katie had died when she was still right here. I took all the posts down, deleted everything.

But now I'm itching for something new. And since painting is no longer an option, maybe still life is better.

I open my phone's camera and get out of bed. I want it to be something random, something with no context. I leave all the lights off and stand in front of my easel. The blinds are open so you can see the skyline of the city from outside the window. I angle the camera toward the floor, showing the tips of my Converse and some of the art supplies in the background. I snap the photo without thinking too much into it.

I post it. Caption it *home*. Tag it with my current location: Toronto. Then I drop my phone onto my bed because I doubt anyone will even bother to like it. Santana will leave some smart-ass comment. Milo will like her comment in that weird, silently pining way.

It's when I'm getting dressed, my shirt halfway off, that I see the screen light up. I grab my phone, not thinking anything of it, until I see the name. *@Edenflora liked your post.*

Everything changes.

4

EDEN

WHEN WE WERE SEVENTEEN, Katie and I spent the entirety of March break at her house, camped out in her bedroom, binge-watching sitcoms and ordering too much takeout. It was still too cold in Ontario for us to do much else; their pool was still closed off for the season. Mr. Falls wouldn't open it up until at least May when the weather warmed up.

That Friday was different. Their parents were out of town—they drove up to the casinos in Niagara Falls and wouldn't be home until Sunday morning.

Katie was already scheming, listing off ways we should spend the next two nights now that her parents were gone.

Truman beat us to it.

"I'm having some friends over tonight," he said. The three of us were camped out on their couch, watching an episode of *Impractical Jokers*. It was sometime in the afternoon.

Katie slurped her juice box noisily. "Like a party?" she asked.

"No. Not a party. A few people," he corrected her.

My head swiveled between the two of them like I was watching a Ping-Pong match.

"I'm assuming Eden and I are invited?"

Truman barked out a laugh. "You assumed wrong." Then he turned to me and said, smiling, "But Eden can come if she wants."

"I—"

Katie cut me off. "She doesn't want to," she said quickly. "So what's in it for us? Because my phone is right here, and it would be *so* easy to send a quick text to Mom and Dad. . . ."

"Katieeeeeeeeeee," Truman groaned. "What do you want?"

She made a big show of stretching out on the couch, lifting her arms above her head. "Hm," she said, thinking. I waited for her to ask me for ideas. "I want the mutual understanding that neither of us will speak a word to Mom or Dad about what happens this weekend."

Truman stopped flipping through the channels and sat up straighter. "What the hell are you planning on doing tonight?"

"Who said anything about tonight? Plus, I'm not sure yet," she said, eyeing me.

"We're still deciding," I offered.

Truman looked between the two of us suspiciously. "Mom and Dad told me to watch you guys."

Katie snorted. "We're almost eighteen. We don't need a chaperone. And you're not exactly the authority on decision-making,

Tru. Didn't you break up with Santana last week for the, what, fifth time now?" she said.

Truman broke up with Santana and no one told me?

Of course no one told me. I wasn't supposed to care—I didn't care.

Truman's eyes darted to me. He was always doing that: stealing glances. "Fourth time," he mumbled.

"Still not helping your case. Do we have a deal or not?"

Truman shut off the television and got off the couch. "Sure, whatever." He stormed up the stairs. I heard the slam of his bedroom door.

"Katie," I warned.

"What?" she said, reaching for the remote. Her hair fell to her shoulders in a sharp bob. She had gotten it cut only a few days earlier after seeing a photo of a model in a magazine with the same style. Katie didn't even spend a day thinking it over. She had the idea in the morning and the appointment was booked by the afternoon. Spontaneity was her thing. And she pulled it off effortlessly.

"What *are* you planning this weekend?" I asked.

Katie flashed me her signature dimpled smile. "Like I said, I'm not sure yet."

She was in an ambulance seven hours later.

Angry red lights are flashing in my head. Alarms are blaring, sirens wailing. I hold my breath. My chest constricts.

Oh no. *Oh no, no, no, no, no.*

I throw my phone, groaning. It crashes into the wall, careening into the floor.

I'm the creepy stalker ex-girlfriend. Wait, minus the ex part. Truman and I never even dated. *So why do you have his post notifications on?* Shut the hell up, brain.

I must have been louder than I thought, because Ramona comes running into my bedroom now. The door slams open, the dim light from the hallway night-light streams in. "What's going on?" she asks. It must be past midnight, because Ramona has her hair up in a messy topknot, her once-smooth gray face mask now cracked against her skin.

"*Eden.*" She fills the two syllables with so much concern it makes my skin prickle. "What the hell happened? Why are you screaming?" She flips the light switch and the darkness vanishes in a poof. I see my messy, scrunched-up sheets, the dust bunnies hiding in the corners, my phone flat on the floor with a new shiny crack along the screen.

Ramona spots it at the same time I do. She walks to the sad little clump of metal, bends to pick it up.

"No!" I bolt upright in bed. "Don't touch it. Just, just . . ."

I liked it. I liked his fucking Instagram post. Not even five seconds after he posted it.

Shit. Shit. Shit.

Ramona freezes, half crouched, half standing. She's watching me like I'm psychotic. To be fair, she's probably right.

I was too careless with my zoom, my stupid stubby fingers

pinching the screen this way and that. I was trying to get closer, see more. What was on the canvas? Was he painting again? What colors were the bottles of paint? The colors could tell me so much—grays and blacks meant he was creating something withering; yellows and pastels meant something happy, something bright. I wanted to see more. I needed more.

Why was Truman back?

Did he miss me?

That thought was unexpected. Because it doesn't matter if he missed me or if he thought of me or if he's painting again. None of it matters. Our chance fizzled away before it ever really happened. We were selfish. Careless. We ruined . . . well, everything.

We ruined everything.

I had been in the middle of zooming in on the skyline, thinking I was a geography expert or something, that I could identify his exact location based on the buildings in the background or if there was a bright yellow McDonald's *M* I could pinpoint, because that is quite literally the height of my culinary knowledge.

And then my finger slipped. The stupid white heart turned red. *1 like.*

I can unlike it, but the damage has been done. He's probably already seen it. Probably thinks I'm still the same fifteen-year-old girl who's obsessed with him. I'm not. I swear I'm not.

Then why do you have Truman's post notific—

For strict research purposes. So I can know when he's back in town. So I can move forward with continuing to avoid him at all costs, same as I used to. For the past two months, I've been able to walk into the hospital to see Katie without having to slowly walk up to the door to her room, peek my head inside, and make sure Truman wasn't there before I waltzed in. Knowing he was miles away was a comfort. A reassurance. I didn't have to worry about seeing him. And I did worry, because seeing Truman was a hit to the gut—it was a reminder of what happened the night of the accident. When I close my eyes, I can still picture his face inches away, the color of his eyes, his dilated pupils. His fingers on my thigh. His lips on mine, right where I had spent so long wanting them. I can feel everything from that moment. That fleeting, terrible moment that still makes my heart race.

Kissing Truman was the most selfish choice I ever made. I regret it every single day that passes. Twenty-four seven.

But then part of me thinks that if he were here, if he stood in front of me right now, that I would run to him, I would collapse into him; I would take any piece of him, no matter how small. Because that moment we had together was terrible, an earthquake, and it still wasn't enough.

"Who is this?" Ramona is holding my phone, staring down at the screen. "Truman Falls?" she asks. "This is why you're freaking out? Because you liked his Instagram photo?"

She doesn't understand. Ramona went to high school with us, but she doesn't know the details, the secrets. To her, it's this simple: Katie was in an accident, Katie's in a coma, I needed a new roommate because Katie was no longer an option, Ramona moved in. It's four simple events that hold no significance to her. She sees it as black and white. But there's so much gray. So much darkness.

Ramona sits carefully on the edge of my bed. Her charcoal face mask has so many cracks on it that it's beginning to chip off her face, little flakes falling onto her pajama top. She sets my phone down on the mattress between us. I can't read her mind, but I know the look in her eyes. She's wondering what's wrong with me. She's wondering what I'm not telling her.

It's not just a stupid photo, I want to say. It's a deer in headlights. It's standing on the edge of a cliff. It's a collision of the before and the now. Truman's return is a reminder of the mistakes I've spent months burying. And now he's returned with a shovel, ready to dig them all up when the soil is still fresh.

"Are you going to tell me what's going on, Eden, or should I go back to bed?" She sounds exhausted, completely sick of my shit. I can't even imagine what it's like to live with me. To try every single day to get closer, uncover my secrets, my tells, and keep walking face-first into a brick wall. Because that's what I am: stone cold and unrelenting.

Part of me screams to tell her. To talk and talk and talk until the secrets pour from me like water rushing downhill. I know it could be so freeing, that some of the weight wearing me down would disappear. And Ramona—Manny too—is here, ready and willing to help. But the thought of reliving those moments that led up to Katie's accident . . . The thought of speaking them out loud holds so much pain. I don't want to see the look in their eyes, the disgust, when they hear what I did, how I betrayed Katie, how I failed her. I don't want them to see me in the same light I see myself. I still need that scrap to hold on to: that there are still people out here who think the best of me.

With my mind made up, I say, "You should go back to bed."

Ramona has been putting up with me for so long now she doesn't even seem surprised. She just up and leaves. Closes the door behind her. I hear her walk down the hallway into the bathroom, hear the rush of water and know she's washing off her face mask, the charcoal swirling down the drain. Then she'll go to sleep and wake up bright and early, at six a.m. like she always does. She'll go for a run, hop into the shower, then go out with a friend and laugh and eat and live the life of a normal eighteen-year-old without a luggage load of issues.

I wanted that simplicity with Katie. That was the route our lives were supposed to take before we reached a fork in the road and strayed.

I pick up my phone off the mattress and I unlike the photo. It doesn't matter if Truman's already seen the notification, because we both decided to cut one another out of our lives months ago. This isn't enough to change that.

Two days pass and I'm at Pollo Loco. Manny and I work right until seven o'clock that night. It's one of the many reasons I love Sundays—we close earlier.

Still, there's no *leaving early* tonight, and surely no late-night-slightly-romantic walks through the city. I don't go on my phone the entire shift, not even to Google another depressing story about a comatose patient. I just sit on my stool in front of the cash register, staring out the windows as the sky turns from orange to indigo. I'm feeling strange. Off. Something has taken a toll on me and I can't pinpoint what. Or maybe I can and I just don't want to. Either-or.

Sometimes I have to question if being so out of touch with my emotions is by choice.

Manny hasn't popped out of the kitchen all night to talk to me. He hasn't offered me food or commented on my newly cured phone addiction. In fact, he's been pretty silent all night. It's quite unlike him, really. I'm wondering if he even smiled at me when I walked in. I'm wondering how I was too absorbed by my own mental distress to notice this.

The clock hits seven and I walk across the faded cream tiles to the door, flip the OPEN sign to CLOSED, and turn the lock. It's the most satisfying sound in the world. People walk past and we make eye contact through the windows. *Don't even think about it. We're closed.* They keep walking. I stand still, my fingers lingering on the cool glass. I need to mentally decompress. I need to wring my brain out like a sponge. I need silence, darkness. But the thought of going home is even worse than staying here.

Ramona's been giving me the cold shoulder ever since the whole Instagram debacle. Which is weird, since she never seems to give up on me. Maybe now she has. Maybe now she's decided that I'm not worth it, that trying to get me to open up to her is like standing in a desert and praying for a thunderstorm. And yet, somehow, this hurts even more than dealing with her pestering.

I don't like this. Not one bit.

God, what is *wrong* with me today. I wish I were an emotionless robot. Can science please hurry up and figure that out?

All the tables have been cleared, and the last hour was slow enough that I've already swept and mopped the floors. Before I pop into the kitchen, I grab my phone. There's a notification from seven minutes ago: *@Trumanfalls just posted a photo.* I swipe on it so quickly my face ID malfunctions. The photo was taken outside, of a weird-looking building with some art structure on top. I realize it's OCAD: Ontario College of Art and Design. Truman mentioned once or twice he wanted to go there. So did he accept an admissions offer for the fall? Was he taking a tour?

This time I rein in my stupid fingers and don't accidentally like the photo. I promise myself I'll turn off his post notifications tonight, but I know myself and she's a big fat liar.

I head into the kitchen fully prepared to grab my bag, walk out the door, and wander around the city long enough that I'm certain Ramona has gone to bed and I won't run into her at home . . . and then I spot Manny hunched over the metal worktable, his head in his hands, looking so far away from the smiling happy-go-lucky guy he relentlessly, and irritatingly, is.

I take a seat across from him. "What happened?" I ask like a

73

therapist. All I need is a pad of paper to flip.

Manny's head lifts up, eyes finding mine. "What do you mean?" He yawns, slapping a hand over his mouth to cover it up.

"You seem off today," I say, putting it lightly.

"I'm just tired."

"Please. That's my go-to lie to avoid talking to people. What's wrong?"

He heaves out a sigh, his shoulders slouching over as he leans onto his elbows, chin propped up on one hand. I notice how his body seems heavy, sloping forward like he can't be bothered to stand straight. There's none of that effortless ease he usually carries himself with. Maybe he really is tired.

"I'm tired, Eden," he says again, reading my mind. "That's it. I'm really, really tired."

I'm not buying it.

"Did your dad say something about us leaving early the other night?" Manny doesn't respond, which tells me everything I need to know. He's biting down on his bottom lip, worrying away at it. "You can tell him it was all my fault," I say. "Blame the entire thing on me. After all, I'm a very bad influence on good boys like you."

"That's not entirely true," he says.

"But it's partially true."

His lips curve up into the tiniest smile. "Partially."

The lighting in the kitchen is alarmingly bright, the kind of light that no one looks good under. Manny still does, of course, but it also heightens all the parts of his face that give away just how exhausted he really is. I want to wrap him up in a blanket, tuck him into bed, and stand guard at his door, making sure no one disturbs him for at least twelve hours.

Then Manny seems to realize something, because he says, "Wait. What are you still doing here? You usually run out the door at seven on the dot."

"That's not true," I lie. Manny only raises his eyebrows, waiting patiently. This is why I don't ask questions. Eventually, they're turned back on you.

"Well? What's keeping you here?" he asks. "And don't say it's me. We both know that's not true."

"You *are* nice to look at it, Manny, but no, it's not you." Now I'm the one sighing, frustration spilling out of me in waves. "I'm not exactly in a rush to get home," I admit.

That seems to catch his attention. He sits up straighter; a muscle in his jaw twitches. "Did something happen?" It's like I pushed a button. Overprotective mode activated.

"My roommate and I got into . . . I don't really know. It wasn't a fight. More of a standoff, I guess." *And if I go home right now, there's a great chance I'll spend the entire night zooming in on various parts of Truman's Instagram post and committing every fact about OCAD to memory.*

"Over what?"

"Me not wanting to divulge every detail of my life to her," I say.

Manny chuckles, his floppy curls bouncing around. "Wow, I can't imagine that at all," he says. "You're so open with me, Eden.

I can't seem to get you to shut up."

"Ha, ha, ha," I say with the enthusiasm of a brick. "You two should meet. You could probably talk for hours about how much of a disappointment I am."

"You're not a disappointment," Manny says gently.

I shrug it off, averting my gaze. Suddenly it's too hard to look at him.

"You haven't missed a shift in two months," Manny points out.

"I'm late all the time," I say to the floor.

"You've been getting better."

"I'm on my phone all shift," I continue because my stupid mouth is so keen on throwing its owner under the bus.

"I didn't see you touch your phone once today," he says. Huh. So he *was* watching.

"I've never gotten a tip that's more than two dollars."

"So customers are cheap," Manny says with a grin. "That's not your fault."

"You're just like Ramona. Always searching for the best in me."

"It's not that hard, Eden. You should try it sometime." He makes it sound so easy.

"This conversation has really gotten away from me." I drum my fingers along the tabletop. It's sleek and shiny, not a speck of dirt because Manny doesn't do anything halfway. Not cleaning, not cooking. Not trying to cheer me up. "Well," I say, standing up. "I should get home."

"I thought you were trying to avoid going home?" Manny says.

"I am, but you're clearly exhausted. I'm not going to force you to stay here with me because I'm too much of a wimp to face my overly kind roommate."

I try to push my chair back to stand up, but Manny's legs have wrapped around it under the table, holding me in place. "You're not forcing me to do anything," he says firmly.

"Manny."

"What are you going to do when you get home?" he asks.

"Honestly? Probably lie down in total darkness until I have to wake up for my shift tomorrow."

"Eden, that does not sound healthy. Like, at all."

"Relax. I'm perfectly fine." Understatement of the century.

"Wanna know what I do when I feel like shit?" he asks. I nod eagerly. "I cook."

"But you're always cooking," I point out.

"Which is why I very rarely feel like shit."

"Except for today," I say.

Manny rolls his eyes. "I'm *tired*. I told you that already. So, what do you say? Wanna hang out for a bit and cook something together?"

I scrunch my face up. "Manny, I'm the worst cook. I thought we established this?"

"We have, but I can teach you a thing or two. Come on."

I think of Ramona's disappointment that seems to hang in the air of our apartment like a cloud; the constant sound of her bedroom door clicking shut; the eerie silence of the kitchen when she's not there bustling around, filming some video.

"All right, let's do it," I say. Manny pumps his fist in the air like the adorable loser he is. I go to the industrial-size fridge and tug open the gigantic stainless steel doors. They're a lot heavier than I thought they'd be, so it takes a few big pulls. The shelves are lined with meat wrapped in plastic wrap, Tupperwares full of bright bell peppers chopped into even strips, endless cartons of eggs, and everything else imaginable. I plant my hands on my hips, searching through all this food like I know what I'm doing, as if I didn't just eat week-old pizza for breakfast this morning.

"Find what you're looking for?" Manny asks from behind me. I don't turn around, but I *know* he's laughing at me.

Maybe it was desperation or embarrassment, but my brain scrounges up a memory from when I was a kid, seven or eight maybe. It's me in the kitchen with my parents. My mom was teaching me how to make gnocchi from scratch like her nonna used to. She boiled the potatoes, then I mashed them; she eyeballed the exact amount of flour while I kneaded the pasta dough into a soft ball. My dad made rissóis de camarão, a Portuguese shrimp patty. My mom couldn't stand them—she hates fish. But they were my absolute favorite. I stood at his side as he fried them in oil. We ate and ate and ate until our bellies were full.

I close the fridge doors and turn to Manny. "Let's make rissóis de camarão," I say.

His face brightens. "You like those?" he asks, not missing a beat.

"My dad used to make them all the time when I was a kid," I share.

It wasn't by coincidence that I started working in a Portuguese restaurant. After moving out of my parents' house and into the city, I started to feel . . . lonely. Well, I was already feeling lonely, but it only got worse. Working here is like a little reminder of home. The smells of the kitchen remind me of my dad cooking up a storm for Sunday dinners. Mr. Álvaro's accent is as thick as my grandpa's was.

Manny is beaming, looking at me like I've just made his entire day. "My dad did, too. The only reason he didn't put them on the menu is because he uses my avó's secret recipe. He said they were too personal. He didn't want anyone outside of the family eating them."

"I'm outside the family," I point out.

"Consider yourself the only exception," he says. Something about those words fills me with so much warmth. "Want to start chopping up the ingredients?"

"Sure." Manny hands me a knife, a huge one with a curved blade. I don't trust myself with it. I'm surprised he does.

"Cutting boards are behind you," he says.

There's a stack of them, both wooden and plastic. I grab a wooden one. When I turn back, Manny's already piling the ingredients onto the table: blocks of butter, gallons of milk, bags of flour, eggs, bread crumbs, salt.

Then he hands me a bunch of fresh parsley and an onion. "Chop them as small as you can," he says. He reaches for the apron on his chair and loops it around his neck.

"Yes, sir."

Manny busies himself with the stove. I lay the parsley across the cutting board and eye the knife suspiciously. It can't be that difficult. I rock the knife back and forth over the herbs, chopping them into all sorts of uneven pieces. They are small, though. At least I've got that right. I scrape the pile of parsley to the corner of the board to make space for the onion. When I look up, Manny's moving fluently at the stove, looking like he's been doing this for hours. He has a stick of butter melting in a saucepan. He pours in milk right from the carton, not even bothering to measure it. I watch him stir it all together before he lowers the heat. The flame simmers down, then he adds in the flour.

"Eden," he calls, glancing at me from over his shoulder. "Can you flour the table for me?" I spring into action, dusting the table with a coating of flour, evening it out with my hand. Manny moves from the stove to the table in one quick step, like a dancer who's practiced this a hundred times. He turns the saucepan over, dumping the dough right onto the floured surface. For a second I've left this kitchen and I'm back at home with my parents, cooking on a Sunday afternoon when hours felt like days.

Manny starts kneading the dough, his arms flexing as he works through it. I'm paying a bit too much attention to him, abandoning my chopping task altogether. His face is scrunched up as he concentrates, thick brows drawn together.

He looks up and catches me staring. "How's the onion coming?" he asks, his face creasing into a smile.

Considering it's still sitting on the table untouched—not too well.

I grab it and begin to peel the skin off. "Your dad taught you to cook?" I ask.

Manny nods, his focus on the dough again. I notice it's smoothed out now. He dusts it with more flour. "My dad worked night shifts at this factory in town, even after my mom passed away. But during the day, no matter how tired he was, he always cooked for me. We lived in the kitchen," he says with a smile. "My grandparents lived with us, too. They'd watch me when my dad was at work."

"I used to cook with my dad, too," I say.

"I can tell," Manny says. "Those are some serious chopping skills." He gestures to the growing pile of chopped onions, which, to my surprise, are all in even little squares. He might be kidding, but I decide he isn't.

"How do you know when the dough is ready?" I ask.

"You do this . . ." He takes the dough in his hands and shuffles it around, smoothing out all the sides until it's a soft ball. He holds it out to me. "Give it a poke," he says.

"Uh, okay." I press my finger into it.

"See how the indent springs back slightly but still leaves a small imprint?" I nod, studying the dough carefully. "That's how you know it's ready. If it springs back fully, it needs to be kneaded more. If it doesn't spring back at all, then you've overworked it."

"What do you do if that happens?" I ask.

"You start from scratch." Manny cuts the dough into two even pieces, wraps them in plastic wrap, and moves them off to the side of the table. "These need to rest while we start the filling. Can you grab me another stick of butter, some milk, and the shrimp out of the fridge?" He says all of this while he's already moving to the stove, holding a frying pan in one hand and the cutting board in the other.

I tug open the fridge again, grab the milk and butter, place it in his waiting hand, then search for the shrimp. "Manny?"

"What's up?" he says. I can already hear the sizzling of melted butter, smell the sautéing onions.

"I can't find the shrimp."

He peeks around the fridge door. "Take this," he says, handing me the wooden spatula. "Keep mixing that around until the onions start to brown."

I shuffle over to the stove as he takes over searching through the fridge. I push the onions around the pan, the steam blowing straight into my face and making me start to sweat. Now I understand why Manny's always wearing T-shirts and dabbing at his face with towels.

I look up from the pan, over at the big metal doors. "Any luck?"

"Not yet."

I turn my attention back to the onions and, shit, they're brown. "Manny, these things are browning fast. What do I do?" I'm beginning to panic. I don't want to be the reason this meal is messed up.

"You're fine," he says, still hidden behind the fridge. "Turn the heat down to low and pour in enough milk to cover the pan."

"Okay. I can do that." I adjust the knob on the burner and the flame dies down. Then I grab the carton of milk and pour until the onions are just covered. "Is this okay?"

Manny's head peeks out from behind the fridge. He eyes the pan and winks at me. "Looks amazing, Eden. You're a natural. Now you can remove that from the heat and add in a dash of salt, pepper, some nutmeg, and all that parsley you chopped up."

I don't even hesitate anymore. I do everything he says, ending with the parsley. I move the wooden spoon around the pan, watching the ingredients swirl together. I'm feeling proud of myself. I pull out my phone, snap a photo, and send it to my dad. I type: *Guess what I'm making?*

"So," Manny says, slamming the fridge doors shut. "We have a problem."

"What's that?"

"We're out of shrimp."

"That's okay," I say with uncharacteristic optimism. "I'll go buy some." I'm already handing Manny the wooden spoon, feeling like a good little helper.

Manny gives me this look like I've lost my mind. "Eden, the fish market doesn't open until six a.m. *tomorrow*."

"Which is why I'll go to the Loblaws down the street and pick up a frozen bag."

"Frozen?" he sputters, like I've just suggested we cut my right leg off and cook that instead.

"We're making this for the two of us, Manny. Gordon Ramsay isn't about to pop in at any second and call you an idiot sandwich for using frozen seafood."

"He'd be right if he did," he says.

"*He'd be right if he did*," I grumble, mocking him under my breath like the immature child I am. I leave Manny with his disappointment and run to the storage room to grab my bag. When I return, he's at the table again, mixing together cornstarch and water.

Manny spots me and smiles. Everything settles back into place. He looks like himself. "Thanks for this," he says to me. "You're a great sous-chef."

I want to hug him. "Don't sound so surprised," I tease. "I'll be back in ten minutes."

Outside, the air has an unnatural chill to it. It raises the skin on my arms, makes me wish I had brought a jacket or taken Manny's. The walk to Loblaws is quick, barely five minutes. I walk as fast

84

as I can without breaking into a run. I'm too lazy to untangle my headphones, so I listen to the cars whizzing by, the chatter of people walking past me, sitting on sidewalk benches or exiting restaurants. The wind whips at my hair, pushing it in front of my face. I picture Katie's wrist and the extra hair tie she always kept with her. That would've been useful right now.

My phone chimes with a text from my dad. He writes, *Look at you! They look fantastic, meu docinho.* My sweet. Then, *Bring some home for your mother and me. Come visit us this weekend, yes?*

I haven't been home in a month. I only made it back that time because Ahmed, Pollo Loco's other waiter, agreed to cover my shift for me if I gave him a week's worth of tips. The look on his face when I handed him a total of nine dollars was priceless. I doubt he'd agree to cover for me again. I'd have to make a trip over in the morning, then leave in the afternoon so I could make it in time for my shift . . . I tell my dad that sure, I'll try to stop by. I mean it, too.

I'm in and out of Loblaws in a few minutes, a plastic bag dangling from my wrist with a bag of frozen shrimp inside. They did have an area with fresh seafood, but I like to push Manny's buttons, so frozen it is. Plus, how much of a difference could it really make? When the patties are made and floating in buckets of oil, all shrimp are equal. Like, there's no way you'd bite into that and think, *Wow, these shrimp were frozen!* And then proceed to arrest me and lock me up behind bars for committing crimes against the culinary gods. Then again, if anyone is picky enough to notice the difference, it would be Manny.

I'm debating turning around and going back for the fresh shrimp when a head of black hair catches my eye. I stop walking, stop breathing; the bag on my wrist stops swinging. Time seems to stop moving. Or maybe the entire world just stops because the cars have frozen, too. First I see the hair like spilled ink, then the dirty Chucks. Everything comes into focus and it's Truman, standing right there, on the sidewalk across the street. I want to keep walking. I want to move before he sees me. I want—I want him to see me. God, do I want him to see me.

And then he does.

He's walking with his head down, eyes on the sidewalk, then his head turns to the right like it was pulled. Our eyes instantly meet. We are so far away from each other and yet we collide.

I see the recognition bloom onto his face, watch his eyes go wide, his mouth pop open.

He looks . . . He looks exactly the same. Like the warmth of the summer sun when we'd lie out by the pool, Katie a barrier between us. Like the crunch of fresh leaves when they fell from trees and we'd rake them into garbage bags. He looks like the past. My mind turns into a kaleidoscope of memories: the warmth of his lips on mine; the tilt of his smile; the streaks of paint caught in his hair; the look of surprise on his face when I pushed through all his barriers and really saw him for the first time. All these memories I've suppressed come trudging back up so quickly it's suffocating.

We stand there, suspended in time, staring at one another. We are barely twenty feet apart, yet miles stand between us. I wait for him to cross the street. To grab me by the shoulders, shake me until I wake up; take my hand and lead me back into the comfort of the past. I think that maybe he's waiting for me to cross the street because he doesn't move. But I can't. I can't do that. Once I'm close to him, I don't think I'll be able to tear myself away again.

And then we both start walking, in opposite directions, on opposite sidewalks on opposite sides of the street. Cars start moving. The wind is howling. I get back to the restaurant and I'm okay. *I'm okay.*

My hands won't stop shaking.

5
EDEN

IT WAS THE NIGHT of Truman's "party." The doorbell started ringing around eight and didn't stop.

I was itching with curiosity, torn between being happy to stay up here with Katie and wanting to run downstairs to see what Truman was up to.

Katie didn't seem happy to be stuck in her bedroom at all. She kept cracking the door open and trying to peer downstairs. "There are way more than a few people here," she said over and over.

We were lying on her bed on our stomachs, her laptop propped up on a pillow in front of us. The floor was littered with half-eaten boxes of pizza, Pepsi cans, and crumpled candy wrappers. Her parents left us one hundred dollars on the kitchen counter for food before they left. Katie spent twenty-five on the pizza delivery, then winked at me as she slipped the rest into the pocket of her jeans. I thought she was so clever, so cool. Mature and responsible, ordering our dinner over the phone, paying the man at the door with all the confidence in the world while I sat at the kitchen table, waiting on her.

I needed a way to distract Katie before she gave in, headed downstairs, and caused a huge scene. Truman said his parents had tasked him with the responsibility of watching her, but it kind of felt as if that responsibility had shifted to me.

"Let's start planning our future," I said.

Katie was lying on her back, scrolling through her phone. "What do you mean?"

"We can start looking for apartments downtown," I offered.

We came up with a three-step plan. We had already checked off the first box: get accepted into the University of Toronto. The next steps were to lease an apartment, then move in together. Katie's parents had already agreed. They agreed to anything she said. Meanwhile, I hadn't even worked up the courage to ask mine yet, but I wanted this more than anything—a life with Katie outside this small town. I wanted to stay up late, dancing as the wooden floors creaked and the neighbors below us complained; waking up early and watching the sunrise from the balcony; getting bagels from the bakery down the street after class and eating them out of the bag for dinner; sitting thigh to thigh on the couch together.

When I told Katie this, she rolled her eyes. "How do you manage to romanticize *everything*?" she said. But she was smiling, like she already had one foot out the door, too.

We distracted ourselves for an hour or two with searching for apartments for lease in the city. I wanted something closer to the lakeshore with a view of Lake Ontario, but that would mean a longer commute to campus, which Katie hated. She wanted to live closer to school so she wouldn't have to worry about taking the subway or walking outside in the winter. It was the only thing we couldn't agree on. Other than that, we had the same thoughts: at least two bedrooms, one bathroom was doable, and the size of the kitchen really didn't matter because neither of us liked to cook.

We looked through dozens of listings, but nothing felt right. Maybe we were being too picky, trying to strive for perfection. But with Katie, perfection always felt attainable.

"We'll order takeout most nights and drink cheap red wine," she said, her voice taking on that definite edge. She was halfway through watching *Scandal* and had decided that wine was going to be her thing.

"Yeah, when we turn nineteen and are actually old enough to buy it," I added. She heaved a sigh, dismissing me with a wave of her hand.

The noise coming from downstairs was growing. Katie seemed to have forgotten about it entirely. She was on the Ikea website, scrolling through photos of bed frames. I couldn't focus. I could hear Truman laughing somewhere below us, people talking, music playing.

I didn't have to go all the way downstairs. I could just peek.

"I'm going to the bathroom," I declared. The bed squeaked

when I rolled off it. Katie just hmm'd and kept tapping away at her laptop. I had to walk by the bathroom to get to the stairs.

My parents' house was, in a word, cozy. "You want people to feel like it's their home, too," my mom would say. The couches were piled with pillows and blankets. All the furniture had some story attached to it: the chestnut trunks in the living room were imported from my dad's family in Portugal; the glassware in the kitchen was my nonna's. Our house was made up of so many different stories.

In comparison, Katie's house was made up of the fanciest furniture money could buy. The floors were cold marble; the couches were hard leather that was imported from Italy; the kitchen had a fancy gas-range stove that Katie and I were too terrified to even turn on. And the stairwell was huge and spiraled right into the middle of their main floor. It had floating steps made of glass, so when I placed my hands on the banister and leaned over, I could see the entire floor. There were people walking around in the kitchen, with boxes of pizza on the counter, cans of soda, cases of beer. Someone had set up beer pong on the dining room table.

I peered into the living room and saw that Truman's friends were lounging on the couch. I recognized some of them from when he was in high school. Most of them were unfamiliar faces. Bags of ripped-open chips covered the coffee table, and the Blue Jays game was on the TV.

This looked like every Saturday night party Katie had ever

dragged me to. So what was the big deal? Why wouldn't Truman let us join? Like Katie and I had never seen people throw balls into cups of beer before.

I left the banister and started walking back to Katie's room, no longer tiptoeing. Then I noticed something strange: the door to Truman's bedroom was open. The door to Truman's bedroom was *never* open. But now it was. It was the narrowest crack, but it was enough to draw me closer, have me peeking through. I could see the dark gray of the walls, the deep brown of the furniture. And I knew I shouldn't, but I wedged my foot into the small gap and the door drifted open even further. I stepped inside and it was nothing like I expected it to be. I was expecting a teenage boy's mess: clothes thrown across the floor, the bed unmade, dirty dishes crusted with food covering the tops of his dresser and empty cups lining his desk.

Instead, everything was neat and organized. The air smelled like fresh cotton. The bed was made perfectly, with crisp edges and tucked-in corners like you'd find in a hotel. A pile of neatly folded clothing sat on his dresser. But what caught my eye, what had me walking through the door and across the space, was the wooden easel placed in front of the large window that overlooked the backyard, the night sky a smudge of skeletal trees and royal blue. There was a painting propped up on the easel, the artwork so striking I couldn't tear my eyes away. The brush strokes were harsh and deliberate, yet soft and gentle. It had the color scheme of Van Gogh's *Starry Night*: the deeply rich blues, the soft greens, the brightness of the yellow. But it wasn't a sky. The swirls were the same, wide and arching across the canvas. Instead, it was a face. A girl, I realized. The blue was the winding waves of her hair. The warm yellow painted the lines of her face, the glow of her skin. It felt like looking through a kaleidoscope, like a warped portrait. It was a person in the same way that it wasn't. It was uncanny.

It reminded me of what Mr. Sullivan, my grade nine art teacher, had said about Van Gogh's paintings. That the unblended brush strokes expressed his emotion, that they made the painting come alive, made it appear to move as your eyes followed along with the striking colors. This painting felt like that. I tilted my head to the left and the colors moved to make it appear like the girl was crying. Then to the right and her mouth tilted upward, the barest ghost of a smile.

I was so lost in thought that I didn't realize I was no longer alone.

"Do you like it?" I shrieked and spun around. Truman was standing behind me. He had caught me red-handed, poking through his life. "Didn't mean to scare you. Sorry," he said, walking into the room.

"Why aren't you downstairs?" I blurted out.

"Why are *you* in my bedroom?"

Dammit. He had a point.

"The door was open," I said.

Truman walked to his desk. It was empty except for his cell phone, which was charging. He unplugged it, typed something, then turned back to me.

"I was just messing with you before. You can come downstairs if you want."

"I'm fine here," I said.

Truman's mouth quirked up. "You're fine in my bedroom?"

"That's not— You know what I meant," I huffed out, my face warming. I didn't want him to notice how flustered I was over being alone with him. I turned back to the canvas. "Did you paint this?" I asked.

"No. I stole it from the ROM."

"How'd you manage to sneak this out of the Royal Ontario Museum?"

"Yes, I painted it, Eden," he said. I watched his shadow on the floor grow larger as he walked toward me. "Do you like it?"

I nodded, my eyes locked firmly on the canvas. I didn't know why, but I couldn't look away. Like if I did, it would vanish. This moment felt weird. Felt fragile.

I had never been alone with Truman before.

I was vaguely aware that Katie was down the hall, waiting for me in her bedroom. She felt so far away all of a sudden, like the hallway had grown, stretching and twisting. The house was ghostly quiet. I waited for the creak of the floorboards, the whir of the air conditioning to kick in, or a car to drive by outside, bathing the room in the glow of the headlights. Nothing happened. Everything seemed to still, except for Truman, who had turned away from the easel—turned toward me, waiting for my response. *Do you like it?*

"It's incredible," I said, my voice slicing through the stillness. "When did you paint this?"

"A few days ago." Truman reached for the canvas. His thumb stroked the ridged lines of paint as I stared at his fingers, the long, slender bones ending in short nails clipped into clean lines. Artist hands. I curled my own hands into fists to hide the nails I bit down to the skin.

"I didn't know you painted." It was a silly thing to say. Of course I didn't know what Truman did in his spare time when he was shut in this room, the door a blockade from the rest of the house. All I had really known about him was that he didn't like haircuts and he never woke up before noon.

Truman and I spoke a lot. We talked about whatever show was on TV. We talked about the weather. We talked out by the pool, in the kitchen eating lunch, or in the hallway upstairs when I exited the bathroom the same moment he walked out of his room. We spent a lot of time talking. The problem was, we never said much. It was all small talk, all filler. All mindless conversations where we tiptoed around what we really wanted to say—or at least what *I* wanted to say: that I found him mysterious and interesting. That I wanted to know his every thought. That he was alluring and sort of mesmerizing, and that if Katie wasn't constantly in between us, maybe we could have more moments than longing glances and boring comments about the summer heat.

Except now, Katie wasn't here. It was him and me.

Beside the easel was an upside-down milk crate. Bottles of

paint were scattered on top, along with a cup of milky water that paintbrushes soaked in. He picked up an opened bottle of white paint. I watched him screw the top back on, set the bottle down.

"It's nothing serious," he said, eyes lifting back up to mine. "Dumb hobby." But the way he painted didn't seem dumb. His eyes kept straying back to the canvas with so much care it felt as if he was dying to talk about it. Like he was waiting for the day someone stepped across the threshold of his bedroom and asked all the right questions, like he was waiting for someone to poke their head inside, dig a little deeper into him.

I wanted him to spill his secrets all over the floor. I wanted to sweep them up and stash them in a jar.

"I don't think it's dumb," I said. I felt a tug toward the door, a reminder I should have left and returned to Katie. But I couldn't. I wanted to know more. "When did you start?"

"I needed an art credit to graduate last year, and it was either painting or photography," he said.

"What's wrong with photography?"

"Nothing," he said. "I just thought that carrying around some paintbrushes would be a lot less work than lugging around a camera." So it all came down to laziness, apparently.

"Who is she?" I asked.

Truman stopped toying with the bottles of paint. "What do you mean?" he asked.

"The girl in the painting," I clarified.

He stilled. His blue eyes flickered up the ceiling like he was thinking, then back to the painting before they settled on me. "I don't know," he finally said. "Someone. Maybe no one."

"How can you not know? You painted her."

He shrugged it off. "I never thought about it."

My eyes followed the pale-yellow streaks of her flesh, soft, ridged edges raised above the surface of the canvas. I wanted to reach out and touch it. I wanted to wipe away her tears. "Is she crying or smiling?"

"What do you think?"

What *did* I think? And why did it matter? "She looks sad. This, right here"—I reached out and pointed to the blot of yellow paint beneath her right eye, unsmudged and untouched—"looks like a teardrop. And the colors . . ."

"What about them?" he pried.

"The blues, the greens. Those were deliberate, right? To use such dark, muted colors. It adds to the melancholy. But then the yellow . . . It doesn't make sense. It doesn't fit."

"It's art, Eden. It doesn't have to make sense." It was such a vague thing for him to say, but it struck me as being so wise. So clever. Instantly, I was dangerously in awe of him and the obvious talent he tried to downplay.

"I guess," I said.

I turned away from the painting and the daze wore off, the heaviness of the moment receding. Then it was just Truman and me, standing in front of the window in his bedroom. He was already watching me, two small lines in his skin where his eyebrows had drawn together. I wanted to know what he was thinking about. I wanted to know who the girl in the painting was and why she was so sad.

I had a feeling he knew and was lying about it.

"You're really good at this," Truman said, walking away from the window and toward his bed. He sat on the edge of the mattress. Creases formed in the comforter around his body. I wanted to run my hand along the cotton, smooth them out. He was still watching me with an intensity I couldn't pinpoint.

"At what?"

"Analyzing. Describing."

I shrugged it off like it was no big deal. Really, I was bursting at the seams. I wanted to say something even more clever, something else he would praise.

"Do you paint?" he asked.

The question made me pause. "I've never tried," I said. I had never thought to. Never thought it would be something I could do.

"You should," Truman said. "I bet you'd be really good at it."

I felt fairly certain that I wouldn't be. Or I wouldn't be anywhere near as good as he was. To spin the conversation away from me and back to him, I asked, "Are there more paintings like this?"

His eyebrows danced upward. "You want to see my paintings?" The question was slow and hesitant, like it was the last thing he expected me to ask.

"*Yes,*" I said a little too enthusiastically. I started to back-pedal. "But you don't have to show me. You probably want to get back downstairs to your friends, so . . ."

"They can wait," he said, already walking over to his closet.

My chest had swelled with this sense of victory, like he had chosen me over his friends sitting downstairs and the baseball game on TV.

It was pathetic how special it had felt—how significant.

I was no longer thinking about Katie, who was in her bedroom, sneaking out the window.

6

TRUMAN

THE TOUR OF OCAD was supposed to end at six. It's bordering on seven o'clock and we're still standing in the Plastics Shop on the first floor. The tour guide—some dude in his twenties with a beard and huge gauges—explains how they take students' digital files and print them into physical objects. Or something like that. I mentally checked out after we left the Photography Centre, where painted canvases lined the walls. There are entire rooms dedicated to being creative mind spaces, where dozens of easels cover the open space and students sit painting portraits, landscapes, still lifes. It's all so different from art class in high school. For one, people willingly choose to be here. Two, everyone's an artist.

I really feel like I might belong here. Which is a good thing, considering I already accepted my offer of admission for September.

The tour ends and I sneak off from the group. I wedge my AirPods into my ears and take the stairs two at a time until I hit the concrete slabs of the main floor. The walls are at least thirty feet high and made entirely of windows. The natural light is insane. It's a painter's dream. The entire vibe of this place is modern industrialism. I can picture myself walking these stairs every day, displaying my work in one of their many galleries. For the smallest second, the future seems bright.

I step outside through the red doors. My phone chimes. A text from Santana. *Send me your location.* That's not creepy at all. I type back, *Why?*

The exterior of the school is my favorite. The main campus is your typical nineteenth-century Toronto building, made with rusted red brick and clouded windows. But a more recent addition is the award-winning structure that stands above it. It's a black-and-white tabletop that looks as if it's suspended in midair. It's held up by multicolored steel legs that were designed to look like pencil crayons. It's the craziest thing I've ever seen. I take out my phone, snap a photo of it, and post it to Instagram with the caption *September*.

I wait a minute, then refresh the page. No likes. Huh, so Eden liking my last post in five seconds flat was nothing more than a . . . coincidence? I'm not cocky enough to think she's, like, creeping my social media every hour. Doesn't mean I'm not vain enough to hope so.

A notification pops up on the top of the screen—another text from Santana. *You're at OCAD??* So at least one person saw my post. *Meet me at the Second Cup on Queen St*, she adds.

I could ask why, but I *am* starving, and getting out of this heat sounds fucking fantastic. My black jeans have turned into a second skin, completely stuck to my legs with layers of sweat. I can practically hear Katie's voice in my head. *Why would you wear* jeans *in eighty-five-degree weather? Don't be so emo.* She'd say it with a smile.

I type *Fine* in reply to Santana and send it.

I'm walking toward the coffee shop when I pass by Fran's—Katie's favorite restaurant. She always made a big show of reading the entire menu front to back, then ordering the same thing she always did: chicken nuggets with fries and honey-mustard sauce. I used to hound her to decide quicker so we could order. Now, I'd give literally anything to have another moment like that with her.

Thinking of Katie is like falling down a rabbit hole. It starts off with an insignificant thought that spirals into me being pulled into a memory so vivid it feels like real. It was March, five months ago, a day or two before Katie's accident. Campus tours had started and we piled into my car, drove an hour on the highway until the two-story houses with immaculate green lawns changed into high-rise buildings, crowded streets, and the CN Tower lining the sky in the distance. Eden sat in the back seat, stuffed into a bright red puffer jacket, a beanie tugged down over her ears. I kept glancing at her in the rearview mirror. Her eyes were stuck on the windows, taking in the sprawling buildings.

Katie sat next to me in the passenger seat. She had the window fully rolled down, letting in the freezing early spring air that felt more like extended-winter air. The weather doesn't warm up until at least April—if we're lucky.

"Close the window, Katie," I said. I was beginning to lose feeling in my cheeks.

"We shouldn't have to suffer because you decided you're too cool to wear a winter jacket," she said, looking smug and warm in her neon-pink puffer.

I looked down at my gray hoodie and sherpa-lined denim jacket. "This is warm enough," I said.

"Then I'll just leave the window open," she challenged.

"It's below freezing outside. I'm not trying to be late to our campus tours because we all froze to death." I rolled up her window and added, "You can sniff as much air as you want when you're walking through U of T."

"But the air smells so good here." She turned around in her seat until she was facing Eden. "Doesn't it smell different?"

I tore my eyes from the road to watch Eden in the mirror. "Definitely." She met my gaze, grinned, then added, "It's probably all the pollution."

I laughed hard enough it's shocking the car didn't swerve into oncoming traffic. Eden's eyes were dancing. Katie rolled up the window and sulked back in her seat like a scolded child.

"Fine. Have it your way," she said. "Excuse me for trying to have a little bit of fun today."

I reached across and nudged her arm. "C'mon, don't be like

that. We're just playing. Here, smell all the air you want," I said, rolling down her window. The wind slammed inside like a sheet of ice. Katie was right—that jacket wasn't anywhere near warm enough.

She rolled the window right back up. "The moment's gone," she said, then raised the radio volume to drown me out. We drove in silence until I turned onto College Street. The street was lined with cars. There wasn't a single spot to park.

"There's one," Eden said, pointing up ahead to a car pulling out.

"Nailed it, Eden." I always found myself saying stuff like that to her. Accidentally encouraging. Look, I wasn't an idiot. Not entirely, anyway. I knew Eden had some sort of crush on me. It was the only explanation for why she always stared, always found excuses to walk past my bedroom like she was waiting for the day I'd ask her to come in. I never did. I never *would*.

Looking back, it probably wasn't the best thing for me to do. I should have drawn a clear line in the sand. Older brother, younger sister's best friend. But then . . . See, Eden was quiet. Or maybe everyone automatically seemed quiet next to Katie. She sat comfortably in Katie's shadow, letting her do all the talking, letting her make all the choices. So when there were these tiny moments of Eden doing her own thing, going against the grain, it caught me off guard. It made me see her in this new, blinding light where she was kind of all I could see.

I was only happy those moments didn't happen too often. It

would have made sitting in that car a lot harder.

I switched on my signal and pulled into the open parking spot, then cut the engine. Katie was still sulking. I knew it would take a least an hour or two before she decided to forgive me for . . . not wanting to catch hypothermia?

She was in a mood that day.

"All right," I said, turning to face both of them and putting on my best dad voice. "Stay with the tour group. Don't talk to strangers—"

"How are we supposed to make *friends*?" Katie butted in.

"Easy—you don't." She hit me with the most dramatic eye roll known to mankind. "Just stick together, okay? Mom and Dad will kill me if something happens to you two."

"As they should," Katie said, smiling sweetly in that sarcastic way. She hopped out of the car.

I turned to Eden. "Watch out for her, will you?" She didn't have to agree. I knew she would.

Eden shuffled across the seat. With one hand on the door handle, she said, "Aren't you coming with us?" Her eyes were shy and waiting. Her hair was sticking out from her beanie in these glossy, dark brown tufts. Rosy-cheeked and sitting there in my car, staring at me like I could make her entire day by saying *yes*.

"I'm off to check out Ryerson. Katie didn't tell you?" I asked. With each second that passed, ditching the campus tour to spend time with her was becoming more tempting.

"No. She didn't."

I watched the disappointment flash across her face. It was for a split second, but it was there. It still counted. I should have let her get out of the car. I shouldn't have kept talking. "Want to meet up later for lunch?" said my big fucking mouth. Eden's eyes were big, brown, and impossibly wide. Her smile was a small slope, the shyest curve. I think she was about to say yes, so I blurted out, "With Katie." I felt my face begin to warm up. I would've done anything for a nice big blast of that freezing air right about then. "Lunch. Like, the three of us," I managed to stammer out.

Eden tugged her beanie farther down until it covered her eyebrows. She was about to say something, about to agree maybe, until Katie's gloved hand knocked on the window. Eden ran out of the car so quickly I was left wondering what the hell I did wrong.

Even now, I wonder if I should have cared less about what Katie might have thought and gone to lunch with Eden. It didn't even have to be lunch. Anything with her would have been great.

The bell to Second Cup chimes. I immediately spot Santana sitting at the most private table in the farthest corner. She waves me down. I notice there are two cups on the table and figure she ordered for me. That isn't going to work. I haven't eaten since breakfast and I'm starving, hungry enough that the food that's been out for hours in that glass display case looks appetizing.

I drop into the chair across from Santana. "There you are," she says. "What's with you and social media again? I thought you went off the grid months ago."

"Not sure," I say. "I've hit a dry spell with painting. This feels like the next best thing."

She takes a sip of her black tea—always black, with almond milk and two Splenda. "I'm totally on board. That's another like and comment on my posts."

"Right, 'cause a thousand isn't enough," I say.

"A thousand and one has a nicer ring to it, don't you think?" She smiles, sets the cup down on the table, leans in. "So, how was the tour? Think you made the right choice with OCAD?"

"It's not what I had planned, but it feels right."

"You had to do some rearranging after the accident." Santana says it so casually it catches me off guard. The accident. Like it's any other memory, another moment in time to easily work into conversations.

She was right, though. I did do *a lot* of rearranging. "I took a year off after high school like Katie wanted, so we could do all this together. University, being in the city. Part of me feels guilty doing all this without her," I say.

"Then don't look at it like that," she says simply. "You're not doing this without her, Truman. You're doing this *for* her. Don't you think she'd want you to continue on with your life?"

Would she? Katie wanted to be a part of everything. She wouldn't let my mom go to the grocery store without tagging along. Is this what she would want? For our lives to keep pushing forward without her? Or would she want us to hang back and wait? I think of her as a kid, sitting on the bottom step of the stairs in bright yellow shorts. She would try to tie her shoelaces so quickly her fingers fumbled. I was halfway out the door, heading to the park across the street to meet my friends. She didn't want me to leave without her.

So is this what she would want? For me to now do everything without her?

It's a stupid question to ask. There really isn't any alternative. At least for now there isn't. Not until she wakes up.

I reach for one of the cups—some frozen, thick white milkshake thing—and Santana smacks my hand away. "That's not for you," she says.

"Then who's it for?"

I take a minute to actually look at her. She's dressed up in this satin shirt with a chunky necklace and even bigger earrings. Her lips form into a smile; they're shiny and red like her burning hair. But her eyes—*those* are what I focus on. Because she's up to something. I've known her for too long to not know when she's scheming.

"What have you done?" I ask too late. The empty chair next to Santana is pulled back, and a man sits down. Thirties, slicked back pastel-pink hair and a moustache that twirls at the ends like some villain in a comic.

"Truman," Santana says, smiling brightly, "this is Angelo."

Angelo. The photographer. The one I've been dodging left and right for weeks now.

Santana set me up. And by the look on her face, she doesn't regret it.

"Great to finally meet you," he says, stretching his hand across the table. "You're a difficult man to track down."

"Artists," Santana adds with a sigh, "always so dramatic with the mystery."

Then they're both staring at me. Watching, waiting. The room snaps back into focus and I realize Angelo's hand is still outstretched, waiting for me to shake it. I don't want to. I can't. Shaking it feels like agreeing to this—agreeing to putting my art up in his gallery, my heart pinned to the walls for everyone to judge. The thought is so traumatizing I can't see straight. The world starts to tilt a little. I need air. Warm, humid air that sticks to my lungs because suddenly I can't breathe in here.

"Truman?" Santana keeps saying my name. Her voice grows lower. My chair scrapes against the tiles. I notice Angelo drops his hand but I'm already halfway across the coffee shop, heading right into the door. A woman is stepping inside and I plow right past her, knocking my shoulder against hers. She yells. I think she yells. Maybe she gasps. I'm already moving down the sidewalk, farther, farther, farther, until I've rounded the corner. I sit on the concrete window ledge of a convenience store and tell myself to breathe. I focus on a rusted bicycle chained up to a tree. I breathe, counting to ten. Colors start to come into focus. I can hear the cars rushing by. My pulse is no longer throbbing so loudly that I can hear it in my ears.

It's okay, I think. *You're okay.* Only it's Katie's voice in my head—

No. It's Eden's.

Before I can dive into whatever that means, Santana's walking toward me. She really is a sight when she's angry. Her red hair turns into flames, licking her face, trailing behind her as she blazes down the sidewalk.

Shit. She's heading toward *me*.

"What the hell was that, Truman?" She stands directly in front of me, blocking off the entire street. She's a wall of fury. "That was so embarrassing. I cannot *believe* you. All he wanted was to meet you! You just had to sit there and listen!"

I need her to stop yelling.

She continues. "Weeks. I've spent *weeks* talking to Angelo about you, hyping up how incredible you are, this underrated artist who deserves his attention. He wants to display your work at his gallery, Truman. You know how many people would kill for that? And this is your response? To literally *run away* like a child? You couldn't have just shaken his damn hand?"

I don't say anything. I stare at the toe of my left shoe. There's a green smudge on it—a grass stain. Huh. I need to figure out how to get that out.

"Well?"

I look up at Santana. She has her hands on her hips, rage radiating off her. It makes me think of the night we broke up. The night she cheated on me. I remember her yelling at me, like it was my fault. *You're so closed off now*, she had said. I didn't care about the yelling or the blame. What bothered me was that word. *Now.* Because what she meant was *now, after Katie's accident.* As if I was supposed to lose my sister and not change a single thing about myself. Like Katie was to blame for our relationship ending, for her cheating on me.

Now.

It made me sick then. It makes me sick now.

"Truman." She says my name like a parent scolding a child. "Are you going to say anything?"

Yeah, I decide. Yeah, I'm going to say something. "It's my art. I'll decide when I want to display it in some gallery or in the fucking MoMA."

"Angelo is trying to help you," she says. "*I'm* trying to help you."

"God, Santana, I don't want your help, don't you get that? You've been shoving this down my throat for weeks now. If I wanted to accept Angelo's offer, then I would have when you first told me about it."

There was a reason I kept going back to Santana. No matter how angry we were at each other, she softened up so quickly. Now the anger fades. Her eyes grow wide, gentle. She looks small, like she's shrinking into herself. It's the easiest way to manipulate me—to have me wanting to comfort her when it should be the other way around.

"I don't get it," she says softly. "I thought you'd want this."

I'm so sick of reassuring everyone around me when no one is returning the favor.

"I don't want this," I tell her. "At least not right now."

"Why?"

Because my paintings are personal. Because a lot of them are about Katie. About Eden. About what if felt like to lose one and then the other. About everything I feel that's too hard to say out loud. Because those paintings are made with my blood and I can't handle someone rejecting them. "I'm not ready," is what I say.

"At what point do you stop waiting to be ready and take a leap, Truman?" I don't know how to answer that. "What are you waiting for? Some sort of sign?"

What I'm waiting for is when the thought of displaying my art to the public doesn't make me physically sick.

"You don't get it," I say.

I see Santana's flicker of irritation. She wants to push me. She wants to drag me back into that seat and force me to speak to Angelo because it's what'll make her look good. But I'm so stretched out from trying to please everyone. Eventually I'm going to snap in two.

"I'll go talk to Angelo," she says, already putting herself back together. She smooths down her hair, fixes the hem of her shirt. "I'll tell him you were . . . I'll think of something."

"Sure, Santana." *Say whatever will make you look good.*

She turns around and walks off without another word. I'm

wondering how we got to this point when there used to be a time when Santana felt like the only person who understood me.

That's not entirely true. I do know what happened. But I'm getting kind of sick of blaming all the bad parts of me on Katie's accident.

It's nearly eight now. The sun is finally starting to set. I want to head over to the hospital to see Katie, but I'm still too riled up. It feels wrong to bring that sort of energy into Katie's space. I decide I'll go tomorrow morning when I've slept it off.

I start the walk home. I don't opt for a streetcar or the subway right now. I want the fresh air; it helps to clear my head. It makes me think of what Santana said. *What are you waiting for? Some sort of sign?* I remember the notification popping up on my phone when Eden liked my post—the overpowering sense of happiness that followed. It was fleeting, but it was still there. Eden was one of the first people who saw my art—who saw *me*. And she didn't run away. Didn't laugh or poke fun at me for being sensitive when everyone had spent so long thinking the opposite. I remember the way her fingers touched the canvas, like it was made of glass. The way she looked at me, like *I* was made of glass. If it was possible to know that every person would treat my work with such . . . such gentleness, such care, then maybe I'd do Angelo's show. Hell, maybe I'd do every show. Plaster my work on the billboards in Dundas Square.

But I'm not in a place to put myself in front of a crowd and wait for them to rip me open when the scars from months ago haven't even begun to fade. I need more time. Hell, maybe I do need a sign.

I cross the street, no longer paying attention to where I'm going. I look up and there's a Loblaws up ahead on the opposite side of the road. I'm thinking I should text my mom and ask if she needs anything when I see her.

Eden.

The flash of dark hair. That round face. The wide eyes that constantly make it look like she's been startled. There's a grocery bag dangling from her wrist. It's so . . . normal. So insignificant. Yet I'm struggling to breathe because it's been months.

It's been months and she's here.

And she's staring right at me.

What are you waiting for? Some sort of sign?

It takes a few minutes after she walks away before I turn around and head back to the coffee shop.

Santana and Angelo are still sitting in the same spot. There's a croissant cut in two on a plate between them. I don't want to imagine what she said to him—what excuse she made up to justify how I acted. *His sister nearly died a few months ago.* That would probably work.

I walk over to their table and all I'm thinking about is Eden. Eden, tumbling into my bedroom and finding the stack of canvases; Eden, reaching out to run her fingers along the rough surface, the raised strokes of paint; Eden, and the way she used to look at my paintings, like they mattered.

Santana spots me first. Then Angelo. "Truman," she says with a hint of surprise.

"I'll do the art show," I say. "Four paintings. That's it." I offer him my hand. He takes it, shakes. Angelo's grinning like he just won the lottery.

"For the record, I was only going to ask for three," he says.

7

EDEN

THE SUBWAY IS DELAYED. No one is surprised. We've been stalled at St. Clair West station for fifteen minutes now. Which wouldn't be the end of the world if I hadn't decided to board during rush hour. It's barely nine a.m., I had to skip my morning coffee to avoid Ramona in the kitchen, and now I'm wedged between dozens of gross bodies. People are coughing and sneezing. No one's covering their mouth because human decency is apparently dead. I'm holding on to the container full of the rissóis de camarão for dear life. I don't want them to be destroyed before they even reach my parents. I can picture my dad picking up the squished patties like, *This is what you brought me?* Then he'd eat them all without another complaint.

After spotting Truman on the sidewalk, I bottled up every emotion that passed through me and tucked it into a neat little corner of my mind. I went back to Pollo Loco and finished cooking

116

with Manny. I must have been a great actress because not even supervigilant Manny noticed something was off with me. We stuffed the patties, fried them in so much oil it was criminal, and ate nearly all of them. I managed to set aside half a dozen to bring home to my dad, just like he asked.

It's not the only reason I'm heading back home. I miss my parents, miss our house. I miss the familiarity, the safety of being in the same four walls you grew up in. Being downtown is equal parts invigorating and intimidating. Usually I stick it out, even when I'm feeling my worst, when the loneliness goes from being an ache in my chest to this shadow that follows me around, nipping at my heels. With Ramona not speaking to me and with Truman popping out of thin air, I need a break. In the span of three days, the entire city has shrunk. Everything feels too close.

The subway jolts, then proceeds to speed down the tracks. Everyone cheers. I eye the subway map above the doors, the yellow line that goes from Toronto to the GTA. There are still twelve more stops until I reach mine. That's at least another twenty minutes. I groan, wishing I had taken the time to untangle my headphones before boarding. Now I try to wedge my hand into the pocket of my shorts, but people are standing too close. I don't want to accidentally grope someone.

Someone sneezes too loudly for it to have been in their sleeve. I look up, ready to pierce them with a glare. I see a flash of blonde hair and it's Katie, holding on to the pole as the subway lurches forward. Her hair fans out around her, shimmering over her shoulders. She's laughing, that alarmingly contagious laugh. She always had a way of making everything feel like an adventure.

I blink and she's gone, her smile fading at the edges. It's just another teen girl. Now that I'm looking closer, the hair color is completely off. It's too brown. Katie's was pure blonde, like strands of sunlight.

The memory collapses. We arrive at the next station. The doors swing open and people rush out. A seat opens up and I run to it, hugging the container of patties to my chest like they're my children, which they very well might be since I made them. Then that would make Manny the father, which would mean—

Yeah, too weird to dwell on.

I snatch the empty seat before anyone else can and settle down into the red cushion. Now I take the time to untangle my headphones and lean my head back, drowning out the noise.

For the next twenty minutes I do the most self-destructive thing I can: I think about Truman. Like, really let myself dig into all that pain. Seeing him opened up an entire galaxy in my mind, and continuing as if it doesn't exist is exhausting. I can't stop wondering what his story is these days—I knew who he was before the accident, but who is he now? I have to imagine that he's changed. I know I have. I'm wondering where he went after Katie's accident, why he came back and if he's doing okay, or if his entire world feels like it's rearranged itself like mine does. There's a loneliness that comes with knowing he's probably the only person who understands exactly what I'm going through right now. Not being able to speak to him about it is brutal, like we're the last two people alive on this entire fucking planet and we're stranded on separate continents.

I could never muster up the courage to ask Truman's parents where he disappeared to sometime in June. The thought of them reporting back to him was humiliating. I didn't need Truman knowing I was asking about him. Or that I still cared about him. Because I didn't. I *don't*. So why am I feeling so off balance after spotting him on the street?

And, honestly, it doesn't really matter where he went. What matters is that he left. Left his family. Left Katie. Left me. I don't understand how he could have done that. Sure, there are days when I want to fold myself into a suitcase and disappear, but I could never do that. Partially because my life is here—my people are here. Mostly, though, it's because going somewhere new wouldn't change a thing. The pain would follow me there like an uninvited roommate. That's how I know that wherever Truman went, he was still burdened with pain. It's impossible for him not to be.

I'm just wondering if he's doing any better than I am. I'm wondering what the baseline for this pain is, because right now it feels like a solid seven out of ten. I'm wondering when it gets better, when it starts to fade. I guess when Katie wakes up. *If* Katie wakes up.

If you asked me five months ago, only days after the accident, I would have bet that Katie would've woken up any day. Maybe she'd be gone for a week. A month tops. But five months? Every single day the hope I feel dwindles down even further, like a flame reaching the end of its wick. I'm beginning to lose all faith that she'll ever wake up. And that's dangerous because without Katie, I don't really know who I am.

It reminds me of Ramona and the contingency of our lease. She told me that if Katie ever wakes up, the second bedroom would become hers. She'd move out with no complaints. Now it seems so silly to even have thought that was a possibility.

The rumination comes to an end when the subway arrives at my stop. It's not until I'm halfway up the escalator that my phone's service kicks back in. One text from my dad, *Here*. That was part of our deal—riding the subway is tolerable, but I draw the line at buses, Ubers, anything aboveground. I don't like to drive. I don't like when anyone else drives me around. My parents are the only exception. I like to think this isn't another *thing* I developed after Katie's accident, but it was. Cars don't feel safe anymore. If they could extinguish the light of someone as bright as Katie, I can't imagine what they could do to a dull spark like me.

Dad's beat-up silver Toyota is parked on the side of the street, directly beside a sign that reads NO PARKING. It makes me smile. It reminds me of one thing the city doesn't offer: family. He spots me and honks the horn to catch my attention, even though we're literally making eye contact. I wave back, holding up the container of rissóis de camarão like a trophy. I can see his grin from across the street. I rush over and hop into the passenger seat. He instantly lowers the radio volume. I prepare for the onslaught of questions.

"There you are," he says, smiling ear to ear. The familiarity of his fuzzy salt-and-pepper hair and crinkled eyes is almost enough to make me cry. He's wearing an old-fashioned tweed blazer and a button-down shirt. I always make fun of him for constantly dressing like his profession, even when he takes a day off to spend it with me. He may as well wear a sign that says UNIVERSITY PROFESSOR.

"Were you waiting for long?" I ask while I buckle my seat belt. The click makes me wince—another memory, another *thing* that could've changed everything.

"Just got here." Translation: he probably waited half an hour.

"There was a delay at one of the stations. We were stalled for, like, fifteen minutes."

"Fifteen minutes is nothing. When I was your age—"

"I know, I know. You had to walk seventy miles to school and cross the Atlantic Ocean."

He wags a finger in my face. "Don't you forget it. Now, what did you bring me?" I take the lid off the container and the smell of oil and salt fills the car. My dad grabs it with greedy hands, holding the patties close to his face for inspection. "Are you sure *you* made these? They look fully edible," he teases.

"Hilarious. I made them with Manny. The chef I work with," I add. His eyebrows shoot up at the mention of, God forbid, a man. "He's a *friend*, Dad. Relax. Kind of my boss but not really. I've told you about him, remember?"

My dad chuckles, low and hearty. "I trust you. But your

mother . . . You know I can't make any promises. Can we dig in?" In my mom's car, no one's allowed to eat. She will find a single crumb on the seat and somehow trace it back to you with DNA testing or heightened mom powers, whichever. But this is my dad's car, where eating is strongly encouraged, if not expected.

"Let's do it."

We sit on the side of the road for another five minutes, polishing off all the shrimp patties. We don't save any for my mom, who feels the need to point out that deep frying only leads to clogged arteries and heart problems. Total vibe killer.

When we've licked our fingers clean like heathens, my dad turns to me and says, "Delicious. Better than mine."

"Now I know you're lying," I say.

"I'm doing no such thing." He turns the keys and the engine revs up. I feel my stomach drop with anxious anticipation. My dad senses it and turns to me. "Need a minute?"

"No," I say quickly, because being eighteen and terrified of driving is ridiculous.

"We're in no rush."

"Dad, I'm fine. Seriously, let's go. We've kept Mom waiting for long enough." The mere mention of her is enough to have him speeding down the street. My mother is where I get all my "lovable" traits from, as my dad likes to put it. Her stubbornness, quick temper, zero bullshit tolerance. All my dad's traits—being overly friendly, patient, calm, and understanding—skipped me entirely.

I spend the duration of the drive looking anywhere but out the windows. It's easier to ignore that the car is moving when I can't see it. My dad pesters me with questions, undoubtedly trying to distract me. *Are you locking the door every night with the dead bolt? Do you need money for groceries? If you want to move home early, your room is waiting. Your mother and I tried this new Greek restaurant that opened up down the street. Do you want to stop there on the way home? My treat.*

I don't have to look outside to know when we're driving by the church, my old high school and elementary school, the bakery that has burned down twice now, and the Italian grocery store with the best wood-oven pizza. Being back home couldn't be more different from the city. There are no high-rises, no cars lining the curbs of every single street. People here walk their dogs and stop to sip their coffee. No one is constantly in a rush, moving on from one spot to the other without taking a minute to breathe. It surprises me that I've missed this, since one of the reasons I moved downtown was for the city's constant frenzy to serve as a distraction.

My dad is back to talking about the Greek restaurant when we pull into the driveway. Something about our old house triggers me because reality begins to ripple until I'm seventeen again and it's Katie's brand-new BMW sitting in the driveway, not my mom's red SUV.

Katie pulled up that winter morning with a smile on her face. When I stepped into her car, she held up a thick manila envelope. "Well?" she said, face flooded with excitement.

I pulled out the matching envelope from my bag. We stared at them in anxious silence. This was it. This was the moment that decided our future, decided if the life we'd planned together would come true or if we had to take a step back, replan, and rethink.

Both of our envelopes were thick—my dad said that was a good sign. The top left corner had the University of Toronto seal, with the school's logo and motto: velut arbor aevo. *May it grow as a tree through the ages.* I wasn't sure what it meant, but it sounded fancy. Wise. All I knew was I wanted to be a part of that. More importantly, I wanted Katie to be there, too.

"Should we open them?" Katie asked. I can still remember her voice when she said that, how small and scared she sounded. I had never heard Katie sound anything but sure of herself. To see her so unsure was like a crack in her armor. A glitch in the system. It humanized her in a way I sometimes forgot to. It reminded me that she was like me: a seventeen-year-old girl on the cusp of the rest of her life.

"Let's do it together," I said.

It took us so long to work up the courage we risked being late to first period. We sat in my driveway for thirty minutes, Katie's car idling, the radio muted, staring at these papers that would alter the rest of our lives.

We ripped the envelope open at the same time. Reached inside and pulled out the letter. I took a deep breath; my entire body was shaking. "Dear Ederia Flora," I read aloud as Katie said, "Dear Katie Falls." Then, in unison, "We are delighted to offer you . . ."

We screamed so loud my parents came running down the driveway. It was the moment we knew our futures would be woven together like ivy snaking its way up a house of stone.

Katie decided we weren't going to school that day, so we didn't.

The moment dissolves into my dad holding the car door open. He must've said something because he looks like he's waiting for an answer.

"What?" I ask, stepping outside into a wall of humidity. My mom's voice echoes in my head: *We don't say* what. *We say* pardon.

"Don't mention the rissóis de camarão to your mother or she won't let us into the house without brushing our teeth," he says.

"I thought Italians are supposed to like fish? How is she the one exception?"

"A fact I wish I would've known before marrying her," he teases, because when it comes to Mom, my dad is a lovesick puppy. He unlocks the door, then hesitates in the doorway. He faces me, points at my nose. "Sure you don't want to remove that thing before we go in?"

"Mom's seen my nose piercing already."

"Doesn't mean she likes it."

"I'm not taking it out," I say a little too firmly. My dad backs off, heads inside.

I kick off my sneakers on the rug. "Mom?" I call, hanging my bag on the hook before stepping in.

"In here!" Her voice echoes from somewhere down the hall.

I walk down the hallway, the tiled floors cool from the air conditioning, and step into our dining room, which has momentarily been turned into a . . . greenhouse? The table is covered in a patchwork of newspapers. There are at least a half dozen potted plants on top and two bags of soil. My mom, the very obvious creator of this destruction, is wearing bright blue gardening gloves and holding a plant up by its stems, the roots dangling in the air like legs.

"Mom," I greet her, "what exactly are you doing?"

She looks up, her face breaking into a grin. In her excitement, the plant drops onto the table. "Huh," she says, now frowning. "I think it survived that." One by one she takes the gloves off and walks toward me. I meet her halfway and she wraps me in her arms.

"So happy you're home, Ederia," she says, using my full name. The familiar scent of lavender engulfs me . . . and soil, which is a lot less pleasant.

"Wouldn't it be a better idea to do this in the backyard?" I ask. She's squeezing me so tightly I can't tear away.

"In eighty-five-degree heat? I don't think so." My mom steps back and appraises me: my hair long and overdue for a trim, the cutoff shorts and cropped black T-shirt. She touches the metal of my nose ring, sighs. "I still wish you hadn't done that," she says, grimacing.

"You're about five months too late on that, Mom. What are you doing in here?" I walk over to the table and flick a piece of soil. Dad walks in, kisses Mom's cheek, then heads straight to the fridge.

"Your mother's doing some decorating," he says, face buried in the double doors. I'm wondering if he's actually hungry or just trying to cool off. Then he pops the lid off a can of lime sparkling water and hands it to me. They always restock it when I'm dropping by.

I take a big sip, the bubbles tickling my throat. "I can see that. Mom?"

She smooths out the apron covering her linen pants and fancy blouse. "I'm repotting the plants. Is that not obvious?" My mother is not the type of person to throw on old clothes to do such a dirty task. Nope. Her hair is blown out into a fancy updo thing with this big turquoise clip and—I look closer. Is that *winged* eyeliner?

"Since when are you this into gardening?" Before I moved out, the only plants in this house were artificial.

"Since my daughter moved out and left me alone in this house," she says, nearly echoing my thoughts.

Dad stops chugging a can of Coke to say, "You have me." Then he burps. Loudly. A bit counterproductive.

Mom presses her eyes shut. "Eden, I'm begging you to move back home." She sounds like she's upset, but she's smiling so wide I can't look away.

Dad crosses the kitchen and wraps an arm around her shoulder. "Thought I was all the company you need?"

"What about the plants?" I ask, smiling too. "They *are* living beings."

"They also don't belch so loudly," Mom chimes in.

Dad kisses her cheek again. Nearly twenty years of marriage and her face still turns the palest shade of red. "But they're a lot less handsome. Don't you think?"

My mom was a professor, too. She taught philosophy, my dad sociology. Their conversations are a lot of big words I never understood as a kid and barely do now. They met in grad school, got their PhDs together, then went on to start teaching.

When I was eight, I remember my parents' smiling faces when they told me my mom was pregnant. It was the middle of winter, but we all felt so warm. I was mesmerized by her growing belly. My dad bought a Polaroid camera and took photos every week, stuck them all right on the fridge.

Then it was June, Mom's belly was gone, but there was no baby. And she seemed sad in ways I didn't understand.

My parents sat me down to tell me I wouldn't be going back to school in September. They wouldn't say why, only that my mom wanted me to be home with her—she had just quit her job to start homeschooling me. Eventually Dad sat me down and said the word *miscarriage*. It took a few years before I fully wrapped my head around what had happened. I was too young to mourn, to feel the weight of the loss like they did.

I was homeschooled until grade nine, when I finally convinced my parents I wanted to be around kids my age again. High school started and I met Katie. Everything changed.

Dad takes a seat at the table. "Okay. Who's ready to spend the day saving some plant life?"

"The two of you know I commuted an hour home for this?" They both nod. "And I have to leave at three thirty to make it back to work in time?" More nodding. "And you want to spend this precious time together doing this? Repotting plants?"

"Isn't this what teens do for fun nowadays?" Dad asks.

I take a seat and tug on a pair of gloves. "Apparently." I follow my mom's lead: grab a pot, place the plant inside, fill in the cracks with soil. She pats it so gently, really going all out for her new hobby of the month. In July it was crochet—I have a scarf for proof—and June was a weird thirty days of candle making. It was pretty fun to wake up to texts from my dad that read *Your mother nearly burned the house down today*, and *Progress!!* with a photo attached of only half his eyebrow singed off.

"How's living downtown in the big city?" my dad asks. "Have you gone up to the top of the CN Tower yet?" My dad moved from Portugal to Canada when he was seven. Almost forty years living here and he still insists on acting like a tourist.

"Not yet," I say.

"I hear it moves." He turns to my mom with all the excitement of a child. She's ignoring him, her attention locked on the plant in her hand. "Did you hear that, *meu amor*? It moves."

"It doesn't *move*, Dad. The restaurant at the top, like, rotates every hour or something so the view's always changing. Can you pass the bag of soil?" He slides it across the table. I scoop out a handful and pack it into the ceramic pot. "Where's this one going?"

Mom eyes the pot. It's white with thick black lines along the bottom. "Maybe in the family room," she decides. "How is Ramona doing? Are you two still getting along?"

"Because if you're not," Dad continues, "you could move back home. University doesn't begin for another four weeks. Think of all the plants we can save. Your mother can even teach you how to crochet."

"These points are not working in your favor," I say.

Mom cracks a smile. "Leave it alone now, Laurentino."

"And Ramona is fine, Mom," I half lie. Suddenly I'm very interested in arranging all the soil on the table into a pile. "We barely see each other anyway with our work schedules. I'm gone all night and she's in and out throughout the day."

"What does she do again?" Dad asks. He's somehow gotten a leaf stuck in his beard. Mom flicks it off with a shake of her hand.

"She's a food blogger. She tries all these different spots in the city and reviews them on Instagram."

"And people enjoy this?" Mom asks, confused.

"People love it."

"Huh," they say together. Then Dad stands, smacks his hands over his belly, and says with impossible enthusiasm, "I'm starving! Eden, I bought your favorite bread from the bakery in town, the one with the hot peppers. Shall we cut some up?"

"He's already eaten half of it," Mom objects.

"Yes, but I saved you half because you're my daughter and I love you very much. What do you say? I'll cut up some soppressata, too."

"Sounds great, Dad," I say brightly, standing up. I walk over to the kitchen and wash my hands, scrubbing the dirt from beneath my fingernails. "I'm going to go for a quick walk to get the mail first, see if I forgot to change my address on anything. Lunch in fifteen?" But he's already standing at the counter, pulling out a large serrated knife and cutting board.

"Sure, dear. We'll wait for you," he says. My mom gives me the slightest shake of her head. He'll have eaten the entire loaf before I'm out the door.

I'm stepping into my sneakers, hooking the mail ring around my finger, when my mom calls out, "Wear your sunscreen! You'll thank me when you're in your thirties!"

I spray some on this one time, just because.

8
EDEN

OUR COMMUNITY MAILBOX IS at the end of the street. The metal groans when I insert the key and tug it open. There are a few bills for my parents. The only thing addressed to me is some expired coupons to DavidsTea. I hold on to all the envelopes and keep walking. I don't head straight home. And because I am the world's biggest idiot, I end up on Katie's street.

Her house sits on a cul-de-sac. It's ridiculously big, with a four-car garage and a heated driveway—something I didn't even know existed until I met her. I can remember going to her house in the winter after it snowed all night. Every driveway was covered in inches of snow; cars looked like mini white mountains. People were outside with shovels and earmuffs, shoveling as much as they could until their noses turned red. Not the Fallses. There was not a speck of it on their driveway. It melted away before even touching the ground.

Her house comes into view, fancy gray brick and matte-black garage doors. I'm hit with a million memories at once: sipping on gas station slushies while we lounged by the pool in her backyard, using pink sticks of chalk to draw hopscotch tiles on her driveway until the rain washed it off, climbing out her bedroom window onto the flat rooftop and staring at the sky. It's as if the entirety of my brain is made up of her. Everywhere I look, she is.

I've made it to the end of their driveway when I feel something soft brush against my ankles. I yelp, looking down to see an orange-and-white tabby nuzzling against my legs. Purrnicus, Katie's cat that she adopted from hell, probably.

He bit me once. I've been wary ever since.

I take a step back, shoo him off me. "Get away, weirdo." His big button eyes blink up at me. He lets out the softest meow before rubbing his cheek against my shoe. I remind myself that he is evil, that this is all an act before this twelve pound cat attacks me, yet I bend down. "Fine. *Fine*. Come here." He strolls right over to my hand. I scratch the soft spot behind his ear.

"What are you doing here all alone when your family moved away, huh?" I say. He begins to purr, rubbing his little head against my knuckles. "Maybe you're not so bad."

Katie went through a phase where she was obsessed with astronomy. She made her dad buy her dozens of books about the solar system, stars, black holes, and read them for a few weeks before shoving them beneath her bed and never looking back. But the name Purrnicus stuck—it was a take on the astronomer

Copernicus. I think he discovered that the planets rotate around the sun.

I'm still petting Purrnicus when a black Mercedes rolls into the driveway. I lost count of how many cars their family owns. The door opens, a shoe peeks out, and my heart is stuck somewhere in my throat because I'm thinking that it's Truman and I'm extremely aware I look like a sweaty mess. Then Katie's dad steps out of the car. I breathe again.

Close call.

He spots me creeping at the edge of the sidewalk and waves.

"Hi, Mr. Falls," I call, standing up and abandoning Purrnicus. He doesn't like that. He aggressively pounds his head against my ankle, then flops onto his back, belly in the air, while staring directly into my soul. *Pet me, human*, his little eyes demand.

"You two are getting along." Mr. Falls is walking over, looking like the millionaire he is. Tailored suit, expensive briefcase, shiny loafers, and a black Rolex on his wrist. I've never seen him with a hair out of place. He's all freshly ironed shirts and fancy cologne.

I'm suddenly very aware that I'm wearing three-year-old Vans with a hole in the toe.

"He's growing on me," I say honestly.

Katie's dad takes off his sunglasses and I really, really wish he hadn't done that. He is the spitting image of Truman: black hair that curls around the ears, sharp angular face. His eyes are Truman's eyes. This deep blue that's like the sky after a thunderstorm.

Like a sapphire. Like velvet. I hate myself for having so many adjectives at the ready to describe Truman's stupid eyes.

Eyes that I haven't even seen in months, thank you very much. Technically that's not true. I *did* see them a few days ago on the street. But it was from too far away to count—

And I'm spiraling.

"Spending the week with your family?" he asks, snapping me out of my blue-induced daydream because I am a middle school girl with a crush.

Crush? *A crush?* Where did that word come from?

I force my mouth to open because I should not be thinking about Truman so much in front of his father. And oh my God, where did these thoughts spiral out of? Is this what happens to my brain when I'm standing twenty feet from his childhood home? It simply malfunctions?

"I just came home for the day," I say, remembering that I am fluent in the English language. "I have to head back into the city in a couple hours for work. How about you?"

"I came by to check in on this little guy." Mr. Falls bends down and pets Purrnicus. I'm so worried he's going to crease his Armani suit that I hold my breath.

You have no idea what an Armani suit looks like, my brain reminds me.

"I didn't realize you didn't bring him when you moved," I say. The sun chooses this exact moment to pop out from behind the clouds, rendering me blind. I shield my eyes with one hand.

135

"We were going to," he says, rubbing Purrnicus's belly because he's plopped down on the concrete again. *Attention whore.* "But he's an outdoor cat. He loves this area. We thought it'd be too cruel to bring him into a building with no outdoor space. So we had a pet door installed here. Now he can come and go as he pleases. Isn't that right?" He tickles beneath Purrnicus's chin. He purrs and purrs and purrs. "I drop by every few days to refill his feeder."

I have this weird, disturbing need to put Purrnicus in my backpack and bring him back downtown with me. He's out here all alone, so far from Katie, the person who loved him the most.

"Anyway." Mr. Falls stands up, smiles at me. It's all Truman. They even have the same smile. And now seeing it on his father's face makes the dull ache inside me throb like a faint pulse. "I'll be on the road in an hour or so to head back into the city if you need a lift."

It's a nice offer, but I'd rather be crammed into a smelly subway than spend an hour stuck in a car with Truman's lookalike. I can already feel the memories pressing at the edges of my brain, waiting to break free.

"No, thanks," I say because my parents did teach me basic manners at one point in my life. "I'll probably hang around a bit longer."

Mr. Falls nods and begins to walk up the driveway. Purrnicus ditches me to follow behind him, and I'm not sure why exactly, but I feel extremely betrayed.

Then Mr. Falls turns around suddenly and says the last thing I want to hear: "Have you seen Truman lately?"

I want to sink into a hole. That familiar feeling washes over me—this urge to instantly change the subject while wanting to unhinge my jaw and ask a million questions at once.

"No . . . ," I begin, then find myself rambling on. "Well, I saw him in passing. Once. Barely. We passed each other on the street. Why do you ask?"

He shifts on his feet and tucks his hands in his pockets, the same way Truman does. And since when do I have such an extensive knowledge of Truman's mannerisms? Some love demon must have possessed me during the brief five minute nap I took on the subway. There's no other explanation. None at all. Nope.

Crush.

Nope.

"Truman recently returned home from Montreal. I figured you two . . ."

He keeps speaking, but I don't hear a single word. Alarm bells are sounding in my head. *Montreal*. It's a clue. The first hint I have of where he went for two months when he seemed to drop off the face of the earth. But what's in Montreal? Aside from the best poutine and, like, crepes.

And *how* did Truman spend so long in another province without posting a single photo on Instagram? We are Gen Z. Our phones are permanently glued to our hands. It's science. So where are the photos? The proof? The evidence for me to obsess over and accidentally like in two seconds flat?

Thankfully, Purrnicus's needy whine ends my Truman deep dive. "I should go refill this guy's food bowl. It was nice seeing you, Eden. Tell your family I say hi."

I spit out some appropriate response like *I will* or *Nice seeing you, too* but my brain is screaming, completely unhinged, demanding for me to follow him into that house and not leave until I've received every single detail about the last two months of Truman's life.

Or I could just ask Truman. . . .

It's so absurd I have to laugh.

9

TRUMAN

THE THING ABOUT HEALING is it doesn't come with an end date. There's no ten-step process for grief or a magic cure that'll have you smiling in a month. It's even harder when the person you're grieving is still alive. It makes everything feel fuzzy, feel off. It's as if the grief is split in two. Part of it is bone-deep sorrow. The other part is blinding optimism that Katie will wake up someday and this purgatory will end.

I really wish she'd wake up right about now, because I could use her decisive skills.

My sister never thought too hard about anything. Her brain must have been wired differently. She was all impulse. When she wanted to cut all her hair off, she grabbed a pair of scissors; when she wanted to learn how to ride a bike, she taught herself in an empty parking lot. She didn't take time to mull things over and weigh out the pros and cons. She just did whatever the hell she wanted. I usually loved that about her. But there were moments when I didn't love it so much. When I think that if she thought things over a bit more, she wouldn't have left her bedroom that night. She definitely would have put her seat belt on. Maybe if she'd thought her choices over a bit more, she'd be here right now to help.

I've been staring at my bedroom floor for the better part of an hour. I still have a shit ton of boxes to unpack, but I've made the incredibly wise decision to put that off for another few days and instead lay every painting I've ever created on the floor. It's a mosaic of mediocracy.

Four paintings. That's what Angelo said. I only need four.

This shouldn't be so difficult.

None of them are clear contenders. A few are too embarrassing to even look at. I stack those ones up and put them back in the milk crate. I'm still left with dozens.

I'm losing my mind, regretting agreeing to this in the first place, when my phone rings.

A photo of Santana sticking her tongue out flashes on my screen. "What do you want?" I answer.

"*That's* how you answer your phone?"

"Yes. What do you want?" I repeat. I nudge the corner of a canvas with my foot. It's a generic painting I did of a food market in Ottawa after a school trip. Not good at all.

"For you to stop being so grumpy, for one. Can you come meet me?"

I stop multitasking and actually pay attention to Santana's

voice. I can hear noise in the background of wherever she is: people talking, music playing. "Meet you where?"

"I'm at Eight Ball," she says. It's one of the city's oldest bars, with green-felt pool tables and actual jukeboxes. People only go there if they're trying to get drunk for cheap.

"I'm kinda busy right now, San."

"Truman," she whines. "Look, I'm here with Milo."

That catches my attention. "You're on a date with Milo and he took you to Eight Ball?" Is he purposely trying to screw this up? A girl as sophisticated and high-strung as Santana needs a two hundred dollar bottle of pinot noir. Not the weekly three dollar beer special. Jeez, Milo. I should send him a text.

"Date? I'm wearing cashmere, Truman. Don't make me throw up."

I abandon the paintings altogether and sit on the floor. "I'm going to need some context."

Everything pours out of her in a rush. "I came with some friends because apparently vintage bars are the new thing. I can't imagine why. This place still smells like the eighties. Anyway, I walk up and Milo's the doorman because apparently that's the career field you choose when you're jacked and tall. And now all my friends have left me to hook up with, if I'm being honest, total fours. Now I'm at this bar alone and Milo bought me a drink and, dear God, Truman, he keeps trying to speak to me and tell me that I look nice, as if I don't know that. I'm literally wearing three hundred dollars' worth of makeup. *Nice?* I look fantastic."

I'm still processing her first sentence when suddenly every-thing goes quiet. The music and chatter abruptly stop. A door closes. "Uh, where did you go?" I ask.

"I'm hiding in the bathroom. So when will you get here?"

"Never," I say. She groans, swears. "Do you want my advice?"

"Of course not. What I want is for you to stop whatever you're doing and get your scrawny self over here."

"Why would I come there when you could just leave?" I ask.

She goes silent. "Excuse me?"

"Leave. If you don't want to be there with Milo, leave. He can handle it." Probably not.

"But . . ." She trails off.

"But you don't want to."

"Of course I want to. Have you not listened to a word I've said? Eighties smell? Terrible music? *Fours?*"

I spot a painting that I carelessly shoved under my bed. Only the bottom quarter peeks out, but it's enough for me to instantly recognize it.

"Truman, what the hell are you so distracted by?" she says, annoyed.

I ignore her and walk to my bed. I crouch down and stare at the sliver of colors peeking out on the canvas: greens, deep brown.

"Leave the bar, Santana," I say. "Or just talk to Milo. The dude's obsessed with you."

"That's— Well, that's absurd," she manages.

"Not as absurd as you insisting you don't feel the same way.

Bye." I hang up before she can scream at me or reach through the phone and rip my head off. It's a weird feeling trying to hook up your ex-girlfriend with the guy she cheated on you with, but I have bigger things to obsess over now.

I tug the painting out from beneath the bed. I can barely even remember painting this. It was a few nights after Katie's accident, when my mind was so full that the only way I could sleep was by transferring some of my thoughts onto this canvas. I painted a few pieces that night. This was one of them.

It's of Eden. There's no denying it.

I can barely remember anything about the drive we took to the hospital together. I had just received the call about Katie. The world had stilled, stopped spinning entirely. I was in some weird fever dream. All I remember is how cold I felt, how quiet the car was with Eden in the passenger seat. It was the first time we were in a car together without Katie. It had only been minutes and we were already feeling the weight of her loss.

It was hours before Katie was out of surgery. Being in a comatose state didn't seem real. You were either alive or dead. There was no in-between. It didn't make sense that my little sister was right there, on the bed directly in front of me, and I couldn't speak to her. Couldn't look her in the eyes again. Maybe not ever.

What I had felt in that moment was crushing defeat. It was guilt. It was knowing I should have been there for her, should have protected her, stopped her, and I didn't. I couldn't because I was a hundred feet away, wrapped up in someone else.

You failed her. That was the thought that kept slamming around in my head. My failure.

My parents were crying. Every time they looked at me, I could see the question in their eyes: *Where were you?*

I don't know why, but I reached for Eden's hand. I think I needed something familiar, something to hold on to, and she was the closest thing. I took her hand and she flinched.

She flinched.

Then she dropped it. She stepped away from me. Never looked at me again, at least not directly. After that I walked into rooms and she walked out of them. I sent texts asking how she was doing and never received a response. It was all the confirmation I needed to understand that she blamed me for that night, too. Of course she did. She *should* blame me. I was the older brother. I was the one who messed everything up.

That was the last night I spoke to Eden. Then I saw her on the street. And it was ridiculous, how the slightest glimpse of her in passing knocked all the air from my lungs.

And this painting—this painting that is wedged under my bed—is of Eden. I painted it in a rush, the strokes of the brush pouring out of me faster than my hands could keep up with.

Eden was easy to paint. All beautiful things are.

It wasn't until the painting was finished that I took a step back and assessed it like I'm doing now. It's a garden. There's lush green grass and spiraling thick trees. A river runs in the background, a faded mountain range behind that. The sky is powder blue with swirls of yellow sunlight. Everything is bright and alive in this utopia.

In the middle there's a bench and a girl sits on it. Grass grows so long it winds its way up the wooden legs. Ivy snakes its way up the girl's ankles, looping around her torso, her arms, her neck. Her hair is the deep amber of honey. Her eyes are lifeless. Everything that touches her is dead.

The grass is the brightest green up until the very spot it reaches her legs; then it's withered and brown. The ivy dies the second it grazes her skin. One of her hands is curled into a low-hanging tree branch that now sags, broken and bent. She's this force of destruction. Nature shrivels away from her, flinches at the thought of touching her.

It's the Garden of Eden, this ruination of something beautiful.

I don't linger too long on the meaning behind it. In fact, I tell myself it means absolutely nothing. Not a single damn thing. It was the product of my mind at four a.m., this beating and broken force inside me that needed to break out.

It's a painting of Eden, a girl I don't know anymore. Simple.

It's the first painting I choose for the four to display.

I go back and forth on that for a few minutes. I'm unsure if it's the right call, to put something so vulnerable on display for strangers to gawk at. The thought of people asking me the meaning behind it already makes me want to hurl myself out a window. Some things are better left unsaid. And isn't art supposed to make you feel? Make you think? Wouldn't standing there and laying out the meaning like step-by-step instructions take away the entire point of creating art? It's up for interpretation. I try to see this painting through someone else's eyes. They might see a girl who's cursed. Or they might reverse it entirely and see Eden as the savior, restoring life instead of taking it.

I decide it doesn't matter what they see as long as they don't see the truth. And how could they? They weren't there in the hospital room. They didn't see her flinch. Didn't see her tear herself away from me like I was poison. They didn't see the look in my parents' eyes, that lifeless disappointment. And they didn't see the look in Eden's—the regret. Like kissing me was the worst choice she ever made.

But now I'm wondering if anyone saw the look in mine. Or if we were all too busy placing blame to realize there weren't only three people suffering in that room.

I head over to the hospital because I can't sleep. I've slowly trained my body to function on five hours a night. I feel tired and miserable all the time, but it seems to be working. It's a lot better than the two hours I was working with before. I don't drive or hop on the bus. I walk, staring down at the cracks in the sidewalk with my hands shoved into my pockets. It's almost midnight. The only people outside right now are stumbling out of bars or huddled together while passing around a lighter. The bars make me think of Santana. I pull out my phone and there's one text from her. *Where are you??*

For a second I consider asking her to meet me at the hospital. I don't like going alone. The silence is overpowering. It's like I'm waiting for Katie to say something. I could ask Santana—she'd show up if I needed her to—but there's no use inviting her. I don't want her there, and she doesn't want to be there, either. She never knew how to act around Katie post-accident. It made her uncomfortable. It's crazy that comfort is a luxury people still have.

On top of that, I always got the vibe that Katie didn't like Santana. I don't know why. Never thought to ask. And now I might never get to.

I stop that thought in its tracks. I will get to. I *will*.

It takes five minutes to get to the hospital. I go through my usual routine: the deep breaths, the counting, the mental prep. The automatic doors slide open and I step inside. I don't notice the smell anymore or squint my eyes against the bright lights. It's another thing I've grown used to.

A short elevator ride to the seventh floor and I'm there. The hallways are quiet when I step out. All the nurses on Katie's floors recognize me and smile. They aren't the same smiles they give Eden—I'm sure of it. These were all full of surprise, all full of pity. All wondering why Katie's older brother doesn't visit more. I can't exactly tell them that the guilt keeps me away. I think only Eden can understand that.

I went to see a therapist after the accident. No one knows. Not Santana, not my parents. It was a month after Katie's coma. I hadn't slept in weeks. Sadness weighed me down like a thousand pound blanket. I couldn't get out of bed. Every time I closed my eyes I saw Katie lying on the ground, cold and alone, trying to yell my name while I was off somewhere kissing her best friend.

I felt like I was drowning every time I woke up from those dreams. My throat closed up. I couldn't take in any air. I was underwater and my body was filled with stones. I could see Katie's face on the surface, rippling back and forth before disappearing completely.

Sometimes it was Eden's face, too.

I told the therapist everything. About the kiss. About the accident. About the guilt and the insomnia and how I never said goodbye. I sat there for the entire hour looking for answers and all I got were questions. I left feeling worse. The next day I decided I needed to leave, get out of this city for a month. Maybe two. It felt like getting away was the only way to find my way back to myself.

For the most part it worked. I feel better. I'm sleeping without nightmares. The sadness is dulled most days. Some days are harder, riddled with memories, but there are fewer and fewer now. The only downfall is everyone thinking I abandoned Katie. But it wasn't about abandonment. It was about . . . It was kind of about saving myself.

Visiting hours ended at eight, but no one says a word as I walk through the hall. I creak open the door to Katie's room out of habit, like I'm trying not to wake her up. The blankets on the couch are rumpled, meaning my mom spent the day here. Katie lies in bed.

There's a reason I mostly come visit Katie at night. Seeing her lying here in the day highlights that something is wrong. Because Katie was a jumble of energy. She'd never miss out on a single day when she could be bouncing around, doing a million things at once. But when I come here at night, I can tell myself that she's asleep. Taking a nap. That the sun will rise in seven hours and her eyes will spring open.

She's just sleeping. That's it.

I pull the upholstered chair right next to her bed and take a seat. Her hair is soft and fluffed out—my mom must've brushed it. Her nails are freshly painted light blue. The blanket is tucked under her chin and her head is propped on a pillow.

I reach out and touch her cheek. "I don't miss you at all," I say. That was our thing. *I don't love you one bit. I better not see you tomorrow. Hope you have a bad night.* Katie and I were so different, but the need to run as far away as you can from your emotions? We both have that.

As kids, no one ever thought Katie and I were related. Her hair is the brightest blonde and mine is black. Her eyes are wide and brown. Mine are blue and hooded, always making me look half asleep. She was the one who kissed all our aunts' and uncles' cheeks and asked to babysit their kids on weekends. I was the older brother who lurked in the corner and wondered when the fuck we'd be able to leave.

People always liked Katie better. She was bright and bubbly. She was outgoing and talkative. She was incandescent and I was unnervingly dull.

The year I spent in high school before Katie started was filled with developing bad habits: hanging out with the wrong people, skipping class, smoking here and there behind the soccer field. I showed up late and left early. I really didn't care. I was fine with sliding by on the bare minimum. I was fine with people associating the name Falls with mediocracy.

Until Katie started grade nine and flipped everything around.

Every single person she met got sucked right in. Teachers loved her. Guys in my grade asked me too many questions about her. Kids decorated her locker on her birthday, wrapping it in rainbow-printed paper and shoving balloons inside. She was an untamable force.

And, suddenly, I was the disappointment. Teachers read my name off their attendance sheets with such high hopes. *He's Katie's brother! He must be as incredible as she is!* It only took them about a week to figure the truth out—I was nowhere near as special as her.

This isn't a sob story. Being the worse end of the Falls sibling duo didn't emotionally wreck me. In fact, having all the attention on Katie was exactly what I wanted. I liked to slide by unnoticed. Unlike Katie, who had people lined up to sit with her at lunch. But she was selective about who she was friends with. I'd see her talk to people in the halls and sit with them in the cafeteria at lunch, but it never extended beyond school. She never brought friends home. Never had sleepovers, never went out after school.

Until Eden.

One day it was Katie. The next day it was Katie and Eden, this inseparable duo.

Eventually I got sucked in, too. I spent my weekends driving them around, going through Starbucks drive-throughs and dropping them at the mall entrance. It was partially because my parents told me to. And partially because I was intrigued.

Eden. She was so quiet, Katie's opposite.

I always wondered why Katie chose her, what brought them together.

I wanted her eyes to open so I could tell her that I was sorry. That I would try better now. That I'd protect her this time.

I grab her hand, assess her blue nail polish that's the color of the sky. I'm hit with that familiar feeling again, like there's this idea rippling under the surface that I can't quite reach. So I try to follow it and see where it leads me. I know that Katie loved the sky. My mom knows that, too. It must have been why she painted her nails this exact shade. My mind trails back to all those times I spotted Katie out in the backyard, lying on the grass, face tilted upward. She always seemed happy like that. In fact, the only time Katie ever sat still was when she looked up at the clouds.

The pieces slowly click into place. Then I'm left with one thought: that it would be kind of incredible to give her the sky.

10

EDEN

MANNY CALLS ME TWO hours before my shift starts. I'm stepping out of the elevator, hugging a basket full of clean laundry to my chest, when my phone rings. I debate throwing it down the elevator shaft. If Manny's calling, it's not with good news. He probably wants me to go in early, which I can't swing right now. I'm obviously very busy doing nothing. And catching up on the chores I've spent the past three weeks putting off. I'm just a busy little bee today.

But if I ignore the call, he'll just keep calling and calling and calling and—

I wedge the phone between my ear and my shoulder. "I'm not currently getting paid to speak to you, so let's keep this brief," I answer.

"Technically you don't ever get paid to speak to me. You get paid to speak to customers," he replies.

I roll my eyes and walk down the hall in my suede slippers. I think they're Ramona's, actually. I should probably stop wearing them. "Will it kill you to laugh? Anyways, what's up?"

"I need you to come in an hour early," he says, exactly like I knew he would. I ask why, even though the reason, whatever it may be, won't possibly change my mind. "It's a lot to explain over the phone. Can you be here in an hour?"

I reach my door and carefully wiggle the key ring out of my pocket. "You've gotta give me something, Manny," I say, sticking the key in the door, turning the lock. I kick it open with my foot, pad inside. Ramona sits on the couch playing *Animal Crossing*; she has her Nintendo Switch hooked up to the TV. I see her character reel in a fishing line. *I caught a squid! It's off the hook!*

"There's an event happening this weekend," Manny continues, "and the man who's running it has reached out to my dad about possibly being the caterer."

"Whoa, Manny. For real? That's huge!" I shut the door with my hip and head inside. Ramona pauses her game and turns to me, clearly intrigued by this conversation. We still haven't spoken much, but some of the awkwardness has faded with time.

"I know. We're freaking out." He does sound a bit frantic, but also happy. This is a big deal. This could potentially really help the restaurant. "It's so last minute. The guy just called and said he'll be stopping by sometime in the next few hours, Eden. We gotta be prepared, you know? Ahmed is here, but . . ."

Ahmed is a twenty-seven-year-old stoner who shows up high

153

for every single shift. His locker is a stash of eyedrops and breath mints. I opened it once by accident and it was an avalanche. I did ask Manny why they haven't fired him. He said something about their dads knowing each other. I wasn't really paying attention.

"But what?" I pry. I take a seat on the couch and start folding my laundry. I pick out all my socks first, match them up into pairs, stack them into a little pile. Ramona still has her game paused. She's leaned in a little to overhear what Manny's saying.

"Ahmed isn't really our best waiter," he finishes.

"You only have two waiters," I say, catching on. "Are you insinuating that I'm your best waiter? No—best *employee?*"

Manny laughs. I look at Ramona and she mouths, *What's going on?* I hold up a finger, telling her to wait a minute.

"If I agree to that, will you be here at four?" Manny asks.

"Agree and we'll find out."

"You're our best employee, Eden," he says.

I have my socks stacked into a cute little pile, and I smile brightly like the cute little idiot I am. "Then I guess I'll see you at four." I hang up before Manny can profess his love to me. It would be justified, since I am saving his ass.

Huh. I realize then that I'm kind of in a really good mood today. Laundry *and* heading into work an hour early? If this is what it feels to have your shit together, I might need to rethink some of my life choices.

I'm debating whether I should finally make my bed when Ramona interrupts. "Well?" she says, her voice adding an extra three question marks. A little curiosity seems to lighten the tension that's been lingering between the two of us. "What was that all about?" I give her a brief rundown because this is me waving a white flag, calling a truce. She seems genuinely happy for Manny's family. "That sounds promising," she says brightly.

"Let's just hope I don't fuck it up," I mumble. I've moved on from my socks. I'm trying to fold my shirts into neat little squares, but they end up looking like sad rectangular heaps.

"This is painful to watch," Mona says. She grabs the shirts and starts refolding them. "What do you mean you're going to mess it up?"

"I don't know." I lean back on the couch, tuck my legs beneath me until I'm a pretzel. Mona has finished with my shirts and moved on to my assortment of pants: leggings, pajama shorts, ripped jeans. "I'm not very good with customers," I say.

Her eyebrows draw together. "Isn't being good with customers your job?"

"I'm not very good at my job," I correct her.

Mona folds a pair of jeans in half, then quarters. "But you care about Manny. You care about his family and their business. So you'll try extra hard tonight. You'll do the best you can for them." I don't say a word. I don't know what to say.

Mona sets the laundry aside. She stares at me in this uncomfortably intense way. "Eden, you're way too hard on yourself," she says.

"No, I'm not," I lie.

"You *are*. You're barely eighteen, working full-time, starting university next month, and, putting all that aside, you're going through a lot. Things I can barely begin to understand," she says gently, an indirect reference to Katie. "You need to cut yourself some slack."

"It's not that easy," I say. Because when you've spent so long beating yourself down, blaming yourself for every single thing that has gone wrong in your life, you can't wake up one morning and decide to just stop. To give yourself a break. To cut yourself *some slack*.

I could blame Katie for getting into a car and not wearing a seat belt. I could blame the driver who drank too much and hit her. I could blame her parents for going away and leaving us alone that weekend. I could blame Truman for kissing me that night and putting all my attention on him. I could blame anyone for what happened that night. But I chose to blame myself. In that split second when I found out what happened to Katie, my first thought was, *I should have been there.* And that guilt just stuck. There was no going back, no rerouting my anger once that thought hit me like a brick. So I went with it. Now, five months later, I'm still going with it.

I don't want slack. It's too late for slack when it comes to Katie, because I already let her down; the damage has been done. But maybe Mona is right. Maybe I don't have to disappoint Manny, too.

Mona has finished with my laundry. She leaves my underwear

and my bras, and stacks all the folded clothing on top in a pile. It makes me think of my mom and the little actions she does to let me know she cares.

"Show up for Manny tonight," Mona says, "in whatever way you can. Even if you drop an entire plate of food on the floor or spill a drink on this mystery man's two thousand dollar suit."

"I can't believe you just spoke that into existence. Now if it happens, I'm sending you his dry-cleaning bill."

"I'll write him a check," she says. "But it's not my fault when it bounces."

I've seen some of the money Ramona has made off her Instagram sponsored posts. There's no way that check's bouncing.

"Well, guess I should take a shower and get ready for work." I stand up, pick up the laundry basket. Mona unpauses her game; the soft island music fills our apartment. "Thanks for folding my laundry, Mom."

"I couldn't sit by and watch you massacre those shirts. It was unethical."

"Or you're just a weirdo who likes folding laundry." Her character on the TV screen reels in another fish. This time the text box says: *I caught a sea bass! No, wait—it's at least a C+!* "And catching fake fish. You're a weirdo who enjoys laundry and television fishing."

"I could have worse hobbies," she says, eyes locked on the television. "Like sleeping in until three and doing my laundry once a month."

"Once *every three weeks*," I correct her.

"Is that supposed to be better?"

"I'm saving water, Mona. Saving the oceans or whatever. Saving real fish, not the ones you're reeling in," I say, waving a hand at the TV. She very maturely sets down her controller to give me the finger. It feels as if we've fallen back into place. Peace has been restored in unit 1519. We really should hang a white flag off our balcony.

I cross the room in a few steps. I'm halfway through my bedroom doorway when Ramona calls, "I missed you, you know!" It's a bit ridiculous that she's yelling when we're barely six feet apart.

I turn back to her. "Mona, I live with you."

"You know what I mean," she says, briefly tearing her eyes away from the screen to hit me with that *don't be so difficult* look.

I study her on the couch: legs crossed, Switch controller in her lap. Her hair is woven into a new fancy braid and her face is scrubbed clean of any makeup. She's wearing her favorite white crewneck with a tiny slice of pizza stitched on it. It says *Cheesy AF*.

She's not Katie. This isn't anywhere close to what I thought my life would look like this summer. But it could be worse. I'm not entirely sure how, but I *think* this could be worse.

"I maybe missed you, too," I say, the words catching even me off guard. "Like, a little. The tiniest amount. Not even enough to be seen with the human eye."

"Go to work," she says, grinning. I close my bedroom door,

but not before hearing that little sound effect again—she caught another fish.

I don't know what I'm expecting when I walk into Pollo Loco at four o'clock. Maybe a SWAT team running around, scrubbing the floor clean, repainting the walls—basically doing anything other than what a SWAT team does. Not that I'm even entirely sure what it is that they do, but I think it involves more guns, hanging from ropes, breaking through windows—and fewer Lysol bottles.

Manny made out that tonight is a big deal, so I'm preparing to walk into some type of frenzied madness. Instead when I walk through the door, the place is deserted. There's not a single customer, and the entire restaurant smells like lemon cleaning detergent. Ahmed is leaning against the counter, staring off into space, probably high, and Manny's dad is bent over one of the dining tables, scrubbing it with so much strength I'm waiting for it to split in two. When he spots me, he straightens up and grins.

"Ederia!" he calls, rushing over. Aside from my parents, he's the only other person I allow to call me by my full name without getting sucker-punched.

"Hi, Mr. Álvaro," I say with genuine warmth. He wraps me in his big, tattooed arms. I'm generally not a fan of people hugging me, but he reminds me so much of my dad that I kind of sink into him. "Manny said it's going to be a big night."

He runs a hand over his bald head, smiling in this sheepish way. "Kid's right. This could be the push we need to help business."

Just like that, he lifts up the weight of the world and rests it on my shoulders.

Manny comes running out of the kitchen like a puppy dog. I can tell he's excited by the look in his eyes. His dark curls that usually flop around are gelled and tamed down. They fall over his forehead in shiny spirals. He's even put on a crisp white T-shirt without a single oil stain. I think there must be something wrong with me for declining his date last week. Like, I should see a doctor immediately.

"Eden, you came." He's looking at me like I'm the freaking sun this restaurant revolves around and it's so completely ridiculous. I don't deserve it. I slack off and spend most of my shift on my phone. Manny is the one who deserves all the smiles, all the praise.

I remember Mona's words: *Show up for Manny tonight in whatever way you can.*

Fine. *Fine.* For one night, I will be a damned good waitress. I will even smile if I have to.

"So what's the game plan?" I say, looking between the two of them. Now side by side, I'm wondering how this place doesn't have a line out the door. Tape a photo of this father-son duo on the windows and people will be lining up around the block.

"I'm finishing off with these tables," Mr. Álvaro says, "and Manny's prepping in the kitchen. He'll fill you in."

Manny and I head into the back, where the kitchen seems to have exploded. The table and counters are lined with ingredients, and there's a fresh slab of dough that's halfway rolled out. Pots

160

are bubbling on the stove and the air smells like tangy garlic and olive oil.

"Manny," I say, stunned, "you don't even know what this dude's going to order."

Manny's already looping his apron around his neck. "He's not ordering. Pop said we're gonna give him a bit of everything." He goes back to the dough, picks up a rolling pin, and starts rolling it out.

I take a seat at one of the stools at the table. "What exactly are you making?" I ask.

"Bolo do caco, bolinhos de bacalhau—"

"English, please."

Manny laughs and starts over. "Warm bread with garlic butter, salted cod fritters, some chorizo and potato bites, piri piri chicken wings, shrimp fritters, fried green tomatoes, salted cod on corn bread . . . And pastéis de nata for dessert. Maybe some bolas de Berlim if I have time." He must see my confusion because he clarifies, "It's a Portuguese donut filled with egg custard and rolled in sugar."

"Yeah, you're definitely making that because I need ten. Shouldn't your dad be in here helping you?"

Manny begins folding the dough in thirds, pinches the edges, then rolls it out again. He brushes it with softened butter, then starts folding it again. "He's been helping me all afternoon," Manny says a bit defensively. "We've mostly got everything finished. I just need to finish rolling this dough and chill it." He does that, then sticks the log into the fridge with a tired sigh. "Bread's in the oven, the wings are marinating . . . I need to start on the cod filling." Manny rushes back over to the fridge and I'm exhausted from watching him. He takes out a bowl of what looks like fish and grabs a pot off the stove that's filled with potatoes. I keep waiting for the door to swing open and Mr. Álvaro to walk in.

"Tell me about this guy coming in," I say.

One by one, Manny places the potatoes in this large silver contraption with little holes on the bottom. He presses the lid closed and the potato comes out through the bottom in small shreds.

"His name is Angelo," Manny says. "He owns this fancy art gallery in Yorkville."

"Yorkville? Damn." It's one of the city's most expensive neighborhoods. Maybe the country's. Any event being held there is not for me. I'd stick out like a sore thumb. Or a broke teenager. Whichever.

"Exactly," Manny says, continuing. "This weekend he's holding a huge exhibit that's all about showcasing Toronto's best undiscovered talent. Every artist is local, and he wants a local restaurant to cater it, too."

I drum my fingers along the tabletop, feeling extremely useless. But Manny's got his flow going, and me asking to help would ruin it. "Makes sense."

"He reached out to my dad this morning and just said he'd stop by sometime tonight."

"A bit last minute. He kinda sounds like a douche," I say.

"*Eden*." Manny stops working on the potatoes and glares at me.

"Relax. I'm not going to say that to his face." I mean, I would. But not tonight when their family's livelihood is quite literally on the line. "So that's why you're making all these finger foods?" I ask.

"Exactly. It has to be foods that are small and portable, that can be, like, carried around on trays and eaten without a fork and knife."

"So no full chickens and plates piled with rice?" I joke.

Manny lets out a breath, wipes his forehead with a towel he has slung over his shoulder, and smiles at me. "No full chickens."

"Have I mentioned that you're a culinary Superman? Seriously, Manny. You're killing it."

His cheeks take on the slightest shade of red. The door swings open and Mr. Álvaro walks in. He grabs an apron off the hook and slaps Manny on the back. "Take a break, Manuel. I can finish this."

But Manny doesn't stop. Of course he doesn't. They start working in tandem. It's mesmerizing to watch. They anticipate exactly what the other is about to do. Manny's dad holds out his hand and Manny places an onion, a knife, whatever he needs in it without his having to ask. They're shuffling around the kitchen, stirring pots and chopping up fish. All the while I'm sitting there watching with my mouth hanging open like the useless moron I am. Eventually I head off to the storage room. They don't even notice me leave. I stash my backpack in my locker. I even put my phone in there for the first time in my life. When I head back into the kitchen, they're still going at it, stuffing dough pockets with fish and slicing tomatoes.

"Anything I can do to help?" I ask.

Mr. Álvaro looks up from the cutting board and nods to the door. "Let us know when Angelo gets here."

"He's got pink hair," Manny adds. "You can't miss him."

I head to the front and wait.

The elusive Angelo doesn't show up for another three hours. The prick. Coincidentally not a single customer does, either. My phone is in my locker. I'm bored out of my mind and in the middle of counting how many tiles are on the floor when the bell chimes. I look up and the door swings open; a head of light pink hair walks through.

I do the most unnatural, weirdest thing I can: I smile at him.

"Welcome to Pollo Loco," I say, already grabbing a menu off the counter and walking toward him.

"Hello—" He pauses, looks down at my name tag, then says, "Eden. Is your boss around?"

Is your boss around? I mock in a whiny voice in my head. Mr. Álvaro comes rushing out of the back. Thank God. I was on the brink of making a snide comment regarding his moustache. How does he get it to *twirl* like that? I want to text Ramona. She'll link me to a YouTube tutorial in three seconds flat.

"Angelo!" Mr. Álvaro has his arms open wide like he's greeting an old friend and not some stuck-up snob he's meeting for the first—maybe second—time.

Stuck-up snob? I really need to tone it down with the judgment. Just because someone's from the city's wealthiest neighborhood doesn't mean they're a snob. Maybe. Possibly. More than likely. But it's not a sure thing.

Okay, it's definitely a sure thing.

I'm so lost in my mental dialogue that I've nearly missed their entire conversation. Mr. Álvaro says that they've prepared him a "special meal" that'll "give him a taste of the food they'd serve at the event." I can almost see Manny in the back with his ear pressed to the door, trying to overhear every last word. I'll give him the rundown later.

I notice the two of them staring at me. Mr. Álvaro says, "Eden will show you to your table. My son and I will bring your food out in a minute. Please, make yourself at home."

I stop standing around like a weirdo, hugging the menu to my chest, and lead Angelo to a random table because they're all exactly the same. I set him up at one closer to the back. He sits down on the tan leather booth and I'm thinking that I should have picked a table closer to the doors, because this one is near the bathrooms and that can't be good. And then I'm spiraling because it's not that serious. I need to relax.

I set down his menu. Smile again. My cheeks are already beginning to hurt.

"Can I get you something to drink?" I ask, my voice sweet as sugar.

"Water is fine. Thanks, Eden." The way he says my name

makes me feel slimy. I nod like a bobblehead and shuffle off to the counter. I watch Angelo flip through the menu as I fill a glass with ice and water. Then I'm wondering if I should put a straw in it or not. Are straws too kiddie? But is it considered gross to sip straight from the cup? Is this the stupidest thing I've ever worried about in my life? Yes.

I opt for a straw on the side and set the cup down in front of him.

"Thanks, darling," he says with a smile. I want to throw up. He smacks the end of the straw on the table until the wrapper begins to peel off. He chucks it aside, then stuffs it in the glass. "You've been working here long?"

"Two months," I say, forcing any sort of disgust out of my voice. Something about this man just seems iffy. And his moustache is really throwing me off for some reason. Seriously, how does it stay like that?

My fingers itch for my phone.

"What's your favorite thing on the menu?" Angelo asks, because apparently this is an interview.

"The pastéis de nata. They're incredible. The best in the city," I add, even though these are literally the only ones in the city that I've tried.

"And those are?"

"It's an egg custard tart. I'm sure Mr. Álvaro will bring you one." I remind myself to smile, smile, smile.

The kitchen door swings open and Manny strolls out, expertly balancing three plates on his arms. I could grab his face and kiss him right now. He eases into conversation with Angelo in a way I'm extremely envious of. How are some people just so good at talking? At being *people*? I notice the plates are filled with warm bread and some sort of herb butter, fried fritters that must be filled with the cod Manny was prepping, and a plate of crispy potatoes with slices of chorizo. Everything smells divine. My mouth is watering.

I slide back over to the counter and let Manny work his charm. Angelo is laughing so loud there's no way he'll pick anyone else to cater the event.

There's no way.

When Angelo finally leaves, Mr. Álvaro locks up and the three of us sit down at one of the booths, eating all the food that was left behind. I'm munching away on my second pastel de nata, Manny has eaten the entire plate of bread, and his dad is very aggressively eating a chicken wing smothered in piri piri—a hot sauce.

"That went well," I say, dipping my finger into the pastry, scooping out the custard, and licking it off. Manny hates when I do this. Now he's too tired to comment.

"He should be giving me a call tomorrow or Thursday with his decision."

Angelo mentioned the art show will have about one to two hundred people strolling through. "But the event is on Saturday," I say. "That's nowhere near enough notice to start prepping to make that amount of food."

Mr. Álvaro only shrugs, smiling halfheartedly. "We'll do what we have to."

I look at Manny. He's leaning back in the booth with his eyes closed.

Mr. Álvaro reaches across the table and pats my hand. "Thank you for your help tonight. We appreciate you, Ederia."

There's something about Manny's dad that makes me feel safe, like I'm back at home with my own family and not miles away.

"Happy to help," I say, returning his smile.

"So," he says, reaching for another chicken wing, "how much do you know about art?"

I think back to dark gray bedroom walls and wooden furniture. To milk crates stacked with canvases and easels propped in front of windows. I see Truman's face in my mind, and the way his eyes got so animated when he spoke about his paintings.

"A little," I say, ignoring the twinge of pain in my chest.

"That's a lot more than I do," Mr. Álvaro says with a laugh. "If we book this event, we'll need you there on Saturday to serve the food. Can you do that? I can pay you time and a half."

"You don't need to pay me extra. I'd do it for free if it meant helping you guys out," I say.

At that, Manny's eyes spring open. He stares at me, not saying a word. Just smiling.

Mr. Álvaro is smiling, too. "What would we do without you, kid?"

11
TRUMAN

MILO AND SANTANA THINK I've given up on my future and that's why I'm dragging my feet with getting ready for this art exhibit tonight. They're wrong. The reason is simple: I don't know if I can mentally handle this right now. The paintings I chose for the exhibit tonight aren't all sunshine and rainbows, either. They're dark. They're sad. They're pieces I created in my most depressed states. They're paintings of Katie when she was here and paintings of Eden when she was here, too. These pieces are filled with real memories and attached to real feelings, and the thought of having a bunch of strangers pick them apart while sipping champagne makes me wish this night were over before it has even begun.

It's too late to change my mind. Not for any personal reasons. If it were up to me, I would blow this entire night off and accept my losses. But Santana and Milo have taken over my bedroom, and they're wrapping the four paintings up in paper, then gently placing them into boxes to keep them safe during the trip to the exhibit.

Santana keeps saying *Oh, I love this one* and *This one hits me right in the heart* and Milo is watching her, huffing out noises that sound like agreement. I think Santana could say the Earth is flat and Milo would look at her like she's the wisest person on this planet before trying to find the edge of it.

"Are you ready to go?" Santana asks. She's wrapped up in a matching oversize sweatsuit, and her hair is thrown up in a knot on the crown of her head, red curls sticking out and touching her shoulders. Clearly, she's not coming to the exhibit. However, she made it very clear she's driving me there to, in her words, "make sure you don't fuck this up for yourself."

Milo's tagging along because Santana is here. Then he's heading to a bar a few blocks over to work for the night.

"What happens if I say no?"

Santana nods at Milo. "He'll haul your scrawny ass over his shoulder and carry you to the car. Milo can hold you bridal-style if that's your preference," she says. Milo grins, flexes. His biceps are the size of my torso.

"I can walk," I say.

We each carry a painting and gather in the elevator. "Are your parents coming?" Milo asks over the soft drone of the ballroom music.

"No."

"Why not?" Santana pries. She balances the box vertically against her thigh, then winds a few tendrils of loose hair around that crazy knot.

"I didn't invite them."

I ignore the identical looks they both give me. They're full of conscious realization that I am, in fact, an idiot. Having my art up for strangers to see is one thing—at least they don't know me. Having it hanging on a wall for my parents to stare at and pick apart? I have boundaries.

"God forbid your family celebrates your achievements, Truman," Santana murmurs.

"Glad we're on the same page."

Milo barks out a laugh as the elevator doors swing open. We head to Santana's car in the parking lot like the most disgruntled trio to ever exist. We stack the paintings carefully in the trunk of her SUV, then Milo makes a not-so-subtle show of sitting in the passenger seat while Santana drives. I'm stuck in the back like a child.

The closer we get to the exhibit, the less air I manage to get into my lungs. Santana sings along to whatever song is on the radio and Milo doesn't take his eyes off her. No one notices that I'm quite literally losing my shit a few feet away. Anxiety winds its way up my body like a snake, squeezing and wrapping itself around all the wrong places. I need Santana to pull over. I need to get out of this car. I need to tuck those paintings back into my closet where no one will ever see them again.

My heart beats so loud I can hear it over the radio; I can hear it over Santana's terrible voice. My palms are slick with sweat. I wipe them on my jeans but it doesn't help. Nothing is helping.

"Santana," I croak out. My voice is hoarse and rough as sandpaper. I sound like I've spent weeks foraging through the desert. I'm about to ask her to pull over because the world needs to stop spinning for a second. The world needs to just *stop* for a second. I want to get off it, whatever ride this is. And then we drive by Katie's hospital and the entire car goes silent. San stops singing. Milo stares out the window, right at the looming building. Me— Well, I feel this rush of ease. Somewhere inside those walls is my sister. This girl who may never be able to look at my artwork again. Or attend an art exhibit. Or sit in a car and sing along to crappy songs. Then everything shifts into perspective. All my problems shrink in comparison to hers. Then hanging my art on a wall in front of a few hundred people doesn't seem like a bother. Instead it kind of feels like a privilege. How many artists would kill for an opportunity like this? And here I am, ready to sweep it right under the rug.

I decide that I don't owe shit to myself anymore. But I do owe everything to Katie. So I'll swallow every burst of pain and push through for her. It's the least I can do.

Santana pulls up in front of the studio the exhibit is being held in. It's floor-to-ceiling windows, so every person walking outside can peer right in. From here, I can see the room is a huge white square, completely open concept in a way that is both calming and completely terrifying. Then everything happens so quickly: The three of us unload the paintings from the car. Santana is kissing both of Angelo's cheeks. Employees rush over and grab the paintings from us. Angelo leads me to the back left corner of the room. *This is your spot*, he says. Or something like that. I stopped paying attention. Then Milo and Santana leave and I'm utterly alone. Just me, my artwork, and other artists, who are all standing around talking. Because of course they have so much in common. Except for me. I'm the black sheep—the odd one out. And even while I know this worry is all happening in my head, it feels insanely real. Then the doors are unlocked and a crowd of people stream inside like someone lifted the gates on a dam. People are drinking and there are servers walking around with trays of food. I don't even bother looking too closely at any of it. I feel like I'm going to throw up everything I've eaten in the past two years.

Then people are standing in front of my paintings. They're mhhhhming and ahhhing and I want to be the one interrogating them. I want to know what they think and if they like it, even though their answers would be insignificant. It's subjective—that's the point. Like it or hate it, it doesn't matter. It doesn't change the way I felt painting these pieces or what they mean to me.

I walk around the room a few times to clear my head. I look at all the other artists' work and feel lucky to even be in here with people who are clearly so much more talented than I am or might ever be. There are sculptures carved of stone and hands made of clay. There are photographs of children's faces and pieces of metal that are wound together to look like melted glass. There are orbs and shapes that hang from rods in the ceiling and a body made entirely of balloons with a single nail next to it, propped up on a silver pedestal.

I feel like I'm in a daze, like my mind is somewhere else entirely. I'm not even sure what I'm doing anymore, just moving aimlessly through this room. So when I spot her, I think I must be dreaming. Or hallucinating at least. Because there is no way Eden is here, holding a tray of drinks, dressed like a server. There is no fucking way she has manifested in my life again.

Then Eden walks by me and stops. Stops because she has seen me. *She sees me.* And then I am in this room again that quickly. I'm tethered back down.

12

EDEN

IT'S HIM.

Truman looks so much like Katie. Too much. I can see her laugh in the way his eyes crinkle at the corners. I stare until it feels like she isn't lying in a hospital bed down the street and she's here, standing right in front of me.

Just like that, the memory from that night—the one I've spent months burying—comes trudging right up with so much force it knocks the air out of me.

I asked Truman to see more of his paintings. He sat on his bed, perfectly placed in the moonlight streaming in through the window.

His eyebrows danced upward. "You want to see my paintings?"

"Yes. But you don't have to show me. You probably want to

get back downstairs to your friends, so . . ."

"They can wait," he said, already walking over to his closet.

Truman dug through the back of his closet and pulled out another white milk crate. Inside were canvases stacked in a neat row, their white edges dotted with a thousand different colors. I sat perched on the bed. The mattress groaned when Truman sank down beside me. He placed the milk crate at our feet and plucked out the first painting.

We sat there for an hour maybe, sorting through painting after painting. Some were from when he was fourteen, but the more recent ones were from this week or this past month. I was in awe of how every single painting was different from the last. There was no commonality. There was no similar use of color or shading. The styles were nothing alike, like it was one big experiment. Some were watercolors, brushed with soft pastel pinks and faded orange. One was abstract, with harsh blocks of yellow interrupted with circles of green, blue, teal. There was no rhyme or reason.

When I asked Truman about this, he shrugged and said, "I'm still figuring out what I like."

There was nothing for me to figure out. What I liked was this: sitting there with him, staring at these paintings, these portholes to his mind.

"You're really talented, Truman," I said when he pulled out the final painting in the stack. It was a frozen pond in the winter. The moon gleamed against the ice, which he had painted in such a way that I could nearly feel how cold it was.

I looked up from the painting to find him looking at me. His face was right there, inches from mine, his eyes a steady blue, that deep swirl of *Starry Night*.

Something shifted in that moment. A curtain had been pulled back. Truman let me in on something special, something secret— some part of himself that I could tell was hidden from everyone else. And he had shown it to me.

I decided I would be cautious. I would handle this side of him with silk gloves. I wouldn't pry. I wouldn't push. I would idle by, waiting for him to offer up more, greedy for every last bit.

If only I had known then that even all of him wouldn't be enough.

"You think so?" Truman said. The vulnerability softened his features until he no longer looked like Katie's older brother. He was just Truman, a boy who loved art and created in secret.

"Do you show people?" *Other than me.*

"No," he answered. "That's why my door's always closed."

"Except for tonight," I said.

Truman's mouth curved up in a slow smile. "Except for tonight," he repeated. "I'm kind of glad I left it open." The words skyrocketed right into my heart and exploded into fireworks.

In that moment, I was exhausted from never letting myself do what I wanted. From tiptoeing around whatever was growing between the two of us but we were both too hesitant to act on. I should have felt guilty that Katie was down the hall, but I didn't.

The only thing I felt was this intense desire to grab Truman's face in my hands and kiss every inch of it.

"You should leave it open more often," I said.

I made my choice. And I chose him.

I shifted closer to Truman on the bed until the sliver of space between us was entirely closed. We were thigh to thigh, shoulder to shoulder. My body buzzed from all the spots his touched mine.

It was nowhere near enough.

I grabbed the painting from his lap and placed it on the bed behind us. Truman didn't move a muscle. He glanced down at me beneath thick, dark eyelashes. I wanted to run my fingers through his hair. I wanted to touch his skin.

I placed my hand on his arm. It was the assurance he needed. *You're not imagining this*, I wanted to say. *Kiss me.*

Then he was.

Kissing Truman felt like one of his paintings, like swirls of the brightest colors and the darkest grays, mixing into one.

His lips were a gentle press, feather soft, like he was unsure of how much of himself I was willing to take.

All of it.

I wound my arms around his neck, pulled him closer. My fingers knotted into his hair, that ridiculous head of raven-black waves that seemed to grow longer every single day. Truman's hands made their way to my waist and he tugged me closer, kissed me harder.

His bed creaked when we fell backward onto it. Then Truman

groaned. I pulled away to see what was wrong. His hand left my waist and reached beneath his back. He pulled out his painting from under him—he had lain down directly on top of it.

"That killed the moment," Truman grumbled.

I grinned the widest I ever had. "No, it didn't."

I reached out and tugged his face back to mine. I laughed against his lips when he tossed the painting across the room without a care.

"Truman!" I exclaimed.

"Not important right now," he mumbled into my mouth. His body shifted over mine, pressing me down into the bed. I took his face in my hands and Truman's lips crashed back into mine with mind-numbing ease. His arms felt so solid around me, warm and safe. I was melting right into him.

We were so reckless. So greedy. But what did we expect? After spending so much time living off stolen glances in rearview mirrors, we were desperate for each other. I was only glad he seemed to want this as much as I had.

Now that Truman was so close, I couldn't imagine ever keeping him at arm's length again.

Until a loud noise sent us flying apart. The house phone was ringing, a wailing siren that ripped the moment right open. Truman broke away; his eyes looked glazed over. Then he heard the noise, realized what it was.

"Dammit. I should get that," he said without moving. The phone stopped ringing. He smiled down at me. "On second thought . . ."

We were already moving back to each other when someone yelled his name from downstairs. He rolled his body off mine with a sigh, then sat up. "What?" he yelled, sounding both angry and annoyed.

"Phone's for you!"

He peeked over at me, his eyes apologetic. His hair was a tangled mess, dark strands stuck up in wild angles and falling over his forehead, hanging over his eyebrows. In a spur of boldness, I reached out and brushed them back.

"It's fine," I said, gently pressing my hand into his chest. "Go get it."

"I'll be right back." He scrambled off the bed and ran to the door, then paused in the hallway and turned back to me. "Don't move," he said with a smile. "Seriously. Don't go anywhere." Then I heard the thump of him running down the stairs.

With Truman gone, I collapsed onto the bed. I was smiling up at the ceiling like a total dork, still reeling from having him so close. I felt dizzy, warm, like everything I had ever wanted was suddenly within reach.

Then I remembered Katie in her bedroom down the hall and I knew I had to tell her. I was so naïve—in my head I was already planning my and Truman's entire future together. I figured Katie would be upset at first, but she'd warm up to it. She'd have to.

With Truman taking forever downstairs, I walked over to her room and rehearsed what I would say. But when I pushed open her bedroom door, none of that mattered.

Katie was gone.

"Katie?" I called. Her bed was empty, her laptop still on it, the Ikea tab open. Her closet door was ajar and clothes spilled out onto the floor—clothes that hadn't been there when I left.

I walked around her entire room. I looked everywhere, even in the spots that were impossible for her to fit in. Then I noticed the window was cracked open.

"Katie . . ." I ran to it and peered outside, sticking half my body out. "Katie!" I called. I yelled her name over and over. There was no response.

I ran into the hall and called her name. No response.

I checked the bathroom. Empty.

I checked her parents' room. Their walk-in closet. Their en suite. All empty.

Then I felt the weight of my phone in my pocket. I pulled it out in a rush, clicked the screen on. One new text from Katie sent thirteen minutes ago. *Snuck out. Cover for me, pleaseeee! See you tmrw.*

There was no tomorrow.

There was only that night and the faint sound of sirens wailing outside. I walked toward the window again to peer out. The black sky was lit up with shades of blue and red that danced across the clouds.

Something felt off. I wasn't sure what it was, but there was this change in the air. It felt like something . . . like something bad had happened.

"Truman!" I was yelling his name, screaming it at the top of my lungs because I knew—I knew she wasn't okay.

I ran down the hallway as fast as I could. My feet kept sliding across the floor. I took the stairs two at a time, not caring that I wasn't allowed downstairs. That didn't matter anymore. All that mattered was finding Katie. Bringing her home to me.

My feet landed on the cold marble and I stopped. It was like someone had hit pause on a movie. Everyone was frozen.

No one was moving.

Truman's friends were standing around. Their mouths were wide open. I could hear people crying.

Katie Katie Katie Katie. Her name was being whispered over and over and over again, like the worst game of broken telephone.

"Truman?" I called. I ran to the kitchen.

I realized something was very wrong when I saw him keeled over, right there on the tiles. He still had the cordless phone clutched in one hand, cradled against his chest.

"Truman?" I said again. I walked to him and the ground was shaking. The walls felt like they were caving in. I couldn't breathe. I couldn't think straight.

The moments we don't see coming are the ones we need to be most afraid of. They sneak up on you, catch you off guard, rip you to shreds without a single warning sign.

This felt like that—like being torn in two.

I reached Truman and he just fell over, right onto his side, curled into himself. Tears were frozen on his cheeks and his eyes were far away, somewhere between the moon and another galaxy altogether.

"Truman?" I asked gently. I tumbled onto the floor beside him, took his hand in mine. "What happened?"

Someone hit play. Everything unfroze. Truman's tears started rushing down his cheeks. He was screaming, wailing; something deep and dark was breaking out of him.

I didn't . . . I didn't know what to do. How to put him back together again.

"Where is she?" I asked. I was crying then too; warm tears slid down my cheeks and slapped into the floor.

Then Truman looked at me, and what I saw in his eyes was . . . it was indescribable.

That was the moment I knew.

Truman drove us to the hospital. He reached for my hand, but I couldn't—I couldn't touch him again. We drove through the dark streets to the hospital Katie had been taken to. The speed limit was sixty but we were flying. A red light wouldn't stop us from reaching her in time.

The hospital was too bright. The halls stretched on forever into a blinding sea of white and I wanted to drown in them. I couldn't look at Truman without feeling a tingle in my lips, and remembering the kiss that left us locked in his room as Katie . . .

It was a drunk driver who hit her. She was only a few streets away. I couldn't remember the number of bones she broke, bones I never even knew were in the human body. Her head took the most damage when her body flew through the windshield. She wasn't wearing a seat belt. I couldn't stop thinking of the hundreds of times Truman said to her, "Katie, put your seat belt on." But this time he wasn't there to remind her. Neither of us was.

She was unconscious now, hanging on by life support.

We stood together in her hospital room. Truman and I were on one side of the bed, her parents on the other. The doctors said that maybe she could still hear us. Katie, this girl who was lying before us, wrapped in so many bandages I couldn't see a sliver of her skin. Her eyes were swollen and bruised. Only her hands were visible, her pastel-yellow nails. So bright, so out of place in all that darkness.

I stood there, searching for the words to apologize for kissing him, for not being there for her, but they never came.

I knew Truman felt it, too. The guilt.

His eyes never met mine again.

We couldn't look at each other.

We couldn't speak without our hearts ripping open into a hole big enough to swallow us both.

We stood side by side at Katie's bed, silent. That kiss felt like a lifetime ago. We were two strangers now, mourning the loss of a girl we loved in different ways. And even though Katie was still alive, she had never felt farther away.

After that night at the party, I never saw Truman cry again. I rarely saw him after that. But his eyes were dry now; there were no tears left. Katie's accident took them all. She took his heart and his tears with her, and I stood there watching, whispering a goodbye to my best friend as the heart monitor continued to beep.

I wished I could turn back time.

I wished I could go back to the days of belly laughs and rainbow nail polish. When we drank juice and had our noses buried in textbooks from sunrise to sunset.

But it was too late.

I had decided Katie's fate the moment I left her side that night, when I chose Truman over her.

And I was left wondering why I thought it was worth it, to lose her for a kiss from a boy who was now broken, too.

13

EDEN

WHY, WHY, WHY DID it have to happen like this.

Spotting Truman on the street was one thing. There was an entire road between us—that's so much safe distance. I could pretend I never saw him. Sure, our eyes locked, but for all he knows my vision has severely declined since our last encounter.

But *this*? Truman standing directly in front of me is too much. Especially when he looks all polished and fancy in a blazer. He even got a fucking haircut. Meanwhile I'm wearing a white button-down shirt with a bow tie, holding this half-empty metal tray in one hand like a dork.

I don't even bother looking down. If he's switched his dirty Chucks for loafers, I might lose it entirely.

And why? Why am I noticing his hair is barely two inches shorter than usual? This is not an appropriate response. An appropriate response would be dropping this tray of champagne on the floor and booking it for the door because this cannot be happening. *I don't want this to be happening.*

The whirlwind of self-hatred lasts for the single second it takes Truman to say my name.

"Eden?"

I'm half here, half somewhere in the past, lying under the sun with Katie. Truman's there too, splashing around in the pool. Katie shrieks because the water hits her hair, her legs.

I could just walk away. My job is to literally walk through this room. I could easily move on, pretend I don't recognize him, go to another guest.

But I don't. I realize it's because I don't want to. I've spent months dreading this happening; months thinking I would storm off the second we were reunited because I don't want anything to do with Truman Falls anymore. Not after what we did that night—what we caused. Yet here he is, and I can't bring myself to move away. It's like that day on the sidewalk when, more than anything, I needed him to see me.

And now he has.

"Truman," I say, my voice somehow sounding hoarse and squeaky at the same time, "what are you doing here?"

His eyes pierce through me, swiping down to the tray, the uniform, the black slacks that are not flattering at all. *Why does it matter?*

"I have some art on display. . . . Do you work here?" he asks.

I suddenly wish I were a lot cooler than this. Because he seems so cool. Too cool. Displaying his work in a gallery? The coolest.

"No. Not really. I waitress at the restaurant that's catering the event," I say. "Wait—some of these are *yours*?"

"Yeah." He smiles down at me. It's the same smile from the closet, that gentleness curling around the edges. "It's a big difference from milk crates in my bedroom, huh?"

He references that moment from our past so casually it catches me off guard.

"Yeah. Just a little."

He laughs, awkwardly tucking his hands into the pockets of his black jeans. I'm shifting on my feet, balancing the tray on one hand, looking around the bright space for something to say, something to do.

Without Katie, what else do we have in common?

"So which of these are yours?" I ask like an idiot because, truthfully, I haven't been paying much attention to the actual art. If I had, I definitely would've recognized Truman's work. At the exact same moment, Truman says, "I should probably stop hogging you and let you get back to work."

"Oh, right," I say. "Yeah, no, of course. I should keep making rounds. You know how rich people get without alcohol. . . ." No idea why I said that, since Truman *is* rich people.

My brain must have fled when my feet refused to.

I stare at this sculpture of a woman's bust a few feet away. Anywhere but Truman's face is the current target.

"I mean, if you have a minute, I can show you my work," he says.

My heart kind of thumps around. When I look back at him, he's still smiling, rocking back on his feet.

Do I even want to see Truman's work? Yes.

Should I allow myself to get wrapped up in a conversation with him? No. Because I am on the clock. Because I'm a responsible employee. Because I am not getting paid to sneak off with Truman Falls, not again.

And because, I cannot stress this enough, *I need to stay away from him.*

Manny must be a mind reader, because he appears out of nowhere. He smiles politely at Truman, says, "Excuse us," and pulls me away by my elbow. The champagne flutes rattle as he leads me over to the booth along the right wall, where all the food is set up. His dad is there, filling trays with some of the appetizers.

"What did I do wrong?" I ask innocently when we reach the booth. I walked my laps around the room. I watched rich people put obnoxiously small food in their mouths. What more is there?

"What? Nothing. Wait— *Did* you do something wrong?" he asks, eyeing me suspiciously.

"Of course not."

"Good." Manny takes my tray and replaces it with one filled with pastéis de nata. "Ahmed's rotating the drinks now. Can you start circulating the food?"

"Aye aye, Captain," I say like the annoying human being I am. He gives my shoulder a gentle shove. I make it a few steps before Mr. Álvaro calls my name. I spin back around. I'm about one spin away from dropping this tray. "Yeah?"

"What's going on out there?" he asks, nodding toward the guests. We're all wearing button-down shirts, so every single one of his tattoos is fully covered. Even the ones on his hands are concealed with gloves.

"Everything's great," I say. I'm assuming he was referring to the food and not my impromptu reunion with a ghost from the past, because that, on the other hand, is not going so well.

"People seem to be liking everything?"

"People seem to be *loving* everything, Mr. Álvaro." I nudge Manny's arm with my free hand. "Relax, okay? This is a good night."

But Manny seems anything other than relaxed. I hurry off and start circling with the new tray before he very politely yells at me to.

The second I begin my rounds, my eyes seek out Truman like two enemy missiles. Luckily I'm at an art event, and everyone is more interested in speaking to the artists than the girl handing out their food. I move through the crowd unnoticed for the most part. A few people stop me here and there for food, but never to talk. Which is fine with me. My brain is doing that thing where it jumps into overdrive and I need a few minutes to think, to process.

So Truman's been busy these past few months, clearly. I doubt he spent much of his time slumming it in bed like I have. He's been a busy artist, probably painting by windows and booking gigs for art galleries on the weekend. But I still don't know what happened in Montreal, why he went there and what he did there. What I'm trying to figure out is, does it matter? Is there a reason that justifies him leaving Katie for months? I doubt he went backpacking through Quebec to find an herb that, once smelled, immediately brings someone out of a comatose state.

The worst part is that none of this is my business. Truman didn't have to run it by me before he left. I definitely did not run it by him when I decided to cut him out of my life and start avoiding him like the plague. So what's the difference? Why did him vanishing hurt me so much?

If I'm being honest with myself, the day Truman packed up and left for Montreal wasn't when the hurt began. It started months before that. It started on that night in his bedroom, when I finally had Truman—the person I had spent so long wanting.

And the second I had him, I lost him.

The tide turned so quickly I barely had time to even sort through my feelings. I was still high off kissing him when the news of Katie's accident hit. It was like the best and worst moments of my life collided into each other. Truman and I never even stopped to talk about what happened between us and what it meant. Or if it had even meant anything to him, because it did to me.

I'm so sick of my life being so complicated. The good is always offset with the bad: Katie's accident and that kiss; Manny's family booking this gig and Truman showing up. For once, why couldn't something good happen without any strings attached?

I'm walking along the left wall. People are standing in tight circles, sipping champagne and trying to sound smart, like they understand half the stuff they're looking at. I keep hearing words like *perspective, subjective, juxtaposition*.

I need a dictionary.

I swerve to avoid a group of women and come face-to-face with a sculpture of . . . I don't know what, exactly. It's made of metal. It looks like a man kneeling on the ground. His hands seem to be trying to pull whatever is stuck over his head. A television? An old desktop computer?

"What do you think it means?"

I look to my right. A girl about my age is standing beside me. Shaved head, septum piercing, bright red lipstick. Her head is tilted to the side as she eyes the sculpture.

"Something way too advanced for me to understand," I say.

"It might be commenting on how technology has completely eliminated any sense of original, individualized thought," she offers.

"Or it could just be a dude with a box stuck on his head," I add like the intellectual I am.

She laughs. "That seems more likely."

The girl winks at me, grabs a pastry off my tray, and walks off. I consider following her for a moment, then stupid black hair catches my attention and I'm one of Ramona's fish being reeled right in.

Truman stands off in the corner, talking to a group of five people. He's gesturing to the paintings on the wall behind him as he speaks. His face is so animated. It's weird to see him look so . . . happy. Because that's exactly what it seems like right now, that he's happy.

And because I'm an evil little monster, I hate that look on him. It doesn't seem right to be happy after everything we've gone through.

He spots me through the crowd, his eyes meeting mine for a brief second. I don't know why I expect him to wave, call my name and beckon me over. He only looks away, keeps speaking, keeps smiling.

A middle-aged man pops up in front of me and blocks my view. His grubby fingers snatch two pastries before he walks off. I want to drop the tray on the floor and let everyone flock to it like pigeons, but I think even sweet Manny would yell at me for that.

With my line of sight clear again, I keep watching Truman. I determine that the four paintings on the wall behind him are his. From this distance, I can't make them out. All I can see are bright swirls of color. I want to get closer.

Instead I walk in the opposite direction.

Manny told me tonight would end at around ten o'clock.

Manny is a liar. It's nearly midnight and people are only now beginning to trickle out.

My feet are aching. The nonexistent muscles in my arms are

sore from holding up trays all night. I feel mentally drained from being around so many people. Also, my brain kind of hurts from staring at all this artwork all night. The only one I really understood was a black-and-white photograph of a cat drinking from a bowl of water. Not much going on there.

I'm standing next to Manny at the booth. His dad disappeared into the back with Angelo five minutes ago. We're putting all the extra food into cardboard take-out boxes that Manny brought. After he leaves, Manny said he's going to drop them off to people who are homeless. I don't know why his goodness keeps surprising me. He deserves a medal, seriously.

I'm fantasizing about taking a bath and sliding into bed when Manny says, "So who was that guy you were talking to?"

"*Manny.*"

He stops boxing the food. "What?"

I take a break too and rest my head on his arm because I really can't reach his shoulder. "This day has been so much. I really can't deal with your jealousy right now," I mumble.

"What jealousy? I'm not jealous," he says too quickly.

I peer up at him. "You sure?"

"No."

We both start laughing. At least he's honest.

He moves on to the cod fritters, picking them up with tongs and evenly distributing them into the boxes.

"He's my best friend's brother," I say casually, distracting myself with closing the lids. Manny stops moving. Poor guy's probably going into shock over learning something real about my life. "I haven't seen him in months."

"Did you know he was going to be here tonight?" Manny asks.

"No. If I had, I wouldn't have come."

Manny whistles. "Damn. It's that serious, Eden?"

"You have no idea." I finish with the lids and stack all the boxes on top of each other. "Tonight went well. Don't you think?

"Subtle subject change," he says. I flash a smile. "But yeah, everything went great. At least I think it did. We'll see what Angelo says."

I pick up the stack of business cards that Manny's dad left on the table all night. "There are waaaaaaay less of these now than we started with," I comment. I hold up the stack for Manny to see.

He nods, impressed. "That's a good sign."

"Is it bad that part of me wants the restaurant to remain dead so I can slack off all night?" I ask.

"Yes. You're a terrible person."

I stick my tongue out at him. Manny hands me a wad of plastic bags and we start placing the boxes full of food in them.

Everything seems to come so effortlessly to Manny. Being nice, giving back to the people who are less fortunate—he's naturally good at being good. I'm about to ask him for some tips when he says, "So this guy from before—"

"Manuel, *please*." I use his full name to emphasize how over this I am.

"No, Eden." He nods behind me like *look, there.*

I don't want to look. "I don't want to talk about Truman. Honestly, what I want is to pretend this night never happened." Manny's still making weird, dramatic chin nods behind me. His eyes are wide open, like he's trying to communicate something without saying it.

"Oh my God. What is it?" I bite out, and turn around.

Truman's standing behind me because of course he is, of course this is the route the night decides to take.

I glare at Manny. "You couldn't have just said he was right there?" I whisper.

"I was saying it with my eyes," he says.

"Next time try using your mouth." I take a deep breath to calm my heart, which is racing for a completely unrelated reason, brush the crumbs off my shirt, spin around, and walk to Truman. The gallery is mostly empty now. There are about a dozen people still walking around—most are heading for the door, which is exactly what I want to be doing.

"How much of that did you overhear?" I ask.

"Not much," he lies.

I stand there playing with the strings of my apron. I can hear Manny behind us, fanning out the plastic bags, the sound of them crinkling when he shoves the containers inside. Maybe if I lie about helping him distribute the food I can exit this conversation quicker.

Then Truman throws a wrench in that plan. He says, "Do you still want to see my paintings?"

I should say no. I should tell him that I am a very busy woman, and that I'm technically still working, so I shouldn't be talking to him. I should tell him—

"Sure," blurts my traitorous mouth.

But it's worth it to see the smile that takes over his entire face.

It's not worth it, I mentally correct myself.

My brain is laughing at me.

"Cool," Truman says. "My setup's in the corner."

He leads me through the room and I see this image of him in the future—Truman walking through galleries just like this, only they're grander, fancier. Like in the MoMA. Or the Louvre. Okay, maybe not the freaking Louvre. I still see him being this super famous artist, though, auctioning off his work for thousands, having fans all across the globe, while I'm withering away at Pollo Loco, my tip jar running on empty, talking back to customers and walking to the hospital on weekends.

When we're close enough to the wall, I don't have to ask which paintings are Truman's. It's so completely obvious. I instantly recognize the frenzied strokes, the delicate balance of rough and gentle. Again, I'm filled with this insane need to reach out and touch them.

Truman stands in front of the four paintings, holds open his arms like *ta-da*. "This is me," he says with an uncharacteristically shy smile.

I stare at the paintings in awe. I want to rip them off the wall and hang them in my bedroom. That way, I can look at them for hours, pick them apart until I see right into Truman's mind.

"Wow," I breathe. I walk closer until I'm standing inches away from the wall. I can see the texture of the brush strokes, the way the paint curves off the canvas.

The first painting is titled *The Garden*. It's of a girl sitting on a bench in the middle of a meadow, I think. Everything she touches turns brown in a sea of green.

"Can I touch them?" I ask. My voice sounds far away. I feel far away.

"Go for it," Truman says.

I reach out and run my finger along the smudges of the river, the branches of the trees.

Truman titled the second painting *Fallout*. It's two people kissing—no, holding each other? They're made up of shadows, smooth black strokes and blurred lines that have no start or end point. The world around them is on fire. Flames lick at their feet. They don't seem to notice.

The third is so obviously of Katie it makes my breath catch. The entire canvas is rippling water. The sunlight is strokes of yellow reflecting off the blue. Truman painted Katie floating in the middle, staring up at the sky so that, in a way, it looks as if she's staring right at me.

"I remember that day," I say so quietly I'm not sure Truman can hear. "It started to rain as soon as she got in the pool." The sun had vanished in a split second. All of a sudden the sky ripped open and rain poured down on us. Me, Katie, and Truman ran inside so quickly, our feet slipping on the slick stones.

"My mom made you two hot chocolate," Truman says.

"It was, like, eighty degrees outside."

Truman starts laughing and I know he's there too, back in that memory, back in the past.

"Katie was obsessed with the sky," he says.

That catches me off guard, tears my attention away from the painting. I never knew that. Katie went through phases of being obsessed with everything: astrology, makeup, Shonda Rhimes shows. But the sky?

I can't remember her ever saying anything about the sky.

How did I not know that?

"She was?" I ask, feeling like the world's worst friend for a whole new reason now.

"She was," Truman repeats.

I want to run to her bedside right now, make her wake up so she can tell me about all the other parts of her I never knew.

I can't let myself dwell on that too long. There must be a memory somewhere of Katie talking about the sky—I just can't remember it right now.

I move on to the last painting. It's the only one I've seen before: the painting of the crying girl. The very one I saw in Truman's bedroom that night.

I feel Truman still beside me. It feels like the entire room shrinks, like it's closing in on me. I'm back in his bedroom, sitting on his bed, leaning into him, filled with greed and want. I remember how badly I needed to kiss him. It felt as if every thought had fled my mind except for that: the thought of Truman's lips on mine.

I shut the door, board up the memory, turn the lock and hide the key. I need to stop allowing myself to slip so freely into those moments. Especially in public, where I might actually do something stupid.

It wouldn't be the first time.

I look at Truman, search his face for any sign that he's remembering that night, too. He stares right ahead. He won't look at me. It tells me all I need to know.

I take a step back. Then another, and another. "Congrats on tonight," I say with a wave. I need to get out of here. Being around Truman is worse than I thought it would be. The memories aren't just fleeting—they practically live inside him. One look at his face and I'm thrown back in time to moments I have no business thinking about.

I don't hear Truman's response. I run back to Manny, sweating and breathing so quickly I feel like I'm going to faint.

"I need to leave. Can you finish this?"

"Why? What happe—" Then Manny looks up from the table, sees the expression on my face, and his glare immediately goes to Truman. "Eden, are you all right?"

"I'm fine. I just . . . I think I need some air."

"Okay," he says, already grabbing his jacket off the chair. "I'll come with you."

"No! Manny, I'm fine. Stay here and help your dad, okay?" I

grab my bag from where I stashed it beneath the table and untie my apron. "I'll see you tomorrow."

I rush to the door, feeling myself beginning to sweat. One second I'm running over shining white marble; the next second it's the stones in Katie's backyard, glistening and white from the sun shower. I think it's her shrieking I hear, but it's really the groan of the metal door when I push it open. The cool night air slams into my face and I stand there, breathing it in. The memory slips away. The sound of Katie's voice fades. It's better. It all feels better.

I pull myself together, sling my bag over my shoulder, and grip my phone too tightly. Cars are driving by. A streetcar barrels down the middle of the road. There's a pizza place across the street with a neon OPEN sign shining in the window. Next door is a twenty-four-hour laundromat. I take in all the little details: the faded noise of a car alarm going off a few streets over, the flickering of a streetlight, the spicy tang in the air from the Indian restaurant a few units down.

I try to soak in as much of my surroundings as I can. I remind myself that this—these sights, these sounds, these smells—is what's real. The memories aren't, not anymore. And no matter how badly I might want to sometimes, I can't live in them.

Eventually, I start to feel better. My breathing slows. The sudden heat wave vanishes. Still, I feel a bit unsteady on my feet. I spot a bench a little ways away and walk toward it. It's in between a garbage can and a row of bikes you can rent out for hours at a time. I take a seat, focus on the weight of my phone in my hand, the bag on my shoulder.

When was the last time I ate?

I reach into my bag and pull out some energy bar of Ramona's that I took before leaving our apartment this afternoon. I read the purple packaging. *Fudge Brownie.* If this is another batch of products she was sent, my hopes aren't high. I take a bite and it instantly sticks to my teeth. And it tastes like dirt.

I snap a photo of myself grimacing and text it to Mona. *These taste like poop*, I type.

She replies instantly. *And how exactly do you know what that tastes like?*

I reply with the middle finger emoji.

I toss the energy bar into the garbage can and eye the pizza place across the street. I debate if it's worth it to spend money on a slice when I have a fridge stocked with food at home. . . . Yeah, it's worth it. I walk back up to the crosswalk, hit the button, and wait for the light to change.

Then I hear my name being called.

"Eden!"

There it is again.

I turn to my left, back toward the direction of the art gallery, and it's Truman. He's jogging down the street, dodging pedestrians heading right for him. I hear him mumbling "sorry" over and over until he's standing in front of me, panting.

He has one of his paintings tucked under his arm.

"Hey," Truman says before pausing to take a big breath. "You left so quick I couldn't give you this." He holds out the painting.

It's the one of Katie.

"Truman . . ." I don't know what to say.

"Take it," he says. "Seriously, I want you to have it."

I hug it to my chest. I don't try to fight him on this. Because I want this. I need this. I blink back tears. "Thank you."

The traffic light turns red. I need to cross the street.

"Wait." Truman holds a hand out like he's reaching for my arm to hold me in place. He thinks better of it and lets it hover in the air. "We've run into each other twice this week," he says. "That must mean something."

"That this city isn't as big as I thought it was?" I offer.

Truman shakes his head, running a hand through his hair. It springs loose, freed from all that gel. It hangs wildly to his ears, the same way it used to.

"Eden. I, um," he stammers. "Look, this is weird. I know that. We haven't seen each other in months, and I'm pretty sure you've been avoiding me. Which is fine—I get it. But do you think we could maybe talk sometime? About, well, everything?"

"I don't think that's a good idea," I say. I look down at the painting of Katie. Her eyes stare right back at me.

"Please." It's the amount of pain I hear in that word that has me breaking all rules and looking Truman right in the eyes. And I realize then that the smiles and the laughs from before were all for show. He was pretending, giving people the version of himself he thought they wanted to see—the same way I do. Because this Truman, the guy standing in front of me right now, looks as if he's going to break down and fall apart in any second.

"The restaurant I work at is called Pollo Loco," I hear myself saying. "It's on Queen Street. I'm there every night."

Then I hold the painting even tighter and run across the street.

14

TRUMAN

MILO COMES OVER THE next day. We've been staring at the
TV screen for three hours already and I'm feeling disconnected
from my brain, which is fantastic. After last night, I want to avoid
thinking and looking at artwork for the next few days. The exhibit
messed with my head. I hated feeling that vulnerable, that exposed,
like my insides were on my outside. At the same time . . . it made
me feel seen and weirdly validated. After painting in secret for so
long, being able to express that side of me in person was sort of
liberating. And being able to share that side of me with people
who seemed to not only get it, but actually *like* what I create? It
was unreal.

If I push the nerves down far enough, I'm already itching to do
it again. Maybe in a few weeks. Now I need a break from thinking
about art. Yeah, just a break from art. That's the only thought in
my mind today. Not Eden. No, that would be inappropriate.

It hasn't even been twenty-four hours since I last saw Eden and I already have to physically stop myself from barreling out the door and heading right over to that restaurant she works at to see her again.

It only took five minutes after our reunion for me to fully understand exactly how pathetic I am. Which is pretty fucking pathetic. All it took was a minute with her to momentarily seal up every crack in my body and make me feel whole again. One look in her eyes and we were back in that bedroom. I was kissing her, and all the pain and guilt from these past months was scrubbed away with an eraser. She transported me back in time. She reminded me of how I felt before all this—how I felt about *her*.

Eden was Katie's friend, this wide-eyed girl who showed up one day and never seemed to leave. She was always somewhere—sitting at the kitchen table, lying out by the pool, perched on the couch, or walking down the hall. Eden was close, but she felt so far away. She existed behind caution tape because it felt wrong to even think about my sister's friend as being anything other than nosy, annoying, and irritating. But Eden had none of those qualities. The problem was, I wasn't entirely sure what qualities she had. Katie seemed to try to keep the two of us apart any chance she could. When we did speak, it was about nothing. When we were alone, it was for two seconds before Katie came running down the hallway, grabbed Eden's hand, and whisked her away. But there were moments that made me think something was there beneath the surface, like the day we drove downtown for the campus tours. We shared these weighted stares, these intense moments, that felt like we were both just waiting for the other to make a move. To cross that line.

It wasn't until that night in my bedroom that everything changed. It turned all these what-ifs into something tangible that, for once, felt within reach. The way Eden talked about my art—like it was important and worth sharing—was the first time I had felt this flare of hope in my chest, because she got it. She seemed to get me. Even this silent, hidden part of myself that wasn't on display for anyone else to see. She took it all in and it felt like it was enough. Or maybe I was enough. For the first time I thought that maybe pissing Katie off and being with Eden wasn't such a shitty thing to do. Maybe it was worth it, to be able to stretch this tiny moment into something much bigger.

Then in five minutes flat, the world turned upside down. We never had a chance to, I don't know, *date*? Just be together for another minute without reality imploding?

Now she's back. And that little spark of hope has been reignited. And how pathetic was that? I could barely look Milo in the eye all morning. If he saw the mess Eden turned me into, I'd never hear the end of it.

There's also still the slight chance that Eden hates my guts. I'll have to ask her.

That is, if she'll speak to me again.

I flick my thumb over the controller and Milo's *Zombie Feast II* character keels over and drops dead. Blood pours out of his neck.

Milo throws his controller at the TV. "You shot me in the head? We're on the same team!"

Yeah, I'm not in the greatest mood.

"Sorry, bud. I had to sacrifice you to save myself," I say. The zombie horde that had us surrounded becomes distracted with eating his character's body, so I slip free. Milo storms off into the kitchen, mumbling under his breath, then I hear the fridge door open. On-screen, I guide my character around the barren wasteland. The map is an abandoned circus, with creepy striped tents and old carnival games that are now overrun with zombies. I reload my gun and shoot them in the head, one after the other. The kill count on the side of the screen increases, but I'm not enjoying this anymore. The distraction was nice at first, but now my head hurts from not eating all day. I set the controller aside and meet Milo in the kitchen.

"You have no food," he says, drinking straight from the container of orange juice.

"Where the hell did you grow up? A barn?" I rip the container away. It's empty. I throw it right into the trash.

"No. Mississauga," he says.

"We have no food because you've eaten all of it." I open the fridge and Milo's right—it's empty, aside from some bagged milk and old Indian takeout that's so far gone not even Milo is interested. Mom's been spending all her time at the hospital. Dad's been working nonstop. I'm not entirely sure if he's that busy or if

208

that's his way of coping. Either way, no one's around to do basic errands. And I've been so distracted with preparing for the art exhibit that I haven't pulled my weight, either.

I check the freezer. Checkmate—a frozen pizza. I turn the oven on and shove it inside before it's even preheated. Then I kick out the barstool, sit at the island, and let my head sink into my hands. If only I could rip my brain out so it stops replaying Eden's face like a torture reel.

"So," Milo starts, "are we deliberately not talking about how last night went, or . . . ?"

"We are not talking about it," I murmur into my forearm.

"Was it that bad?"

"You're talking about it," I point out, annoyed.

I hear the stool beside me scrape against the floor, then the air that's let out of the leather in a quick *whoosh!* as he sits down. Ginormous fucker.

"I think I'm in love with your ex," Milo says out of absolutely nowhere.

That has me sitting right up. "Excuse me?" I choke out.

Milo looks so beaten down. The love-sick idiot. "I saw her at the bar the other day."

"She may have mentioned it," I say, wincing as I think back to that conversation.

His entire face brightens like a light being switched on. "Yeah? What'd she say?"

"Uh . . ." I don't think it's very useful for me to point out how Santana hid in the bathroom, or spent the entire call asking for tips to avoid him. I settle on, "She's playing hard to get."

Milo lets out a grunt. "I figured. I don't know what it is about her, man, but she's so . . ."

"Irritating?"

"Yeah," he says.

"Mean?"

"Oh, so fucking rude," he agrees.

"She has this weird way of making you feel like she's crushing your entire ego while giving you a compliment?" I ask.

"Exactly," he says. To my amazement, he's grinning. Ear to ear. I listed every trait about Santana that I couldn't stand, all the reasons I replayed in my head every time I broke up with her, and here this guy is, loving all those qualities.

Dammit. Maybe they'd be good for each other after all.

"Santana doesn't like empty promises," I hear myself saying. "She's too independent for that. What she wants is actions. Show her that you want to be with her. And tell her she looks nice."

"I always tell her she looks nice," Milo says, confused.

"And?"

"And she goes, 'I know,' and stomps away."

"That's how she is," I assure him. "You need to crack through the icy exterior and then you're golden, dude."

Milo runs a hand over his shaved head. His forearm is covered in a winding tattoo I always thought was a snake. I realize now that it's a frayed piece of rope. "Can I be honest with you?" he asks. "I know I never met your sister, but after hearing what happened to her . . . It makes you think. At least it made me realize that everything could change in an instant."

I nod along. I've already tried the whole look-on-the-bright-side bit and it's fine. What works best for me is living half on the bright side and half in absolute darkness. Like they say, you can't look directly at the sun for too long.

"You're spot on," I say.

"Maybe I'll take a shot with Santana. What's the worst that can happen?"

"She stomps all over your heart and tears you in two?" I offer because I'm an unhelpful asshole.

"At least she'd finally be giving me some type of attention," he says with a laugh.

The oven beeps. It's finally preheated.

Milo grunts. "I'm not really in the mood for pizza," he says.

Truth be told, I feel the same way. And after listening to Milo's declaration of love for my ex, it gives me an idea. It's probably not a good one. Scratch that—it's definitely not a good one. *What's the worst that can happen?* I'm about to find out.

"You know what? Me either." I grab my hoodie from where it's hanging over the chair and pull it over my head, even though the sun is shining so brightly outside that our entire apartment is flooded with light. "I'll be back," I say. My car keys are still on the counter from where I threw them last night. I shove them into my pocket, grab my phone, and head for the door.

"Where are you going?" Milo calls after me.

"I'm kind of in the mood for Portuguese food."

I walk into Pollo Loco and the place is dead. I wasn't expecting that. The waiter at the counter looks up from his phone and instinctively reaches for a plastic menu.

"Table for one?" he asks.

I walk over. His name tag reads *Ahmed*. I'm trying to place where I know him from, then realize he was there last night at the art exhibit. "No, thanks. I'm looking for Eden?"

He just blinks. His eyes are glazed over and bright red. "What?" he says.

"Dude—are you high?"

"Shhhh!" He glances over his shoulder then shoots me a glare. "Why would you say that so loud? I'm not high. I'm . . . tired. Haven't slept in a while."

Looks like he hasn't slept in a year. Not that I'm one to judge.

"Look, I don't care. I'm looking for Eden. Is she working now?"

A light bulb seems to go off in his mind. "Oh. Right. Yeah, her shift doesn't start for another . . ." He looks down at his watch. "Two hours."

I want my dumb ass to sink into the floor. What did she say

yesterday? *I'm there every night.* Dammit. I was so caught off guard by her actually agreeing to speak to me that I barely listened to what she said.

This is fine. Two hours is only one hundred and twenty minutes. That's like sitting through three episodes of a forty minute show. No time at alllllll. Easy peasy.

I thank Ahmed and head over to a booth, prepared to wait for the long haul.

"Still don't want that menu?" he calls.

"Sure," I say. I left the apartment in such a rush I didn't have any of the pizza, and all I ate this morning was a bagel Milo brought over. Shit. I probably shouldn't have left him alone in my house. Why does my brain malfunction whenever Eden is mentioned? I need to rewire it.

I read through the menu front to back because I want to get a feel for this place that Eden apparently spends all her time at. The first thing I notice is that the menu is sticky, like someone spilled soda all over it and it was never cleaned. And the menu is in both Portuguese and English, which my idiot self appreciates greatly. I'm reading through the dessert section, distracted by something called pastel de nata. There's a photo of them in the middle of the page, and I recognize the pastries Eden was carrying around last night.

Last night, when she happened to show up out of nowhere during one of the biggest moments of my career. And when did I start viewing painting as my career? I'm not sure, but it kind of feels right. It's really the only thing that seems to bring me any sort of happiness, no matter how fleeting. So maybe I should stick with it, take it more seriously.

The art exhibit didn't have an auction portion. Angelo had said it was strictly to show off local talent and help "get our names out there." When the night ended, he pulled me aside and said he thought it went really well. A few people had asked him about me—my name, if I had a website, how much my paintings sell for. It seemed bizarre that they didn't simply ask me directly, but whatever. I wish I would've thought to bring business cards to hand out.

Actually, I should probably make a website, too. And maybe consider pulling back on the anonymity of my Instagram account. Not for a while, though. Last night was a lot. If my art does happen to take off, I want some more peace before I decide to attach my face to it.

Like a naïve fool, I'm already picturing myself walking down streets and being recognized. People asking for my photo, for my *autograph*.

Ahmed appears at my table at exactly the right time. My ego needs immediate deflating.

He's staring at me, holding a pad of paper. "Ready to order?" he asks. The guy is so clearly high it's hilarious.

"Yeah . . ." I get the lunch special: roasted chicken, potatoes, rice, and one of those pastries on the side because I think Eden would recommend that. "And a water. Please," I add because I always hear my mom's voice in my head: *Say please and thank you.*

He walks off and disappears into the back. I hear him call out my order. I look around the place. I try to see it from my mom's design eye. It's a bit tacky, with banged-up linoleum tiles and faded leather booths. The counter that runs along the far wall has stools lined up along it. It kind of feels like this place used to be a diner. The owner must have tried to reconstruct it into a restaurant and gave up halfway through. The food's good, though. At least the few pieces I tried last night were. I barely had an appetite; the nerves had my stomach tied up in knots.

That and how I kept waiting for Eden to realize my paintings were of her.

I don't think she noticed. I would have seen that moment of recognition flash on her face, like it did when she saw the painting of the crying girl. She hadn't realized it was her sitting on the bench in *The Garden*, or that it was us holding on to each other in *Fallout*. It must be for the best. Eden spent the past five months avoiding me. Somehow, I don't think she'd be very pleased to find out how I spent these past months: painting her.

I look around and try to spot the curly-haired guy she was talking to last night at the exhibit. I feel relieved when I don't see him. Not because I'm jealous or anything. That would be entirely ridiculous. Completely uncalled for.

Ahmed walks over with a steaming pile of food. He sets it down in front of me, then stalks off. The portion is *huge*. Like, I doubt Milo could finish this. The rice is piled into a mini mountain, same with the potatoes. I dig into the pastry first—a little ode to Katie, who was a big fan of eating dessert before dinner. A few bites in and I'm shocked there isn't a line out the door. This is one of the best things I've ever eaten.

While I eat, I check my email, texts, Instagram messages. I've gotten a few new followers since last night, but that must be a coincidence since my account is anonymous. Angelo told me he'd "be in touch regarding any other opportunities." Problem is I have no idea what that means. Is he going to email me? Ambush me at another coffee shop with Santana? I can probably ask Santana to pester him for details the next time they work together, but I don't want to come off as being desperate, even though that's exactly what I am.

I check the time. There's still an hour before Eden's shift starts. I try to focus on something else, like the sky project for Katie that's finally coming together. I stood in her room last night and realized everything I need is right there: the walls and the ceiling. After I get my hands on some blue and white paint, I'm all set. Well, that and the furniture I'm missing to complete her bedroom. I start hunting on Facebook Marketplace for a bed, a dresser, and a nightstand that I plan on painting clouds all over. If it turns out the way I see it in my mind, her bedroom will feel like standing in the sky when I'm done with it.

I scroll through listings for a while but nothing is right. It needs to be wood so I can sand it down, and a color light enough that

216

the pale blues and whites can peek through. Maybe oak or birch. I type that into the search bar too and hit refresh. A new listing pops up: *Four-piece oak bedroom set for sale. Gently used!* I click through the photos the seller posted. Parts of the wood around the edges are a bit banged up, but nothing a coat of primer can't fix. I message the seller, asking if the set is still available. He responds in seconds. *Yes. Can you come grab it today?* He lives in Parkdale, which is only a few minutes away . . . I type back *Yes.*

If I really crack down, I can have Katie's new bedroom finished in a week or two. Not that I'm following any sort of timeline. Katie could decide to open her eyes tomorrow or next year. Whenever it happens—because it will happen—it'll be ready.

The door to the restaurant chimes. I look up and it's Eden, forty minutes early. Her hair is settling around her face, and she has the smallest backpack I've ever seen slung over one shoulder. She stomps inside, her headphones shoved in her ears, and is nearly at the back door when she skids to a halt.

She turns around, slowly. Her eyes land right on me. Then they widen considerably, the same way they did last night.

I wave. She doesn't move.

"Hey," I say. She takes out her headphones.

I'm slowly realizing this wasn't a good idea. She's looking at me like I'm the last person in the world she wants to see today, which is a bit of a blow to the chest. Then Eden's walking over so slowly, like she's regretting every single step.

Yeah, I shouldn't have come.

"What are you doing here?" she asks, sounding like a drill sergeant barking out orders.

"You told me to come by."

"I didn't think you'd show up *the next day*, Truman."

I'm not going to admit that I couldn't stop thinking about her. I say, "I had a craving for Portuguese food."

She snorts, loops the loose strap of her backpack over her bare shoulder. "Convenient." Then her eyes narrow, zeroing in on the half-eaten plate of food in front of me. "How long have you been here?" she asks.

I take a sip of water, stalling. "An hour." Eden presses two fingers to her temple, squeezes her eyes shut. "Headache?"

"Yeah. Came out of nowhere," she says in a way that implies she knows *exactly* where it came from.

I still can't wrap my head around how weird it is to see her standing alone, without Katie at her hip telling her what to say, what to do. That's kind of how their friendship seemed to go. Katie pulled the strings, Eden followed along for the ride. Now, seeing her alone, when she says what she wants and does what she wants, it's kind of like I'm talking to Eden for the first time—the real her, at least.

"I talked to Ahmed. Is he always—"

"High?" she asks. "Yeah."

"He said your shift starts at five," I say.

Eden looks like she's heavily considering finding him and knocking him out. "So Ahmed chose today to become talkative.

That's fantastic. Did he divulge any other personal details of my life to you?"

"Uh, no?"

This is wrong. She doesn't seem happy to see me at all. I don't think I was even expecting her to be happy. I just wasn't expecting *this*.

"Look, I'll go." I dig out my wallet and start counting out a few bills. Clearly Eden isn't ready to stop avoiding me. Which is fine. It sucks, but it's fine. I don't blame her. What does she possibly see when she looks at me? *Oh, here's the guy who's responsible for Katie leaving me.* Yeah, can't exactly blame her for putting me dead last on her priorities list.

Some optimistic part of me hoped last night had changed something. I must've read too much into nothing.

I slap the bills on the table. I'm about to stand up when she says, "Truman, wait." Then she shrugs off her backpack and sits down. I'm waiting for her to say something when I realize she's staring at my plate of barely eaten food.

"Are you . . . hungry?" I ask carefully.

"A little. I came early so Manny could make me something before my shift starts. Manny's the chef, by the way. You may have seen him last night." She says all of this to the plate of food.

Finally I just slide it across the table to her. "You can have it," I say.

"What? No. You barely touched it."

"I ate some of it. And I had one of those pastries."

Her entire face lights up. "Aren't they incredible? Hold on." Eden runs off, bends down behind the counter. She comes back with a clean fork in hand, slides back into the booth, and digs into the plate of food.

"Do you not eat at home?" I say, then I want to kick myself. It's none of my business what she does at home. Which leads me to another thought—where is home for Eden? I have no idea what the last five months of her life have looked like.

The lack of knowledge I have about her life is alarming.

"All we have is cardboard cereal," she says, not offering up an explanation. I want to ask who "we" is. Actually, there are about three trillion questions I want to ask her.

My phone rings. It's Santana. I send it to voice mail.

"You can get that," Eden says, stabbing her fork into a potato with alarming aggression.

"It's not important," I say. Santana's probably calling to complain about whatever Milo's done now. He may have looked her directly in the eye—that would be enough for her to bite his head off.

My phone rings again. Santana.

Eden's eyes lift up to mine. "Sounds important," she comments.

I shut the thing off and shove it under my leg. "How long have you been working here?" I ask.

"Is this why you waited two hours for me? To discuss my budding career as a waitress?" she says.

I rack my brain and try to remember Eden ever being sarcastic. I can't remember a time when she wasn't being . . . quiet.

"Well, that and to feed you," I say, "because clearly no one else is."

She frowns. "Manny feeds me. And like I said—cardboard cereal."

"Sounds appetizing."

"It's not. Tastes like cardboard."

I laugh. I'm kind of unable to take my eyes off her. "Never would've guessed."

Eden pushes the empty plate toward me. Then she plants her elbows on the table, crosses her arms, and leans forward. She's staring at me like she's trying to read my mind. Meanwhile I couldn't get her to look me in the eye last night. What changed?

"I have a lot of questions for you, Truman," she finally says.

"I have a lot of questions for you too, Eden."

"Like what?" she pushes.

I want to ask who her roommate is, where she's living, why she's working here, and if she's still going to university in the fall. I want to ask if she thought about me and why she spent months ignoring me—well, I know the answer to that one. What I really want to know is if she's done pretending I don't exist. Because I haven't been able to stop knowing she does since the night I kissed her.

There's a list of questions I need answers to, and none of them seem appropriate to ask right now.

I shake my head, drag my finger through the condensation on my water glass. "Cardboard cereal?" I ask. It seems like the safest starting point.

"My roommate, Ramona, is a food blogger. She gets sent a bunch of products from different brands for Instagram collabs. The most recent were these boxes of protein cereal that taste like cardboard. Wait, that might actually be an insult to cardboard."

Roommate. Ramona. Food blogger. I try to rearrange all these clues to her life like puzzle pieces.

"You were the last person I expected to run into last night," Eden says out of nowhere.

"We can agree on that," I say.

Eden picks up the napkin on the table. She starts folding the edges, then ripping it into tiny shreds that fall down like snowflakes. "I didn't mean for it to seem like I don't want you coming here," she says, staring down at the table. "It's just . . . Well, I don't know how to act around you." Eden pauses, keeps ripping the napkin until there's nothing left but a pile of destruction.

I grab a new napkin and offer it to her. Eden takes it, keeps shredding.

"What do you mean?" I ask. I'm scared of saying the wrong thing. Like one misstep will send her running and it'll be another five months before she turns up in my life again.

"It was always Katie and me. You were there too, sure, but we never really spoke about anything real." Then she adds, "It feels weird to talk about her out loud."

"You don't talk about her?"

"No," Eden says. "At least I try not to."

"Why?"

She shrugs. "Hurts too much."

"Probably hurt a bit less if you did," I offer.

Eden pins me with that gaze again, like I'm a math question she can't solve.

"Maybe." The way she says it makes it sounds like there's more—an idea growing, something else she wants to say but holds in. Then she checks the time on her phone and gets up in a hurry. "Shit, I have to get back there. Are you planning on sitting here all night?"

The idea doesn't sound terrible. "Would you let me if I tried?"

"No," she says easily.

"Then I won't." I start packing up too, leaving a few bills on the table to cover the meal. I have to go meet up with the dude selling the bedroom set before he snubs me and finds a new buyer.

Eden loops her bag back over her shoulders. "Well," she says. "Thanks for the food."

She hurries off before I can get another word in.

15
EDEN

RAMONA STOMPS INTO MY room that morning and drags me out of bed. Not literally, but she might as well have. She's babbling about this new French patisserie that opened near Dundas Square like a kettle about to boil over. I haven't gotten a word in since my door creaked open.

"I'm going to die if we don't leave right now, Eden," she says, looking übersophisticated standing at the foot of my bed in a floral button-up dress, her hair slicked back in a tight knot.

"I promise to write you a great eulogy," I grumble, pulling the comforter straight over my head.

"Don't go back to bed—they sell out before noon!"

I peek out from beneath the covers. The swath of sunlight slinking in from the hallway has me squinting. "Why do I need to come with you? I thought our entire dynamic was that *you* leave this place, experience the world, and bring me back some mementos in the form of a to-go box."

Ramona glares at me so intensely it reminds me of the way my mom used to sit at the foot of my bed, listing off my punishments because I stayed out after curfew with Katie, or skipped class twice in one week because of . . . well, Katie.

Some faint form of realization slams into my chest, but I can't exactly pinpoint what it means. Or if it means anything at all.

I swallow it down, leaving it to sort through later when I'm not half-asleep.

"I need to post photos on Instagram," Ramona says.

"And this requires my presence because?"

"I need you there to take cute candids of me eating a croissant, or sipping a café au lait."

"The front camera exists for a reason, Mona," I say, a yawn puncturing my words.

She plants her hands on her hips and ages ten years. "Will you please come with me? I don't want to go alone."

"What happened to Lolo?" Lolo's her friend-slash-photographer. She's tagged at the bottom of every single one of Mona's Instagram posts next to a camera emoji.

"She's somewhere being happy with her girlfriend. Will you come?"

"I'd rather—"

"Great!" Then Ramona is somehow digging through my closet, throwing a hoard of black clothing onto my bed. "Your closet looks like a black hole."

"That's the point." I pick at the denim shorts and T-shirt she's chosen. "These are different shades of black," I point out.

She stops ransacking my closet to pierce me with another withering look. "And?"

"Nothing. I love wearing different shades of black. Doesn't bother me at all."

Then for some godforsaken reason, I'm getting changed while Mona waits in the hallway, tapping her foot like an impatient teacher, yelling out different items from this patisserie's menu. The only word that resonates in my brain is *croissant* because I'm a terrible, uncultured person.

The painting of Katie that Truman gave me is right where I left it: leaning against the leg of my desk. I tell myself to scrounge up a hammer and nail to hang it somewhere, but I'm not sure I want that. Something about staring into Katie's face is eerie, so I leave it untouched for now.

I meet Mona in the hall, and she gives me a look that I wouldn't quite define as *approving*, but not completely *disapproving*, either. I seem to pass the test, though, because then we're shuffling out of the building, down the street, and onto the subway. We emerge onto Dundas Street West and then I see it: a line of people outside a cute little café called Bonne Journée.

I turn to Ramona. She plucks her expensive sunglasses out of her hair and sets them on her nose. "You never said anything about waiting in line," I say.

She loops her arm through mine and tugs us down the street. "I thought it was implied."

"Definitely was not." There are at least twelve people waiting outside the café. We stand at the back of the line behind two girls wearing pearled berets. "This better be a life-altering experience."

"You stepping outside in the daylight should be life altering enough," she says. "Seriously, I'm buying you a vitamin D supplement. I don't know how you're still alive."

Easy. It's simple mental compartmentalization and suppressing an extremely wide variety of emotions. "I'm doing just fine, thank you very much," I lie. If I said the truth, Mona would probably call my parents and they'd stage an intervention.

The doors to the café open, and a strong whiff of butter and bitter coffee clouds into the street. A group of girls exit before a few more people head inside. The line dwindles down and we move up a few spots.

"So, how was that art exhibit thing?" Mona asks in a way that's too poised to be casual.

"It was fine," I say like the big fat liar I am. I stare straight ahead of me. I can still feel Mona's gaze, searching my face like a radar for any signs of . . . what? Sadness? Pain? Silly for her to think those only show externally.

"Did everyone like the food?" she nudges.

"People seemed to," I say. Although Pollo Loco has still been a ghost town at night, so I'm not entirely sure how successful Manny's plan to boost business was.

"How was the artwork?" she asks. We move up in line again. "Any noteworthy local artists?"

"Not a single one," I say. It becomes clear to me that she's up to something—she *knows* something. I'm not sure what exactly, but I have a few ideas that all start and end with one head of infuriatingly dark hair.

Ramona actually places her sunglasses farther down her nose to stare at me directly. "That's interesting," she says. Then the doors to Bonne Journée open once more. A smiling employee gestures for the girls in front of us to step inside, then us. I trail behind Ramona because suddenly I'm feeling very out of place. The café is even cuter on the inside, with gold wall sconces, white marble counters, and flowery chandeliers. The ceilings are high arches, and a raised seating area is nestled toward the back behind a small set of stairs. I can smell the bitterness of dark chocolate and the warmth of fresh bread. It makes my stomach rumble.

Ramona has her phone out already, snapping photos of everything—the ceiling, stacks of antique plates, puffs of steam bubbling through the air as coffee roasts. I'm locked onto the glass display of sweets. Glazed croissants, colorful macarons, chocolate éclairs, tiny porcelain dishes of crème brûlée, apple palmiers. I'm suddenly very grateful Ramona decided to drag my ass out of bed.

While the two girls in the pearl berets order, Ramona studies the menu. "What should we get?" she asks.

"Is one of everything unacceptable?" I ask with complete sincerity.

"No, but my bank account might say otherwise. Want to go save us a table while I order?"

I head to the back of the café, up the three tiny steps to the seating area. Every table is full except for one near the back window. I head over, dust a few crumbs off the metal because waitress mode is never deactivated, and take a seat. Music filters in through the speakers, this soft lull that can only be Bon Iver. Not exactly on brand for a French café, but I enjoy it. Sunlight streams in through the window in a warm haze; it slants across the tabletop, warms the side of my face. I stare up at the sky.

Katie was obsessed with the sky.

That's what Truman said. It's what I keep going back to over and over again. How did I not know that about her? It's such a small thing. Still, I can't stop thinking that if I never knew that about my best friend, then what other secrets was she keeping?

Then there's Truman, who showed up at Pollo Loco last night like a fever dream. He sat right down and managed to turn that familiar, safe space into something so jarring. So overwhelmingly full of him. His presence seemed to stretch across the entire restaurant. There was no escaping the onslaught of memories and feelings. I could have walked away from him—I *should* have walked away from him. I definitely should not have sat down with him, and I can't exactly figure out why I did.

Maybe it's because when everything seems so unfamiliar, he's this reminder of the past, like a sinking anchor or a steady oak. And I shouldn't latch on to him, but even now I can feel my fingers beginning to curl around memories I have no business being wrapped in.

None of that matters anymore. I have simply rewired my brain to not think about Truman Falls. Any thought of him slips into my mind for a single second before dissolving completely like a biscuit dunked in hot tea.

Ramona trots over to the table with a smile lighting up her face, holding a metal tray that's overflowing with tiny plates. She sets it on the table with a *ta-da*. "I've secured the goods," she says, sitting down across from me.

The tray is filled with so much dough covered in chocolate that I feel like the Grinch—my tiny heart is growing right in my chest.

Ramona takes two cups and saucers off the tray, sets one in front of her, and slides the other over. "Black coffee for you," she says, "and dark hot chocolate for me."

"What happened to your café au lait?"

"They don't have nondairy options," she says with a pout.

"Lame."

We dig into the food. Mona uses the daintiest knife I've ever seen to cut everything in half. The croissant is stuffed with Brie and fig jam, the crème brûlée splits with a satisfying crack, and we share a pastry filled with sweet cream and topped with fresh fruit. Then Mona seems to remember the entire reason we came here, because she hands me her phone and begins fixing her hair.

"Is the lighting okay?" she asks, alternating between tilting her face toward and away from the window. I pull up the camera app, center her face in frame.

"It's fine," I say. "Stay right— Yeah, like that."

"Take it so that it looks like I'm drinking," Mona orders. She pretends to sip from the cup, smiling with her eyes and staring directly into the camera. I try a few angles to get other customers out of the shot, then snap some photos.

"Cute," I say, handing her phone back. She flicks through them, nodding approvingly. The thought of having a career that's solely based off taking photos of yourself is exhausting. I don't know how she does it.

Mona sets her phone aside. "Thanks for that," she says.

"Aren't you going to post them?"

"I need to upload them to my laptop first, do some light editing. I'll probably post them tomorrow and do, like, a little review of what we ordered." She pauses, sips her hot chocolate, then gives me that look again. "Back to the art exhibit. . . . Nothing stood out to you?"

I sigh. "Mona, just spit it out."

She blinks, scoffs. "What? I'm not implying anything."

"You've been poking around the subject all morning. Seriously, ask me whatever you want to know." No guarantee I'll answer, but she can try.

Mona sets her drink aside and leans froward. Her entire face softens, which means she's going to bring up a topic I most definitely do not want to speak about. "Look," she begins, "Lolo was at the exhibit that night."

"She was?" I ask. I think back to the crowd of unfamiliar faces that were just that: unfamiliar. I don't remember seeing Lolo. Then again, I was supremely distracted with someone else.

Oh shit. Truman. I know exactly where this conversation is going.

"She only popped in for a minute or two. But—"

"But what?" I interject with anger that surprises me. "What exactly did Lolo see that she desperately had to report back to you?"

Ramona hesitates. "She said she saw you talking to Truman Falls. I'm not trying to be nosy, Eden. I'm making sure you're doing okay."

Sometimes I forget that Ramona and a few of her friends went to high school with me. After moving into the city, it's difficult to keep track of what parts of my old life followed me here.

Sometimes, I also forget that there are other people who knew Katie. Other people who miss her, too. That I wasn't her only friend and that I'm not the only person grieving her.

"Eden?" Mona says.

Normally this is where I'd stuff all the feelings I can't sort through inside me like a suitcase, then zip myself up nice and tight, not divulging a single word. For some reason, I don't want to. Seeing Truman twice was explosive. That's what it feels like: as if my head and chest might physically combust if I hold all this messiness inside me for a single second longer. I'm not going to tell Ramona every excruciating detail from the past few months, but a starting point would be nice. I'll leave a trail of bread crumbs for now.

"Truman was at the art exhibit," I say. I look out at the sky. It's easier than seeing whatever look of surprise will shoot across Mona's face when her stoic roommate finally begins to open up. "Nothing happened. He had some art on display. We talked for a few minutes."

"What did you talk about?" Ramona asks. Her voice is like a feather landing on ice, soft enough that it doesn't crack right open.

"Mostly his artwork," I say.

"Did you talk about Katie?"

Her name is enough to send a fit of pain searing through me. Katie's smile flashes through my memories, her face a streaking light across the sky. It's a knife to the chest. "A little."

"Okay," Mona says. She reaches across the table and pats my hand. "How's Truman doing?"

"He seemed okay," I say, which doesn't offer much reassurance. There's a difference between *seeming* okay and actually *being* okay. I'm sure I seem okay to a lot of people, but only I know that I'm nowhere near that. And I have a feeling it's the same with Truman.

"What exactly happened between the two of you?" I turn away from the sky, back to Mona. She's running her finger along the rim of her cup.

233

"Between Truman and me?" I ask.

Mona nods.

This is where I draw the line.

"It's not something I like to think about," I say.

Ramona smiles reassuringly. I can sense she's pulling back, laying off. She knows I've reached my breaking point. Pushing any further will only crack the surface of the ice.

"I understand," she says. I'm grateful when she changes the subject. "Do you want to get out of here? I was going to hit up Whole Foods for some groceries. You can come with?"

Then the sunlight completely disappears. A cloud has pushed through, blocking the rays entirely. How rude. But it feels like a sign. So I tell Mona that no, I don't want to go spend seven dollars on a carton of eggs. There's actually somewhere else I need to be.

There are fresh flowers on the table in front of the window in Katie's room, bright red and pink roses. The blinds are pulled open, right up to the ceiling. Was that Truman's doing, giving her that view of the sky?

I tiptoe to the edge of her bed and stand there, staring. Five months later and the words still can't come out. They're stuck in my throat, lodged behind a million forms of *sorry*.

There is so much I want to tell her about: Truman's artwork, my job at Pollo Loco, Ramona's *Animal Crossing* addiction, U of T in the fall and how she's finally made it here—right into the heart of the city she loved so much. I want us to pick right back up from where we left off. If I close my eyes, I'm back in her bedroom—only the window is closed. Katie hasn't snuck out. In my mind she's curled up in bed with her laptop perched on a pillow. She's shopping for furniture. She's preparing for our future. She's there. And she's alive, she's alive, she's alive.

When I'm around Katie, my brain latches on to the tiniest inkling of hope. Because, standing here in front of her, it seems absolutely impossible that her light has been dimmed forever. There's no way. Someone as bright and all-encompassing as Katie can't just lie here. There must be more to her story. More to her life. There are so many more people she has to meet; so many more people she has to love. There are all these hidden parts of herself she has to tell me about. I need to ask why she's obsessed with the sky and why she never thought to tell me. I need to know every thought that has ever entered her mind. And I'm sinking, completely sinking with the realization that I might never have another minute with her.

This is us now. This is where laughter and driving mindlessly through town has led us. To a bed in a hospital. To abandoned hope and so many what-ifs that they suffocate me entirely.

I take Katie's hand and look at her nails. They're still sky blue from when I painted them last. On the table in Katie's room, there's an old makeup case her mom brought over. It's filled with bottles of bright nail polish. I grab it and get to work. I soak cotton pads with polish remover and tell Katie about the art exhibit. I take all the polish off her fingernails and detail the food I ate today with Ramona. I pick a new polish color—still blue, but this time a deep indigo—and swipe it over her nails. I don't do the greatest job because this was one of Katie's talents, but it's good enough.

Physically I'm here—standing at Katie's bedside, painting her nails, listening to the sound of her heartbeat on the monitor. Mentally I'm somewhere else entirely. A different year. A different life.

It was early August, the humidity so thick it pressed down on us like a cloud. Katie passed her driver's test and her parents bought her a shiny black BMW with tan leather seats that our sweaty legs stuck to. She'd blast the air conditioning and we'd spend days driving around town with nowhere in mind. On Tuesday we drove to the twenty-four-hour diner and ate nothing but plates of fries. On Wednesday we sat in the high school parking lot and rolled all the windows down when it began to rain. Our town was cramped but we took up so much space.

On Thursday Katie decided we had to drive to the beach. I woke up early and borrowed my mom's tote bag. I filled it with sunscreen, lotion, lip balm, granola bars, magazines, and a polka-dot towel. Katie picked me up at noon and we flew down the empty streets. She played the radio so loud it drowned out both of our voices. I didn't ask how she knew the directions without looking at a map—I trusted her to head the right way. Every few minutes we looked at each other and smiled, these big, toothy grins. *Look at us. We're so grown-up.*

We drove for two hours until the streets opened up and water took over. I followed Katie through the sand. I kicked off my sandals when she did. I walked barefoot through the sand when she did. She chose a spot right along the shore. I thought we were too close to the water, that one big wave would cover us entirely, but then Katie was flapping her towel out and I did the same without saying a word.

The water from the Georgian Bay was freezing cold. The ground was rocky and the sand piping hot. We ran into the waves, screaming and giggling. Then we collapsed on our towels and shared a pair of headphones, listening to whatever song Katie had queued up. I told her that I didn't really like it. "You need to expand your taste," she said. She was probably right, so we kept listening.

Her hair was golden in the sunlight, fanning out across the sand. I could see the rise and fall of her chest, hear her humming along to the music. I glanced up at the sky and the world felt both bigger than I could even begin to wrap my head around, and like it somehow began and ended with us.

The heart monitor continues to beep, a steady rhythm. A searing reminder. And this is the worst part, the very worst part. She's still here. She's *right* here. And yet somehow she is oceans away.

I finish up with Katie's fingers, swipe the blue polish across her thumbnail. Now her hands look like they've been dipped in the night sky. I know I have to leave. I rarely make it longer than fifteen minutes.

"See you later," I say before heading out the door.

My eyes begin to burn when I step outside. I'm so sick of crying that I just blink the tears away, shove them right back inside like prisoners in a cell. The city streets are still relatively quiet at this time. Rush hour won't begin for another few hours, then people will be racing to the subway. Now there's only one person, sitting on a metal bench outside the hospital.

Because I seem to attract all sorts of disasters, that person is Truman.

He's sitting down, staring straight ahead of him. His arms are draped across the bench in a way that takes up so much space. This time, I walk toward him with purpose. There's something I want to say—something I need to say. The worst part is, I'm slowly realizing he's the only person who can give me what I want.

I suck in a breath, hold my head up, walk over. I order my eyes to not shed a single tear or I will *kill them.* "Truman," I say with defiant force.

He doesn't even seem surprised, just turns his face toward me, blinks those narrow blue eyes. "Eden. Hey." Then he looks behind him, toward the hospital entrance. "Are you leaving?"

"I am." I toy with the strap of my bag to buy time. Since I figure the best way to get this over with is to simply spit it out, I do just that. "Look, you mentioned something about Katie being obsessed with the sky and I can't stop thinking about it."

He seems puzzled. "Why?"

"Because I never knew that," I say. "Because she was my best friend and I never knew that."

My eyes start to sting again. *Don't you dare.*

Truman runs a hand through his hair but I wouldn't know that because I'm not looking. I'm not looking, I'm not looking, I'm not—

"It's one small detail about her," Truman says. "You know everything else. You know all the important stuff."

"But what if I don't?" I hate how my voice crumbles.

Truman scoots over on the bench, freeing up space. "Do you want to sit?" he asks. I shake my head. No, I don't want to sit. The way he is staring at me is distracting enough. It's not the usual pity people hit me with. Truman's eyes are full of understanding, like he's weighed down by the same shit that's been living on my shoulders.

"I feel far away from her," I say. The words shoot out of a secret place inside me, somewhere I haven't let free in a long time. "Like the memories are drifting away and then I'll have nothing left."

Truman smiles. "You don't have to explain it," he says. "I know exactly how you feel."

That's what I was hoping for.

Time to get to the point. "I think we both know I've been avoiding you for some time now," I say.

"Hadn't noticed," he says in a way that is very clear he definitely has noticed. And then my brain is heading down a dangerous track, because how much exactly has Truman noticed about me?

"Anyways, I have an idea."

"An idea?" he repeats, eyebrows flying high.

"Maybe we can start spending small amounts of time together." I force the words out. Spending time with Truman Falls is quite literally one of the most worrisome things I can think of. But if I'm thinking about this honestly, he is also the only other person in this world who knows all the parts of Katie I failed to pick up on. I could ask their mom, but the only time we speak is at Katie's bedside, and I'm not exactly lining up to spend ample amounts of time there with my heart on fire.

"To do what exactly?" Truman asks. I seem to have gotten his attention. He's staring right at me. Those blue eyes hold me in place.

"I want you to tell me about Katie," I say.

"You're her best friend. You know everything there is to know."

"No," I correct him. "I didn't know she loved the sky." I know it sounds a bit ridiculous. The look Truman gives me confirms that.

"That's one random fact, Eden."

"I want to know all the random facts," I say. I don't care how small or insignificant. If it's about Katie, it matters to me because *she* matters to me.

"You think this will help you somehow?" he asks.

"I don't need help. I need . . . information."

"On my sister," he clarifies, stretching his legs out in front of him. People are walking by on the street but I'm not paying much attention. When Truman's around, I can't seem to focus on anything other than him, really.

God, that's a terrible realization.

"Exactly," I say, reeling in my silly brain.

"And what's the catch?"

That makes me pause. "What does that mean?"

"You said yourself that you've been avoiding me," Truman says. "This sounds like the opposite of avoidance."

I realize now that I never considered how Truman would feel about all of this. "Do *you* want to avoid *me*?"

"No." He says it so quickly—too quickly. I try not to read too much into that. "At the restaurant, you said it hurts to talk about Katie." I nod because, yeah, I did say that and I'm not entirely sure why or how that slipped out. "So maybe this will be good for the both of us."

"How so?"

"You have someone to talk about her with," he says.

I ask the burning question. "And what do you get out of this?"

I don't miss the way Truman changes. His eyes fall to the ground, his arm that's outstretched across the back of the bench slides down against his leg. He's shrinking into himself. "I have someone to talk about her with, too," he says quietly.

"You have your parents," I say. "You have your friends." And suddenly I've made this into a grief competition. It only reminds me that I don't have many people left who share my memories of Katie. Except for Truman. He's in nearly all of them.

"It's not the same," he says simply. "Moving on, I think talking about her can be good for the both of us. It'll be nice to remember the other version of her before all this."

241

Right. All this, like the hospital currently serving as our back-drop.

"Exactly what I'm hoping for. Do we have a deal?"

Truman stands up. He's walking toward me and I'm back in his bedroom, back craving the feel of him. He holds his hand out like he wants us to shake on it. Only I don't want to. I don't want to touch him. I don't want to know what touching him will feel like now. Everything has changed, and it only makes sense that has changed, too.

I stare at his hand long enough that he lets it fall back to his side.

"Guess so," he says with the tiniest bit of offense.

"Well," I say. I start walking backward, one step after the other. I'm already regretting this. A big gate I had firmly shut is now open wide and Truman has stepped right on through.

"Give me your phone."

I stop walking. "What? Why?"

"You need my number," he says, as if he somehow knows I deleted it from my phone in a sad attempt to delete *him* from my life. "How else are you going to plan these meetups?"

"No one said anything about a meetup," I stammer.

"Do you want me to pass the information on to you telepathically?"

"That's my preferred method of communication, yes."

Truman actually laughs. "Or you can just message me on Instagram."

My entire body *freezes*. "What does that mean? I don't even follow you on Instagram," I say. My face is as hot as the damn sun.

"You liked my photo in four seconds flat, Eden."

I . . . I want to disappear. If the sidewalk opened up and swallowed me whole right now, I would not complain. Drag me into the center of the earth. Burn me to ashes.

"My phone was clearly hacked," I say to salvage what's left of my dignity.

"Clearly," he says, smiling. Or he might be smiling. Not sure. I'm not looking, of course.

"*Fine.*" I reach into my pocket, hand Truman my phone. He types his number in, I'm guessing, then hands it back. I make a big effort to not touch him. If he notices, he doesn't say.

"Let me know when you want to talk," Truman says. The bench groans when he sits back down. The wind picks up, blows his hair around his face. I want to . . . God, I want to run my fingers through it.

I'm the world's biggest fool.

16
TRUMAN

BEGINNING THE PROCESS OF painting Katie's bedroom is a painful reminder that I haven't stepped foot in a gym in my entire life. The cans of paint weigh my arms down so heavily I give up and drop them on the elevator floor. Even the gray-haired grandmother standing next to me gives me this sad, pitiful smile, like she could pick the cans up no problem and run laps around me. I tuck my tail between my legs and slink off into our apartment. It's dead quiet. Dad's at the office and Mom must be at the hospital with Katie. Works for me—I focus best in silence.

Katie's room is the last one in the hall. It feels weird calling it *her* room because it's really just an empty room. All her belongings are still frozen in place in her bedroom at our old house. I saw the way my parents lingered in the doorway; how they could never actually step foot inside. I get it. I used to do the same thing. Being in there was suffocating. Memories lived in the walls, and it was impossible not to feel her absence even more when surrounded by all the things Katie loved.

I nudge the bedroom door open with my foot. The room is stuffy and humid—I left the windows open overnight to let the primer I applied to the walls air out. The secondhand furniture I picked up is in the middle of the floor, wrapped up in a blue tarp. It doesn't really matter if it gets flecked with paint, since I'm going to repaint it once the walls are done. And that's my goal for the day: finish off the walls. Or at least *mostly* finish them.

I drop the cans of paint on the floor and leave them alone for now. I stare at the walls, try to picture what I'm trying to create before I even begin. I don't want the bedroom to feel like four walls and a ceiling. I want them to blend into each other so they are seamless. I want the sky to feel endless, to feel vast. I want it to feel like you are floating, suspended right in time.

I search the floor for the pencil I tossed in here last night. It's rolled around and gotten stuck in the air vent. I pick it up, press the point into the pad of my finger.

I'm reminded that I've never taken on a project this large before. I have no idea where to start. I could watch tutorials. I could hire someone to do this for Katie. But that feels wrong. It has to be me. I want this to come straight from my mind and onto these walls. As dumb as it sounds, I want her to know that I put a big part of myself into this. It doesn't feel as if there's much I can give or do for Katie right now. This is all I have.

Screw it. I start off with quickly sketching clouds onto the wall in pencil. There's no rhyme or reason to where I'm placing them. I draw heavy ones near the floor, hovering inches off the baseboard. Light, fluffy ones float closer to the ceiling. Then I sketch more of them in between to fill the area, leaving enough space for the blue of the sky to shine through. I leave the ceiling bare for now until I can locate a ladder.

When the pencil tip has dulled into a soft smudge, I stop, look around. I don't know what I'm expecting. I don't really know what this will look like when it's completed. But I'm trusting my gut and seeing where it takes me. It takes a few tries for me to open the can of blue paint. I pour it into the tray and mix in some white, slowly adding more until it becomes the exact shade I'm looking for: pale blue, like faded denim.

I dip the roller into the paint and rock it back and forth, coating it evenly. I start off with the larger areas in between the clouds. The first press of blue onto the wall is startling, this explosion of color that, for some reason, fills me up entirely. I keep painting, keep gliding the roller across the area, and my mind begins to slip away.

It was last summer, early August. One of those days when the sun felt like it was in our backyard instead of the sky. The pool took up the entire space, but Katie and Eden were lying near the fence, right on the grass in their swimsuits. My mom had made them lemonade in these pink cups with twirly straws. There was a hose wrapped around one of the tree branches nearby. The water poured out in a soft mist. When the wind shook the branches, the water blew right over them.

"Impressive," I said, using my hand to shield my eyes from the sunlight.

"Eden's idea," Katie said. Her voice sounded far away, hidden behind the summer haze.

I waited for Eden to turn and look at me like she always did. But she continued to stare up at the sky, kicking her toes through the air.

"Truman," Katie said, "can you go get us some more lemonade?"

I stood underneath the hose, shaking my hair through the water like a dog. "Have your legs stopped working?" I asked.

Katie took her sunglasses off to glare at me. "We're tanning."

"You look like two overcooked lobsters," I said. Katie's skin was bright red. I knew she hadn't thought to put on sunscreen— her mind was always rapid-firing. She never paused to consider the consequences.

Eden . . . Well, I was trying very hard to not look at her.

"You look like Casper the *Not* So Friendly Ghost," Katie shot back. Eden looked right at me, fighting off a smile.

"Ouch. Sick burn, Katie," I deadpanned. Then I grabbed the hose in the tree and turned the dial. The water shifted from a mist to a hard spray, drenching the two of them. I was doubled over, laughing my ass off, while Katie shrieked.

"Truman!" She jumped up squealing, trying to use her arms to shield her face from the water. "I'm telling Mom!" Katie whined before stomping inside through the patio door. Katie was a lot of things—and she was also a pretty big baby when she didn't get her way.

Then I realized that Eden hadn't moved. She was still lying on the grass, drenched head to toe. What struck me most was that she was smiling.

I claimed Katie's spot and lay down right next to her. "Hey," I said while the water kept hailing down on us. I couldn't see her eyes from behind her sunglasses, which were now dotted with droplets.

"That was mean," Eden said, that smile unwavering.

"I'm the mean older brother," I said. "It's my job."

Eden lifted her sunglasses into her hair. Her brown eyes teetered on gold in the sunlight. The water had her hair sticking to her forehead and her cheeks. I remember wanting to reach out, brush it back. But that was weird. Very weird. And slightly inappropriate.

"Katie told me you're not starting university next month," Eden said, brushing the wet strands off her face. I had just graduated from high school two months before. Instead of heading off to post-secondary in the fall, I'd decided to take a year off.

"Thought I'd take some time off and figure out what I want to do," I said. It sounded way better than the full truth: that my life was starting to feel like I was blindly stumbling through a forest at night with no recognition for left or right.

"It's dumb that we're supposed to have everything figured out by eighteen," Eden said. Even though I'd thought the same before, it sounded like the smartest thing I'd ever heard. Somehow, for that second, I stopped feeling like being a kid with no direction was wrong.

The water from the hose kept raining down on us. My entire shirt was soaked through. Eden was drenched from head to toe. I thought that I should get up and shut it off, or at least turn the dial back to mist.

I didn't move.

I didn't really want to.

"It is dumb," I said, because I was trying to remember how to think while watching the water drip off Eden's eyelashes as she blinked.

"Katie doesn't like when I talk to you," she said out of the blue.

"She told you that?" I wasn't entirely surprised. Katie made it crystal clear that I shouldn't be talking to Eden because it was "weird" and "totally creepy, Truman."

But Katie wasn't there. And it was rare for me to have a moment alone with Eden that lasted for more than a couple of seconds. Maybe I was feeling greedy, maybe a little risky. Maybe it was a combination of Eden and the searing sun that had me not really caring about Katie's disapproving voice in my head.

Eden nodded. "She did."

"She's scared you'll like me better than her," I joked.

Eden put her sunglasses back on, turned her head back up to the sky. "Impossible," she said. "I don't think I can like anyone better than her."

I looked at her hands resting on her stomach. Her nails were lime green. "I can paint nails, too," I said. "Just throwing that out there, you know, in case it's crucial in determining who your favorite Falls sibling is. I can also come up with fun ways to hang a hose."

"*You* can paint nails?" she asked, giving me her full attention again. Which was a lot to take in.

I wanted to tell her that I could paint many things. Instead I just said, "I can."

Her mouth quirked up into the cutest of grins. "Without getting polish all over my fingers?" Huh. So she was teasing me.

"I make no promises."

I realized then that we were flirting. Why had this taken so long?

Then the patio door squeaked open and Katie walked out holding two cups. "Truman!" she yelled, marching over to us, lemonade sloshing over the rims and down her hands. "Leave Eden alone, weirdo, and get out of my spot."

Feeling like I had been caught doing something wrong, I stood up and let Katie take her spot back. Then I fixed the hose, set it back to a light mist.

"Santana's inside, by the way," Katie said as she sat back on the grass.

I remember standing there, waiting. I didn't know what for. Maybe for Eden to say something. Maybe for her to ask me to stay, which was beyond idiotic.

"Did you hear me, Tru? Santana's inside."

"Okay," I said. I glanced at Eden one last time, but she was already looking away, wrapped back up in whatever Katie was talking about.

Then the sun fades away, the water dries up, and the only blue sky is the one I'm painting onto this wall in Katie's bedroom. It's almost entirely covered now. I switch from a roller to a small brush to outline the curves of the clouds, painting over the soft strokes of the pencil. Then it's . . . done. Not fully. I'll have to do another coat of blue tomorrow. This time I'll add more white to lighten the color, give the sky more depth. Right now it's looking a little too one-dimensional for me. Then I can brush on the clouds and that's it. Add a few strokes of yellow for the sunlight, then finish off the ceiling. After that, the only thing left will be for Katie to walk in. And when she does, her entire face is going to light up.

I try to remember the last time I saw Katie's face light up, and my mind takes me back to the night of the party. I only had to do one thing: keep an eye on her. Just watch over my little sister, protect her. That was it. Something so simple that I screwed up in a way that feels quite literally unrepairable. I lost my sister that night. It feels like I've lost a lot of love from my parents. I lost the ability to look at myself in the mirror without hating what I see. I've lost that in other people, too.

Eden comes to mind.

At the hospital today, it was nearly impossible to notice the way she couldn't stand too close to me. Or how she wouldn't touch me, like shaking my hand was some tainted curse. And I can't even blame her—that's the worst part. She *should* be hesitant of me. She shouldn't want to get too close, because I let her down once. Who's to say I won't do it again?

But . . .

But somehow, I find myself hoping I can change her mind. And why is that so important to me? To show Eden that I, what, am a good person? That I can redeem myself after losing Katie that night? She's the last person I should be trying to impress and yet here I am, making pacts outside hospitals to talk about my sister, the one thing that seems to slowly rip my heart out of my body in tiny shreds. Yet I didn't even hesitate when she asked. Of course I'll talk to her. I'll tell her anything she wants to know. Because after that night in my bedroom—after everything that went so wrong—I'm still here hoping that maybe one thing will go right. Because that's exactly what kissing Eden felt like. It felt right.

I want to go back and do everything differently. I want to text all my friends and tell them not to come over. I want Katie's window to stay locked and for her to have never climbed out of it. I want to have noticed she was gone.

There are so many things I want. And a lot of them are more important than any sort of affection from Eden. But here I am, thinking of how great it would feel for another moment with her before our lives collapsed around us.

I shake it off. I tuck those thoughts away. Obsessing over a girl should not be my main focus right now. Instead I seal up the paint cans and open the windows again, letting the paint fumes air out. I'm readjusting the tarp when I hear voices from down the hall. Huh, guess my parents are home.

I don't even think to tiptoe down the hall because why would I? There's nothing to hide, nothing to whisper about. But when I round the corner and step into the kitchen, my parents are doing just that. They're standing at the counter, heads bent together, talking so low it raises the hairs on my arms. My mom, whose sadness hasn't left her for months now, looks even more broken. And my dad is holding on to her arm. Maybe he's holding her up.

My heart drops to my feet. I'm thinking it must be Katie. Something must have happened.

"What's going on?" The question startles them. They look up at the exact same time, eyes filled with identical frenzy. I notice a look pass between them. *How much did he hear?*

"Truman," my mom starts, then stops. "You're covered in paint."

"I was working on Katie's room. What were you talking about? Has something changed with Katie?"

I'm already spiraling out, expecting the worst, running through a million terrible scenarios in my head. Then my dad walks over to me and the room shrinks. Or maybe I shrink because I feel like a kid again. Like a kid who just wants someone to tell him everything will be okay. Even if it's a lie. I don't care at this point.

"Your sister is fine," my dad says. Looking at his face is like staring into a mirror. It still catches me off guard. "How's the room coming?" I notice the change in subject. Something is off. Something has changed. I'm not sure what.

"It's coming along," I say. "You can go take a look."

My dad pats my shoulder. "In the morning. I'm calling it a night." Then he leaves, walks down the hallway. *In the morning.* That means, well, never. It's a nice way of saying *Hey, I don't really care.* Not in a malicious way, either. I get it—art isn't for everyone. My parents never took much interest in my paintings. They never asked questions or even said they were good. It was just something I did, something that passed the time. It wasn't serious. It wasn't a job and it definitely wasn't a career. But for the longest time, it felt like all I had. And now, it kind of feels like the only thing keeping me going.

My mom's still standing at the counter, watching me.

"Is she really okay?" I ask again. I can't shake the feeling that something is wrong.

"Nothing has changed, Truman. Katie's fine," she says. Then she smiles, the lines in her face deepening. It's enough to make me shut up, make me turn around and go back to my bedroom. Then I'm lying down, staring at the ceiling. The moonlight is streaming in because I still haven't found the energy to put up blackout curtains. The thought of having to locate a hammer and a ladder physically sucks all the life out of my body. I want to lie down like this, in silence. In the dark. Because this is nice. This is easy.

Then my phone lights up with a text. And it's from Eden. And the darkness fades a little.

Done work around 10. Meet me there?

Right, our agreement. Talking about Katie. That's what she wants: memories, stories. Lucky for Eden I've got tons of them that I'm dying to share. Talking to Santana and Milo about her isn't the same thing—they don't get it. With my parents there's too much heaviness. But with Eden . . . Well, I really don't know what it'll feel like. Kind of want to find out, though.

I text Eden back: *And go where?*

I don't know, she writes. Then, *We'll think of something.*

Well, okay then.

I pull my car over in front of Pollo Loco and have no clue where to take this girl. Or what to say to her. Or how to even act around her. Eden said she doesn't know how to act around me. Well, the feeling's mutual. I spent so long staring at her from far away that my mind can't wrap itself around the mere fact that she's . . . here now.

Through the restaurant windows I can see Eden mopping the floor with her headphones in. The first time I met her she was fourteen with braces, camped out on the couch in our living room, watching reruns of *One Tree Hill* with Katie, their fingers entirely covered in Cheetos crumbs. I remember she looked at me and her eyes shot open. Then Katie went, "Oh. This is my brother, Truman." And Eden just nodded and kept nodding, like a bobblehead. And that was it. She was there. Four years passed and she never left. And now she's here, working full-time, living on her own in a different city, trying to find her place in this world that feels relentless and unforgiving. I have no idea who she is anymore. I barely even knew who she was back then. But I knew who she was that night in my bedroom. I knew her—I saw *right through her*. And if there's more of that—if she's more of that—then I might be in way over my head.

I might be fucking doomed.

My eyes follow Eden around the restaurant. She's wiping down the counters now, then heading into the back. Suddenly I'm nervous because in a few minutes she won't be in there and I won't be out here. There won't be a window between us. She's going to be here, beside me, waiting for me to do whatever it is she wants me to do. And I'm such a goddamn idiot who will undoubtedly find a way to mess this up and scare her off one more time.

I'm an idiot who should drive away. Turn the engine on. Return home because Eden hasn't even seen me yet. It's the smart choice. It's the right choice.

But I never claimed to be smart. So, I wait. Keep waiting. Then wait some more. I reread the text she sent: *Done work around 10. Meet me there?*

Well, here I am, waiting to see what happens.

A few minutes later the restaurant doors open and Eden's on the sidewalk, standing beside a guy I recognize from the art exhibit. He locks up, they talk for a second, then she's walking to my car, knocking on the window to get my attention as if she hasn't had it this entire time. Her dark hair's been let down and it blows around her face, falls over her eyes. I unlock the door and Eden seems to fill up the entire space.

"Hey," I say because one syllable is basically all my brain can manage right now.

She sits down with a huff, throws her bag at her feet. A cloud of food follows behind her, filling the car with the smell of frying oil. "I don't understand why you even bother owning a car here," she says because saying *hello* is clearly overrated.

"Uh— What?"

She glares at me in the dark. "Public transit exists for a reason. So does walking. It's the entire point of being downtown."

My brain jumps from point A to point Z, trying to figure out what's happening right now. "Did something happen at work?" I ask.

"No."

"I'm trying to figure out what put you in such a great mood."

She glares again with enough force to burn multiple cities to the ground, Khaleesi style, then says, "If you must know, I got a customer complaint. It's not my first one." Then she pauses. And she's piercing me with this look, like she's waiting for me to jump in and say something. "This is when you act surprised, Truman," she finishes.

Oh. Of course. So I gasp on cue.

"What'd you do?" I ask before realizing my mistake.

"Why do you think I did something?" she fires back.

I decide the best way out of this is complete silence.

Right choice, because Eden continues. "I was on my phone and may have, potentially, forgotten to bring a customer their food. And it may have—"

"Potentially?" I offer.

"—potentially been a bit cold when I did manage to bring it to them," she finishes.

I nod along, secretly studying Eden in the dark. She does seem a bit sad. Maybe she's tired from working. Either way, her face is missing that usual animation: the startled eyes that shrink into a glare in half a second. Nice to know a heavy mood doesn't affect the sarcasm that rolls off her tongue like burning-hot lava.

"Want to know what I think?" I ask.

"No, but you can tell me anyways."

This ballbuster. "I think," I say, "that it wasn't your fault at all."

This seems to catch Eden's attention because she stops staring out of the windshield. She looks right at me and I'm suddenly wishing she hadn't because her eyes are just, well, *a lot*.

"You're right, of course. But what makes you say that?"

"Did you mean to forget their food?" I ask.

"Of course not."

"Then there's nothing more to it. You made a mistake, big deal."

Eden seems to consider this for a moment. Her eyes track over my hair, which must be a mess even after my best attempt to tame it, my face that's probably weighed down with sleep, and then to my jacket that I thought looked cool but now I'm not so sure. I wait a little too eagerly for her to say whatever it is she's thinking about me.

She only looks away. "Where are we going?" she asks.

The dreaded question. "I don't know," I admit. "Have somewhere in mind?"

"No," she says slowly. "Do you? Like, some place Katie used to like?"

"Uh . . ." How had I managed to forget this entire arrangement is about Katie? It's definitely not about Eden wanting to spend time with me. And of course not the other way around, either. That would be nuts.

Eden doesn't say a word. I hear her drum her fingers along her thigh. It's so different from Katie, who could never seem to stop talking. My parents always said that her mind moved so quickly her mouth couldn't keep up. She would always babble about places in the city she wanted to go someday—restaurants she wanted to try, museum exhibits she wanted to visit, plays she wanted to get tickets to. But that's just it: these are places Katie *wanted* to visit someday. She never got the chance to.

Then I'm thinking that maybe we can experience them for her.

"There's this diner my grandmother brought Katie and me to one year for her birthday," I say. "They make her favorite strawberry milkshake."

Eden scrunches her face up. "Strawberry?"

"Katie was a real weirdo, huh?" I turn the key in the engine. It roars to life and Eden jumps in her seat. The entire car shakes.

"What are you doing?" she says quickly. The girl sounds entirely breathless.

I force myself to concentrate on what Eden's saying and not the way her fingers graze her skin when she swipes a lock of hair behind her ear. "Driving to the diner?"

"We can't drive there. We have to walk."

"Eden, it's pretty far—"

"We aren't driving there," she repeats. Her voice has me thinking something's wrong. I take the keys out of the engine. I shut the car off. Silence hits us and she collapses against the seat. Deflates. Breathes again.

I don't know what's happening. I don't know what to say. My brain is the most useless one on the planet right now. I can't figure out what I did that triggered her, but I want to take it back. Because what the hell was that?

"We won't drive there," I say softly. "We don't have to drive anywhere."

And then everything slams into me at once. The accident. The *car* accident. Katie. The windshield. The drunk driver. Of course.

I want to reach out and take her hand. Something tells me that'll only make everything worse. I saw the way she flinched at the hospital when I reached for her. And this is delicate. There's no room for trembling fingers when you're dealing with glass jars.

"Eden?"

She's staring down at her lap, picking at a loose thread in her jeans. "Sorry," she says.

"Nothing to be sorry about," I say. "Seriously. Not a thing."

Eden keeps picking at the thread. She knots it around her finger and yanks, ripping it right out. "I don't like driving anymore," she says.

"You don't have to explain yourself." But I want her to. I want to know more about her.

I roll down the windows, thinking that maybe fresh air will help. The car is feeling a bit stuffy, a bit suffocating. I don't want her to feel trapped. Especially not with me.

"Katie loves the sky," Eden says. "Can you tell me why? There must be a story behind that."

"There is," I say. I relax in the seat, since Eden seems to have abandoned the idea of walking to the diner. "She went on a school trip to the Ontario Science Centre in grade five—it might've been grade six, not sure. Katie came home that day glowing. No joke, Eden, this girl was *beaming*. She spent the entire night going on about this exhibit they had on all the different types of clouds. Cumulus, stratus, other ones I don't remember. They had this demonstration with water and ice droplets that literally re-created a cloud right there in the science center. I guess Katie touched it and she was hooked. She spent weeks going on about clouds, researching them, becoming obsessed with airplanes. She even made this comment once that she wanted to live up there with them. I don't know, maybe it's dumb. But it was something she really loved. Or at least she used to."

I can feel the weight of Eden's stare. It's feathers and bricks all at once. I don't look at her. I don't want her to see what these memories do to me, how they take me someplace that's weightless and suffocating at the same time.

"That's a really great story," Eden says.

"Yeah."

I'm slammed with this urge to go back home, lock myself in Katie's bedroom, finish giving her that sky. Maybe that's what she's waiting for. Maybe when it's complete, she'll wake up.

Stupid, stupid thought. Still, it has me itching for a paintbrush.

"Where did you go this summer?"

Eden's question snaps me right back to the present, to this stuffy car. "Uh, what?"

"This summer," she repeats. "You were gone for a while. Where'd you disappear to?"

First, I'm floored that she even noticed. Second, I'm falling to pieces that she cares enough to ask.

"Montreal," I say. "There was a summer art program at a university there." Then I keep going, keep rambling, because suddenly it's very important that Eden understands this. "I applied and got accepted before Katie's accident. Then everything changed. I wasn't going to go, but . . ."

"But you needed to get away?" she asks.

It leaves me speechless. "Exactly. Yeah."

"I get it," she says quietly. "That tug to be near Katie but to also be as far away as possible from any reminder of her. Kind of cruel, huh?"

"Very," I say because my brain has reverted back to one-word answers.

Eden understands. This girl fucking understands. And of course she does. Eden sat on my bed with me for an hour going through my artwork. She saw right into my brain, my entire heart, and she just sat there and—and *cared*. Listened. Learned. So of course she would understand this, too. Of course she would be the person to offer me the smallest amount of comfort that I've been searching for from my family and friends. But no. I find it here instead, in a girl I haven't spoken to in months. A girl I kissed one night and have spent five months regretting.

Five months wanting to kiss her again.

"Do you think she'll wake up?" Eden asks. She says it so carefully, like she's testing the words out. It must be the first time she's asked someone this.

"Yes," I say with 100 percent honesty. She will. She has to.

"How are you so sure?"

"Because I don't think this world can exist without someone like her in it."

And then I'm squinting because Eden turns the light above us on. She's leaning across, getting right up to my face. What is she—

"What is that?" she says. She's pointing to my cheek, keeping a safe distance between her finger and my skin, of course.

"What is what?" I look in the mirror. There's a smear of blue paint right under my eye. Another on my temple. There are a few flecks in my hair, too.

"Oh," I say, embarrassed. I start wiping at it with my fingers, trying to smudge it off. "It's paint."

"What are you working on?" she asks so earnestly my heart implodes.

I want to tell her. I know she'll understand. Hell, she'll probably love it. But talking about Katie's bedroom doesn't do it justice.

I'll have to show her.

"What are you doing tomorrow morning?" I ask.

Eden sinks back into her seat, letting the distance between us grow again. She must have reached the limit to how long she can look at me for, because she's back to staring out the window. I think three seconds is her max.

"My schedule's pretty jam-packed," she says.

"Oh yeah? With what exactly?"

"Sleeping, not getting out of bed, that cardboard cereal I previously mentioned . . ."

"Sounds like you're a busy girl," I say, not sure why I'm grinning.

"Very busy," she says. "You're lucky I'm here right now, actually."

I feel lucky. "What are you doing before work?" I try again.

"Why do you ask?" she counters.

"There's something I want to show you."

17
EDEN

IT RAINS ALL MORNING. The sky is gray and dense, the sidewalks are sleek with water. The wind howls against the building. It sounds even louder from this high up in our apartment. It reminds me of Truman's painting from the art exhibit, of Katie in the pool that day the sky opened up and poured down on her, completely out of nowhere. She was laughing, smiling, beaming. Like nothing could dampen her, even when she was soaked through and through. My heart feels a little heavy today. But it's a little less heavy than it usually feels when I think of her. And I can't exactly figure out why that is or what has changed. My mind keeps going back to Truman. Maybe he was right—maybe talking about her does help. Maybe it's the reminder that she does exist outside of my mind, that there are other people who experienced her before the curtain drew closed.

A rainy day is what I need. It's the perfect excuse to stay in bed and do nothing. Sure, I would do that even if the sun were out, but now it's socially acceptable, so.

Except rent was due last week and I still haven't paid Ramona back for my half of it. My check is somewhere in my locker at Pollo Loco, shoved underneath stained Tupperware and balled-up sweaters. So when Mona asked if I could go by today and pick it up, I told her that no, I would just bring it home tonight when my shift is done like any logical person would. And she expertly pointed out that I've been saying that for a week now, because I have. The conversation somehow ends with us outside, huddled under an umbrella, down the block from Pollo Loco.

Ramona insisted on coming because I'm a child who she doesn't trust to do anything alone. Plus I think the foodie in her has always been curious to see the restaurant I work at.

We step out of the rain and into Pollo Loco. Two booths are taken up by customers, which is two more than normal. Ahmed is sitting at the counter in my usual spot, holding his phone horizontally and probably playing some game I hope to never hear about. The *Animal Crossing* theme song already lives rent-free in my head thanks to Ramona.

"This place is . . ." Ramona doesn't finish her sentence. She's taking in the chipped tiles, faded paint, worn-out furniture, and general murkiness that lurks in the air. It does smell good, though. We have that going for us.

"Do you want something to eat?" I ask her. Ahmed looks up from the counter and glances at me without a word. I lead Ramona to a table and she sits down; the faux leather squeaks.

"If you want something, sure." She's looking around the space, probably trying to locate a cute corner she can photoshop the shit out of so it's somewhat Instagram worthy. I don't think we have any of those here.

"I'll see what Manny's cooking," I say, then head into the back. It feels criminal to be here when I'm not getting paid. I push through the kitchen door and Manny is working away at the stove, stirring a wooden spoon through a gigantic pot. He spots me, smiles. There are tiny beads of sweat dripping down his forehead.

"What are you doing here?" he says. "Wait—is it already five?" Then he frantically checks his watch.

"You've still got a few hours before you have to deal with me. I need to grab my check." I head into the storage-room-slash-washroom and rummage through my locker. I should probably clear out some of the crap in it. I should probably do that right now, actually. I don't, of course, because what is life if not a gigantic game of procrastination? I grab my check and head back to the kitchen, the steam from Manny's latest recipe warming me entirely.

"What is that?" I ask.

"Caldo verde," Manny says in Portuguese, two words I actually recognize.

"Green soup?"

Manny shuffles around in a drawer, pulls out a spoon. "It's

a Portuguese classic. There's chorizo, kale, potatoes, chicken broth—the gloomy weather made me crave it. Wanna try?"

"Hell yes." Manny dips the spoon into the pot, then holds it out to me. It's piping hot, with little swirls of steam curling off the metal. I blow on it a few times, then sip. I'm not surprised to find out it's delicious. Manny knows what he's doing in the kitchen.

"Like it?" he asks, beaming.

"It's delish. Can you spare enough for two bowls?"

Manny tugs the white towel off his shoulder and dabs his forehead. "I can't sit right now—"

"Not for you and me, Manny, sheesh. My roommate, Ramona, is here with me."

"Oh. Yeah, sure. Give me a second and I'll bring it out."

"You're the best!" I say, running off before he can make fun of me for it. Ramona is still sitting at the table, scrolling through her phone. It's almost noon, which means it's time for her daily post. Ramona says the key to social media is consistency: you want to annoy people, but in a way that makes them *want* to be annoyed by you. Makes no sense to me.

"Manny's bringing us some soup," I say.

"It's, like, seventy-five degrees out, Eden."

"I'm sorry—are you saying *no* to free food?"

Mona shuts her mouth. I pull my phone out of my pocket and peek at the screen in a very casual way. I'm not, like, waiting for anything exactly. Not a text from a specific person regarding a suspicious fleck of blue paint and a promise to show me more. Nuh-uh.

"You keep checking your phone," Mona says, reading my mind.

"No, I don't."

"You pulled it out every two minutes the entire way here," she says. "Even on the subway where there's no service."

"I'm just waiting for *Mario Kart Tour* to update," I lie.

Mona kicks me under the table. "What's going on?"

I huff like the big bad wolf. Fine. *Fine*. "I might be waiting for a text."

"From?" she pries.

"Truman."

I have to give it to her, because Ramona does not react at all to his name. I know it's taking every ounce of her strength, but she actually holds it together. Interesting.

"What is he texting you about, exactly?"

"I don't know," I admit. "That's the point."

Mona scoops her long hair off her shoulder and starts mindlessly braiding it. "Care to elaborate?"

Normally this is where I would shut the vault, spin the lock, make sure it's nice and secure. Instead I . . . I kind of want to tell Ramona about whatever is transpiring between Truman and me. Maybe then she can help me make sense of it, because I clearly can't.

I tell her about sitting in his car last night and the blue paint. I leave out my little freak-out when the engine started. I need to retain some sort of boundaries.

"Sounds like it's something for Katie," Mona says when I finish.

"That's what I was thinking." I just don't know what it is. And the curiosity is driving me up the wall.

"So how has it been, talking to Truman again?" Mona asks.

"Weird," I tell her honestly. "Like somehow talking to a complete stranger and someone you've known forever at the same time."

Mona finishes her braid and flicks it over her shoulder. "Sounds like a mess."

"You have no idea, dude."

Then I lose Mona's attention entirely. Manny is walking toward us, smiling like a puppy dog, two huge bowls of steaming soup in his hands. I see the exact second he notices Ramona. He literally *stops*. Just stops walking. Stops smiling. They stare at each other like absolute morons before Manny remembers how to walk and makes it to the table.

"Two bowls of caldo verde," he says, setting them down in front of us.

"Thought you were going to drop them for a second," I say. "Manny, this is Ramona, my roommate. She's a tough critic when it comes to food."

The smile that takes over Manny's face is blinding. He turns it on Ramona and she melts like a Popsicle left on the sidewalk. I realize that I am witnessing something special happening. Something cute. Yet all I want is to eat, so I do just that.

"Eden's told me a lot about you," Manny says, crossing his arms against his chest. Is he—*flexing?*

"He's lying," I say in between slurps. "I haven't said a word."

Ramona laughs, and it's way more high-pitched than usual. "Not surprising, Eden." Then she holds out her hand and Manny shakes it. "Nice to meet you. Is this your place?"

"My family's. I'm the head chef," he says with so much pride it practically oozes out of him. They're still holding hands over the table. I want to dump a bowl of soup over each of their heads.

"I'm excited to try your food," Mona says, tugging the bowl of soup across the table. The same soup she was just complaining about, may I add.

Manny runs his hands down his apron, takes a step away. "I gotta get back in there before the pot boils over. Enjoy, ladies."

Ladies?

He disappears into the kitchen. I glare at Mona from over my spoon.

"What?" she says innocently. She takes a sip and her eyes go wide. "Wow."

"You know what."

"You never told me your boss is that cute, Eden."

"He's not my boss," I say, blowing on the spoon. "And Manny has questionable taste in women."

"Did he ask you out?"

"The fact that you figured that out so easily is incredibly offensive," I joke. "But yeah, he did. Nothing happened. Well, we kissed once, but it didn't mean anything. And Manny is, like, the greatest guy on this planet. You should go for it."

Ramona sips, sips, sips her soup, not saying another word, just smiling to herself.

Sickening.

Then my phone chimes and I jump so quickly I spill soup all over the table. Mona watches me with raised eyebrows that spell out *I told you so.* "Shut up," I grumble.

I grab a pile of napkins and wipe up the spill, then grab my phone. It's a text from Truman, of course. It's his address. Then, *Can you get here in thirty?*

Uh, yeah. Yeah I can.

"What did he say?" Mona asks.

"He sent his address." And even the street name sounds fancy. I just know it's one of those luxurious high-rises with a doorman that wears white silk gloves. They probably speak in British accents. They're probably so posh. So fancy. So cool. I'll walk in with my banged up sneakers and track mud all over the plush cream carpets. They'll chase me out the door. I'll probably be banned for life. A washed-out photo of my face will be taped to the wall in the security room: *Beware of Gross Low-Life Girl, Do Not Let Her Enter.*

It's probably for the best if I don't show up. That way I can avoid the embarrassment that comes with feeling out of place. Plus, it's not like I even want to go and see what Truman's working on. Or even go and see Truman, for that matter. I really don't want that at all. Like, it totally does not irk me in the slightest to just go an entire day *without* seeing him. I really don't—

I pick up my stupid backpack and shove my stupid little arms through the loops, because who am I kidding?

"I have to go," I tell Mona while typing the address into my phone.

"Thought so," she murmurs.

Truman's building is a short walk from the hospital, and only a few blocks from here. Perfect. A ten minute walk is way too little time for me to overthink everything. And definitely not enough time for me to start feeling nervous about seeing Truman. What's there to be nervous about? Absolutely nothing, that's what.

"Have fun with Manny," I say, then head out the door before she can begin to freak out and beg me to stay. Manny is a golden retriever. A human teddy bear. He's also a chef and Mona lives and breathes for food. I'm sure they'll be fine.

Heat knocks the breath out of me as soon as I step outside. Not sure why I keep being caught off guard by how grossly humid it is every day, since it's been like this for months now. I tell myself I can't wait for winter, only to spend all of winter hoping for summer. The cycle is endless. I watch my train of thought roll into a full-blown collision.

At least it stopped raining.

I follow the directions on my phone to Truman's building. I'm slowly starting to familiarize myself with the streets here, but I'm nowhere near pro enough to go rogue. I know certain routes like the back of my hand—hospital, Pollo Loco, our building. Anything unfamiliar is uncharted territory. I run across the street when there's a gap in the traffic like Katie used to. She never waited for red lights and walking signals. She just went, trusting that people would stop for her. They usually did. Until they didn't.

I don't want to think about that. Instead I think about whatever Truman needs to show me so desperately. Because that's exactly how he seemed when he brought it up: desperate. I'm curious, but it kind of feels like I'm rooting for him, too. Like I want him to prove me wrong. To show me that there's this hidden part of him that's worth caring for.

Mostly, I want to know that he didn't give up on Katie when he left. Maybe then I can trick myself into believing he didn't give up on us, either.

And then I want to lie down in the middle of the road, because where did that thought even come from? *Us?* There is no us. We never had a chance for there to be an *us*. And if we did, was that something I would have wanted?

I arrive at Truman's building and it's exactly as I imagined: incredibly tall and unnecessarily fancy. The doors are wrought iron and huge. No doorman, though. I got that wrong. I step inside the little entranceway and there's a touch screen for visitors. I type in Truman's unit number, then the code he gave me. The door slides open and I walk in. It smells like eucalyptus, and I can hear water tinkling, like there's a Zen fountain somewhere. The concierge desk is empty—there's a little sign that says *We will return in thirty minutes.* I walk across the marble floors and round the corner to the elevators. I stab the up arrow with my finger, feeling self-conscious and out of place.

And then I'm in front of Truman's unit and it's time to face the facts: I'm nervous. Like, heart-beating-so-quickly-I-can-barely-breathe nervous. Because this is weird. Because I shouldn't be here. Because without Katie to break the ice, being around Truman feels like stepping too close to a fire. In the same second I tell myself to book it to the elevator and go home, the door is being tugged open and Truman is standing in front of me. And he's smiling. And his white T-shirt is covered in blue paint. And there are flecks of it in his hair again, on his cheekbones, dotting his neck and disappearing under the collar of his shirt.

On second thought, the elevator is a far walk. I should probably just stay.

"Hey," Truman says, that slender mouth of his turning up into a smile. He actually looks happy to see me. "You came."

"You piqued my curiosity," I say casually. That's what I am: cool, calm, collected.

"That was the plan." He tugs the door all the way open. "Come see what I've been working on."

I step inside and our shoulders briefly touch, but I, of course, do not notice this insignificant piece of information. And then I actually take in Truman's apartment, and I want to move in. It's sprawling and clean. Everything is shiny and neutral. There are no stains on the plush white rugs and the chandeliers look like they've been imported from a country I've probably never heard of.

Wow. Mona and I have quite literally been living in a shoebox.

"Nice place," I say.

It seems to make Truman uncomfortable. He tracks a hand through his hair, which only turns a larger portion of it blue. "Katie's room is this way," he says. He starts walking through the living room, then down the hallway. So that's what he wants to show me, Katie's bedroom?

The door to the bedroom is cracked open and the smell of paint floods the hallway. I can see bursts of blue as we get closer. It's identical to the shade smeared over Truman's skin. My curiosity has surpassed a ten. I'm a solid twelve right now. Then I follow Truman into the bedroom and . . . And we've left the apartment completely. Somehow we're standing in the middle of the sky.

The walls are a morning blue that goes right into the ceiling. There are clouds that have been painted with so much texture and depth that they actually look fluffy. They're on the ceiling, too. And when I look up, I am surrounded by this endless sea of blue.

"What is this?" I ask. I want to cry. I think I might.

"What I've been working on for Katie," Truman says from somewhere behind me. I'm not paying attention. I'm walking to the wall because I want to touch the cloud. I want to be like Katie, pinching a piece of cotton between her fingers and having it alter her forever. I'm about to run my fingers across the white paint when Truman grabs my hand.

"Paint's still wet," he says.

He's touching me. His hand is on mine. It's that night in his room again. It's the impending kiss. The doom that follows.

I pull my hand away quickly. "Sorry," I say. Then everything comes together and I understand what I'm looking at. It's Katie's bedroom. That Truman *painted*. He made it possible to give her a piece of the sky.

My heart feels like a stone that has sunk deep down into the middle of my body. I am so mesmerized by him and what he's able to create. His fingers are made of magic—they must be. How can you take four walls and turn them into the sky and not be the most incredible person in the world? I'm hit with so many feelings at once it's staggering. I might topple over. I might need to forget everything I thought I knew about Truman Falls. I might need to start from scratch.

"You painted this?" I ask. Of course he painted it. I just want to hear him say it.

He smiles this soft, embarrassed grin. "I did, yeah. Do you like it?"

"Do I *like* it? Truman—" I do a little spin, soak in every wall, every inch of space he transformed. "It's . . ."

"It's a lot to take in," he offers.

"When did you start this?"

There are paint cans, paint trays, and paintbrushes littering the entire floor. There's a pile of something in the middle of the room, covered in a blue vinyl tarp. Truman picks up one of the paintbrushes and begins fidgeting with it. He runs the clean bristles against his palm.

"A few days ago," he says.

"You did all this in a few days?"

Truman shrugs, his eyes lift up to mine. That straight and narrow face of his is usually all angles and sharp lines. Except now it's softened. He hasn't stopped smiling since we walked in here. "I don't have a whole lot going on right now," he says.

"Are the walls finished?" I ask.

"They are, yeah. I finished off the clouds this morning."

I point to the tarp. "And what's under that?"

"Oh. Right," Truman says, like he had forgotten it was there. He lifts the tarp and uncovers a few furniture pieces—a headboard, nightstand, and a dresser, all in this light, nearly white, colored wood.

"Is this the part when you tell me you're a carpenter too and built all of that from scratch? Because I might need a moment."

Truman laughs and I hate myself because, dammit, it's a nice laugh. "Would it impress you if I did?"

"Maybe."

"Hate to let you down, Eden, but I didn't build it. I bought it secondhand from this dude online."

I'm happy to hear it. I don't think him having another secret talent would be good for my well-being right now. I'm still a little dizzy from the paint reveal. Or the paint fumes. Probably the fumes getting to my head, making me feel things that aren't really there. Et cetera, et cetera.

"What are you going to do with it?" I ask.

Truman runs his hand along the wooden dresser. He's so tall, so thin and lanky, and yet his presence somehow stretches from wall to wall. I can see the veins running through his pale skin, spot every fleck of paint that decorates it, too.

"I'm not sure," he says after a minute. "I was going to paint it, but I'm worried it might be too much."

"What do you mean?"

"Like . . ." Truman sets the paintbrush on top of the dresser, plants his hands on the side of it, and starts to push it. He pushes it flush up against the wall, right near the large window. "I can't decide if it'll be too much, having both the furniture and the walls painted like the sky." He gives me another one of those embarrassed smiles. "I'm really indecisive," he explains, "but I kind of want this to be perfect for her. You know?"

"It looks pretty perfect to me," I say.

"What do you think I should do?"

It catches me completely off guard. "With the furniture?" Truman nods, watching me. "Uh. I think you should probably ask someone who's actually creative. I haven't painted anything since, like, kindergarten. And even then it was pretty terrible."

"I want to know what you think," he pushes.

"Paint the furniture," I say without thinking. It just feels right for the sky to be everywhere.

Then Truman picks up that paintbrush again and holds it out

to me. I take a step back because I definitely should not be trusted with that, or with a project this precious. I'll find a way to ruin it. I'll spill the entire can of paint and destroy the sky entirely.

"You want *me* to help?" I ask. Is that why he asked me to come here?

Truman takes another step toward me, poking the brush through the air like it's a lethal weapon. In my hands, it very well might be.

"If you want to," he says. He kind of shrugs it off, but his face looks so open, so earnest. Like he . . . Kind of like he wants me to say yes.

"I do want to," I say. Of course I want to be a part of something that'll be so special for Katie someday. My brain tries to interrupt with the usual *if she wakes up* but I'm not in the mood for that right now. Right now, I want to live an entire day with the hope that yeah, Katie will wake up. And one day she'll walk into this room and be able to live in the sky. It'll feel so nice to know that I played some tiny role in giving her that.

"Then take the paintbrush, Eden," Truman says, offering it up again.

"I can't guarantee I won't ruin everything," I warn.

"Impossible."

"I might spill an entire can of paint everywhere."

"Then we'll clean it up. I saw you at Pollo Loco the other night. You know your way around a mop," he teases.

I scoff. "I only know how to clean when I'm getting paid for it."

Truman's mouth quirks up. "Is that what it'll take? I have to buy your time?"

"My complete lack of art skills is worth every penny. Promise."

Now I'm smiling, too. Which is weird. I never smile around Truman.

Scratch that. I never smile. Period.

He waves the paintbrush toward my chest one more time. Reluctantly, I take it. How hard can it really be to run some blue paint over wood? Easy peasy. If there were lemons, I could squeeze them.

"Where should I start?"

Then Truman kicks into instructor mode. It reminds me of Manny in the kitchen and that very rhythmic, purposeful way he moves. Truman pours a small amount of the blue paint into a tray that's on top of a small foldable table. Then he lays the tarp flat on the floor, picks up the nightstand, and puts it right on top. I don't know if that's standard practice or if he doesn't trust me not to spill paint everywhere. Either way, good call. He eyes the brush in my hand with pursed lips. I can practically see the little artistic gears turning in his brain. He rummages through a plastic bag and pulls out a mini paint roller, just small enough to fit the width of the nightstand.

"Use this instead," he says, swapping it with my paintbrush. "It's a lot easier to paint with. And the paint will go on smoother."

"So where do I begin?" I'm standing there like a total moron, paint roller in hand, my brain empty of any and all thoughts.

"Dip the roller in the paint," he says. I do that. "Then roll it around in the tray to get any excess off," he says. I do that, too. "Then start painting." Easier said than done.

I roll the roller around a little more until the majority of the paint drips off, then carry it over to the top of the nightstand. Since I've already come to terms with my own failure, I just go for it. I run the roller against the wood in long, even strokes. And just like that, it starts to turn blue.

"Huh," I say, kind of amazed. "This isn't that hard." I keep going until the entire top portion of the wood is painted.

"You're a natural," Truman says. I feel like a child. I want a gold star sticker to put right on the center of my forehead. "You can do the same thing to all the sides. Then switch to the bristled brush to get into the crevices that the roller can't reach. After it dries overnight, I'll put on a second coat."

I'm nodding along like I'm actually very handy and know exactly what he is referring to. Bristled brush? Use them all the time. Second coat? Of course. Truman starts with the dresser, first pushing it onto the tarp, then laying on the first coat of paint. I multitask—painting the sides of the nightstand and watching him work. It's sort of mesmerizing. He handles the brush with such ease, like every stroke is this extension of his mind and not some measly little swipe of paint. I want to crack his mind open like an egg and see everything inside it. And this time, not just the parts about Katie, but the parts about him, too.

"So Montreal," I say. It feels like an olive branch. Like I'm trying to bridge the space that's opened up between us these past few months.

"What about it?"

"What was the art class like?" I say, rolling the paint across the right panel of the nightstand.

"Different than anything I've done before. It was all about the human form. Bodies, faces, lines and curves. We painted a lot of people." Truman pauses, then adds, "A lot of nudity."

I stop painting. "I'm sure you enjoyed that." He flicks his paintbrush at me. A few blue droplets fly across the room and fall onto the tarp. "Ha, missed me."

"It wasn't like that," he says, bending down to coat his brush in a fresh layer of paint. "It's not, like, sexualized. It's more of a mutual appreciation. We're not focusing on any specific body part. It's more about how all the lines of the body connect, from limbs to muscles, that sort of thing."

"Interesting. What's your favorite thing you painted from the class?"

Truman forgets about the brush in his hand entirely. He's watching me with wide eyes. I realize they're kind of the exact same color as the paint. "You really want to know?" He says it like it's the craziest thing in the world. Like it's been ages since anyone has taken any sort of interest in his life.

It hits me that maybe it has been.

"I wouldn't ask if I didn't," I say.

Truman tells me about this one project they worked on where he had to paint a stranger. Like, literally find someone on the street and ask their permission to be painted. "I barely speak a word of French, so no one had any idea what I was saying. Then this older lady spotted me and started translating for me. Every single person said no."

"So who'd you paint?" I ask.

"The lady," he says.

"The translator?"

Truman nods. He's kneeling on the floor, painting the bottom of the dresser. "I bought her a coffee afterward. We talked for about two hours."

"Huh," I say.

"What's that mean?"

"Nothing. Nothing at all."

"*Eden.*"

"*Nothing,*" I say, returning the dramatics. "I simply wouldn't have guessed you spent your time in Montreal with women three times your age."

"What exactly did you think I was doing in Montreal?" he asks, laughing.

"Not having coffee with grandmothers, that's for sure. Plus, I didn't know you went to Montreal until you told me in your car."

"So where did you think I disappeared to?" he asks.

I'm aware that it's very, very quiet in this room. That if we stop talking, we'll be able to hear the rain that's started up again, or the whir of the wind blowing outside.

"I didn't really think about it," I tell him. It's the truth. Sure, I wondered where he went. Sure, I was even a bit upset that he was gone. I couldn't wrap my head around how he could just up and leave when the stakes were so high. You don't go all in, then walk away from the table before the cards have even been dealt. Unless you're desperate. Unless your life feels like it depends on it.

"You never asked my parents?" he says. "You're at the hospital with my mom all the time."

I set down the roller and switch to the brush, dipping it in the paint. "We didn't talk about you," I say.

We lapse into this heavy silence. The rain trickles down. I can hear the soft rhythm of our paintbrushes coating the sanded wood.

"My parents weren't too happy that I left," Truman says. No— *whispers*.

"They probably don't get it," I say.

"They don't. They don't get it at all. I had to leave for a while. It had nothing to do with abandoning my sister. I . . . I needed a minute," he says.

"I said *they* probably don't get it, Truman. But I do." And I don't know why I can't seem to leave it at that. I keep going, like my creaky old tap has finally started to work again and all the water that has built up for weeks simply rushes out, full speed ahead. "I sleep a lot," I say. "My roommate makes fun of me for it. So do my parents. They think I'm lazy. That I want to lounge around in bed all day like a lump. But there's this moment—this tiny, tiny moment that happens whenever I wake up. It's like my brain hasn't turned on yet, like it hasn't remembered everything that's happened these past months. And for a single second, Katie is still here. There's no accident, no coma, no *nothing*. She's here. And it feels so real that I cling to that moment. I keep trying to go back to sleep so I can wake up and feel it all over again."

And then the words are out there. This grand reveal I haven't told a single person before. I don't even know why I said it. Maybe because it feels like I'm finally talking to someone who understands this very specific kind of grief. It's not every day you lose someone and they're still here. Grief is final—it's funerals and cemeteries and the understanding that that person is gone, that you'll never see them again. It's pain, but it's acceptance. Grieving Katie is different. It's blunt pain and dull hope. It's knowing I'll probably never speak to her again, but that there's a chance I somehow still might. It's one-sided conversations in hospital rooms and clinging to memories that feel too far away. I don't know how to mourn her because she is still here. She is still here. She's here, she's here, she's here.

She's so far away.

I don't know when it started, but I'm crying. Tears are dripping down my cheeks, gathering on my shirt. I step away from the nightstand because I don't want to ruin it. Because I can joke all I want about how funny it would be for me to spill an entire can of paint, but if I actually did, I would crumble into a thousand twisted pieces. What Truman is doing here is so good. It's far better than anything I've done in the past five months. And if I ruined so much as a fraction of it, just one speck of paint that looks off, it might very well undo me. I'm that spool of thread again, unraveling across the bedroom floor.

Then Truman is kneeling beside me. He's taking the paintbrush from my hand. *Good choice*, I think, *save the furniture*. But then I look up from my lap and he's staring right into me with this overwhelming amount of concern and I don't understand why. Maybe he's not trying to protect the furniture. Maybe he's trying to protect me.

"I'm fine," I say, sniffling like an idiot. "Sorry. Let's pretend I never said that. And never cried."

"We can do that if you want," he says gently. "Or we can acknowledge that this shit is hard. And there's nothing wrong with struggling through it, Eden."

"It feels like there's no end in sight," I say. Like I'm walking through a narrow black tunnel that stretches longer every single day.

"Then we'll keep painting," Truman says.

"Wish it was that easy," I say. I blow my nose with my shirtsleeve because I simply love oozing sex appeal. Then I notice Truman is trying so hard to not laugh his entire face is turning red.

"What?"

"Nothing," he says, about to bubble over.

"Truman—"

"When you rubbed your nose, you got a little . . ." He points to my nose, where I'm realizing there must be a shit ton of paint because this man is falling apart.

"It can't be that funny," I say, hating that I'm fighting off a smile.

"It's like if Rudolph had a blue nose," he says.

"Wow. *Wow*. I hate that image." I rub at my nose, which must make it worse, because Truman has finally burst. His face is split wide open, he's grinning so wide, his laughter floating up right into those clouds he painted. I'm trying to fight it off but he ropes me into it, too. And then we're both laughing like a bunch of children, doubled over, half crouched onto the floor, braced on our hands for support. And Truman is so close. So intoxicating with paint swirled onto his skin, disappearing between the fabric of his T-shirt. I'm filled with this insufferable urge to take it off and see where the blue and white lines touch his skin. I want to kiss him again. It would be so easy to. Maybe it'll feel like no time has passed. Maybe it'll feel like it did that night in his bedroom, like we were teetering into something great. The past and the present are blurring together. These feelings stir in my chest. I remember how his lips felt, how his hands felt cradling my face. It's so strange how effortlessly you can slide back into someone's life and it feels like no time has passed, like nothing has changed—yet everything is different.

"Let's even the playing field," I say. I swipe my paintbrush onto his forehead. A faint blue smear covers his skin. I hate how it only brings out his eyes more. Of course he can pull off being covered in paint. So incredibly cruel, this guy.

I must be scowling. But Truman is smiling. He looks . . . happy. Like genuinely happy, through and through. I can't remember the last time I saw Truman happy. Or the last time I felt, well, whatever it is I'm feeling.

Truman holds up his paintbrush up to my face like a threat. "Don't make me, Eden."

"You wouldn't dare," I say with as much fear-inducing vigor as I can manage. It seems to work because Truman drops the brush onto the floor, then lies down right there, on top of the tarp.

"Wow," he breathes. "It really does look like we're under the sky."

So I lie down beside him. I want to see, too. And he's right. He is so, so right. From down here, we could be anywhere. Lying in a meadow. A park. On the chair in Katie's old backyard all those summers ago. Instead we're here, under the sky that Truman created. It's somehow better than the real thing.

Truman tilts his head to the side. He's looking at me now, but I'm not sure which version he is seeing: Eden, his sister's quiet best friend; Eden, the girl who sat on the edge of his bed and waited for a kiss. I am hoping that what he sees is the person I am now: Eden, the girl who is trying her hardest to push forward, who wants to feel happiness again. And I don't know how or why, but I think that when Truman looks at me, he very well might see just that.

The paint has already dried on Truman's face, little blue flecks dotting across his skin. I do the one thing I'm scared of—the one thing I want to. I reach out and run my fingers through his hair. I separate the strands that are stuck together with paint. I watch as his chest rises and falls, this gentle reminder that we are here.

"Let's call it a truce," he says out of nowhere.

I don't ask if he's talking about the paint fight or everything else—the five month silence, the distance, me avoiding him. For so long it's felt like we've been on opposite sides, existing so far away from one another. And now we're beginning to drift back to each other, closer and closer toward the middle. So I say, "Okay."

My heart is beating so quickly that I can hear it more than feel it. It's right here, pulsing in my ears, ringing through my mind.

So we lie there, blue paint on our skin, smiling at one another. I know that time is still ticking away, that somewhere outside these four walls, people are rushing through the city, running off to work, to class, to meetups with friends. But here, watching the paint dry on Truman's skin, we are in a separate world entirely.

"Your eyes look like the sky," I say. They are blue and vast and terrifying.

When Truman's fingers curl around mine, I let them.

18

TRUMAN

I KEPT WAITING FOR the flinch. For Eden to recoil. To move away from me. Drop my hand and, I don't know, get as far as possible. We lie here and I keep waiting. It never happens.

It's the first time Eden has touched me since that night when I kissed her. The first time she hasn't tried to keep this distance between us. Here and now, with our fingers stained blue, interlocked together.

"Yeah, well, blue's your color," I say. The paint is smudged across her nose and onto her cheeks.

She rests her cheek flat on the floor, turns to me. Her eyes are molten brown, smoldering and inescapable. "You think?"

"I think."

I tell myself to get my shit together. I feel winded from holding Eden's hand. From being inches away from her. I wonder if oxygen seems to disappear when we're so close for her, too. Or if her heart is pounding against her rib cage like the world's fastest drumbeat. I can't be the only one feeling this charge, this electric storm building inside me. She looks so calm with her hand on her chest, the other in mine.

This is Eden, the girl I've spent every single day for the past five months thinking about and hoping to see again. The same girl who has made it her mission to ignore every aspect of my life. Which was fine once I had started to accept it. Until now—now when she lifted the lock and let me inside. And I'm stuck here wondering how the hell I'm ever supposed to stay away from her again.

"You need to go get Purrnicus," she says suddenly.

So that's what she was thinking about: Katie's cat. Forget about different pages. We're on two completely different *books*. "Why?"

"He's Katie's cat. He should be here, don't you think? Like, closer to her."

"He's an outdoor cat, Eden. He would hate it here."

"But he's at your old house all alone," she says.

"My dad goes to check on him. And I thought you hated that cat?"

"I do," she says quickly. "He's a terrible, terrible cat. Maybe the worst cat."

"For a terrible cat, you seem to care a lot about him."

And now she is glaring. God forbid someone finds out this girl has a heart.

"Do you ever go back there?" she asks, swiftly changing the subject.

"I try not to," I say, swallowing the lump that has appeared in my throat.

The thought of having to explain why I stay away from that house is exhausting.

"I get it," Eden says.

The lump disappears. So this is what it feels like to talk to someone who understands you, huh? To not have to harp on and explain every deep feeling or troubling thought. To have someone pull back the curtain guarding your mind and not run for the hills. Eden gets it. I think she's the only person who really does.

"Let's talk about something that isn't completely depressing," Eden says. "What's your favorite movie?"

I laugh. "*Good Will Hunting*. It's this movie my dad loves. He used to watch it with Katie and me all the time. Have you seen it?"

"I don't watch movies," she says. This girl is the strangest person on the planet. And I can't get enough of her.

"So you hate happiness—got it."

I notice the second Eden lets go of my hand. She's staring up at the ceiling, holding her hands to her chest. The smell of paint is heavy as a cloud. I should get up and open the window . . . I don't move.

"I have a short attention span," she says. "Anything over forty-five minutes is torture."

"So at forty-six minutes you're mentally checked out?"

"I pack my bags and leave."

"Weirdo," I say.

"I'm unique," she says matter-of-factly. Then, "I know those paintings you had at the art exhibit were of me."

I don't even know what to say to that.

"It's fine," she says quickly, still not looking at me. "I'm not mad about it or anything. I didn't realize at first, actually. But I'm right, aren't I? The girl sitting on the bench? The two people holding each other?"

Of course she's right. Of course I'm a complete fucking dumbass. In my defense, those are two of my favorite paintings I've ever done. And Eden showing up at the exhibit that night and seeing them never even crossed my mind. I would've bet on a meteor striking me directly before that ever happened. Then she was there, staring right at these creations of her. I had hoped to God she wouldn't realize. I thought I had gotten away with it. Clearly I'm an idiot.

"You're right," I say. There isn't a big enough shovel to dig me out of this hole.

"Why'd you paint me?" she asks.

This is the fork in the road. I can tell her the truth or I can lie.

I decide on the truth. "Because I kissed you," I say, "and I couldn't stop thinking about it. Then Katie was gone. Then you were gone. I felt gone, too. And anytime I stared at a canvas and tried to create something, the only face that came to mind was yours and hers. You can guess which was more painful to think about."

I tear my eyes away from the ceiling and look at Eden, who seems to be trying very hard to not look at me. "Oh," is all she says. It might be for the best, because if she were to say she never thought about the kiss, that would hurt. But if she were to say that she couldn't stop thinking about it either . . . that would almost be too much to process. And suddenly the sliver of space separating us is way too big.

"Eden?" All I want is for her to give me something: a laugh, a smile, another syllable. Then she props herself up on her elbows, her hair falling around her shoulders in these insanely dark waves. Her eyes meet mine before falling to my mouth, and she doesn't have to say a single word. I know she's thinking about the kiss. Not only that, but she's thought about it, too. Maybe she really has replayed it and fixated on it the same way I have.

I wait for her to reach out, lean forward, give me some sort of hint that she wants this, too. Then she's standing up and dusting off her clothing. "I should get going. I have to be at work soon," she says.

I have to try really hard to not ask her to stay.

Once Eden has left, I fall onto the couch and unlock my phone. I try not to overthink it as I open up Instagram. I switch to my anonymous art account. The profile photo is my reflection in a bathroom mirror. I edited the picture so that it's blurry and my face can't be made out. Now I replace the edited photo with the original so that my face is right there for all my followers to see. I replace the alias *Capote* in my bio with *Falls*. And just like that, there is nowhere left for me to hide.

It feels sort of nice.

19

EDEN

I LEAVE TRUMAN'S APARTMENT and I'm feeling giddy in a way I most definitely do not approve of. I'm like a slab of marble that someone has finally begun chipping away at, and it feels strange to be . . . happy. Even if it's the tiniest amount. But if I'm being honest with myself, it doesn't feel strange at all. It feels good. It feels *nice*. It's a feeling I can get used to, even if I'm still not entirely certain if it's a feeling I deserve.

I get home and Ramona is nowhere to be found. And our apartment is so tiny that there are barely any places for her to hide. She must have gone out with a friend or is taking up a booth at some new restaurant. I could check her Instagram but I'm already running late, so I say a little prayer that Mona hasn't been kidnapped, quickly change into my work clothes, and head over to Pollo Loco.

It's an effort to stop my thoughts from replaying every detail of the day. I keep seeing the fluffy clouds Truman painted and then trying to imagine how Katie's bedroom will look once it's been completed. I speed through our time together and my brain gets stuck on one detail: Truman's hand in mine. And not because it felt strange or foreign, but rather because it felt warm and right. That might be the scariest realization of all—that spending time with Truman was nothing like I thought it would be. I expected the memories of Katie to be playing through my mind at full force. Being near her brother was enough of a reason for the past to catch up with me and weigh me down.

Instead it felt effortless. Like that bedroom was a safe space to talk about Katie, and talk about her in a way that made me want to *keep* talking about her. Her memory wasn't painful anymore. It was healing. And that was the strangest part, because it's never felt like that before.

Now I'm stuck dealing with the realization that spending time with Truman Falls might be exactly what I've needed all along.

It's a startling realization. Extremely inconvenient. Definitely borderline inappropriate.

And yet here I am, stepping off the subway, a few minutes away from Pollo Loco, already wondering when I can see Truman's lanky self again. Dammit.

None of that matters right now. I walk into Pollo Loco and I skid to a halt like a cartoon character. No wonder Ramona wasn't at home. She's *here*, sitting in a booth across from Manny.

The bell chimes when I open the door. They both look at me

in sync. I'm in such a good mood that I find it kind of adorable instead of insanely annoying. Manny is grinning so wide I think his face might split in two. Ramona has the decency to be embarrassed.

"Eden!" Manny calls, waving me over. "Come sit."

I walk over, thinking about how weird it is to see Manny anywhere but in the kitchen. Mona slides across the leather seat to make space for me. I settle in, eyeing the two of them and waiting for an explanation.

"What are you guys up to?" I ask suspiciously.

Mona's phone is resting on the middle of the table. She picks it up and holds it out to me. Her Instagram page is pulled up to a post of her outside an ice cream parlor, licking a chocolate cone. "Remember this gelato shop I posted last month?"

No, I don't. "Yes," I lie.

Mona rolls her eyes, seeing right through me. "Their business was struggling, Eden. After I made that post, they blew up on social media. Remember? I've told you all of this. The owner reached out to thank me for that post. They even named a flavor after me?"

Ah, yes. Now I remember. "The Mona-Lime-A," I say to prove that I do in fact pay attention when people speak to me. "Lime gelato with graham cracker chunks."

"Sounds delicious," Manny chimes in.

"What does that have to do with Pollo Loco?" I ask. Then realization hits a second later. "Oh. *Oh*."

"I'm going to work with Manny and make some posts for the restaurant," Mona explains, her fingers doing that unconscious habit of twisting pieces of her hair into a braid. "I think it can really help bring in some business if I market it correctly. Fill this place up with some younger people."

I'm totally on board with that. "Young people do leave the best tips," I point out.

Manny chuckles. I notice that his T-shirt is crisp, without a single stain on it, and that his usually fluffy curls have been tamed down with product. Huh. I decide I'll bug him later for trying to look cute for my roommate.

"My dad's really going to appreciate this, Ramona," Manny says, staring at her from across the table like he's ready to get down on one knee and propose.

"It's no biggie. And I'm excited to work with you," Mona says in that sweet-like-sugar voice of hers. It's so adorable I think I might be physically sick.

I make a big show of prying myself off the booth and standing up. "I'm going to clock in. You two keep doing whatever this is." I head off to the back, leaving Mona and Manny to talk business and probably fall in love. The collab is somewhat of a great idea. If Mona can really play a hand in filling this place with customers, she'll be helping out the Álvaro family in an unrepayable way.

In the back room, I'm in the middle of shoving all my belongings into my locker when something catches my eye. Since this is the storage-room-slash-washroom, there's always a bunch of random stuff stored in here: Christmas decorations, boxes of old plates, an entire shelf stacked with bottles of dish soap. Now I'm interested in the box of tools. Specifically the hammer. . . .

At the end of my shift, I ask Manny if I can borrow it. He says yes.

When I'm in my bedroom that night, the painting Truman gave me is leaning against my desk, right where I've left it. Katie and I are locked in a staring contest— Well, *I'm* locked in a staring contest with a painting, but it's so realistic that I'm expecting it to blink at me any second.

I analyze my bedroom again because my indecisive self cannot choose a spot to hang it. The painting can go above my bed, but the irrational fear that it'll fall in the middle of the night and knock me unconscious has me leaning more toward hanging it above my desk.

Fully aware that I should grab a measuring tape and make sure it's centered on the wall, I opt to go in blind. I grab the nail I also stole from Pollo Loco and pick a random spot on the bare wall above my desk. I eyeball it and find what seems to be the middle. I hit the nail with the hammer, knowing full well that Ramona is sleeping down the hall and will probably wake up and kill me. Still, I hit the nail again, then again, then one more time, until it's really wedged in there and only the circular head is peeking out.

I'm careful when handling the painting of Katie. I balance it on the nail, push it a little to the left so that it's even. Then I take a step back and stare at my best friend's face, because there is nothing left to do. She's there, in the water, staring up at the sky in a way that makes it feel like she's staring right at me.

The strangest realization hits me: I don't feel entirely alone anymore.

20
TRUMAN

I SPEND THE NEXT two days working on Katie's bedroom. The walls are fully painted, the furniture is shining with its second coat, and the only thing left is the ceiling. I realize my mistake when it's too late: that I should have painted the ceiling first to avoid paint dripping down. There's nothing I can do about it now. I buy an extended paint roller and have the first coat finished in a couple of hours. Then my arms are aching and I'm dying to visit Katie and tell her that her bedroom is almost complete. At this rate, it should be ready at the end of the week.

It's the middle of the afternoon and I need to physically stop myself from falling into bed. I rinse the paint off, then head over to the hospital. When I'm there, the weirdest thing happens. This time when I walk through the hospital's automatic doors, I don't need to take a deep breath and prepare myself for what's about to happen. I think it's because I've never come here with good news before. But telling Katie about her bedroom *is* good news. And it sort of dulls the pain these visits usually offer.

When I exit the elevator on the seventh floor, I spot my mom lingering at the end of the hall. She's talking to Katie's doctor. They're looking down at the chart he's holding. I can't hear what they're saying, but it doesn't seem to be anything good. Not that people ever smile in hospitals, but a smile right about now to cure my nerves would be great. The doctor hands my mom some pamphlets before walking away.

"Mom!" I call out, halfway down the hallway. Her eyes fly upward and she looks nearly panicked. I watch, confused, as she shoves the papers the doctor gave her into her purse.

There are two chairs in the hall outside Katie's room. My mom sinks down into one. It looks like she hasn't slept in days. Thinking about it now, I can't remember the last time I saw her at home.

"I thought you weren't coming by until later," she says. Her eyes are red and puffy. She rubs at her temples with her fingers like she can feel a headache coming on.

"I finished off Katie's room earlier than I planned . . ." Then because I need to know, I ask, "Is everything okay?"

"Everything is the same," my mom says.

The same. It's both good and bad. Good because it means nothing has changed—Katie is still here, still hanging on. Bad because it means nothing has changed—Katie is still here, eyes unopened.

"What were you talking to him about?" I pry. I sit down on the empty chair, fully aware that Katie is a few feet behind this wall.

"We were discussing Katie's treatment going forward."

I have no idea what that means. "Wouldn't it be the same as her treatment now?"

My mom does the strangest thing. She puts her hand over mine on the armrest. She pats it a few times, gives my fingers a squeeze. "We'll see," she says in a way that sounds too final, like there's something she purposely isn't saying. "I need to head out. I'm taking a client furniture shopping. Are you going to stay with your sister?"

Another moment she has swiftly swept under the rug. "Yeah, I'll stay for a while."

My mom leaves and I sit at Katie's bedside and tell her everything about the room: the clouds, the furniture, the colors, the way the ceiling will look when she's lying in bed.

"Now the rest is up to you," I say. "You need to wake up and see it for yourself."

Then the exhaustion from the past few days creeps up on me. I fall asleep on the couch for a few hours. When I wake up, the sky has darkened. The first thing I hear is the machine attached to Katie that always beeps; it's the sound of her heart beating in little red waves that fill the screen. Then I spot Eden sitting on the chair beside Katie's bed. She's running her fingers through Katie's hair.

"Morning, sunshine," she says to me, voice dripping with an expert level of sarcasm. "Sleep well?"

I rub my eyes, blink at the bright lights. "What are you doing here?"

"Didn't know I needed your permission to visit," Eden says. Her hair is tied back in a ponytail, showing off that full, heart-shaped face. She's wearing a faded gray hoodie that's at least three sizes too big. It swallows her whole in an unnervingly adorable way. I really want to cross the room and kiss her.

I don't, of course.

"You must've missed the email. How's she doing?"

"Sleeping," Eden says. I like that. This pill is easier to swallow if I simply imagine her sleeping.

I haul my ass off the couch and every bone in my body cracks. I'm nineteen going on fifty, apparently. I grab a bottle of water off the table, take a sip, then move the empty chair right next to Eden's.

"I know the doctors say maybe she can hear us," Eden says with a soul-crushing amount of hope. Her eyes are wide and red when she turns to me. I can't tell if it's from not sleeping or crying. Maybe both.

"I think she can," I say.

"Have you told her about the sky room?"

"A little bit." It's a tiny white lie. I have a feeling Eden would like to be here when Katie finds out about the room. Maybe I should've waited to begin with.

"Tell her," she all but demands. So I take a deep breath and do that all over again. I sit there and talk to Katie about the room I've nearly finished. I tell her about the blue walls, the fluffy clouds, the furniture, and how if you lie down on the floor, it feels like you're outside in the middle of the world. The weirdest part is that it doesn't feel *weird* sharing any of this in front of Eden. Instead it feels nice to know that she's listening to what I say. That she cares.

"He's taking too much credit, Katie," Eden says. "I practically did all the work. He just stood there and twirled his hair."

"Twirled his hair?"

She's trying so hard not to laugh. "What other reason do you have for keeping it so long?"

"It looks good?" I offer.

The look Eden gives me has me contemplating a trip to the barber for the first time in years. God dammit, this girl. This shot to my heart.

"Anyways," Eden continues, clearing her throat, "I helped out with the room, too. Some would even dare to say I carried the project on my back. Might even have the back pain to prove it."

"Care to put your money where your mouth is?" I ask.

Eden's entire face brightens. "What do you have in mind?"

"If you're such a great painter, paint something."

"Like what?" she pushes.

"Like me."

I'm certain Eden will laugh it off and say something along the lines of *fuck, no*. So when she grins, holds out her hand, says, "You have a deal," I'm glad we're in a hospital because I might literally pass out.

"You're serious," I say.

"Dead serious."

I shake her hand. "You're going to have to excuse us, Katie. This should be interesting."

It's a little past six when Eden and I get back to my apartment. The sunlight is perfect for painting, so I tug open all the curtains and let it pour in. Eden waits on the couch as I gather everything she'll need: a blank canvas, paintbrushes, paints. I'm so excited my hands are kind of shaking. Not sure if it's from spending time with Eden or waiting to see what sort of catastrophe this girl is about to create. On the other hand, it would be very much like her to completely blow me away with the hidden fact that she's an incredible artist. Jury's still out.

I set up the living room, display all the materials on the coffee table, then sit back on the couch. Eden takes the chair across. I watch as she picks up the tray, pours different colors of paint onto it, her eyebrows scrunched together as she concentrates. It makes me wish I was the one painting her.

"All right, Eden. No pressure. We're just laying everything on the line here," I tease, relaxing into the couch cushions while she keeps squeezing paint bottles.

"Will you be quiet? I need total silence. Pretend you're a stone statue," she says, "those ones that can't talk."

"Woooooow. You're in a mood."

"I'm always in a mood," Eden shoots back. She crosses her

307

legs on the chair and places the white canvas on her lap, holding a brush in one hand and the tray of paint in the other.

"You can still admit defeat," I say. "We don't have to suffer through this."

"What makes you so sure I'll be a terrible painter?" she asks, swirling the brush around in black paint. Wonder what part of me she's starting with. So predictable.

"I'm kind of expecting the opposite," I admit.

"I appreciate the confidence boost. Now can you lean back a little? Just relax. And brush your hair out of your face— Yeah, like that. Turn your head to the side a little so the sun . . . Perfect. Now, don't move a muscle."

"And if I do?"

"Don't."

"And if I have to sneeze?"

"Hold it in," she grits out.

"Can't that kill you?" I ask.   •

Her eyes are narrowed into slits. *Slits.* "I don't know, Truman. Let's find out."

I'm laughing away. I can't help it. She's something else entirely.

"What are you starting with?" I ask.

"I thought I said no talking."

"You're a mean one, Eden Flora."

"Have any tape? Wondering if it'll fit snugly over your mouth."

"Any excuse to get close to my mouth, huh?" Now she looks like she might actually lunge off the chair and murder me on this couch. I lift my hands, surrendering. "Fine. I'll shut up. You win."

We sit there in silence. The only sound is the stroke of Eden's brush and her occasional sigh. I can't see a single thing she's painting, but I can tell she's annoyed by the look on her face. And she keeps holding the brush between her teeth to let her hair down, then tie it up, then take it back down. I can't stop looking at her. Not even at her face. But her hands. Her neck. The way the canvas is propped against her knee and the spot of black paint on her fingertip, the color I know she chose for my hair. Looking at Eden is like standing in the middle of a museum. There is so much to see. It's like my eyes are fighting each other to find somewhere to land.

She's mesmerizing.

"Your eyes are annoying," she says when too much time has passed in silence. "There's no paint that's the right color blue for them. They're like glass one second and the sky the next."

"You're obsessed with my eyes—I get it."

"Missed the point entirely."

"Good. Are you almost done?"

"I guess. It's not very good. I'm not good at art, just so you know. Don't expect, like, the *Mona Lisa* or something."

A laugh bursts out of me. "I was never expecting that."

Now Eden smiles. This time, my eyes know exactly where to look. "Good," she says, unfolding herself from the chair. Eden crosses the room, the painting secured tightly in her hands. She angles it away from me so I still can't catch a peek. I'm dying to see

309

how she painted me. It's not lost on me how drastically our roles have flipped. The couch lets out a little groan when she sits down next to me. Her knee knocks into mine. What a ridiculous thing to notice. Still, I do.

"Can I see?" I ask in a way I hope sounds patient and cool, not like I'm practically desperate to see something she's created.

Eden props the canvas on her lap, resting the base on her thighs. She purposely angles it away from me so I can't see a sliver. "It's bad," she says. Embarrassment creeps into her voice in a way I'm not familiar with. Eden is rarely embarrassed. In fact, she's rarely anything other than sarcastic and ready to fire some highly destructive witty remark.

Except now she's gripping on to the painting too tightly. And if anyone can understand the vulnerability that comes with sharing something you've created, it's me.

"I'm not exactly expecting it to be *good*, Eden."

She silences me with a glare. It takes one second for any trace of softness to crumble entirely, then she's back. "My hatred for you reaches new heights every single day," she says. But she's grinning. So I'm thinking that maybe she doesn't hate me at all.

"Just show me. I won't laugh," I promise.

Eden chews on her bottom lip. She tucks her hair behind her ear that's covered in four different piercings. I think Eden's stalling, but then she makes up her mind and, with a weighted sigh, turns the canvas toward me. I study it for a minute. She got the black hair right, the pasty skin, the blue eyes. It sort of looks like me. Or my fraternal twin. Maybe a third cousin at best.

"You were right," I say. "This is definitely *not* the *Mona Lisa*."

"Truman!" Eden holds up the painting like it's a weapon—and I don't doubt this girl can find a way to make it one. Then she thinks better of it and punches my arm, and I'm sure this isn't safe. I mean, the paint is still wet. She's going to destroy my couch and the canvas all at once. But I don't care. I don't think she does, either.

"It's not that bad," she says, studying her work. "Your head is kind of lopsided, and I don't think one of your eyes should be bigger than the other, but it's all right."

"Maybe one of my eyes *is* bigger than the other," I offer.

Eden makes this soft little "hm" and then she's sliding closer to me, leaning in slightly until we're nearly face-to-face. She takes my chin between her fingers, holds me still, and analyzes my face in a way that is too calm to be natural. I don't think I breathe the entire time. In fact, there's a good chance 90 percent of my brain simply stops working. Having her so close, feeling the soft touch of her fingers, is such a startling contrast to how she usually is. Her steely gaze turns soft and liquid, and there's nothing hostile about the way she looks at me.

"They're definitely the same size," she says. Right. My eyes.

"Good to know," I say, sounding winded. God, I might need to lie down.

And then she's moving away, shuffling back over across the cushion, taking all the light and softness right with her.

311

"Not bad for my first try," Eden says. She's trying to change the subject, like that'll sweep whatever that moment was right under the rug.

"It's an A for effort," I say, because my brain is still scrambling to put itself back together.

Eden is setting the painting down on the couch. Something in her brain is telling her that, yes, putting a wet painting down on a white leather couch is a good idea. But she's handling the canvas with so much care it's painfully adorable, so I don't say a word.

She looks at me over her shoulder, hits me with that familiar look of disdain. "Don't be such a dork," she says.

There's a smudge of black paint on her cheek that loose strands of hair have stuck to. I can't stop staring at it.

"Would you rather I be cool and charming?" I say.

Her laughter is a hit to my ego. "If you're even capable of that, sure."

"Can I keep the painting?" I blurt out.

Eden's stunned. "Why would you want it?"

She's right. I shouldn't want it. It's not very good and I can definitely see it haunting my nightmares. But I'm completely fixated on the fact that she made this. That this fiery girl who could barely stand to be in the same room as me a week ago sat down and painted my stupid face, which really isn't much to look at. And if I'm being honest, I think there's a good chance that this thing will get destroyed before Eden even makes it home if I leave her in charge of it.

"I want to frame it," I say, pointing to the blank wall above the couch. "Right here."

"I don't think your parents will like that," Eden says.

She's probably right. "Maybe in my bedroom, then."

Her eyebrows shoot up. It's her only tell. The rest of her face is stoic, pensive, and I want to know what she's thinking. Although I'm fully aware that if I were to ask, she probably wouldn't tell me. 'Cause this is Eden, the girl who covers herself in layers of humor and sarcasm to keep everyone at bay.

"You don't really want it," Eden says. She's wrong. I do want it, so I reach across her to grab the painting. And she . . . She stops me. She clasps her hand over my wrist. It's barely anything. It's insignificant. But we both notice it.

Eden pauses, her eyes locked on the exact spot her fingers are touching me. I don't know how it's possible to feel so aware of someone else's presence, and yet this is how it's always been with Eden. When she's here, she's blinding and bright. When she's not, I can't get her out of my mind.

She's here now.

I move in a little closer. All I can think about is our kiss that ended too quickly. Our future that we never got to explore. The *feelings* that we never got to explore. And maybe it's too late for a lot of things, but it's not too late for us.

"Truman." Eden says it in that voice, the one that warns me that she's going to try to push me away any second. But suddenly, it's urgent that I don't let her. I don't want to be pushed away and cast aside. I can't let another five months pass before I get a chance with her again. All I want is to be right here with her.

For once, I stop thinking about everything that might go wrong. I forget about guilt and regret, about every person who exists outside these walls, and I take Eden's face in my hands. Her mouth falls opens, probably to yell at me, but I kiss her before she can get the words out. I kiss her because it's quite honestly the only thing I want to do.

Eden caves. She leans forward, her body relaxing into mine. I lose myself somewhere in the feel of her hands on my face, then on my back. I can feel the wet paint on her fingertips as they touch my cheek. I can taste the anger and the temptation and how wrong this might be, but neither of us stops. Because we need this.

Because five months was too long.

Because I think this is where we were meant to end up.

21

EDEN

TRUMAN KISSES ME AND my mind is completely empty, like a chalkboard wiped clean. In the smears I see the tilt of his face leaning closer; I see the sky in the blue of his eyes. I replay it over and over again. I commit it to memory. I memorize the way he holds my face. The way he tastes. The way he feels, like the past and the present swirled into this one moment that is teetering on perfect. It is the first time my brain goes completely silent. There are no whispers, no trickles of noise. In the silence Truman kisses me and I feel something soft, something easy. Something that feels like peaceful acceptance, like standing on the brink of happiness.

And still that memory of our first kiss weighs me down. It's always there in the back of my mind, waiting to remind me of why I should stay away from Truman—even in a moment like this when I don't want to.

The second Truman pulls away, he's smiling. "Huh," he says. Not exactly what I want to hear. "Huh?"

"Just didn't really think anything could top that first kiss," he says in the dorkiest way possible.

"Bad things happen when we kiss," I say, partially because it's true, and partially because some part of me feels like ruining this moment is what I deserve.

"I think us not kissing is a bad thing." Truman's hands snake around my waist. I stare up into this face of his that I just spent an hour painting. I really did not do it justice. I'm not sure if anyone can even capture the essence of Truman's face, because it is so much more than the sum of its parts. It's not about the curve of his mouth or the color of his eyes—that's where I was wrong. It's about the way his entire demeanor softens when he speaks; the way he offers the smallest smile at the mention of Katie; the way the lines of his face smudge into gentle arches when he's near me. It reminds me of the way he paints, with this perfectly measured amount of precision, not too light but not too much pressure. He softens in all the right ways.

"Can I ask you something?" Truman says. He's still pressed against me, his forehead resting on mine. His words tug at my heart. I worry he's going to say something that will ruin the moment and have reality crashing back in.

"Okay," I say slowly, already feeling the moment slip away.

"I always wondered why you avoided me after Katie's accident." He says it with so much hesitation that it splits me in two.

"Is it because you blamed me?"

I must've heard him wrong. "Blamed *you*? The only person I blame is myself."

I feel his hands tense on my waist. "Blame yourself for what?"

"Katie's accident," I continue. I could never admit this to anyone. Anyone but him. "It was my fault. I was the last person to see her. I spent the entire night in her bedroom with her. And then I left. I got distracted by you—by kissing you. If I hadn't, Katie wouldn't have climbed out her window. She wouldn't have gotten hit by that car. She wouldn't be in a hospital instead of here with us right now. I convinced myself it was all my fault and I still think it was. And looking at you was a reminder of that night. So I stopped looking at you. I stopped thinking about you. Started avoiding you however I could. I tried to block out all the bad things that happened that night and I think that I managed to block out the good things, too. Because I don't think kissing you was a bad thing. Only what happened afterward was."

I've said too much, but it feels like it isn't enough. I want to dig deeper and tell Truman that I think I have felt this way for him for so long now, like he is the flicker of a light switch when a room gets too dark. That his artwork is a masterpiece and so is his mind, as well as his heart. That I hate how his hair curls behind his ears and I never want it to stop. That kissing him that night in his bedroom destroyed me entirely because I regret it so much— but the worst part is that I don't regret it at all. I would kiss him one hundred times over again. In any bedroom. In any art exhibit.

317

With any color paint on my hands. I would choose him time and time again because he is remarkable in every single way.

"That's why you ignored me?" he asks. "Because of guilt? You think this is *your* fault?"

"Whose else would it be?"

"Mine," he says so quickly. "It's my fault, Eden. Everything has been. I'm Katie's brother. I should have been looking out for her that night, not you. None of this was because of you."

His words stop me entirely. "Truman," I say, "not for a single second did I ever think Katie's accident was your fault."

"I never thought it was yours," he whispers. His fingers tighten on my waist. I lean into that pressure, that gentle reminder.

"So you thought I ignored you because I blamed you for Katie's accident?"

"I did," he says.

Everything starts to click into place. We have both spent the past five months convincing ourselves that we are to blame for Katie leaving the house that night. At what point do we stop? Stop pointing fingers and chipping away at ourselves? I don't think hearts and minds are built to withstand this much self-inflicted damage. I think I need to stop. I think we both need to stop. But how do you quit a habit that's wrapped itself so tightly around your brain? That has seemed to rebrand your entire existence? Because for the longest time I haven't seen myself as Eden anymore, an eighteen-year-old girl who is going off to university in the fall, who moved to a new city and made new friends, who

318

kept her life moving forward when the world tried to pull her back. For months I have seen myself as this: a failure, a terrible friend, the cause of Katie's coma, and the girl who chose a stupid crush over her best friend's life. But in that moment, how was I even supposed to know that Katie's life was on the line? It had only felt like my heart was. I only realized how wrong I was when I was too late. Was that my fault—for not predicting Katie would sneak out? I don't know anymore.

"Maybe we should have cleared all this up five months ago," I volunteer.

At that, Truman laughs. It's like clouds floating across the sky and the sun peeking through. "Maybe," he says. "Or maybe we're allowed to mess up sometimes."

"Maybe," I agree, hoping one day I'll be able to believe it.

"I finished her bedroom, by the way. Well, not the ceiling. But the rest is done."

It feels as if my entire body is smiling. "No way."

"Come on." Truman grabs my hand and pulls me after him. We are down the hallway in seconds, where the smell of paint still lingers in the air. We step into Katie's bedroom. Then we are standing in the middle of the universe.

The walls are incredible, like they were last time. Now the furniture, the pieces we painted, are here, too. The sky continues through and through. I glance to where Truman stands beside me, arm to arm, and he is radiant like the sun.

"I finished it this morning," he says with so much pride. "The walls needed some touch-ups, and I had to fix a few of the— Eden, are you crying?"

Of course I'm crying. I'm a freaking mess and my heart has lodged itself somewhere in my throat. I use the sleeves of my shirt to dry the tears, then push my hair in front of my face to hide the heat rushing to my cheeks. "No," I say, awkwardly waving my hand through the air. "I think it's just the paint fumes. Like, the chemicals and stuff making my eyes water."

Truman doesn't buy it. He doesn't call me out on it, either. "Sure. Of course. So, what do you think?"

"It's perfect." It's the only word I can manage without turning into a puddle with a few pieces of black clothing floating on top like the world's worst life raft.

"This is the best part." Truman pulls me down to the floor until we're lying on our backs like we did that day we spent painting. "Squint your eyes," he says, "like you're staring at the sun." I do. Between the haze of my lashes, all I can see is the blue and white. It really does feel like we are staring up at the sky.

"Whoa," I breathe.

"Yeah," he says. "Do you think she'll like it?"

I'm so lost, so completely out of it. I feel so angry that Katie might not ever see this. I feel so happy that someday she might. I feel soft and warm because Truman gave her this—he gave me this, too.

"Eden," Truman says. "Do you?"

"I don't know," I say. "I can't think right now."

"I can move farther away if you want."

"Not because of *you*."

Truman pokes my stomach. I slap his hand away.

"The paint fumes?" he says.

"The paint fumes," I say, turning my head to the side to meet his eyes. They are there, waiting, knowing that *paint fumes* is just a cover for something that is too hard to say.

I feel his pinkie touch my wrist in this gentle, hesitant way, as if he wasn't kissing me a few minutes ago. I wonder how long he's going to make himself be this careful with me. I wonder how long it will take for the scars we both got that night to begin to fade.

"I was upset that you left this summer," I whisper when the silence has stretched on long enough that my voice sounds far away. "I couldn't understand how you left Katie. How you left me. I get it now, honestly, I do. But at the time I didn't."

This time, when I look at Truman, his eyes are closed and his head is facing the ceiling, but his fingers are still there, on my wrist.

"I hated you for leaving Katie," I say.

"That's okay."

"But I think I was really upset that you left me."

"I'm sorry," he says, eyes still shut.

"Me too," I say.

I don't know who moves first, but then our faces are only an inch apart, and I'm wondering why Truman needed to replicate the sky when all I have to do is stare into his eyes to find it.

"I need you to do one thing for me," Truman says. "You always used to tell me that Katie didn't like when we spoke or hung out."

"She didn't." She never really said why. Maybe she was jealous for my attention to be on anyone but her.

"Well, I don't want you to stay away from me anymore, Eden. So you might need to break your word to Katie."

"Break my *word*? You make it sound like I took a blood oath."

"Sounds like the type of weird shit you two liked to do."

"We drank juice boxes and got sunburned by your parents' pool. I don't think blood oaths were very high on our to-do list, Truman."

His chest convulses as he laughs, eyes dancing in this dreamy, sparkling way. And then I'm sick to my stomach for using such nice adjectives to describe this dude. But maybe he deserves it. Maybe.

"Point is," he continues, "are we doing this or what?"

"And they say romance is dead." This time it's me who inches closer. "Katie's not going to like this," I whisper.

"She doesn't have to like it," he says.

Then Truman is kissing me again. The sky above feels like it's entirely ours.

22

TRUMAN

IT TAKES EDEN A few days to decide that the most important task in her life right now is reuniting Katie with Purrnicus. "He's her cat, Truman. She hasn't seen him in *five months*." She keeps emphasizing the amount of time that's passed like it's the strongest point in her argument. I don't even know if cats can recognize the passing of time. I'm pretty certain they can't.

"All we need to do is drive to your old house, pick up Purrnicus, bring him to the hospital for an hour or so to be with Katie, then we'll plop him back outside before his curfew," Eden says. She is sitting on the floor in my bedroom, digging through a milk crate of old paintings. The memories I have of her doing that are so sharp I have to peel my eyes away.

"We can't take a cat on the subway," I say.

"Have you forgotten you own a car?"

"You don't like being in cars," I point out.

She goes silent, then says, "I'm willing to try."

That is when I realize how much this cat means to her.

"Are you going to keep asking me until I say yes?" I ask.

Eden pulls out an old shitty painting I did of a sunset, stares at it for a second, then puts it back in the crate. "I'll wear you down eventually," she says. "You might as well save us both some time and say yes now."

I leave my bed and walk over to the desk. My keys are right there, thrown on top of my laptop. I pick them up, twirl them around my finger. "Let's get this over with."

Eden is jumping around in a very un-Eden-like way. It's sort of alarming, actually. "Katie is going to love this," she says, already running out of my room and down the hallway. She's hurrying down the stairs, still talking about this cat.

"I thought you hated Purrnicus," I say, remembering all the times Eden hissed at him and called him a variety of nicknames, the most popular being *loser* and *this fucking cat*. Clearly she's had a change of heart.

"Oh, I can't stand him."

On second thought.

"But Katie loved him," she continues, "and reuniting them feels right. Plus, I went by your house a few weeks ago and he seemed really lonely. He kept scratching his fat little head against my ankle. That's when you know he's desperate—when he looks to me for affection."

It takes Eden a while to get into the car. I don't say a word.

I don't push her because it's not my place. I can't begin to understand how this must feel for her, how scared and nervous she must be. I leave her to it. She sits in the seat for fifteen minutes before strapping on her seat belt. Then she sits there for another ten. I place my hand on her knee. "How's it going?" I ask.

"Let's go," she says.

"Are you sure?"

"Yes," she says, steel through and through.

The drive back home takes an hour. The traffic is backed up and consistent; it doesn't let up until we're off the downtown streets and taking the ramp onto the highway. Then the skyscrapers and endless shops turn into long stretches of greenery and industrial buildings. Hotels, car dealerships, places of worship. We're heading back home.

Eden has a Tupperware balanced on top of the cup holders. It's filled with food from Pollo Loco. She asks me—or orders me, actually—to stop by her parents' place so she can drop it off for her dad.

"What is it?" I ask. She won't let me peek inside.

"Just some chicken and potatoes Manny made last night."

I take my eyes off the cars for the smallest second to look at Eden. Her hair hangs down her shoulders in thick dark waves. Her eyes are wide and bright, and she's smiling while squinting against the sunlight. I think back to all the times we spent driving around together in the *before*. When Katie sat in the passenger seat, Eden in the back, and I was their chauffeur. Then I would glance at her in the rearview for barely a second. It was all the time I could risk. Now I can't take my eyes off her. And I feel lucky to be able to.

"Why don't you bring me some food that Manny made, huh?"

"Why don't you come visit me at work and buy it yourself, huh?" she fires back.

"If you want me to come visit you at work, just ask. Enough with the hints already," I tease.

My eyes are back on the road. I can feel her glare like two burning hot lasers, piercing through my skin, breaking right through my armor.

I drop Eden off at her parents' house and she runs inside, carrying that silly container of food like it's the Olympic torch. The front door opens and I recognize her dad, who pulls her into a hug. Then he waves to me and I'm wondering what he must be thinking, or how much he knows, or if Eden has told him anything about us. Is there even an *us*? I don't want to harp on labels. I'm happy she's back in my life. It's as simple as that.

Barely five minutes pass before Eden is running back down the driveway and hopping into the car. I notice that this time she doesn't even hesitate. She sits right down, buckles her seat belt, and we're driving the short distance to my old house. I've only been back here once in the past couple of months, to grab some supplies after returning home from Montreal. I had no interest in revisiting this place and all the memories that live there. But I'm realizing that facing it with Eden by my side makes it seem a bit more manageable.

I begin to pull into our driveway and, sure enough, Purrnicus is sprawled out right in the center of it, sleeping on his back under the sun.

"I guess he's sort of cute," Eden remarks. She's lying through her teeth. That cat is fucking adorable.

I park the car off to the side, giving the little guy all the room in the world, and then Eden is kneeling down beside him, scratching the tufts of fur behind his ears. I crouch down beside her and rub his belly. He's purring so loud it sounds like someone's turned on a chainsaw.

"Hey, bud," I say, running my hand along his tail. Eden is plopped down right on the driveway, legs crossed and everything. "Uh, you coming inside or what?"

"Is it okay if I wait out here? I really don't want to go inside there," she says.

"Oh. Yeah, no problem."

"Unless you want me to come with you!" she says quickly. "Do you? Because I will."

"No, no, I'm fine. Keep an eye on Purrnicus so we don't have to search for him through the entire neighborhood."

Eden smiles up at me. "Remember to grab the cat carrier. I think it's in the front hall closet," she says, because of course she knows my own house better than I do.

The walk up to the front door feels strangely long. I realize my hands are shaking when I go to put the key in the lock. I can't seem to get it to fit. I twist it this way and that, but my hands are trembling so hard the lines won't match up.

I'm not entirely sure if I can do this. And it makes me wonder what must be wrong with me to find it this difficult to open a damn door. But the memories inside are begging to be let out. I don't want to drown in them. I don't want to be caught in the undertow. Because the second this door opens, Katie is everywhere: she is sitting at the kitchen table with the fridge door left open; she is lying on the couch, flipping through television channels; she is the soft footsteps heading up the stairs; she is the girl standing in the hallway in bunny slippers; she's the early riser brushing her teeth at six a.m.

I begin to feel crushed with this onslaught of the past until I feel a hand close over mine. It's Eden's. She guides the key into the lock. She pushes the door open. She takes my hand in hers. "Come with me," she says, and leads us into the house.

We step inside and the silence is haunting. Everything is right where we left it. Katie's shoes are still set at odd angles on the carpet from where she tossed them off. Her coat still tilts off the hook. I try to find an inch of space she hasn't touched and fail.

Eden knocks her shoulder against mine, squeezes my hand. "She's everywhere, huh?"

"Everywhere," I repeat.

I watch in awe as Eden walks toward the closet, digs inside, and pulls out a pale-yellow pet carrier. "Knew it was in there," she says. Then she is back by my side and the heaviness lifts a little. "Need anything else?"

I don't. We leave. Eden takes the key this time and locks the door behind us. Outside, the air is stiff and the sun is blinding. I try to gasp for breath as quietly as I can so Eden doesn't realize the extent of how messed up I am.

I join her back on the driveway. She has the carrier right next to Purrnicus. She opens the little metal door and tries to push him inside. He's not having it, though. He keeps wiggling on his back, belly thrust in the air, sun warming his skin.

"*This fucking cat*," she seethes. Somehow, it makes me feel ridiculously better.

I pick up Purrnicus and plop him into the carrier. Then we're back on the road. Purrnicus meows the entire ride and I keep shooting Eden looks that say *told you this was a bad idea*, but she is smiling so wide at that freaking cat that she doesn't even notice.

"Are we even allowed to bring cats inside the hospital?" she asks.

Then we both realize our mistake.

"Probably should have figured that out before driving here," I say.

"Probably."

I call the hospital and manage to speak to Celia, Katie's nurse. I explain the situation and she agrees that it's fine to bring in Purrnicus, just for an hour or so. Then we are back in the city, Eden is glowing, and the hospital pops into view.

The second we step into Katie's room, Eden shuts the door and opens the carrier. Purrnicus is hesitant. He stays inside it for a few minutes, making a big show of sniffing around. Then his paw touches the tiled floor, then his other ones do. Then he is walking around the room with all the curiosity in the world, smelling every inch and crevice.

"All right, you scoundrel, we brought you here to see Katie, not sniff to your little heart's content. Let's go." Eden picks him up and plops him on the bed, right on top of Katie's legs.

We both stand back and watch. Purrnicus sniffs at the blanket, then walks up Katie's stomach to her pillow. He smells her chin, her hair. And then he just falls down right there, curled into her chest. The room is so silent we hear him purring.

I keep expecting Katie to wake up right now. There can't be a better moment than this. But no matter how much Purrnicus nudges his head into her cheek, her eyes don't stir. Still, I think she'd be happy to know he was here.

"You made the right call," I say to Eden.

Her eyes are filled with tears when she turns to me. "Don't sound so surprised."

Eden goes to work that night and I bring Purrnicus back to the apartment. I'll drive him back home tomorrow when I don't feel completely wiped out. I'm lying in bed, Purrnicus balled up at my feet, when my parents step into my room. It's so jarring to see the two of them standing in here. Especially when they look like this. My mom is giving me the same smile she gave Katie before breaking the news that her hamster had died.

"What's going on?" I ask. I barely have time to worry about the last time I vacuumed in here. My mind is already prepping for the worst-case scenario.

"There's something we need to speak with you about," Dad says in that detached lawyer voice of his.

My heart sinks.

"Okay," I say. *Okay. Okay. Okay.*

This doesn't seem like it's going to be okay by a long shot.

"Can we sit?" Mom asks, quite obviously stalling.

I sit up in bed and free up space at the end. They take a seat, taking turns petting Purrnicus, who instantly begins purring. *Read the room, bud.* Then Mom grabs him and cradles him against her chest. She looks like she has aged backward, turning into a child as she rubs her cheek against his.

Now they both are staring at me, the same way they did that night when I walked into the hospital, Eden in tow. I remember my mom couldn't speak. She just stood there, frozen, staring at something no one else could see. My dad was the one to grab my shoulders, whisper the details of Katie's condition, and lead me into the waiting room.

This feels like that.

My entire body goes cold, like oxygen and blood and whatever else it's made up of just ran for the hills.

"We were talking to Katie's doctors last night," Dad begins.

I stop listening sometime after that. Mom's crying came easy. It's her smile that is forced. I wonder why she thinks she has to pretend this is a good thing. We all know it isn't. My dad is saying words like "quality of life" and "Katie wouldn't want this" and I'm thinking this is ridiculous. The only person who knows what Katie wants is lying in a hospital bed right now, unable to speak.

There is no air in this room.

I never really thought about how long Katie would be in a coma for. I always assumed she'd wake up one day and I'd drive her home. She'd see her new bedroom furniture and smile, probably call me lame and tease me for missing her. I'd deny it, then eventually tell her that I did. There was never a point where I imagined us having to make this decision for her. I tried not to imagine any type of future my sister wasn't a part of.

If not for the permanent oxygen tube allowing her to breathe, she'd look like that princess she loved, like she was asleep. But she flew through the windshield when the car hit her, and her brain wasn't the only part of her that was damaged. She couldn't breathe on her own.

"Truman?" It's my mom's voice this time. Gentle, like the way she used to call my name in the middle of the night when I was little, peeking her head through the doorway to check if I was asleep.

"Yeah."

"What are you thinking?"

"I don't know," I say. I'm screaming on the inside. I'm breaking straight through the bone.

"It's almost been six months." Dad this time. He's crying for once. "You know she wouldn't want this," he whispers.

The worst part is that he's right. Katie wouldn't want to spend years in a hospital bed, holding on because we want her to.

"We don't need to decide tonight," Mom says, "but it's something we need to think about."

"Okay."

The conversation is over.

I wait for my parents to leave. After they are gone, I don't move. I pretend my body is lead and sit in that same spot until the sun rises. I imagine what this would feel like for years, not being able to move. I realize it sucks. Then I'm thinking that this might be Katie's life forever.

She wouldn't want this.

No one would.

Is it selfish to keep her alive? To visit her in a hospital room for the next decade because none of us have the strength to say goodbye?

My parents want to take her off life support, but I don't think they realize Katie isn't the only one on it. I am, too. Pulling the plug might take me down with her.

23

TRUMAN

A WEEK HAS PASSED and my parents haven't changed their minds. We are sitting in Katie's hospital room, which has now become our new family room, the only place where all four of us are together. My parents are on the couch and I'm on the edge of Katie's bed. Her feet stick out from the blanket and her toenails are painted yellow, no doubt Eden's work.

I look away. I close my eyes, clench my jaw. I want to be anywhere but here, anywhere but stuck inside my own life, my own mind.

The doctor walks in, long white beard and round stomach. He is smiling in that soft way doctors smile around us. Like anything a bit rougher will rip us to shreds. It very well might.

He and my parents begin talking about Katie's options. Again, I tune out.

I think about Eden. About how I still haven't told her. I think

I'm waiting for my parents to change their minds. For a banner to roll down from the ceiling that reads *Gotcha*. Once Eden knows, it's all over. It becomes real. And it's easier for me to keep all this pain inside. I don't want to pass it on to her. Not when she's only begun feeling happy again.

But if my parents go through with this . . . I don't know how much time Katie would have left. How many days we'd have to say our goodbyes. They have to make their choice so I can make mine.

I close my eyes. All I see is black and I wonder what Katie sees. I hope she sees blue. That there are clouds and sunshine, and that sound the sunrays make on summer days. I don't want her to spend eternity staring into endless darkness.

How do I say goodbye to my little sister? How do I say goodbye to someone who isn't here to hear it? I need her to wake up, right now, for just one second. I need to tell her I'm sorry. There are so many more words I need to say to her.

Then I hear those two words again: life support. It's my dad's voice this time. I open my eyes and the doctor is nodding. I read his lips. *Whenever you're ready*. That's the problem. I never will be.

Pulling the plug feels like giving up. And I can't give up on Katie. Not before I can give her the sky.

When the doctor leaves, my mom is crying with her head on my dad's chest. I don't have it in me to feel sorry for her. She did this to herself—didn't she?

It's a cruel, disgusting thought.

"Don't do this," I say, not recognizing my own voice. "She can still wake up. She's still fighting. I know she is."

I turn to my sister. I grab her hand, brush the hair off her face. Her eyes are closed. Her skin is pale. The steady hum of the heartbeat monitor fills the room. I squeeze her hand so tightly, begging her to wake up. "Please," I whisper, blinking through tears. "Show them you're still here, Katie. Show them."

But she only lies there, lifeless. Not moving. Not breathing on her own. No witty comeback this time. No yelling. There is no smile, no grip from her fingers. She's here but she isn't and, God, I know what that feels like.

"Truman?" My dad again. He is crying through the words. I don't look. I already know what he will say. "We have two more weeks with her."

I can't breathe. Pain rips through my chest. My heart is burning. Breaking. Shards slicing right through my skin. I try to stand up and stumble back down. I grab Katie's face. I say her name. I might be screaming her name. I beg and I beg and I beg for her to wake up. Right now. There's no time left. *You have to wake up.*

I feel hands on my shoulders, pulling me back. I try to push them off. I need another minute with her. Fourteen days will never be enough. I need these sixty seconds, too.

I keep saying her name. *Katie Katie Katie.* I try to reach out and grab her hand, but I can't move with my dad holding me. So I give up. I fall to the floor. My head hits my knees and I curl into a ball beside my sister. I want to shrink into myself. I want to disappear. More than anything, I want to switch places with her.

I push past my dad. I ignore my mom's tears. I stumble out of the hospital room and down the hallway like a broken man.

I must have been losing my mind because I keep wishing for Eden and then she is here, right in front of me. The elevator doors open and I run to her. She looks like an angel, bathed in yellow. I tug her to my chest and wait to feel whole again. Wait for the love I'm beginning to have for her to stitch me up and sew me shut.

It never happens.

I grab her face. I let her go. I step into the elevator and watch the doors shut. Eden spins around, watching me. Her lips are moving, eyebrows creased in the middle.

Her hands reach out, but the doors are already closing. And then I am moving, down, down, down. Sinking right into the floor. My eyes are so blurry I am seeing double, triple.

When the elevator doors open, I run through them, down the hallway, and straight outside. The sun hits my face first, then the wind. I sink down right there, on the sidewalk, in the middle of the hospital entrance. I lie down, rest my head on the cold ground.

I stare up and all I see is the concrete ceiling above me. It isn't right. This isn't right. I get on my knees and crawl until I see the open sky. Then I lie down and stare at the blue. *Better*, I think. *This is better.*

It might be an hour that passes before I hear someone call my name. There are footsteps. Then a hand is shaking my shoulder. I crack my eyes open and Eden is kneeling beside me. Her eyes are red. Her cheeks are stained with tears.

I reach up to touch her and she pulls away.

She isn't saying my name—she's yelling it.

She isn't shaking my shoulder—she's hitting it.

Eden is screaming. Crying. And I force myself to sit up. Force myself to focus, to stop staring at the sky. I hear my own voice but can't make out the words.

"You knew!" she yells. "You knew about this for a week and you didn't tell me? She's my best friend, Truman! My best friend! You're not the only person who loves her!"

I am teetering off the edge of the world.

Eden grabs my face, focuses her eyes on me. "Truman?"

"I'm sorry," I say, stepping away from her.

Her hands fall to her sides. I can see the heartbreak in her face. I deserve this. I must.

"I thought they'd change their minds," I say. "I couldn't tell you. I couldn't make it real."

Eden is sobbing so hard her entire body is shaking like a leaf in a steady breeze. I want to hold her to me. I want to protect her the way I couldn't protect Katie. But it's too late now. I've let them both down, haven't I?

"You should have told me," she says, hiccuping through the tears.

"I think I might love you," I say. They are the only words that come to mind.

Eden shakes her head. "You don't," she says. "You shouldn't. *We* shouldn't love each other. We can't." She looks down at her hands, reverting back to that old habit of not looking at me, not touching me. "We kissed and Katie's accident happened. Then we kissed again and look at where we are, Truman. We can't do this anymore."

Whatever shred of light that is left inside me burns out when Eden turns around and walks away.

I don't know how I do it, but I manage to pick the broken parts of myself back up and walk home. I'm thinking that Katie's favorite color was pink, but I can't remember. It may have been blue, like the sky she was so intrigued by. Or it may have been orange. She was always painting her nails orange. There are flecks of it all over our kitchen table at home. My mom always told her to paint her nails somewhere else. Katie never listened.

I am thinking that maybe her favorite color was yellow when I walk back into the apartment. I shut the door behind me. The sound of it banging echoes through the space, but I can't really hear it. I'm thinking of yellow: Katie always wore this yellow sweater. It was knit, with a hole at the neck. My dad tried to sew it once, but it only made the hole bigger.

Then I'm sitting on the couch, thinking that maybe her favorite color was red. And then I'm thinking of Eden and how it felt to kiss her.

I didn't see it, but Katie's blood was red, too. When she flew through the windshield and landed on the road. Red. Everywhere.

My dad said it took the ambulance seven minutes to arrive. Traffic stopped when the cars hit. I think the whole world may have stopped as she lay there.

I remember what it felt like when I got the phone call.

I remember what it felt like to kiss Eden in my bedroom that night. It felt like, for once, something good had happened to me. And then I was downstairs at the party, the phone ringing. It was my mom. She was crying, screaming. It took her a minute to even get the words out. *Accident* was what she said first. Then *Katie*. I fell to the ground sometime after that.

And then Eden was there that night, kneeling down beside me. I remember wondering how I had just felt like I could breathe for the first time, and now I was crumpled on the kitchen floor, drowning.

I'm thinking of how white the hospital walls were when I walked in with Eden. I remember blinking against how bright it all was. It smelled clean. Too clean.

I remember seeing my mom standing at the end of the hall, wrapped against my dad. I could hear her crying as soon as the elevator doors opened. I didn't like to hear her cry. It was like her heart was shattering inside her, and the pieces were using her mouth to break free.

I know that's how she felt, because it was how I felt. How I still feel sometimes.

I remember walking into Katie's room with Eden beside me. We had to wait almost six hours while she was in surgery. I don't remember how many bones she broke or what they were called. But I do remember how it felt to stand there and see my little sister lying in front of me. There were too many bandages. They covered her face, her arms, her hands, and her ankles.

I only knew it was Katie because two of her fingers were sticking out. Her nails were yellow.

Eden was crying beside me. This time she sank to the ground first. I had already reached for her once and she pulled away. I couldn't look at her. Not then. Not after what happened. So, I walked to Katie and I held those two fingers. I didn't say anything. I couldn't find the words—they wouldn't come.

Now I close my eyes, rest my head against the couch. The sun is too bright. I try to block it out. I realize that I've lost Eden. I let everyone leave and I'm here sitting on this couch, going through every color of the rainbow trying to figure out which was Katie's favorite.

I decide that it's blue.

I convince myself that it's true.

24
EDEN

RAMONA TRIES SO HARD to help me. She comes into my bedroom and brings me plates of food. She sits on the edge of my bed and tells me that she went to Pollo Loco to see Manny. She tells me that they have hired a new waitress in the past week to replace me because I'm unable to do anything at all. She tells me about how she and Manny are still brainstorming ideas to help business—that she took some photos at the restaurant today to post. She doesn't stop speaking. I stop listening.

How am I supposed to care when the world is falling apart? With Truman gone and Katie about to leave me too, there are no more Falls siblings in my life. And I haven't felt this lonely since before I entered grade nine and met Katie for the first time.

I was the new girl. The weirdo. The kid who had been home-schooled so long she forgot how to make friends or act around people. I was in English. We were reading *The Boy in the Striped Pajamas*. I remember sitting in the last row and feeling alone. Invisible. The teacher said the words I dreaded the most: *Pair up and discuss chapters one through three*. Everyone had someone to turn to except for me.

I was preparing to work alone until this girl sitting in front of me, this girl with the yellowest hair I'd ever seen, turned around and smacked her hand flat on my desk.

"Want to be partners?" she asked. I noticed all ten of her nails were painted a different color. She had red cherries hanging off her pierced ears.

"Sure," I said.

She told me her name was Katie. That was it. That was us.

And now I lie in bed and wish I could go back to that day, to any moment before that spring night when a man drank too much and got behind a wheel and hit my best friend; when I watched Truman break down on the kitchen tiles when he learned his sister might be dead.

I squeeze my eyes shut and hope that these past few months have been a horrible dream. That I'll wake up to Katie snoring beside me in a light pink sleeping bag and Truman sitting on the kitchen counter, feet dangling in the air and a bowl of cereal on his lap.

If I had known there was a drunk driver on the roads, I wouldn't have let Katie leave the party. If Katie's parents were aware of how fragile their son was, they wouldn't take their daughter off life support. If Ramona knew the pain searing through my heart, she wouldn't be bringing me trays of cold leftovers, thinking that it'll help at all. She would just leave me alone. I want everyone to leave me alone.

There are seven days left. Seven more days with Katie.

I fall asleep. I don't wake up for hours. Maybe the entire day. The next morning, I am lost completely, moving through spaces I don't recognize. Our kitchen feels smaller than usual. The entire apartment may have shrunk, like Ramona put it on the wrong dryer cycle. I force my feet into a pair of sneakers and make myself leave this place. I need to get to Katie. There are only seven days left. My time with her has an expiration date now.

Ramona isn't home. She must have gone to some brunch date or to Pollo Loco to visit Manny. It doesn't matter. The only person who understands is Truman. And he lied to me. He kept the most important piece of information from me right when I was foolish enough to think something was happening between us.

I think I might love you is what he said.

Impossible. It is impossible for either of us to ever love each other. There is too much pain, too much grief that will always be between us, stopping us from getting too close.

When I leave the apartment building, I realize that it's nighttime. It's pitch-black outside and I hadn't even noticed. I check my phone—it's nine thirty. Weird.

The route to the hospital feels less familiar than usual. I am wound up like an old broken clock, my thoughts are amplifying by the second, I am ready to unravel completely.

At the hospital, I can't get myself to walk inside. I say this to myself: *There are seven days left. You cannot waste a single second. Do you get that? Stop standing around. Go inside. Stop wasting time you don't have.*

But I can't. I can't, I can't, I can't.

Going inside makes everything real. It makes the clock move forward when all I want is for it to freeze entirely. So I sit down on the bench outside and wait for . . . Well, I don't know.

My mind slips to Truman and how he must be handling this. If I am broken into a hundred pieces, he is in the thousands. He is back in that kitchen, phone clutched in his hand, hearing the news over and over again.

And my thoughts seem to work some sort of evil magic, because then Truman is here, standing in front of me. His details come at me fast—the red smudge to his eyes, the way his hair is messier than I have ever seen it, this indescribable weight that seems to push him closer to the ground.

"Eden," he says.

I blink once. Twice. I wipe away my tears with shaking fingers. I reach out to touch him, to make sure he is real. His hand lifts to fill the space between us. Then his fingers touch mine.

I pull my hand away instantly. "What are you doing here?"

Truman looks broken, even worse than he did that first night in the hospital. At least then there was still hope Katie would wake up one day. Now we have nothing. Only a crushing reality and a life after her.

"I came to see her." He speaks so softly. I notice the look in his eyes, the same one I see in the mirror—this emptiness.

"It doesn't have to be like this," I say. "It shouldn't be like this."

He doesn't even wince. Doesn't show any type of pain. And why should he? His sister is going to die. A few harsh words from a girl he used to care about won't have the same damage. It's hard to split your grief in two like that.

Truman sits on the bench beside me and buries his head in his hands. I don't know why I sit there waiting for him to say something, some lighthearted comment poking fun at me. Of course he never does. Why should he care now? Everything seems insignificant in the face of tragedy.

But still I wait. Wait for some glimpse of this guy I was beginning to know.

When Truman lifts his head and his eyes meet mine, I wait for my heart to skip a beat.

I wait for that familiar feeling of wanting to run into his arms, but all I can think of is the girl who stands between us. The girl who has always stood between us. And I don't want to despise Katie for keeping me from her brother. I don't want to blame her for anything. None of this is her fault.

It is easier to blame myself. To blame him.

Truman removes his head from his hands. His hair is untamable, blowing in the night wind like tendrils of ink spilled on a canvas. "Will you come with me?" he says out of nowhere.

I don't want to speak to him. I don't want to go anywhere with him.

"Come where?" I ask.

It doesn't matter. I know I'll go wherever he says.

25

TRUMAN

I LISTEN TO THE wind howling against the hospital as Eden's eyes search my face.

"I want to go say goodbye," I say.

"Say goodbye?" she repeats. I nod, cross my arms over my chest to fight off the constant coldness I feel. Or maybe I need something to do with my hands so they won't reach for her.

I thought she would have more questions about me appearing out of fucking nowhere. I came to the hospital because I can't sleep. Because there is a countdown on my life now, and it only feels right to spend every second of it at Katie's bedside. But then Eden is here, sitting on this bench alone, looking as broken as I feel, and I can't help myself. I wait for her to ask me to explain. Instead she nods and follows me to my car without a word.

She must know this has something to do with Katie. It always has something to do with Katie. But it isn't just about my sister now. It's about me, too. About Eden. About us. A lot of things have come to an end in these past few days.

A lot will come to an end tonight, too.

The streets are quiet as we drive. There are no cars and barely any light. I have the radio shut off and Eden is silent as we make our way out of the city once more and back to our hometown. I can't find a single word to say. Nothing feels natural. Nothing feels right.

When I turn into our neighborhood, Eden perks up. She looks outside the window, straining her neck to see the houses passing by.

I don't know if she remembers this route. The one I've driven time and time again after the accident. It is branded in my mind, in my eyelids. It is always here, waiting. Haunting. And it's eerie to drive back down this street, to think back to what happened here that night.

Eden must realize where we are going, because she looks away from the window. Turning to me, she says, "Why?"

I don't say anything.

I don't know what to say.

I glance at the clock. Ten thirty. I sneak a glance at Eden. There are goose bumps up her arms. I turn the heat on and look away from her because it hurts too much. Simple as that.

We reach a red light, and my eyes follow the shape of her face in the moonlight. The curve of her lips, dip of her nose, the way her eyelashes kiss her cheeks. I drink her in, every last bit, knowing this might be the last time I get to be this close to her.

Then I look away. But like this route, the image is still there, burned into my mind.

My mind spirals, leaving my hands shaking. My vision blurs. My legs begin to twitch. I can't focus on the road and the traffic lights blur together into a solid rainbow.

I try to pull myself together. Instead I pull over.

"Truman?" Eden says in this quiet voice when the car has stopped. Her words are so gentle. Just like that first night. "What is it?"

"I need a minute."

She sighs. "I get it," she says. "The memories." And she does. She is the only person who does.

And then she reaches across and holds my hand. And I hate it. Hate how good it makes me feel. How whole. How happy. Because I shouldn't feel any of those things. It feels like I'm cursed to be broken. My sister is about to die and it's wrong for me to feel anything but the weight of that.

"I should have told you about Katie," I say when the silence drags on too long. "It didn't feel real, Eden. And I couldn't accept that it was real. That my parents would do this to their daughter. I was trying to protect you by keeping it a secret. I was trying to protect myself."

She pulls her hand away. "Keep driving, Truman."

So I do. I turn the engine on, pull myself together, and wipe the tears from the corners of my eyes. Then I say, "I missed you," because it is impossible to hold this in.

It's there, on the corners of her mouth, the ghost of a smile. It is fitting for the ghost of a girl she has become and the ghost of a boy sitting beside her. That's what we are now: shadows, living in darkness. Waiting for each day to end.

My heart beats too fast when she looks at me like this. Like all she wants is to crawl across the space between us and plant herself around my heart. But I think we both know we can't. That the days of pretending we are happy and able to be together are over.

Because I love Eden. I think I really might love her. But I've gotten used to saying goodbye to the people I love most. And tonight, I am saying goodbye to two.

I can still see the marks of the tires on the road, even though they're long gone.

Eden is hesitating, still leaning against the car. I am walking on where the tire marks once were, tracing the spot the car was driving. Tracing the spot where the accident took place. Tracing the spot where Katie's car flipped, landing on the grass.

It feels surreal. Like a different time, a different life. Like it happened to someone else. Not Katie Falls. Not my little sister.

I kneel on the ground, run my finger along the asphalt. If I close my eyes, I can hear the squeal of the tires. I can hear the sound the cars made as they hit. I can hear Katie's scream, hear the glass breaking as her body goes through it. I can hear the silence of her lying on the ground, barely breathing. And I can hear the sirens in the distance, rushing to her.

That's why I don't close my eyes. Why I always leave them open. Wide open.

I lie down, right here on the street, right here on the invisible tire marks. I don't know where Katie's body landed, but I imagine it was here, right beneath me. And I wish I could sink into the asphalt, turn back time, and let it be me who lay here instead.

I am crying when Eden lies down beside me. We stare into the night sky together, not a cloud in sight. Only stars, littered across the open blue.

I want to give her the sky.

Now I never will.

"I never came back here," Eden says. "After the accident, I refused to drive down this road. I'd take the side streets; I'd walk along the ravine—anything to not come back here."

"I was here every night," I say. "When I couldn't sleep, I'd walk here, lie in this exact spot, and I'd just wait."

"For what?" Eden asks.

"I don't know," I admit. "Maybe for a car to come. For Katie to walk out of the trees. To wake up and find out this was all a dream. A bad, terrible dream."

"Truman . . ."

"She would have wanted this, Eden. Katie wouldn't want to live like that, on life support."

"The Katie I knew would have never given up," Eden says so forcefully I know she wholeheartedly believes it to be true. "She

352

would have kept fighting." And then she is standing up, moving so quickly, walking back to the car and away from me.

I follow suit. I follow her.

Eden leans against the car door. She's crying. I hate how often I've seen her cry. "I'm angry, Truman. Just let me be angry. Let me be upset. Let me scream and let me believe that my best friend is a fighter. That she wouldn't want to die."

I reach out to wipe the tears from her eyes and she pulls away. She won't touch me again.

It's like time is going backward.

26

EDEN

IT STARTS TO RAIN sometime later. It pelts down onto the road, turning the asphalt a sleek black that shines beneath the moonlight. Truman is soaking wet. My clothes are dripping water. I don't know how this night ended with us standing here in the rain, on the road that almost took Katie's life, and it is as if she is here with us, somewhere in the trees or the shadows or even the rain that streams down our faces.

I watch Truman unlock the car, his movements stoic. Reflexive. I can see the weight he is carrying in his bones, see it sink him closer into himself. He sits in the back seat, shuffles over, and holds the door open for me.

When I sit beside him and shut the door, we are bathed in silence aside from the rain hitting the roof of the car. I want to look at him, but the promise of goodbye lingers too heavily between us. This rain may as well be an ocean between us, an endless expanse stretching between our hearts.

Because I am so fond of self-hatred, I turn to him. His hair hangs across his face; water droplets slide down his skin. His blue eyes are impossibly bright in the darkness. I lower my gaze to his hands, which are tapping against his thighs. He looks broken, tormented with ghosts that riddle his mind and cloud his heart.

I think I love him. Or I could love him. I think I could love him for a long, long time. But time was never in our plan. Instead we have moments, short moments like this, where we can steal a kiss and a gaze, and we hold on to them, hoping it will be enough someday when the rain turns to dust and the sky brightens up, when our paths cease to cross and we are nothing more than two people with a doomed past.

"Eden." My name feels so right in his mouth. "I don't want to say goodbye to you," he whispers.

I feel him move closer, feel the heat that warms me from head to toe whenever Truman is within reach. And when his hand finds its way to my thigh, I stare at it.

"This is too hard, Eden. It's too hard to go through without you. I need you here," he repeats.

And, God, it is so selfish. The weight of his words. The desperation in his voice. Of course he needs me. Of course I need him. I need Truman like the oxygen in my lungs. He is a lifeline and he is an anchor and I can't be with him without drowning, too.

We are this terribly ironic tragedy, doomed from the very second we laid eyes on each other.

And still, I reach for him. I grab his head in my hands and, for the last time, I kiss him. I press our mouths together so fiercely until I can feel the cracks in my heart, the ones etched deeply into my soul, start to mend with every touch of his tongue and every graze of his fingers.

I unzip Truman's jacket. I peel the wet fabric from his skin and run my hands across his chest, the curves and the soft lines that pull me from my mind and lift me somewhere above the clouds. I feel his breath on my neck, feel his hands on my bare skin as my clothes find their way to the floor with the rest of his.

I am terrified. I am desperate. I am drowning in guilt and floating on love and I hold him as close as I can because this is the last time my fingers can touch his skin like it is mine for the taking.

He says my name and I hold his gaze, watch his steely eyes pierce my heart and ignite a fire somewhere deep within me. I should tear my body away. I only pull him closer.

"Truman." It is a breath, a release of air, and his mouth is there, on mine, without me having to even ask.

And then he is everywhere. I feel him in my heart, on my eyelids, on my fingertips. He is on my chest and my back and my legs and his breath is clouding my mind and *this is fine*, I think, *I don't want to see a world without him hovering somewhere at the center.*

When Truman whispers *I love you* it feels wrong, but I say it back anyway. I run my mouth across his skin, wet with rain and sweat, and I wrap my legs around his back, pulling him tighter until there is no space left to close.

Maybe it is therapeutic. Maybe it is destructive. Maybe there isn't a difference.

We lie there until the rain stops pouring and thunder no longer vibrates throughout the night sky. The storm is over. So are we. It's final now.

I pull my head from Truman's chest and peer up at his face resting against the glass window. His breath fogs it up with every exhale. Feeling me awaken, he turns his face to mine. We don't smile. There are no flutters in my chest this time. Only aches.

Truman nods and looks away. I slip my clothing back on and climb into the passenger seat. Truman gets dressed, too. A minute later, we are driving through the dark, deserted streets.

When Truman rolls the windows down, the night air blows in. The windows defog, like it erases everything we just did—everything we just were.

We sit in silence until I say, "What now?"

Truman stops at a red light. We are halfway back to the city by now. My apartment building will pop up on the right side of the road in ten minutes.

It is all we have left. Ten minutes to feel like we live in a world occupied by the two of us.

"I don't know," he says. Then, "That's a lie. I do know, Eden. But it's not what you want to hear."

With that, we stop talking.

I already know what Truman wants. He wants us. He wants me. He wants a life of happiness and kisses and heartfelt moments that will forever be trampled on by the guilt that snakes its way around my heart whenever I lay my eyes on his beautiful face.

And I have spent so long going back and forth with myself. Trying to decide whether I could love Truman Falls and live a life consumed by happiness, too. The answer is that I can't. That the guilt will always be there. That as long as we are together, I will constantly mourn the loss of Katie, and he is a walking reminder of the girl I am losing and the choices that led me here.

Truman pulls over in front of my building. I reach into the space between us and find his hand waiting.

"I've always needed you," I tell him. "I always will. But it's not enough, because for how happy you make me feel, the guilt is there, pressing down ten times stronger. I can never be happy with you. I can't be the girlfriend you want me to be. I can't forget Katie or how I let her down. I can't shove it all to the back of my mind. You need to let me go. You need to go be with your sister and spend these last few days with her. You need to forget about me because we can't be happy together. We can't."

I think he is crying, but his eyes are pressed so firmly together that it's difficult to tell.

"Are you going to be okay?" I whisper, feeling his hand go limp in my own.

"Yes," he says. It's a lie. We both know it.

I lean across the seat and kiss him, one last time. I taste the memories and everything we shared and the moment our mouths part, I let it go.

I let him go.

I watch him from outside the car. Watch him in the darkness and shadows he always seems to be in. His gaze is locked on the road ahead. He just sits there, the car idling, like he is too afraid to drive off.

Then his door opens and Truman runs to me, wraps his arms around me, crushes me to him. I press myself into his chest and feel his heartbeat beneath my cheek. It is bright and alive, and I know that one day he will be like that, too.

Truman murmurs something into my hair. I can't make it out. I don't think I am supposed to. This moment is for him.

When he pulls back, he smiles, the smallest of them all—the saddest, too. "I can't promise I won't stop painting you," he says.

As he walks away, I call his name one last time.

He pauses, turns around.

I drink him in, every last detail. His beauty is painful. His heart is beautiful.

"You're an incredible artist, Truman. And a better person than I am."

He gets into his car and drives off.

The words are the truth. He is good. He is loving and kind and the greatest brother Katie could have asked for. It is me who brought him down, me who chipped away at his goodness.

But now he is free. Free to be good without me.

27
TRUMAN

I BARELY SURVIVED LOSING Katie the first time. But the second time, I am ready.

I stand at her bedside. I grip her hand as tightly as I can. I fill the room with her favorite things: yellow nail polish, the stuffed bear that always sat on her bed, her favorite knit sweater, and an old friendship bracelet.

My parents stand on the other side of her bed. My mom is crying. My dad is a stoic anchor. I couldn't cry if I wanted to. I'm hollow from the inside out, a barren desert. A wasteland.

I glance at Katie's face and see all the life it once was flooded with. I can picture her toothy grin, her bright laughter, feel her scrawny elbows jutting out when I gave her piggyback rides. I can feel her ruthless gaze, that hard steel that melted into silk in a flash. Katie is more like me than I ever realized. We are jagged around the edges, but soft as cotton within.

Her doctor enters the room and suddenly, the lights are dimmed. He asks my parents a question. From the corner of my eye, I watch my father nod and pull out his phone. Then a song is playing. I barely register it, but I pull the memory out from somewhere deep in the past. It's Katie's favorite song. The one she'd be dancing to every summer night when I fell asleep on the couch.

As the doctor prepares for the end, I can smell the s'mores Katie used to burn. The vanilla perfume she loved to drown herself in. The waffles my mom baked for her every Sunday morning. I can feel her tiny hand holding mine when we were kids; I can see her wide eyes staring up at me, making me feel like the bravest kid in the world.

I need time. Hours or days. Seconds, even. I will take anything. Any last moment to sit here with her, thinking maybe she could still hear me. Maybe she could wake up. Maybe she would make this all okay again.

"Wait," I say. The doctor turns toward me. My parents watch, confused. "I need a minute with her."

When the room clears, I pull back the blanket on Katie's bed and lie down beside her. I wrap her in my arms, cradle her head against my chest. Something tears through me, ripping me open from the inside out. I wait to cry. Nothing comes.

After all this time, I still can't find the words to say to her. *Sorry* and *I love you* don't seem like enough. Instead I hold her hand and close my eyes. I picture her asleep beside me and we are kids again, tucked away on the grass in the backyard, grass stains on both our knees. I can see the vast open sky above us. Feel the sun on my skin, the wind in my hair. I picture her up there, finally sleeping on the clouds. Safe and happy. Alive and bright. Katie, the girl in the sky.

My eyes open and we are back in the dim hospital room. Her eyes are closed. I brush the hair off her forehead. I kiss her cheek. I tell her that I love her. I hope that wherever she is now and wherever she will soon be, that she can hear me. That she will believe me.

The door creaks open and the room fills with people again. I stand at Katie's side, clutching her hand. *Don't leave me*, I think. *Not yet. Not ever.*

My mom fluffs out her pillow as she shakes with sobs. My dad tucks her in, pulling the blanket right up to her chin.

Faintly, I hear the door to the room open. Someone walks in. We all turn to stare, and it's Eden. She is standing in the doorway and she is holding . . . She is crying, holding dozens of cardboard clouds in her arms. They look like she's cut them out of old boxes and painted them white. There's string attached to them. She holds a roll of tape, too. And then she looks at me with this broken, tiny smile. Because she has done the one thing I failed to do: she has brought Katie the sky.

We all get to work. Even Katie's doctor helps. We tape the clouds everywhere: on the windows, to the walls; my dad even stands on the chair and hangs some from the ceiling. The clouds are bent and the cutting is jagged, but it's absolutely perfect.

I meet Eden's gaze and I hope that she knows what this means to me. What it must mean to Katie. If I ever doubted if I was in love with her, I know the answer now.

And then we are back, gathered around Katie. Eden stands behind me. My parents are together, arms wrapped tightly around each other. I stand there, a buoy out at sea, lost somewhere in the night. I never take my eyes off Katie. Not for a single second. Not when the machines turn off. Not when my mom buries her head in my dad's chest. Not when the room falls silent and I know she is gone.

Eden's hand is on my shoulder. I know there are tears falling down her cheeks like water ebbing downhill. It is pulling me apart, limb by limb. I shut my eyes. I choke back the tears.

The world seems to shift on its axis. Everything goes dark when Katie does. All the light is pulled from the universe, disappearing with her. And every scar on me that had begun to heal is torn right open. She is gone. *Gone.* I want to sink down with her. Bury me with her. Take me with her. Anywhere but here, in this crushing world that feels impossible to breathe in.

I sink onto the bed beside her. I hold her face in my hands. *You're okay now*, I think. *You're okay. It's okay. It'll be okay.* I tell her all the words I wish someone would tell me.

It is our second time in this hospital now, losing the same girl. I thought the pain the first time would end me. But this—*this* is endless. A black hole. No other sadness will ever compare. I'd give anything to feel the pain I felt that spring night. It was a fraction of this. This is crushing, inescapable. I am ash littering the ground. The fire has fully burned out.

Unaware of where I am going, I stand up. I don't want to leave Katie's side, but these four walls are moving in, threatening to crush me. *Why run?* I think. *Let them.* I squeeze my sister's hand for what is, painfully, the last time and stumble into the hallway. Everything is spinning. My eyesight is blurry.

I make it down the elevator and push through the hospital doors. I gulp down fresh air like a drowning man. I keep walking, keep moving. Cross the street and then another one. It's the middle of the night. There are no cars, no people. I stop when my feet give out, just fall to the ground and tuck my head between my knees.

I feel like a stone plucked up and dropped into a lake, doomed to sink beneath the murky tide; like a wanderer dropped in a forest with trees lining every side, without a compass or a sign; like a boy who lost his youth too soon and scrambled hopelessly to put his life back together again, piece by broken piece.

The agony feels endless. The pain is a deep well inside me. I am weighted by grief; it has only been minutes and I am already too weak to survive this. How can I go on? Continue? Stand back up and keep living some semblance of a normal life?

And then the wind blows. It rattles off wind chimes at a nearby shop. My heart stops. That sound, that carefree jingle—it's Katie's laughter. All of a sudden, the shadows seem to part and some shred of light returns. I can see Katie skipping down the sidewalks. I can see her smile, bright as the morning sun. The world is still filled with her. Memories and moments take over the air. She is everywhere, alive through me. I want to wrap my hand around her arm. *Stay*, I'd say. She would this time. There is nowhere left to go.

I'd tie a string around her arm and the other end around mine. I'd tether her to me. We'd get lost together this time. We'd fly through the clouds as one. She wouldn't need to be scared anymore; I'd be with her every step of the way.

I can picture her standing in front of me, seeing the mess I have become. Sitting on the sidewalk like some broken lump of clay. *Get up*, Katie would say, rolling her eyes. *So dramatic.*

Katie, the girl who never sat still.

Katie, the girl who never gave up.

My sister, the girl who held my hand and walked with me.

And I know, deep down, this is the last thing she'd want. She wouldn't want her death to be the end of my life, the end of my happiness. She'd want it to be the beginning. She'd want me to be restless. She'd want me to be like she was on those summer days when she'd bounce around the house, full of movement and life until her very last breath.

Would Katie want me to sink to my knees? Would she want me to stop keeping score and give up? To barricade the doors, lock them up, and swallow the key? I know the answer.

My bones scream, my heart is in shambles, but I stand up. I keep walking with no idea where I am going. Just knowing that she'd want me to go somewhere.

I'll do this for you, Katie, I think. I'll fight for her. I'll live for her. I can't believe that she is gone for good. I know she is up there somewhere, nestled between the clouds, looking down, smiling.

I have to believe it. I have to.

28

EDEN

NO MATTER WHAT HAPPENED this past year, I never thought I'd be spending a Sunday morning at my best friend's funeral.

My heels sink into the soil as I walk across the cemetery. The sun is barely pushing through the clouds, the grass still damp with morning dew. A chill fills the air, nipping at my bones. I remind myself to breathe. I remind my feet to move forward when they so desperately want to run back.

A small group of people has gathered for Katie's funeral. Her casket sits closed beneath a willow tree. A priest stands behind it, a figure of black, a looming reminder of death. The rows of seats are sparsely filled. I remember her mom mentioning the funeral would be small, intimate. Not crowded with rowdy kids from school and the boys whose hearts Katie had once broken.

Truman and his parents sit in the front row. I recognize Santana behind him, her red hair impossible to miss. A weighted silence fills the air, like a dark cloud looming after a storm, one that will never lift. I watch Truman from across the grass. I haven't seen him in a week, since the hospital. We haven't spoken since the night we said goodbye in his car and went our separate ways.

He looks hollow, all bones and sharp edges. His eyes are hooded, clouded with dark circles. His black hair is rumpled, blowing lifelessly in the wind. He is a shell of the boy I used to know. I know if he were to look at me, he would think the same.

Since the night Katie died, time has ceased to exist. Minutes, hours, and days all bleed into one another. There is no sunrise and no sunset. Just the ticking of the clock, waiting for each day to end so I can close my eyes and pretend none of this is real. The sadness is bone deep. It is impossible to describe. I'll carry it in my chest for the rest of my life. It will always be there, gently weighing me down until the day it fades to an ache.

Minutes tick by and the seats began to fill with aunts and uncles I have never met. Old family friends, grandparents, a few faces I remember from hazy summer mornings and chilly fall nights. I watch Truman stand, shake their hands, hug a few of them. He is a corpse brought to life, a flame completely fizzled out. I can see he's trying—trying to keep his composure—but I don't think there are enough bandages in the world to put him back together again.

Eventually, nearly all the seats are filled. I keep telling myself: *Go, sit down, pay your respects. Hug Katie's mom and then her dad. Touch Truman's shoulder, let him know you're here.* But I physically cannot move. The thought of stepping one inch closer to her casket makes me want to crawl out of my skin.

I settle for standing beneath a nearby tree. The funeral begins. The priest says a few words, rekindling the past and the highlights of Katie's life. I want to shove him away. *Get out,* I'd say before taking over and telling my own memories. The real memories of the real girl who lies there, moments from being gone forever.

I want to run away and never look back. But I don't. I stay until the priest says his final words. Until the casket is placed in the ground. Until the soil is piled on top. Until her mom cries so loud it shakes the trees and scares away the birds. My eyes are trained on Truman. I wait for him to break, wait for him to fray at the edges and disappear entirely. It never happens. He stands tall and firm like a steady oak. He holds his mother as she cries and wipes the tears from her face. He is there, present. I see it in his eyes, see him snap back into himself for the briefest moment. I know he is doing this for his family. I know that when he is alone in bed tonight, he'll be stone once more.

And then the funeral is over. She's gone. I wipe the tears from my cheeks. I make myself remember Katie as the girl who was bright and bold and fearless. That's who she was and always will be.

I tell myself I'll come back one day and sit by her grave. I'll finally say all the words that have been locked up in my throat for months now. Once I know the words to say, I will. I will make it okay. She will forgive me. Everything will be okay.

On the way back to the street, I stop at a bench nestled along the sidewalk. I wait for my breathing to slow, for the haze to clear from my eyes, for my thoughts to feel weightless again.

I am sitting there, waiting, when Truman comes out of nowhere and sits beside me. Benches seem to be our thing. I don't need to look to know it's him. It's like I can feel the life pulsing through him—my body knows when he is near; my heart knows to speed up the way it always does around him.

I wait for him to speak. What does he want? A shoulder to cry on? Company to sit with? Someone to tell him it will all be okay? I won't lie to him.

I keep my face forward, eyes locked on the cars parked along the street. I see Truman stretch his long legs out before leaning back against the bench. His hands are clasped in his lap. His body is rigid, stone cold. His breaths are puffs of white in the chilly air that now teeters on fall.

Then his eyes are on me. I feel them graze my face. I can feel every glance, every blink. It shoots through me like electricity sparking off a live wire. I keep my face forward, knowing I'll be a goner the moment our eyes meet.

I'm still not certain if I loved him. I think I did. I want him to be happy, but that happiness can't come from me. At least not right now. There will always be too much guilt, too much pain wedged between us. Every time I look at him, I see Katie's face, hear her voice. And I wonder if years passing and my heart healing will change anything, if it will ever be enough for me to let my guard down and truly feel happy with him someday.

I think it might. I think we can find our way back to each other.

But for right now, Truman and I had our moment. And for the time it lasted, it was sort of everything. It was nearly enough to calm the storm we had stirred up. I know I will never care for someone that way again, never feel that same familiar warmth that blossoms inside me when his eyes find mine, and that will be okay—because it has to be okay. We are like winter and summer, made to exist in the same world, but not together. Never at the same time. We both need our own life, our own moments to grow and still have those memories to look back on.

Now, sitting on the bench, Truman reaches across the space between us and grabs my hand. I feel myself still, like a single movement will scare him off. Tentatively and ever so slowly, he intertwines our fingers and rests our hands against the cold wooden bench.

I take a long breath to calm my racing heart, and then I look at him. My eyes find their way to his easily. They are waiting, the palest blue in the cold air, like sea glass broken along a salty shore.

We hold each other's gaze as the rain begins to fall, hitting the ground and the barren tree branches. His eyes hold every moment of our past: that first stolen kiss in his bedroom; the summer mornings lying on the grass in backyards; painting the sky in Katie's new bedroom; taking his clothes off in the back seat of a beaten-up car. It is all there, every last moment laid bare between us.

And then the most incredible thing happens. Truman smiles. A real smile. The kind that splits across his face. The kind that tears the world in two. The kind that is radiant sunlight after a cold winter.

For that moment, that briefest of moments, the world settles into itself. The wind calms. And for a faint second, everything feels okay. Everything will be okay.

I squeeze Truman's fingers. I smile back. I want to say a million different things, but every word would cut through the peaceful moment we have built around us.

Then I stand up. I move a little easier, like gravity has loosened up the slightest bit. The heaviness has faded—barely, but it's still something.

As I walk home, the clouds clear. The sun pours down and warms my face. The sky turns a startling blue, the color of his eyes.

For the first time in an endless stretch of darkness, I feel an inkling of light.

Acknowledgments

I can't believe I got to do this again. Thank you to the team at HarperCollins—you keep making my dreams come true.

The biggest thank-you to my editor, Elizabeth Lynch, for two things: leaving comments like "Beautiful!" that made rewrites a little bit easier, and for her thoughtful understanding that helped make this book the best it could be. Thank you to Catherine Wallace for (once again) dealing with the chaotic messes that are my first drafts. And for helping with the first half of this one. (And for giving me the idea to move the sky to the hospital.)

Thank you to the people who read this book when it was merely a disaster available for free online. (Shout-out to Wattpad!) Thank you for rooting for Truman and Eden from the first chapter to the last—that support was what inspired me to make it to the end of their story.

Thank you to my family, who were absolutely *thrilled* to know about this book from the get-go, and not a week before it hit bookstores like last time. Oops. Thank you to my mom for offering the idea to write my second book about her. (Thank you to myself for not listening to that advice.) And thank you to Alessia and Antonio for existing, basically. I guess being one-third of the Triple As would be boring without you two. Like, a little bit.

Thank you to my writer friends who are, quite honestly, the absolute best. They're the first people to experience my unfiltered blabbering and, somehow, have stuck around from book one to book two. Thank you for the constant advice, brutal honesty, and for not yelling at me for writing characters that wear too much black. And to Olive, my nonwriter friend, for keeping me sane the other half of the time.

I saved the best for last: Misty, Bella, and Chico. For being the fluffiest and best to cuddle with when my stress levels reached new highs because, spoiler alert, writing a book is kind of hard.